friction

friction

Best Gay Erotic Fiction

Edited by Gerry Kroll

alyson books

LOS ANGELES · NEW YORK

Manufactured in the United States of America.

This trade paperback original is published by Alyson Publications Inc.,
P.O. Box 4371, Los Angeles, California 90078-4371.
Distribution in the United Kingdom by Turnaround Publisher Services Ltd.,
Unit 3, Olympia Trading Estate, Coburg Road, Wood Green,
London N22 6TZ England.

First edition: April 1998

02 01 00 99 98   10 9 8 7 6 5 4 3 2 1

ISBN 1-55583-471-X

For a listing of publishing credits for each article, refer to the "About the
Magazines" section on page 394.

To the memory of
Harold Robbins,
the master of sex and story line

Contents

Foreword ix

Karma *by R.J. March* 1
Dads *by Bob Vickery* 13
Anyway *by Roddy Martin* 27
Snowbound *by Lee Alan Ramsay* 38
Toddy's Twick *by Lew Dwight* 63
Pinch *by R.J. March* 73
Jock Talk *by Leo Cardini* 88
Fantasies *by Bob Vickery* 101
The Innocent Predator *by Evan Robertson* 115
Souvenir *by Barry Alexander* 126
Fever *by R.J. March* 140
The Man at the Gym *by Derek Adams* 153
Blind Date *by Bob Vickery* 164
Checkmate *by Todd McGuire* 178
Boystown *by R.J. March* 186
Gaijin *by Ron Templeton* 199
Liberation! *by Cain Berlinger* 211
Taking Out the Trash *by Michael Boyd* 223
The Canadian Censor *by Bob Vickery* 238
Bringing Up Robbie *by Mark Caldwell* 253
The Golden Boys *by R.J. March* 266
A Queer Turn *by R.J. March* 278
In-Tents Encounter *by Christopher Morgan* 288

Traction *by Lew Dwight* 295

When Luddy Goes *by R.J. March* 303

Physical Therapy *by Bob Vickery* 317

Discretion Sought, Discretion Served *by Lew Dwight* 331

Coaching Session *by Steven Lundquist* 342

The Roommate *by Grant Foster* 352

Tuesdays We Read Baudelaire *by R.J. March* 364

Looking for Mr. Right *by Michael Cavanaugh* 376

Contributors 389

About the Magazines 394

Foreword

It's been said that writing a book is like appearing in public with your pants down. Editing a book of short stories—erotic short stories, no less—and calling them the best of the year undoubtedly has something of the same self-revealing nature about it. "Look, everybody," you guilelessly exclaim. "These stories turned me on! I bet they'll turn you on too."

As a matter of fact, that is precisely the process I went through when I originally bought many of these stories for *Men, Freshmen,* and the former *Classifieds* (now *Unzipped* magazine). Slogging wearily through a pile of unsolicited manuscripts—"slush," as the industry calls it—and at last uncovering a gem can be as rewarding as anything an editor ever experiences. Naturally we want others to know about our exciting discovery, and if that exciting discovery turns out to speak volumes about our own tastes in matters erotic, well, that comes with the territory. So go ahead—deduce what you will about the editors at Alyson as you peruse this list of the year's best gay erotic short stories. They stand by their choices, as do I and all the other contributing editors—from magazines around the country—from whom Alyson solicited entries for this anthology.

As it happens, several of the writers included in this anthology are men with whom I have had a close working relationship for some time. To say these relationships have been fruitful seems, for me, to be stating the obvious. All you need to do to check on the accuracy of my boast is to start at the top of the table of contents and begin to read these tales. Among the authors are such talents as Leo Cardini, Michael Cavanaugh, Grant Foster, and the amazingly prolific Derek

Adams, regular, always-welcome contributors to the magazines I edit. I believe they're equally welcome in other editors' offices too.

This book is loaded with what I think are standout writers, but I feel it's only proper to give special mention to three men who are heavily represented here, writers whose versatility and imagination leave me utterly satisfied (and not a little awestruck) each time I receive a submission from them. The first is Bob Vickery, a man whose stories are each as different from the other as any editor could hope. Bob approaches situations that might not normally occur to other writers and weaves them into stories of great erotic and emotional depth, whether those situations involve sightlessness ("Blind Date"), homelessness ("Physical Therapy"), single parenthood ("Dads"), or the death of a lover to AIDS ("Fantasies"). His endlessly fertile gift, I'm happy to report, shows no evidence of running dry.

Lew Dwight is another writer who finds erotic potential in the most unlikely setups; witness "Toddy's Twick" and "Traction," two offbeat stories that would have been disasters in the hands of a lesser talent. As gifted as he is eccentric, Lew can also take classic mainstream gay erotic fodder and transform it into a story so emotionally and sexually charged, you'd swear the subject had never been tackled before "Discretion Sought, Discretion Served."

Finally, it is my belief that no erotic anthology should ever go out the door without having a healthy sampling of stories by the brilliant R.J. March. My association with R.J. began nearly five years ago, and my appreciation of his talents has only grown stronger with time. I am as proud of having given his fiction a consistent home as I am of anything I have ever achieved in my professional life. Not for nothing does R.J. have eight stories included in this volume—nearly one quarter of the book. His understanding of what makes a situation erotically charged defies explanation. But, then, magic should never be explained.

Fred Goss, Editor in Chief
Men, Freshmen, Unzipped
Los Angeles, December 1997

Karma
by R.J. March

Micah sipped his coffee; the heat of it hurt his tongue, which he'd
apparently injured the night before while eating out Kelly's ass.
He could see Kelly now, facedown, legs spread. Kelly had a
smooth little fanny that appealed to Micah, a young man's rear
end: blemish-free, peach-fuzzy. His balls spread out between his
thighs like something spilled, easily slurped up and rolled about
in Micah's mouth—but only one at a time because of the size of
the things. Nothing boyish about them or his prick, with its
horselike dimensions. Pink and straight, with a network of blue
veins coursing under its surface, it had a downward point, a beautiful helmet.

"Mikey," Dick Jones barked, startling him and causing him to
spill some coffee. Dick laughed; Micah didn't.

"You had this dreamy look on your face," Jones said. "You
know how the Gland is about that."

"The Gland is playing golf with some du Pont." A brown stain
spread across a report Micah had just finished. This, oddly
enough, wasn't his day. Despite the awesome ass-licking, butt-
fucking time he'd had the night before, this day was shaping up
miserably. It was pouring when he went out to start his car that
morning, only to find it wouldn't.

"Not the wrestling lover, I hope," Jones said.

"She might like wrestling," Micah responded. "I didn't receive
a profile."

"I didn't know you had a brother," Jones said, pulling tissues from a box on Micah's desk and dropping them on the spill.

"I don't have a brother," Micah muttered.

Dick's mouth squirmed to fight a greasy smile, his hand going inside his gray flannel vest. His white shirtsleeves were rolled to the middle of each forearm. He had the upper body of someone who crewed the Delaware. Micah glanced away from the oar-hardened wrists and sneezed.

"Getting a cold?" Jones said. "Out in the rain without your rubbers?"

Micah looked up, making his features dull, feigning incomprehension. Jones sighed.

"Oh, Mikey. No ear for irony."

"I told you about that 'Mikey' shit, didn't I?" Micah said, blotting up the rest of the coffee.

Jones rolled his eyes. They were that strange contact-lens blue, but natural, his own. He looked through glasses that looked borrowed from someone named Fritz. His blond hair was cut short to combat a natural kink and underplay a slightly receding hairline, which Micah secretly found attractive.

"So who was your celestial twin?" he wanted to know from Micah. "I seriously thought he looked like your brother."

"My ride this morning?" Micah said. "Friend of mine." He waved the report to dry it, giving himself the air of a coquette with a fan. Dick grabbed the fluttering papers.

"Sometimes I think I don't know you very well at all," he said. "Print up another copy of this, Micah, that's all you have to do."

"What do you mean?"

"I mean, open up the appropriate file and click on the print icon, for Christ's sake."

"No, I mean about not knowing me very well."

Jones looked at his watch.

"I've got a lunch meeting in fifteen," he said. "What are you doing after work?"

Fucking, I hope, Micah thought, his mind running through his "good excuses" file and coming up with a wake for a dead aunt—why, he didn't know. Easier than explaining Kelly, he figured.

Jones regarded him drolly, looking very close to shaking his head admonishingly.

Micah had met Kelly at the gym. Kelly was the chiropractor's assistant on duty when Micah turned his head sharply to check out a wagging bob in someone's shorts. He was all but crippled immediately. *Instant karma,* he thought, carrying his head crookedly to the back of the gym. "Pinched nerve," he grimaced, pointing to the back of his neck.

Kelly jumped out of his swiveling office chair and bounded over to Micah like he was a code-blue emergency. He led Micah gently to one of the rooms in which the doctor manipulated bones.

"I'm not licensed to do anything but give you ice," Kelly said, his voice deep. He wore spandex shorts and a cropped T-shirt—typical gym gear for someone in as good a shape as he was. *But can I trust him with ice?* Micah wondered, trying to check out the boy's basket. His damned nerve throbbed, preventing inspection.

"Dr. Glenn will be back soon," Kelly said. He wore a name tag that made his T-shirt swing, its sleeves long gone, his pesky, pert nipple popping into view every now and then. "Would you like to lie down?" Kelly asked. His red hair was combed back with gel, just long enough to flip up in back. There were freckles running across his arms, his shoulders. *Is his dick freckled too?* Micah wanted to learn.

"I've got two or three fused vertebrae," Micah said, pointing again to his neck.

Kelly brought an ice pack and placed it with care on Micah's neck and came around, squatting before his patient. "Does it help?" he wanted to know. His legs were spread, and the heavy wad in his skintight shorts became Micah's focal point.

Micah nodded as best he could.

He left the gym with the ice pack and Kelly's number, feeling like a smooth operator despite the odd tilt to his head and the shooting pain that made him see stars.

He dialed Dick's extension.

"Yallo," he answered.

"My car's not done yet."

"Can't your, um, friend drive you?"

"He's at work," Micah told him. "Never mind. I'll call a cab."

"What about your aunt's wake?"

"Canceled," Micah said.

"Canceled? They canceled a wake?"

"Hang up, I'm calling a cab," Micah said.

"Like hell you will."

There was an accident on 176, and traffic was stopped dead. Dick put the car in neutral and popped in the latest Dave Matthews Band CD. "This guy's gay, isn't he? I think he's gay."

"How the hell would I know?" Micah snapped. He hadn't any plans for his evening, but he never thought he'd be stuck in a car with Dick Jones. *He wouldn't be so obnoxious with his mouth closed,* Micah thought, *or biting a pillow.*

"So why'd you lie to me this morning?" Jones asked. "Don't you like me anymore?"

Micah looked at his clasped hands in his lap. "Look, I'm sorry," he said, unable to come up with anything suitable to follow that up with.

Jones shrugged. "I'm callused, buddy, don't worry. No feelings to worry about since that nerve-ending removal. Hurt like hell for a little bit, and then—nothing. Haven't felt a thing since. Just ask my wife."

"How is Candace?" Micah asked, putting his shoulder to the window.

"Gone," Dick said, taking his hands off the wheel. He laughed. "Our first anniversary is next week."

"Jeez, I'm sorry," Micah said, feeling like an ass, and for some reason he remembered a dream he'd had that morning in which the roof of his house was gone and it was raining like hell. It started to rain in real life, drumming the roof of the car like anxious fingers. Jones switched on the wipers, but there was nowhere to go and nothing to see. He turned off the engine. "I'm low on fuel," he said, and then, "So who's the guy?"

"This morning?" Micah stumbled. He was not comfortable talking about his personal life at work—those were two worlds he did not like to overlap.

"And last night," Dick said. "It's none of my business. I'm just interested lately in people who are enjoying a healthy sex life. I'm simply making idle conversation."

"We're no longer idling," Micah said.

"That is subject to debate," Dick said, then added, "So what's he like?"

"Are you sure you want to know? Why do you want to know? When did you suddenly become bi-curious?"

"I've always been curious. I watch the Learning Channel."

"His name's Kelly. He collects grenades."

"Hand grenades?"

Micah nodded. "They're nicely displayed, though."

"No doubt," Dick answered. He sat quietly for a while regarding the view through the rain-streaked window.

"What happened at home?" Micah asked.

"Are you sure you want to know?" Dick said, turning, fixing his blue eyes on the knot of Micah's tie. He shrugged. "The usual, I guess. Candace collects grudges. She remembers every shitty little thing anyone's ever done to her."

Micah said nothing, keeping his ill opinion of Jones's wife to himself. "You all right?"

"Oh, I'm just fine," Dick answered him with a fake smile.

They picked up a six-pack close to Micah's house. "Just wasn't working," Dick said, scratching himself. His shoes were off, and his tie undone. Micah sat across from him trying to be a good listener, trying to maintain eye contact. His gaze tended to drop down the stretched-out length of the man before him, though, and he'd find himself unaware of what Dick had been saying.

"You know what I mean?" Dick said, breaking Micah's concentration.

Micah nodded slowly.

"You're a good friend," Dick said, leaning forward, obscuring his crotch.

No, I'm not, Micah thought, *I'm a fucking pig, so lean back again, because it makes your crotch look like a mountain in those trousers.*

Micah held up his empty bottle. "Another?" he asked.

Jones made an iffy face. "What about your plans?"

"No definite plans," Micah said. "I'll call him later. Anyway, he's working."

"What's he do?"

"He works," Micah said, stalling, "in a gym."

Dick nodded. "I thought I saw deltoids this morning."

"He's a chiropractor's assistant."

"Is that anything like a dental hygienist?"

"He's really sweet," Micah said.

"Again, no doubt," Dick said, rolling his blue eyes.

Dick looked at his watch, then looked up at Micah. "Hungry?" he asked. Micah shook his head. "Me neither."

The beer was gone, and they opened a bottle of gin somebody had given Micah for Christmas. "Mixers?" Dick asked.

"Diet Coke?" Micah offered.

Dick shook his head.

Micah found some reconstituted lemon juice, so they drank the gin on ice with squirts from the plastic lemon.

"You should change," Dick said.

"I thought you liked me the way I am."

"Your clothes, I mean," Dick said, not impatiently. "I like you fine the way you are."

"I like you fine," Micah returned.

"You should get out of your work clothes, though. You look like you're at work."

"I wore these to work today," Micah said.

"Go change or something," Dick said.

"OK, all right," Micah said, getting up and making his way down the hall to his bedroom. He was feeling more than a little buzzed—he'd skipped lunch and now dinner, and the alcohol was feeding on him. He stripped down to his T-shirt and boxers, humming the Dave Matthews song he'd heard in the car. He stood in front of his bureau opening drawers and looking into them. He had no idea what to put on.

Dick was standing in the doorway. Micah saw him there and said, "I don't know what to wear."

"Have I ever seen your legs before?" Dick asked him. "You have big legs. Is that what your boyfriend is doing for you? Making your legs big? Lots of squats?"

"He's not my boyfriend. I don't even know his middle name."

"You know mine, though," Jones said, and Micah nodded. "And I know yours."

"You do?" Micah asked.

"Yup," he said.

They both stopped talking, but the voice in Micah's head was loud and rambling and wary. *Not a good thing,* it said. But look at him, his compact form there in the doorway, framed and backlit, the blond fuzz of his head, his 31-inch waist—each a siren song to Micah. *But he's married,* came the voice of reason, *and straight and a coworker. He's disconsolate and kind of drunk and probably just horny. To take advantage of him now would be like raping a paraplegic, wouldn't it?*

Micah blinked, and Jones was suddenly standing very close to him, his juniper-berried breath like cologne to Micah's nose.

"You're thinking way too much," Dick said. He put his big hands on Micah's chest; they were warm and moist through his T-shirt. "Jesus, you've got pecs too," he whispered.

"They were on sale."

Jones's left hand trailed down Micah's torso, stopping at his polka-dotted shorts. "I had you pegged for a white Calvins kind of guy," he said, swirling a finger into the fly.

"These were on sale too," Micah said. "Are you sure—" he started but stopped when he felt Jones's finger poking his soft prick into a doughy semierect state. Dick went to his knees, pushing his face against the front of Micah's shorts, mouthing the burgeoning head of Micah's prick.

"I'm not sure if this is a great idea," Micah continued, palming the back of Dick's head and forcing it harder against his groin. "I mean, what will we say to each other tomorrow? Are you going to talk to me at all?" Jones pushed up Micah's T-shirt, exposing his crunched abdominals, the smooth six-pack that was his glory—they were like leather-covered rock—and Jones exhumed his face from Micah's crotch.

"Jesus," he exclaimed. "You've been hiding all this!"

"I didn't think you'd be interested," Micah replied. His cock had become engorged and pressed itself insistently against the front of his boxers. Dick dragged the garish shorts down, unveiling the quivering rod. He stabbed his tongue at the hardened, goosefleshed conduit, licking up to the bulbous head that had always seemed to Micah a little odd, a little overboard, and so unlike all the other aerodynamic, arrowheaded cock heads he'd seen in his lifetime. He'd always felt strapped with a tom-tom. Odd or not, though, Jones was not averse to licking it up and down and handling it like a drumstick and sticking it all into his mouth.

"It's better than I thought it was going to be," Dick said.

"That's good to hear," Micah returned.

"I was always bugging Candace to buy bananas and zucchini and cucumbers. Was I sending some heavy subliminals, or what?" He unshouldered his suspenders and unknotted his tie. He looked up from what he was doing. "You OK? You look a little sick."

Micah nodded—he was feeling anything but sick. His cock tingled, needing to be touched more and more. He thought about the next day at the office. This was totally fucked-up, he decided, looking down at his shiny, rosy knob not eight inches from Dick Jones's mouth.

Dick talked as he undressed, about Candace, his lack of sex experience ("You know, with guys, I mean!"), even about some account they were working on. "Talked to Joe about that media plan for Westways. He thinks they're going to go with it." He got himself down to his T-shirt, trousers, and dark socks. He wasn't lean, and he wasn't fat, but he hovered somewhere in between, which was perfection as far as Micah was concerned. Jones wrinkled his brow, looking up at Micah, taking a deep breath. Standing, he unlatched his slacks. He himself was wearing the white Calvins, their pouch filled with a lot of flaccid dick. He gripped himself, pulling on his soft package.

"Guess I'm more nervous than I thought," he said, making a sheepish face. He let go of himself and grabbed hold of Micah. He got down on his knees again and took the man's prick into his mouth. He played his tongue along the underside when he went down and used it to lash the sensitive head when he drew back, his teeth lightly dragging and causing Micah to gasp. He was able, despite his inexperience, to bring Micah closer than he wanted to be to shooting. Micah pulled on Dick's meaty earlobes, pushing into his tight-lipped mouth and hitting the back of his throat, liking the muffled sounds the man made. His balls were bathed in drool that leaked from Dick's sucking mouth.

"Enough," Micah said, tugging on Dick's ears. Dick sat back, his fanny resting on his dark-socked heels. The pouch of his briefs had doubled in size. His plumped dick rode downward along his balls. His crotch was camera-ready, picture-perfect. He had the look of an underwear ad.

"Take off the rest," Micah said, and Dick pulled off his T-shirt. He was covered with golden brown hair. His pecs were fat and accented with small brown nipples that were pointed and widely spaced. He put his thumbs into his shorts.

"This is a pretty definitive moment," Dick said.

Micah laughed, his cock bobbing. "I think you had your definitive moment a while ago, pal, right before you started giving me head."

"Guess you're right," Dick said.

"We can stop here," Micah said. "We don't have to do anything else. We can forget this ever happened."

"No way," Dick said, shaking his head. "No fucking way."

The shorts came down.

Dick Jones had the kind of cock that Micah dreamed about: fat-shafted and topped with a tiny gumdrop of a head that pointed up and out.

"Jeez," Micah breathed.

They waltzed to the bed and wrestled across the mattress, kicking off pillows and bedsheets, seeking a flat and uncluttered surface on which to fuck. Micah had already decided that it would be a nice gesture to let Dick fuck him. He got himself down on all fours in front of the man and started licking the perfect pecker. Little pearls seeped out and were tongued away. He chewed on Dick's fuzzy bag, bringing the whole tight thing into his mouth, sucking and snorting like a pig at a buffet.

"Mikey," Dick said softly, touching the side of the man's face, and Micah came off the bag, dragging his mouth up the sweet, curving shaft, up to that little point of a head. He went down hard, swallowing Dick's dick and breathing hotly into his bush.

When Micah crawled up Dick's torso and sat down on his cock, Dick said, "No way."

"You don't want to?" Micah asked.

"No. I mean, yeah, I want to, I just can't believe it, that's all. I read my horoscope this morning, and it didn't say anything about fucking you."

"You want to, though?" Micah asked, wanting to be sure.

"Abso-fucking-lutely," Dick said, pushing up with his hips and stabbing into the hole. It was an easy slide in; the sweet, pointy prick was perfect for fucking, although it thickened quickly and felt like a fire plug once it was all the way in.

"Shit," Dick said, cupping Micah's ass. "This is nice, man."

Micah squatted on the cock, playing with the brown points of Dick's nipples. He maneuvered his rear end so that his prostate bore the brunt of Dick's sharp-headed cock. His own dick bobbed happily and untouched, tapping away on Dick's stomach and leaving sticky dots.

"Am I doing it right?" Dick asked, and Micah laughed. "It doesn't take a rocket scientist, I guess," Dick said. "But are you enjoying yourself? Does it hurt? Am I equipped with a monster cock that is eviscerating you as I speak?"

"I'm in fucking heaven," Micah said.

"You look like an angel, man," Dick said, thrusting up sharply, making Micah gasp. He reached up and grabbed the back of Micah's head, pulling him down for a full kiss that made Micah's head swirl. He felt compelled suddenly to reach down between their bellies and start pulling on his cock.

"Shit," Dick whispered, his mouth full of Micah's tongue. "I'm—" He struggled to unpin himself, but Micah rode him out, taking the full blast of Dick's load up his ass. Then Micah sat up straight, his hand on his bone, and aimed for his coworker's face.

When it was all over, Micah unseated himself and stretched out beside Dick.

"I'm sorry, man," Dick said.

"What for?"

"Coming early."

"You were right on time, as far as I'm concerned."

"It's just that I haven't had sex in 32 days."

"Not at all? Not even jacking off?"

Dick turned to look at Micah. "You consider that having sex?"

"Well, yeah. Kind of. It's pretty much the same, isn't it? The end result, I mean."

"Well, then, I haven't had sex, according to your standards, since this morning in the men's room at work after I left your office," Dick said.

"That's so sweet," Micah said, putting his head close to Dick's.

"Yeah," he said. "So tell me, buddy, do you really know my middle name?"

Micah made a face. "Sure, I do. Sure," he said, trying to think of it. He was sure he'd seen it somewhere, on some interdepartmental mail or something. *It began with a* j *or an* m, he thought, *or maybe an* s.

"It's John," he said.

"Nope."

"Jacob."

"Jacob?"

"Not Jacob," Micah said. "So what's mine, then, smart-ass?"

"Jacob?"

"Nice try, asshole," Micah said.

"Steven," Dick tried.

"Close enough," Micah said, licking a running drip of come from Dick's chin.

Dads
by Bob Vickery

I glance at my watch and make a mental calculation of how much time I have before I need to make my appearance at Jason's school. It's early evening now, and the park is getting dark; there are only a couple of streetlamps off in the distance that provide any kind of illumination—that plus a half-moon rising in the east. *A mugger's paradise,* I think and then push the thought out of my head. When my dick is doing all the thinking, I try not to let practicalities like that get in the way. Every now and then a break in the shrubbery gives me a glimpse of the city: the streets fanning out below, ending in the greater darkness of the bay. Solitary figures lean against trees or emerge from the shadows and saunter by, the sharp, cruisy looks in their eyes giving the lie to the casualness of their stride. Over and over the ritual repeats itself: our gazes locking together, the quick scan of each other's bodies, then the eyes locking again, this time asking, *Interested in a little action?* Or else the turn of the head with the unspoken message: *Move on.*

I don't think it's excessive vanity on my part to note that I get a hell of a lot more of the first reaction than the latter. I'm wearing a T-shirt tight enough to feel like a second skin, showing off the cut of my muscles, the pumped-up biceps and pecs (I came straight to the park from my daily workout at the gym; my hair's still slicked down from the shower). I've busted my ass to look good, and I have no qualms about strutting my stuff. Alice tells me I've become quite a peacock since our divorce.

I see him perched on the back of a park bench, his knees wide apart, his feet planted on the seat. A cigarette hangs loosely between his index and middle fingers, smoke lazily curling up. I get the impression that he's young, maybe more from the posture of his body—half self-conscious, half bored—than from anything I can discern from his face, which is hidden in shadow. His body is lean and well-defined; like me, he's wearing a T-shirt that shows off his physique. But unlike me, he doesn't appear to be on display; he sits slouched over his knees in an attitude that seems without pose. I begin to wonder if he might be some straight dude who's wandered into this gay feeding ground, clueless to what's going on around him. I find myself very interested.

I sit on the bench next to his feet and lean back, my arms resting along the back. There's not the slightest shift in his posture or attitude to give any acknowledgment of my presence. I look up at him. "It's a nice night, isn't it?" I say. OK, as an opening line it doesn't exactly sparkle. But any successes racked up in park cruising rarely result from verbal wit. He turns his head and looks straight at me, a gesture that pulls his face out of shadow for a moment. His features are regular and smooth: a strong jaw, deep-set eyes, high cheekbones. I can see that my first impression was right. He is young, early 20s maybe, a good eight or nine years my junior.

He takes a puff from his cigarette and exhales out of the corner of his mouth. "I guess so," he says. A silence lies between us like roadkill.

I make another stab. "What's your name?" I ask.

He looks at me again for a few seconds. "Don," he finally says. He doesn't ask me mine.

After a few more seconds, I stand up. "See you around, Don," I say.

"Do you want to fuck?" he asks my back.

I turn around and face him. His face looks pale and chaste in the faint light from the streetlamp. I try to imagine what he would look like naked. The image I come up with is very nice. "Yeah," I say. "As a matter of fact, I do."

Don swings his legs around and stands up. He drops his cigarette and grinds it out with the toe of his boot. "Let's go," he says.

Don's dick thickens out nicely as I suck on it, twisting my head from side to side for maximum effect. His hands lightly grasp my head, and he fucks my face with long, slow thrusts, like a runner pacing himself. My hands slide under his T-shirt, kneading the hard flesh, tweaking the nipples. I give them gentle twists, and Don grunts his appreciation. I work my hands down his back and over his smooth ass, squeezing the cheeks. Don slams his dick down my throat and then leaves it there, grinding his hips, his balls pressed against my chin. When he pulls out again with killing slowness, I nibble at the meaty shaft, my tongue working on it feverishly. Don gives a long, drawn-out sigh, a hair's breadth shy of a groan. "Yeah," he says gruffly. "That's good."

He pulls me to my feet and kisses me, ramming his tongue into my mouth the way he had his dick a few seconds ago. I wrap my arms around him and press my body hard up against him. My pants and shorts are down around my ankles, and my hard dick stabs against his belly. He reaches down, wraps his palm around both of our dicks, and begins stroking. Both of our dicks are leaking precome, and they slide up against each other with a slipperiness that makes my body tingle.

Don drops to his knees, and I feel the warmth of his mouth around my cock. I start pumping my hips to maximize the sensation. He's a good cocksucker, energetic and skillful, and the shivers of pleasure that ride over my body are coming quicker and harder. He takes me to the brink, and just when I'm ready to shoot, he pulls back. His mouth drops down to my balls and sucks on them as the threat of shooting recedes. We're surrounded on all sides by high bushes, and the darkness is nearly total; my only contact with him is the feel of his invisible wet tongue sliding over my balls and dick. Don's lips move up my cock, kissing the shaft wetly, and then he swoops down and starts sucking me off again. Once more the sexual tension rises inside, building up to climax, and once more, when my dick is at the point of spitting out its load, Don pulls back. I groan my frustration.

"Yeah," Don growls. "You're just dying to shoot, aren't you?" Before I can answer he's sucking me off again, pulling my load up from my balls once more. I thrust hard and deep down his throat, a spasm shoots through my body, and this time I go over the edge, squirting my load into the warm, wet confines of Don's mouth. He sucks greedily, squeezing out every last drop. He finally stands up and starts beating off. I reach down and squeeze his balls, and with a loud groan he shoots, splattering his jizz against my shirt. When he's done he leans forward and kisses me again, pressing his naked body against mine.

A couple of minutes go by. I gently disentangle myself. "Listen," I say, "I have to go."

The moon has risen above the tops of the bushes, lighting up his face with a dim glow.

"What, you got a date or something?" he asks. I can't tell whether he's being flippant or genuinely resentful.

"No," I say. "It's a PTA meeting."

I wander all over the damned school building before I finally find Jason's classroom. I'm half an hour late, and I've missed the orientation. The parents are milling around, waiting for a chance to talk with the teacher about their children. Alice spots me and fixes me with a murderous glare. I go up to her, adopting a contrite expression.

"Listen, I'm sorry I'm late," I say. "Things just got piled up, and I lost track of time."

"The least you could have done is wear something a little dressier," she whispers vehemently. She looks down at my T-shirt. "What's that you've got spilled down your front?"

Oh, jeez, I think. *Don't load.* "Nothing," I say, crossing my arms in front of me. "Just some coffee. I was in such a damn hurry, I wound up spilling half of it." I put a slightly aggrieved tone in my voice, like somehow the accident was her fault for making me hurry. Alice just rolls her eyes and walks away.

When I finally meet Jason's teacher, she tells me that Jason is doing fine. "He tends to daydream, though," she says. "It's not a serious problem, but sometimes he seems a little distracted."

Like father, like son, I think.

The next day Jason and I are in my car crossing the Bay Bridge; one of the lanes is closed for maintenance, and the traffic is bumper-to-bumper. Jason has recently picked up an interest in Greek mythology, sparked by some project in school, and every time we ride together lately, it's been my job to tell one of the stories (I bought some books a couple of weeks ago just to bone up on this stuff). We've already covered the Trojan War and Ulysses' long, problematic sail back to Ithaca. Now I'm telling Jason the myth about the Golden Fleece. He's particularly caught up in the story because of the fact that he shares his name with the hero. I get to the part where Jason is trying to steal the fleece from the king only to find that it's guarded by a dragon.

"If a dragon is guarding the fleece, then how could the king get to it?" Jason asks. He's always looking for ways to trap me in an inconsistency, as if I wrote the damn myth.

"He couldn't," I answer. "Nobody could get to it."

"Well, then, what good was it?" Jason asks. "Why did the king care if Jason took it or not?" He gives me a look like, *Explain that, sucker!*

"It was a tourist attraction," I reply. "People would come from all around to look at it from a distance. The locals made money selling souvenirs: ashtrays, key chains, T-shirts that said MOM AND DAD SAW THE GOLDEN FLEECE, AND ALL I GOT WAS THIS LOUSY T-SHIRT. That kind of thing."

Jason is 11 and too old to let on that he thinks any of my jokes are funny. He rolls his eyes in a way that is pure Alice, but I can tell he's amused. I decide that now is a good time to bring up another subject. "I saw your teacher last night," I say. "She's worried about your being too easily distracted."

Jason shrugs and looks out the window, searching for a distraction. I switch back to the Golden Fleece and capture Jason's attention again. I'll leave the edifying lectures to Alice.

Later, after I fix dinner for Jason and myself, the two of us go to a Jackie Chan movie. Jason loves these action flicks, which Alice won't take him to because she thinks they're too violent. Tonight Jason gets to watch the bad guys get the pummeling they deserve while I sit in my seat lusting after Jackie Chan. God help me, I've always had a special weakness for athletic clowns. The movie is longer than I anticipated, and I don't get Jason home till after 10. "Tell your mom I'm sorry I kept you out so late," I tell him as I give him a good-bye hug. I watch him as he runs up the sidewalk; I don't pull away until he's safely inside.

Whether it was the movie or something else, I'm really feeling an adrenaline pump. I turn on the radio and find a good rock-and-roll station. Mick Jagger comes on, singing about how he can't get no satisfaction, and I join in, my fingers tapping time against the steering wheel. I feel completely uninspired by the thought of returning home and going to bed—at least alone. What I really want, I decide, is to get laid. Barring that, then at least a little social mixing.

I tick off my options and finally decide on one of the bars on Castro. Now, I am not, by nature, a bar person; I don't like the cigarette smoke, and I don't normally deal well with crowds and noise. But I decide, *What the hell, it's been a while. Maybe it'll be fun this time.* I make my way through the city streets, turn on Castro Street, and grab the first available parking space.

I pick the Detour for no other reason than it's the first bar I stumble across. It's after 11 on a Friday night; the place is packed.

I push my way through the crowd until I can belly up to the bar. After a couple of minutes, I catch the bartender's eye and order a Michelob. I pull out my wallet and drop a couple of bills on the bar, and the barkeep scoops them up.

"Is that your kid?" a voice next to me asks.

I turn and see a man to my right, about my age, maybe a couple of years older. He's smiling at me and indicates, by a nod of his head, the picture of Jason I keep in my wallet.

I smile back. "Yeah," I say. "His name's Jason."

"How old is he?" the man asks. He has an easy smile that is very engaging. His eyes are brown and friendly, and his face gives off a comfortable masculinity.

"Eleven," I say. "Going on 30."

The man laughs. He reaches back, pulls out his wallet, and flips it open like a cop showing his badge. Inside is a picture of a young boy wearing a baseball cap, a bat slung over his shoulder. "This is my boy, Matthew. He's nine."

I take in the boy's brown eyes and wide grin. "He looks like you," I say.

The man's smile broadens, like I just paid him a compliment. I like the way he likes being compared to his kid. I bet the guy's a good father. I quickly take in the broad shoulders, the chest hairs poking above the top shirt button, and the muscular forearms beneath his rolled-up sleeves.

I hold out my hand. "My name's Joe," I say.

"I'm Pete," he says. We shake hands. He raises his bottle of beer. "To fatherhood." We clink bottles and each take a sip. Pete looks at me. "So is Jason a turkey-baster baby?"

I blink. "I beg your pardon?"

"Artificial insemination," Pete says. "Matthew's mom is a lesbian. We were friends for years before deciding to parent together. It was a real job getting her pregnant. I'd go to her bathroom and jerk off into a pimiento jar, give it to her, and she'd go to her bedroom with a turkey baster. It took months before she conceived."

I grin. "Maybe you should have taken the pimientos out of the jar first." Pete laughs. I take another sip of my beer. "Actually, Jason was conceived the old-fashioned way: by good old traditional screwing. I was married to his mom for five years."

Pete raises his eyebrows. "Kinky."

I shrug. "Yeah, well, that was my experiment with normalcy. I've pretty much worked it out of my system."

It doesn't take long before we start comparing notes about our kids. Pete's boy is a pitcher in Little League, loves soccer, and is a huge fan of Michael Jordan. "He gets all this jock stuff from his mom," Pete says, laughing. "He sure as hell doesn't get it from me. I have to read the sports section every morning so I can talk to him about Barry Bonds and who the Giants are going to trade for next, all that stuff. It's fuckin' murder."

I tell Pete about Jason's drawing and writing skills, about how, at the ripe old age of 11, he can kick my ass in chess, and about the huge battles Alice and I have over his joining the Boy Scouts. "She tells me the Boy Scouts will give Jason a chance to meet new friends and learn important values. I tell her the only 'value' he'll learn from that snake pit of homophobes is intolerance of gays and lesbians. She's totally clueless about this. She thinks I'm just being politically correct."

Pete shakes his head sympathetically.

We order more beers and keep talking about our kids. I have never done this before—comparing notes with another gay man on raising a son—and I surprise myself with what a good time I'm having. After a couple of hours, my voice is getting hoarse from shouting over the noise in the bar. "Listen," I say to Pete. "You want to come over to my place and continue this conversation?" Pete agrees instantly.

Back at my apartment I fish a couple of beers out of the refrigerator and join Pete in the living room. He's picked up a photo album from a bookshelf and is going through the pictures. He looks at a shot of Jason and me on the Sausalito ferry. "Jason looks like a nice kid," he says.

"He is," I agree. I sit next to him, going over the photos with Pete. Our knees brush together, and I make no effort to break the contact. After a while I put my arm around Pete's shoulder and pull him toward me. We give each other a long, wet kiss, our tongues finding their way into each other's mouths like foxes coming home to their burrows. The photo album slides off my lap and onto the floor as I push Pete back onto the couch, wrapping my arms tightly around him. We hold each other in wrestling clenches; Pete thrusts up, and we roll off the couch and onto the shag carpet, our mouths never separating. I slide my hand down the front of Pete's jeans and cup his crotch. The bulge I feel under the frayed denim is a promising handful.

"You got something there for me, buddy?" I croon. "Something meaty I can swing on?"

"Yeah," Pete says, his eyes bright. "Just come and get it."

We begin a feverish undoing of buttons and zippers. I pull Pete's jeans down, revealing a pair of boxer shorts with rocket ships on them. I give a small laugh. "Who the hell are you, Buck Rogers?"

Pete gives a sheepish smile. "Matthew gave them to me for my birthday last month."

"Well, I'm sorry," I say, grinning, "but they have to go." I yank them down below his knees. Pete's hard cock flops against his belly. This is one of my favorite moments in life, getting acquainted for the first time with the dick of a hot man. It's like unwrapping the main gift on Christmas morning: Sometimes you find you're stuck with a box of underwear, but sometimes you get a full Lionel train set. Pete's dick definitely falls within the train-set category: fat and long, the head flaring into a wide red knob. I tug his T-shirt up and straddle his legs, looking down at his body, taking in the solid torso, the cut of his pecs, the hard belly. "You are one hot fucker," I say, wrapping my hand around his dick.

I begin stroking it, then bend down and press my lips against the meaty shaft, kissing it softly. I let my tongue trail along its length, swirling around the head, probing into the piss slit. This is the dick he stroked in his lesbian friend's bathroom, a pimiento jar clutched in his free hand as he thought the sexy thoughts needed to coax out the load that would later become his son. For some reason I find the image incredibly erotic. I slide my tongue down to the base of the shaft and then onto the hairy scrotal sac. I pull down my own pants and begin stroking my dick as I bury my nose in Pete's balls, inhaling deeply. The musky, ripe smell of a male in rut fills my lungs. I open my mouth wider and suck in his balls, rolling them around with my tongue, savoring their taste and texture. My own cock is hard and urgent in my hand. I look up, and my eyes meet Pete's. His pupils are wide and dark, and his gaze bores into me as I tongue his ball sac. I reach up and squeeze his nipples, and he closes his eyes and groans.

I pull my head back.` "Let's go back to the bedroom."

Pete nods. "I thought you'd never ask."

We pull up our pants high enough to stumble down the hallway to the bedroom. Pete walks ahead of me, affording me a sight both comical and very sexy: his rocket-ship boxers pulled up as far as his thighs, his ass exposed to my lecherous gaze. It's a beautiful ass, smooth and tight, creamy white beneath a sharp tan line. I quickly play in my mind all the things I intend to do with that ass in the next few minutes. My dick gives a throb of anticipation.

It just takes us a minute to throw off what clothes we're still wearing, and we fall onto my bed, naked. I spread out on top of Pete, my mouth fused to his, feeling his bare flesh against mine. The guy is beautiful, and I want to taste every inch of his body. I cover his face with kisses and then work down along his neck, his shoulder, finally nuzzling under his armpit, drinking in the acrid-sweet taste of his sweat. I swing my head around and suck on his nipple, nibbling it gently between my teeth, rolling my tongue around it. Pete sighs deeply, and I repeat this with his other nipple.

My tongue pushes through the forest of his chest hairs, tracing their path as they descend down his hard belly and into the thicket of his pubes. I hold his dick in my hand again and gaze at it for a couple of seconds, enjoying how its warmth spreads into my palm, how it pulses with every beat of his heart. I bend down and take it in my mouth again, working my lips down the shaft, rolling my tongue around it. Pete begins pumping his hips, and I match his movements, bobbing my head with each thrust. I close my eyes, concentrating on the sensation of having a mouthful of dick.

"Holy shit!" Pete exclaims.

I quickly open my eyes and look up. "Did I nip you too hard?" I ask, concerned. But Pete is staring over toward a box on top of my dresser. "Are those the shoes that flash red lights when you walk?" he asks.

I give Pete an exasperated look. "Yeah," I finally say. "I bought them for Jason. What about them?"

"Matthew's been bugging me for weeks to buy him a pair, but I can't find a store that sells them." Pete is all excited. "Where the hell did you find them?"

"Look," I say, trying to keep the testiness out of my voice, "could we squirt our loads first before we get into a discussion of shopping?"

That shuts Pete up for a moment. He flashes me an apologetic look. "Sorry about that," he says. His mouth curves up into a slow smile. "Why don't you sit on my chest and fuck my face?"

Somewhat mollified, I straddle him, swinging my dick above his face. I shake it at him. "You sure you don't have any more questions about shoes?" I ask him. "It might be a while before you have your mouth free again." Pete grimaces and then just lifts his head, swallowing my dick. He works his tongue around it as I start pumping my hips. The mood returns to me as I watch my dick slide in and out of the mouth of this handsome man. I lean back and let the sensations ripple over me, stroking Pete's cock behind me.

But I find I'm still hungry for dick in my mouth. I pivot, and in the space of two heartbeats, we're both just slurping away like two pigs at the trough, both of us sucking cock like there's hell to pay. I run my hand over Pete's firm ass and then burrow it into his crack, rubbing my fingers lightly against his hole. Pete quickly shifts so that I get better access. I push my finger inside up to the first knuckle, then worm it in deeper. Pete's ass clamps around it in a tight, velvety grip, and as I move on to the third knuckle, Pete groans loudly. I push hard against his prostate, and he goes wild, thrashing his hips, kicking his legs. I finger-fuck him energetical-ly, his groans bouncing off the ceiling and out the window. *Well,* I think, *I guess we're giving David Letterman a little competition with the neighbors.*

I pull my finger out. "I think it's time I give you a good fuck-ing," I say.

Pete just grins and spreads his legs wide. "Go for it, man."

I reach over to my bedside table, yank open the drawer, and pull out a packet of condoms and my jar of lube. Pete watches in-tently as I grease up and sheathe my cock. I sling his legs over my shoulders, and carefully, with excruciating slowness, I impale his sweet ass. Pete starts groaning again. I can tell this guy likes to make noise in bed. I settle into a rhythm of quick, sharp thrusts. "Tell me, Pete," I grunt between strokes, "where'd you buy those neat Dockers your kid was wearing in that photo of yours?"

Pete looks at me, startled, and then laughs. "OK, are we even now?" he asks.

I shove my dick all the way up his ass and leave it there, grind-ing my hips against him. Pete gasps. "No," I grunt. "Not till I fuck you silly." I bend down and plant my mouth over Pete's. We play dueling tongues as I pummel his ass.

Pete twists around, and we switch to doggy style, my hands an-choring his hips, his body pushing hard against mine. I slide my hands up his torso, kneading the hard muscle, my thumbs rub-bing against the tough little nubs of his nipples. I twist them, and

Pete groans. I wrap my arms around him and pull his body tightly against mine, my chest sliding over his sweat-slicked back. I reach down and wrap my hand around his dick, stroking him in time to the thrusts of my hips. He shudders and leans his head back, and I seize the opportunity to thrust my tongue deep in his ear. "Sweet Jesus, can you ever fuck!" he groans.

We settle into a steady rhythm—me plowing Pete's ass; Pete fucking my hand; our bodies pressed together, front to back; the sweat shining on our skin. My breath rasps in and out of my lungs, I can feel the sweat trickle down my face, and each thrust of my dick sends a thrill of sensation through my body. Pete gives a low whimper, and as I skewer him the whimper turns into a long, trailing groan. I reach down and cup his balls in my hand; they're tight against his body, ready to drop a load. I give them a squeeze, and Pete's body shudders in my arms. He cries out loudly as his load squirts into my hand, coating my fingers with his thick, creamy jizz. I hold on to his body as it bucks in my arms until he falls forward, spent. I continue pumping his ass, feeling my load being pulled out from my balls. I give a loud groan.

Pete turns his head toward me. "If you're going to shoot," he growls, "I want to see it."

"OK," I pant. "Here goes."

I pull out of his ass and rip off the condom. Pete turns in the bed so that he's facing me, his eyebrows pulled down, his eyes watching intently. A few quick strokes of my hand is enough to push me over the edge. I groan again and push my hips forward. My jizz splatters against Pete's face and chest in ropy wads. "Yeah," Pete growls. "Shoot that load." He reaches up and twists my nipples as the last of my jizz spews out. I bend down and lick it off him, my tongue trailing along his cheeks and eyes, kissing his lips.

We lie in bed together for a long time, my head on Pete's chest. I can feel his heartbeat against my cheek. After a few minutes I drift off into sleep.

The next morning is a repeat of last night, only this time Pete gets to fuck me instead. By the time we finally crawl out of bed, it's almost 11 o'clock. I fix Pete a cup of coffee and pour one for myself as well.

We sip in silence, feeling the morning-after shyness that descends upon strangers who have fucked the night before. "Does Jason like miniature golf?" he finally asks.

"Yeah," I answer. "He loves it."

"There's a really good course right across from the Oakland Coliseum," he says. "Maybe the four of us can take in a round sometime."

We make a date for golf on Tuesday night. As I kiss Pete goodbye, I press up against his body. "The Mervyn's over on Geary Boulevard," I whisper in his ear. Pete gives me a quizzical look. "That's where I bought those shoes."

Pete grins. "Thanks. Maybe I can pick Matthew up a pair this weekend." He kisses me again and leaves.

I close the door, return to the bedroom, and slip off my robe. As I shower I imagine the sensation of Pete's naked flesh pressed against mine. My dick begins to stiffen as I think about next Tuesday. After miniature golf is over and the kids have been dropped off at their respective moms' places, then it'll be the dads' turn for fun and games. I can hardly wait.

Anyway
by Roddy Martin

I was sweating on the StairMaster beside my best friend, Duncan, trying not to covet the glances his workout shorts were pulling from the boy at the pec deck. "Guess what," I said.

"What?"

"I got hit on today at work by a customer. First time that's ever happened."

"What did he want?"

"Who knows? I wouldn't talk about it, not at work. And besides, he was married."

"Wedding ring?"

"His check. It had her name on it. Unless he's got a joint account with his mother."

Duncan mopped his face. "Jeez. What a pig."

Well...

The truth is, that afternoon at the art store, when I looked up and saw him—charcoal suit; red silk tie; boyish face; big, round glasses—the air was suddenly thin. "Hi," he said. "I need those letters you rub down."

"Any particular typeface?"

"Can you show me? I'm pretty ignorant."

Our elbows touched several times as I flipped through the type catalogs. He nodded a lot and smiled. It lit up his face, made him beautiful. That and the blue eyes. My eyes are blue but not like his. His had...

I don't know. Anyway, he was going to pick (yawn) Old English. "What's it for?" I asked. A flier for an organ recital. I talked him into Garamond Condensed, a restrained but elegant face that plays well against looser scripts like Mistral.

OK, I was a little solicitous.

But he took what I suggested. Rubber cement, clip art, graph paper, a nonrepro pencil, a steel-edged ruler. His $8 purchase ballooned to $45. "Are you the one giving this concert?" I asked as he wrote his check.

"Yes," he said. "I play for St. Luke's."

"That's impressive."

"Not really."

His cheeks grew red at roughly the same rate as mine grew hot. I looked at his check. I looked at his ring finger and felt way stupid. I asked, "May I see your driver's license? Do you need a parking stamp?"

"Yes, thanks." He turned. Then he turned back. "Are you feeling what I'm feeling?"

"Maybe," I said. "Probably."

"I'm learning," he said, pausing for a breath, "that it's best to be honest about these feelings. Don't you think?"

"Um…"

"Can I see you? What time can you…I mean, when do you get off work?"

"I can't discuss this."

"Please."

"Not now, not in the store. But you can call me at home if you want. We'll talk." I scribbled my number on a business card.

Duncan bent over the watercooler. His shorts crawled up his crack. "Learning to be honest?" he asked.

"At least he was cute. He looked like Joseph Steffan."

"Right. So you're going to see him?"

"Hell, no. I'm going to turn him down nicely." The man's name was Thom. He was just shy of 24, four years my junior. His check had Bible quotes on it. His wife was Carol. "Besides, he probably won't even call."

But he did call. He left two messages on my machine before he caught me at home on my day off. "Remember me?" he asked.

"Sure. How's the flier coming?" It wasn't. The $45 worth of layout supplies sat in the bag. He wondered if we could get together. "To talk about the flier?" I asked.

"No. Just to get together. Are you doing anything?"

"Watching *Love Boat*."

"Sorry," he said. "I guess you're not interested."

"It's not that I'm interested or not interested. It's that you seem sort of married."

"That's true."

Long pause. I asked, "Are you gay?"

"Something like that. Are you?"

"Ninety-seven percent. Can I ask you, do you do this often? God, that sounded awful."

"No, it's a fair question. I'd really like to see you. Please."

"I don't think it's a good idea."

But inside of an hour Thom was sitting on my sofa, staring at the floor. "I don't mean to be a pest," he said. "Maybe I should go."

"You're not a pest. Want a Coke or anything?"

"Thank you, no."

I looked at Thom's suit. It probably cost more than my sofa. There was a scuff on my coffee table, lots of scuffs. Gingerly I eased my foot over the worst of them. And saw that my toenails needed trimming.

Thom said, "Um…"

"What?"

"Nothing." His hands found mine. We laced fingers and sat. At length I said, "Your hand is soft."

"Yours too."

"You think?" I glanced up. "Thom, I don't know what to say. I just don't know." Our lips met.

"That was nice," Thom gulped.

"Wasn't it?"

We kissed our way from the sofa to the bedroom. It took a while, and we left a trail of clothes. "You're a great kisser," I gasped.

"I never kissed a man before."

"Never?" We tumbled onto the bed.

"*U-u-um.*"

I lied. Thom was a rotten kisser. But I loved kissing him and rolling with him. I asked, "Did anyone ever tell you that you have beautiful eyes?"

"Not recently."

"Well, you do."

By now we were down to our Fruit of the Looms, though Thom still wore a V-neck undershirt too small for his muscles. His slacks were tangled around his shoes. I remember thinking this might be a problem.

I put his hand on my chest. "You can touch me, you know. Touch me here; I like that." His hand was shy but warm. His erection poked my thigh. I wanted him. I wanted to feel his skin on my skin. I'd worked his T-shirt halfway up his back. Now I rolled us over so we were side by side.

I kissed his eyes. I kissed his ears. I pushed up his shirt. His stomach was flat and smooth. He was breathing hard.

I pinched his pec. He went, "Uh!" He closed his eyes and bit his lip, and...

Gasped, "I'm sorry."

We peered at the wet spot growing on his briefs. I said, "That looks awfully sticky."

"It is."

The spot grew to the size of two half-dollars. He said, "I guess that broke the mood."

I smiled and patted his thigh. Ten minutes later he stood clutching the brown paper bag I'd given him. He planned to pitch it in the Dumpster. It contained his briefs. "Forgive me," he said for the third time.

"Please. There's nothing to forgive."

Thom stared at the doorknob in his hand. "Well, thank you." He turned and threw his arms around my neck. "Thank you. You're the only guy I've done it with."

"Oh?"

"I mean in a bed."

"Oh."

He left. The room felt empty. Later I went to the gym with Duncan and Ned, this boy he was sort of seeing. Ned was all of 22. His sandy hair fell over his right eye. He glowed at Duncan with adoration, like a baby brother. This was easy to envy.

Duncan said, "Did that married guy call back?"

I nodded.

"And?"

"Don't ask. It's boring. Anyway, I'm pretty sure I won't hear from him again."

Good thing too. Thom was young and sweet, and I figured that if we got involved, he'd need me a lot, but in the end I'd need him even more.

I knew how that worked.

It rained the rest of the week, and the days dragged. Friday night I settled down with *Playgirl*. "You are masturbation fodder," I told the Man of the Month. "I love your tits. Great ass…"

The Man of the Month had half-moon pecs. His spaghetti-string tan line widened at his lower back dimples into a pale wedge that ran down his crack. The blurb said he was a third-year theology student.

"Oh, I *love* your tits! You have great tits. I'm gonna come looking at your tits. Your tits are giving me a great big orgasm…"

And so forth. I was spending a lot of Friday nights like this. I made myself get out. I made myself go to the bar, where I met a slender redhead who was a colleague of sorts. He worked at Crafty

Crafts. We compared notes on glue guns and origami paper. "Do you sell a lot of Flower Faeries?" he asked. He had pretty lips.

"What's a Flower Fairy?"

"*Faery.* Faeries. They come in packs."

He had lovely lips. But… "Great talking to you," I said, standing. "I've got—"

A slight headache?

"—to work tomorrow. Have a nice night."

"OK." He looked up. "You could make it nicer."

His name was Brian. He wore pleated slacks; an elegant, slender belt; a beige shirt; an olive-green tie. I mention this because once inside his apartment, he was all over me. And I was all over him. God, his tongue. God, his hands…hands everywhere. *Hard.* "See how much you excite me?" he said, thrusting his crotch against mine.

"Yes."

He gasped, "I like the way you…you're very…"

"Yes."

"You're very masculine."

"No, you."

I found myself flat on Brian's bed, shirt open, fly open, dick pointed at the ceiling, watching Brian peel off the olive-green tie, the beige shirt, the belt, the slacks. He had red hair on his chest. His Calvins bulged. I thought, *This is great porn. How'd I get cast in it?*

And, *How come my head still aches?*

Then the porn got truly great. Brian buried his face between my legs. His lips, his lovely lips…his lovely head bobbing up and down. I tried to stroke it—his hair looked perfectly soft—but my arms were tangled in my shirt, and he was sliding my pants down, spreading my legs. Kissing, licking. I just sank back, and—

Whoa! He bit my perineum.

—somewhere in my heart a wish sprang up. "What's the matter?" asked Brian.

"Nothing."

"Your cock is so big."

"Yeah, well. You know what they all say: big feet, big—o-o-oh!" First time anyone stuck his tongue *there*. What a sweet kid, so eager to please. So lovely—sitting up, stripping off the Calvins. Cock all hard and pink in a nest of fluffy red hair. I tried not to wish what I was wishing.

Brian asked, "Wanna see my butt?" His butt was the color of French vanilla. "Like it?"

"It's beautiful."

"Wanna, you know, plug it?" Condoms and lube appeared from a drawer like magic. Steadying himself with his hands on my pecs, Brian winced and bore down. I asked, "Are you all right?" Dots of sweat popped up across his brow.

"I'm in—u-u-uh!—heaven." He began to bounce. "I love your tits," he puffed. "You have very arousing tits. Oh, I *love* your tits!"

"God." I wished I were with Thom.

Next morning at the art store, I stood watching the rain flood the gutter. It would be one of those Saturday rains that kept customers at home rather than brought them out. The day would be fucking long.

I'd sent Heather, my young assistant, downstairs for a box of pencils. The light for the basement phone extension promptly went on and stayed on. That was half an hour ago. "Heather to the sales floor," I said through the intercom. *"Now."* I had to go to the bathroom.

The phone rang. "Do you sell art kits?" wheezed the caller.

"What kind of art are you doing?"

"It's for my granddaughter."

"What kind of art is *she* doing?"

"She asked for an art kit. Don't you have them?"

"We have drawing kits, painting kits, pastel kits—we have all kinds of kits."

The caller considered this. "I guess I better find out what she wants. Oh, sir, are you familiarized with those Faery Fingers?"

"Do you by any chance mean Flower Faeries? I know for a fact you can get them at Crafty Crafts."

Five minutes later Heather sauntered up, batting her round, ingenuous eyes. "Want half of my caramel apple?" she asked.

"Heather, where are the pencils?"

"Pencils?"

Upstairs I sat and studied the cracks in the bathroom wall. I was 30. I didn't feel 30. Guys who were 30 made twice as much money as I did. They wore suits and had jobs with pensions and responsibilities I didn't want. I wanted to read plays. To go to the gym with Duncan and buy compact discs and be shattered by an orgasm once in a while. On the other hand, you'd think that by now I'd have matching furniture and a man to take care of, not just a stack of *Playgirl* magazines.

Time was getting a little scary.

While I was gone a paper bag had materialized by the sales terminal. "You'd better get me those damn concert tickets," Heather hissed into the phone, glancing at me warily over her shoulder. I picked up the bag. It contained rubber cement, clip art, graph paper, a nonrepro pencil, a steel-edged ruler...

"Heather?"

"All right, gotta go." She hung up and announced, "Someone returned that."

"A tall man with glasses?"

"He wasn't that tall. Can I take lunch now?"

"Wait a second. Did the gentleman say why he was returning all this stuff?"

"No."

"It was a *return*. Didn't you ask?"

Heather's eyes widened. She looked like Tweety Bird.

But there was a note that she'd forgotten to mention. Folded and stapled twice, it said: "My friend offered to design the flier on his computer, so it turns out that I don't need these supplies after all. But thanks—for *everything!* Sincerely, Thom. (P.S.: I admit, I came to the store in hopes of seeing you. I'm disappointed, but it's probably for the best.)"

Friend? Computer? For the best?

Silly, I felt like I'd been slapped in the face. And yet...after work I found Thom on my doorstep. "I've been driving around," he said.

"Have you?"

"I've been fighting with myself."

We gazed at each other. "Yeah," I said. "It's a bitch, isn't it?" I opened the door for him.

My hand floated over Thom's stomach. He sighed. "That feels nice." Most of our clothes lay in a pile by the bed. "I like you a lot," he said. "Do you like me?"

"Um-hmm." I licked my way from his ear to his throat.

He laughed. "Your chin scratches."

"Is that good or bad?"

"Good. It gives me goose bumps."

"It's because my"—kiss—"5-o'clock shadow"—kiss—"comes in at 2:30." I set about washing Thom's left pec with my tongue. I blew on the wet skin. "You have a great body."

"I play racquetball."

"Yeah? You must"—kiss—"play an awful lot."

"I do isometrics...too."

Sucking Thom's hard pink nipple ("Uh!"), I slid my hand under the waistband of his cotton briefs. His cock was in a state of great excitement, and so I ("Uh!") rolled my thumb over it. Once. It jerked. And...

"Damn," he gasped. "I'm sorry."

I peered at the semen dripping from my fingers. "You say that too much. Stop saying that."

"But...sorry."

I held him. What else could I do? "Hey," I whispered. "Relax."

The rain splashed outside, and I marveled at the nape of his neck. "Can I ask you something?" he said. "Are you glad that you're gay?"

"It's been a while since I thought about it."

"If you had a son, would you want him to be gay?"

"I guess I'd want him to be whatever he was."

"Oh," said Thom. "I have a son."

This piece of intelligence was off my radar screen. I asked, "How old?"

"He's two."

"Ah." I pressed my cheek to his skin. "Can you stay for a while?"

"A little while."

"Let's take care of these knots in your muscles." Soon I had Thom flat on the bed. Straddling him, I spread oil on his back. I kneaded his shoulders. His muscles were firm, his skin smooth and pale. The crotch of my briefs kept brushing the seat of his.

"Better?"

"Much."

Thom's hair was cut in a precise V. Lying on top of him, I traced it with my nose. I kissed his shoulders, his shoulder blades, all the way down his spine. I kissed his tailbone. Sliding his briefs down, I kneaded his buttocks. I buffed them with my 2:30 shadow.

Thom shuddered. Marveling at the small of his back, I knew I was headed for trouble.

"Thom, roll over."

I took him in my mouth. "Oh," he sighed. "Stop."

"Nmph?"

"No, don't stop."

The man had a wife and a child. I didn't want to hurt them. I didn't want to get hurt, which was inevitable if... But...

I found myself staked out flat, Thom between my legs. He thrust.

"Ouch!"

"Sorry." Pumping and snorting, he grabbed my face and slurped. His tongue was in my nose. "I want this," he panted. "I want this. I want this." We rolled around and around and landed on the floor.

"Are you all right?"

"Yeah. Faster."

"I'm…"

"Oh, God."

We wound up entwined, kissing and jerking off. "Know," I said, "what I like about you? Your eyes."

"Mmm."

"And your smile."

"Mmm."

"And…"

I came. He came. It was lovely, warm. I spread it on his chest. "Mind? Sometimes I like to play with it."

Thom sighed blissfully. "I'm so confused."

My heart went into free fall, and I thought, *I wasn't doing anything with it, anyway.*

We lay there being sticky.

Snowbound
by Lee Alan Ramsay

I hadn't seen a highway sign in maybe 40 minutes, not that I was traveling that fast. Since there was close to half a foot of snow on the ground, I wasn't sure I was on a highway at all; it could have been a mere trail. If this was indeed the shortcut I saw on the map, then I would be breaking out onto 89 within the next five miles.

However, the deeper I got into the thick, heavy forest and the narrower, bumpier, and more twisted the roadway—whatever it was—became, the more I started thinking I had taken a very wrong turn. When flurries added to the already blowing snow, I decided to find a wide place to turn around. With the gas gauge indicating that I had about a quarter of a tank, I didn't have the luxury of a lot of time to experiment, and roads that the state kept plowed were preferable to the meandering thing I was on. It would be dark in another hour.

I saw a slight break in the trees to the left. I headed the hood ornament slowly in the direction of the gap, came to a stop, and put the car in reverse. I was just about to stop and begin another swing when the right rear of my Saturn gave way with a loud metallic bang.

There must have been a ditch—a very deep ditch by the feel—on the right-hand side of the roadway, and I was now partly in it. When I put the transmission into drive once again, the heavy clanking and whirring sounds issuing from the rear of the vehicle told me I was also in serious trouble.

I got out and surveyed the right rear tire, which was at a crazy angle to the rest of the car. I had broken an axle.

Getting back into the driver's seat, I did some quick thinking. I had a heavy parka that would keep me warm through the night. On the seat beside me were a half-filled bag of Doritos and a quarter of a cup of cold coffee. Even with nothing to eat, I could last the night.

It was too close to dark to strike out on foot in any direction, and at least with the closed car, I'd have some protection from the wind. And if I idled the engine for just a few minutes at a time, I could provide myself with a little heat. In the morning I could head back to the road and flag someone down.

I tried not to think too much about how stupid I'd been to turn off the marked roads. It wasn't like I was desperate to get back home to L.A. or anything.

It was then that I noticed a small sign up ahead, partially obliterated by the swirling snow. I squinted just in case desperation was making my eyes play tricks on me. No, it was a small white sign with black letters, which I couldn't read at that distance. I zipped up the parka and got out again.

On closer inspection I saw that the sign read RANGER STATION 3 MI., with an arrow pointing up, indicating straight ahead.

I looked back at my stricken Saturn and decided to try for the station. If it was locked up solid, I still had enough daylight left to get back to the car. But plan B held out the hope of warmth, a little food, and a means to communicate with the outside world. I trudged off in the deepening snow; I hadn't a moment to lose.

After 20 or so minutes, I saw light in the distance. It was still snowing lightly, but I could see square yellow windowpanes. A few more steps, and I could discern the outline of a rude cabin.

The cabin was small and square with a sharply pitched dormerless roof, and smoke poured from the huge stone chimney. On the wide front porch, raised and relatively sheltered from the snowfall, was a stack of cut wood.

I hammered on the rough-hewn panels of the windowless door and shouted, "Is anyone home? "

I heard stirring from inside, and eventually the knotted panels of the door creaked open. A huge bearded man in black briefs and a red tank top stood there to greet me. He was frowning heavily and seemed outrageously disturbed by my presence.

"Yeah?"

"Uh, sir...I broke an axle down your road a ways, and I wonder if you have a phone."

I could feel the warmth of the cabin flowing out the open door. The stranger seemed not to mind the cold air replacing it around his scantily clad body. He stood there mute and scowling.

"Maybe I could also warm myself by your fire while we're waiting for the tow truck?" I added tentatively.

The man was large; he must have been six-five at least, and he was heavily muscled. But there was a bigness about him that went beyond stature, a presence that must have commanded attention when he walked into any room. His ruddy, florid face was surrounded by unruly wisps of black hair and a full beard of the same raven shade. Dark eyes shone out from his face, twinkling even in the gathering dusk.

It seemed that the stranger needed a long time to frame his comments, as if he were being charged money for words and had to be efficient with them. "No tow trucks comin' out on a night like this. No business on this road anyway."

I was cold and beginning not to feel my feet anymore. And it suddenly occurred to me that this man was being cruelly hostile. I'm only five-six and certainly represented no threat to this Paul Bunyan.

"Gee, I'm sorry to have bothered you," I snapped. "I'll just knock on your neighbor's door instead. Maybe he'll be a little more civil than you."

The stranger snorted. "Snotty little article. You'd never know I hold out salvation for you."

"Not if you don't let me in," I countered, unflustered by his blustery manner.

At this he stood aside from the doorway and bid me enter with a gesture.

The interior of the cabin was clean but claustrophobic. The single room was no bigger than the average square living room. One side of the chamber was dominated by an overstuffed easy chair and a double bed with heaps of plain cotton quilting. There was a braided rug in earth tones on the floor. The other side of the room held a huge black wood-burning stove of ancient vintage and a small wooden kitchen table of perhaps the same decade of manufacture as the stove; it had plain sturdy square legs and a distressed mahogany-colored surface. There was a single kitchen chair of a different design from the table.

Behind the table and stove was a wall of shelves, floor to ceiling, obviously the pantry. The deep shelves were lined with cans, bags, and boxes. To one side of the shelving was a niche with a two-way radio. My spirits brightened when I spotted that detail, not having seen a telephone in my opening scan of the room.

"My name is Oscar," I said, pulling the parka hood off my head. "I was heading back to L.A. from Greenboro—that's a little town in the upper northeast corner of California. Thought I'd see a little of the Sierras on my way back. I saw a chance to cut 20 miles off the trip with a little shortcut. Guess that map's mismarked or something…"

From the stranger's stark silence, I suddenly realized I was carrying on like a demented magpie. I offered my hand.

"Darien," he said. He had a firm handshake, tough but not bone-crushing. He went to the stove and poured me a mug of coffee from the speckled blue pot. He moved with a pantherlike grace, silently on bare bony feet that had to be size 15s at least. He handed me the steaming mug and pointed to the easy chair, bathed in a pool of bright light from a floor lamp with a yellowing fringed shade. There was a book facedown on one of the arms;

I had interrupted his evening reading. I glanced at the title as I sat: *Lady Chatterley's Lover.*

Darien pulled the kitchen chair into the center of the room and sat within conversation distance of me. He had beautifully sculpted thighs, which he spread wide, and a bulge in the black briefs that could possibly have taken my breath away had I been at liberty to stare at it for a few consecutive minutes. From the rather rude greeting this man had given me so far, I decided not to press my luck.

I looked over at the radio. "So can we contact the outside world from here?"

"Sure."

There was nothing more. No more words, nothing in the way of movement toward the sacred microphone that might have spared me any more anxiety over my situation. I pondered what I was doing wrong. Was I not communicating my desire to leave? Was there some kind of a language barrier? Perhaps I was to use the radio myself. Perhaps Darien needed to be told exactly what I wanted: *Darien, baby. I want you to go to the radio, activate it, call the nearest similar radio, and relay the message that Oscar has a broken-down car, a reasonable amount left on his MasterCard, and a stern desire to return to the City of the Angels, otherwise known as La-La Land.*

It seemed that my host had an inertia problem. Bodies at rest tend to remain at rest...

"Darien, sir...I realize I've interrupted a quiet evening at home for you, but if we could just make some kind of call out to civilization..."

My host interrupted me. "What makes you think this place is uncivilized?"

The question gave me cause to ponder a moment. "Well," I began slowly, "I don't see a gas station nearby. There aren't exactly a lot of hotels and bars around with lighted signs. We're not in the real thick of a lot of people."

"And lights, buildings, people make up civilization?" Darien asked matter-of-factly. "One person alone can't be civilized?"

It was warm in the room in more ways than one. I used the time to pull off my parka to think. "I'm sorry if I've offended you, sir. I didn't mean to demean your situation here. As rustic as it is, it is obviously not uncivilized."

For the first time Darien smiled. The beautiful Santa Claus lips spread wide, and the thick hair around his mouth moved. "I could call now, but no one'd come out till morning, maybe day after tomorrow morning if it snows all night. Why don't you just plan on staying the night, and we'll bring someone out for your car when we can?"

"Sounds like a plan to me," I said. I sensed my host was growing a trifle more at ease with my presence. Perhaps he was one of those people who is shy with strangers; that could account for his apparent status as a hermit in a rather inhospitable section of wilderness. Surely he was not bothered by very many visitors, even if he was a forest ranger.

I was in the mood for a hearty meal and a good stiff drink or two, but if he had already eaten and was a teetotaler, I could survive. At least I was warm.

My spirits brightened significantly over the next moment.

"I was about ready to start supper," said Darien. "Can't offer much more than tinned stuff, but you're welcome to join me."

"I'm pretty handy in the kitchen, sir. And though I've never cooked on a wood stove before, it's always been a fantasy of mine to try. Maybe you could let me put something together, and you could go back to just relaxing with your book. A little effort on my part to thank you for your hospitality."

Darien nodded, his pensive lips extended. Oh, those thin rust-colored lips in that vast nest of black hair! At length he made a slow sweeping gesture to the pantry shelves and indicated the row of clean pots and pans on the warming shelf over the stove. He pointed to the stack of wood in a huge hod next to the firebox.

He sank into the easy chair I'd just vacated, absorbing himself immediately in the pages of Lady Chatterley's sexual Olympics. *Pity,* I thought. *Hairy, masculine, built, hung…and getting his jollies off on a het sex book. Sigh.*

I found some chipped beef, one jar among dozens on the shelf. Though nonfat dry milk was no substitute for the real thing, I mixed it thick enough for a creamy nuance; there was enough thyme and oregano to bump up flavors and make cream chipped beef over soda biscuits, something you'd order again at a truck-stop beanery. I tested the heat of the oven for the biscuits by sticking my hand into its dark depths, like I knew what 350 degrees felt like on my bare skin! And when I finished preparing a side of French-cut string beans heavy with garlic powder, I was ready to call my host to the table.

During that half hour I watched him "unconsciously" scratch his crotch 14 times by actual count, and I got the feeling it was not because his bulging genitals were itchy. He sat in the huge wing chair—done in a faded gold brocade that looked like a relic that had tarnished—with his legs as wide apart as when he was sitting in the kitchen chair, which point raised the serious question of where I was going to sit at the dinner table. There was only one table chair in the tiny room.

That's not all there wasn't.

There was no sink and consequently nothing to draw water into. But this was no tragedy since there was nothing to draw water from either, not even a pump with a curved metal handle. I ladled water for the meal from a huge pot on the stove; I guessed it was melted snow.

There was also no door in the room leading to anything resembling a bathroom, which I was going to need within an hour or so. And since I had been on the road a day and a half without bathing, I was especially curious about this strange home's other sanitary facilities.

"It's soup," I said to my host.

He looked over the top of his book and smiled. Setting the volume down on the brocaded chair arm, he rose and went to the door. A gust of cold snowy air burst in; he didn't bother closing the panels for the time he was on the porch. After 30 seconds of chilly blasts, he returned with a captain's chair in scuffed and warped maple, which he slid toward the table. That answered the question of where the second of us was to sit for dinner. My other questions—and some I had not even thought of—would be answered within the hour.

My host was apparently not used to eating in close quarters with other people, at least not people with genteel tastes. Darien hunched over his plate, clamped all four fingers over the handle of a spoon, and shoveled food into his mouth like an Aborigine. I tried not to notice, though his table manners and the fact that he chewed with his mouth open were nauseating.

I disarmed the situation with chitchat.

"So I was visiting my Aunt Charity, she's the one I told you about earlier, the one who's been real generous with me over the years, especially at Christmastime. Anyway, I wanted to make sure she was settled in the new retirement community, Lazy Acres; you remember, I mentioned that earlier too. Well, I just wanted to make sure the place was decent and that they were taking care of her OK. Anyway, I talked to the resident manager and made sure she'd get the best of care, then I just headed home. Aunt Charity isn't too coherent anymore." I paused in my monologue to make a twirling-finger gesture at my temple.

"Anyway, it's not that I really need to get home or anything. I can't *tell* you why I decided to even look for a shortcut back to L.A. I have this dippy roommate, Greg; I told you about him. Well, I'm not exactly desperate to get back to his craziness." Though in Chatty Cathy mode, I decided not to go any further with the part of my story concerning Greg, my ex-lover. "And I mean, like, a mail-room job at Moist Erotic Entertainment Enterprises isn't anything you'd want to put on a résumé these days.

I think they could actually struggle through an extra day or two without me. Besides, stuffing *Harvey Takes a Dive* and *Bambi's Audition* into boxes for shipping isn't anyone's idea of a career these days, take it from one who knows."

I'm not sure when I noticed it, but I was the only one talking during dinner. I'm not even sure Darien acknowledged my efforts at conversation with the proper grunted monosyllables. I just prattled on as if what I was saying was the most important talk in the world.

When I finally sat back and relaxed in the captain's chair, sated and silent at least for a moment, Darien stood and in a single motion lowered all the dirty dishes into the water pot on the stove. It was my guess that they'd simmer for the night, a very convenient and most effective dishwasher, and the water would be discarded in favor of new snow in the morning.

My host checked the firebox, threw in another two chunks of split wood, closed the wrought iron door, and damped it down to nearly zero air for the gentle blaze within. "That'll go the night."

Starve the blaze of air, and it lasts a long time.

I decided the time was right to get bold about sanitation facilities. "Uh, Darien, sir, I need to use the euphemism, if you could point me in the right direction. And if it wouldn't be a huge imposition on your hospitality, I'd like to shower...or bathe, as the case may be in your establishment."

My host stood in the middle of the room and deliberately pulled the red tank top over his head, revealing a thickly muscled chest, tanned and covered with a matting of black hair. The man then casually bent over and lowered the black briefs from his crotch. I had to stifle a gulp.

He was gorgeous. No more than a 30-inch waist, yet he bulged everywhere else: pecs, ass cheeks, biceps. His thick flaccid penis dangled a quarter of the way to his knees, and his heavily muscled thighs pushed the softball-size nut bag out from his body. And all of it was covered with black hair—not thick, kinky, fluffy hair but smooth black fur that hugged his ruddy skin. I was having a lot of difficulty remaining civil.

Standing buck naked in the middle of his single room, my host bowed slightly at the waist and gestured to the front door, the only door. Maybe he misunderstood what I had just asked for. Then again, I was the one most likely to misunderstand anything in this realm.

Darien motioned with one upturned palm that I was to stand. I complied. Then he pinched at garments he no longer had on and gestured "nakedness." I shook my head in disbelief but complied with his oblique orders. I sat to take off my shoes and socks, pulled my T-shirt over my head, lowered my jeans, and stripped off my Jockey briefs.

"Hul-lo," I said. "Bathroom? Shower? Toilet?"

The huge man grabbed me by the wrist and pulled me to the cabin door, opening it with his free hand. I was led out onto the porch and down the front steps into a pool of moonlight on the snow-covered front lawn.

I couldn't believe what was happening. He took me to the side of his home, where he squatted and promptly relieved himself. Unable to come up with a reason why not, I imitated him, right beside him, though my bare feet were being assaulted by icy knives of cold.

He moved a few feet from his steaming pile of urine and excrement and began scooping up handfuls of snow, first to wipe his crotch area and then, with new clumps of white powder, to scrub the rest of his body: armpits, face, chest, legs.

I was getting shivery with the cold, so as long as this was going to be my evening toilette, I decided to make it quick. I moved away from my own relievings and doused myself wildly with snow. Actually, I have to admit, not only was the notion of bathing in snow just kinky enough to make it exciting, but romping about on a mountaintop naked with this incredible hunk of male sinew was beginning to turn me on. I rubbed snow thoroughly in my crack area and shampooed my reddish brown hair with snow as well.

Then I felt the cold invading me to a point that I knew was dangerous. Beginning to shiver more violently, I scrambled up the steps of the cabin and raced inside, followed by my bounding, laughing host. Our bare feet pounded on the rough boards and braided rug.

"As long as the core doesn't get cold..." he bubbled.

I raced for the stove and spread my arms, putting as much of my body in contact with the radiating heat as I could. I felt both clean and invigorated. And my natural functions had been satisfied as well. As rude as his ways might be, I was somehow getting in tune with this rough mountain man.

Darien turned toward the bed and bent over, showing his beautiful hairy cheeks and his livid wrinkled ball sac sagging between the backs of his thighs. He began turning the quilts down. "OK," he pronounced, "I'm turning in. Ya got yer choice. The floor, the easy chair, or in here with me."

"Uh..." I fumbled, still not sure of my status in this household. "I guess I'd better tell you straight out so there's no misunderstanding: I'm gay—you know, homosexual—and it might be best if I take the floor or the chair, just so nothing untoward happens during the night."

Even as I delivered the last of that ridiculous line—like I would force myself on this man, who was roughly twice my size and weight—I realized how utterly stupid I could get sometimes. Then I realized I was even stupider still.

Darien stood up from arranging the bed and turned toward me to reveal a semi–hard-on that was beginning to angle away from his magnificent loins. The thick penis was still curved slightly downward, but it was veined and rugged, like the mountaintop we were both standing on, tough and demanding. He had an almost exasperated expression on his face, as if to say, "Gay? Why, whatever do you mean?"

"Oh, God," I heard myself saying into the yellow light of the cabin. Then something like "Darien, please, could we just sit and talk about this for a minute..."

My host simply snapped his fingers in the direction of his open bed. I must say, I've been seduced by the direct and very effective "Let's fuck" line in bars before, but Darien had these amateurs beat by light-years!

I left the warmth of the stove and slid under the quilts; Darien slipped in beside me and immediately enfolded me in his arms. He extended his tongue and licked around my neck slowly, like a snail leaving trails. Then he journeyed up my neck to an earlobe and began nibbling on it. I could feel the steady puffs of air on the side of my face.

I became a puddle of goose pimples. I let out a guttural moan of pleasure that has meaning only in an animal realm. I let my hands roam about his massive back; he was hairy even there. As he pressed our bodies closer and closer together, I felt his mighty organ growing stiff between us. This was the kind of penis that moved solid objects out of the way as it engorged itself.

He began caressing me slowly, very delicately. His palms were rough, like sandpaper, but he put so very little pressure on my skin that the sensation of iron fist–velvet glove sent me into waves of shivering ecstasy: my arms, my chest—with lingering stops at the nipples—my abdomen, my thighs. I had been hard for some minutes now but became totally aware of just how aroused I was only when he closed his fist around my throbbing dick.

Aroused? This man was arousing me in ways that went way beyond the mere physical. It was as if I were not a slave to just my nerve endings anymore—or perhaps he was stimulating nerve endings in my mind and imagination. His clean, musky scent invaded my nostrils, unclouded by manufactured perfumes.

I got bolder. I wanted to caress him too. No, that was a lie—or at least not the complete truth. I did want to let my palms explore his hairy skin but only after I thoroughly explored and fondled his penis and testicles. I wanted to hold the organs in my hand, actually feel their bulk and weight. Perhaps I wanted to feel how demanding they were becoming. I reached down and drew my fingers around the warm, pulsating cock. I inched a few centimeters closer to utter erotic insanity.

He did not thwart my efforts to grope him. Rather, I sensed he might have shifted his body ever so slightly to give me room to probe his crotch.

As I let my fingertips explore the hard shaft of male flesh, I think I made some trashy reference to the Almighty. I let my fingers inch their way down to the rod's base, where I gathered up the balls and pressed them against his hairy crotch. The bulging sac felt like a living cactus plant, bristling with black stubble. I fondled each testicle in turn and returned to holding the cock in my curved fingers.

Then I delivered the line of all ridiculous lines: "Are you going to rape me with this piece of meat?"

"It's going up your ass. If you don't want it there, then I guess it'll be rape."

I deserved that.

I could have simply said, "Fuck me." I could have just rolled over and presented my upturned cheeks to let him know that I wanted to be fucked. In the end, though, I just succumbed to his pace, his way of making things unfold. I didn't become a limp, unresponsive blow-up buddy doll, by any means, but I would do what he wanted us to do. And I definitely opted for not saying anything further.

He rolled on top of me and pressed his lips against mine. I allowed his tongue to begin a long, slow exploratory journey into my mouth. With the actual invasion of my body, I soon realized just how strong and passionate Darien was. Perhaps it was pent-up desire, a long time in the wilderness without another body nearby to seek release. Yet somehow, in some tiny remaining chink of reason—reason was quickly being swept away by my own passions and animal lusts—in a small recess of reason, I wondered if this man ever really wanted for anything. He could not be in love with me: We'd known each other only a few hours. But there was something, a galvanic force that was almost literally drawing me toward him.

I felt his mighty legs shifting position under the quilts. They were between mine now, and he was forcing my legs apart. I offered no resistance whatsoever. In a quick succession of movements that did nothing to shatter the sublime mood, he threw off the quilts, reached to the floor next to the wall for a towel and grease, slathered his dick along with my upturned hole, and positioned my ankles for the optimum angle of thrust. The cabin's air was still warm; there was no chill on my naked skin.

I braced myself. I'd taken some huge dicks in my time, but this one was going to take concentration. I didn't want to ruin everything by wimping out or, worse yet, screaming in pain. I would have to relax. I let my head fall back into the pillow and released both nerve endings and muscles to the inevitable. He sensed when the moment was right.

Oh, God, did he go slow! At times I thought he wasn't moving into me at all, then I could feel the next increment spreading me apart. Slowly, ever so slowly, he came down and into me.

I opened my eyes for a brief second, just to see his face. He was staring intently at the place that connected us, staring fixedly, face contorted in riveted concentration. Then, when he sensed that enough of his organ was inside me, he relaxed, pushed forward in one long, brazen thrust, and sent me over the edge.

I felt no pain, just massive bulk and pressure, as if I were being inflated. He locked my legs in the crooks of his elbows and slumped down on me. I felt my body doubling up, my knees pressing against the sides of my chest. I was completely helpless, and yet I was soaring the updrafts of raw, unadulterated lust for another man. My mind started to reel out of control as if the room itself were spinning on an unseen axis. I was intoxicated.

Then he started to stroke, slowly at first, then with a mounting savagery that pushed me even further into the oblivion of passion. The lower regions of my body started to catch fire with the friction of his huge pole. I started to squirm within the limits of my entrapment beneath him but not in an effort to get away by any means. Rather, I wanted him deeper in me if that were possible. I wanted to open myself further to him, to press myself up toward him even harder than he was pounding me. I let out a long moan that must have shaken dust from the rafters of the cabin.

Then, almost without warning, I heard his voice begin to fill the cabin's air: low and raspy at first, then mounting inexorably to a steady roar over my head. He slammed his pelvis home, welded it there, and then in another few seconds the whole room quaked with an orgasm I was certain was affecting seismographic equipment in at least three states.

I could feel his mighty organ pumping into me, shooting load after load of liquid. Though I could not see inside my bowel to make certain, I would have bet he set records with the amount of sticky fluid he was releasing. He seemed to go on twitching for hours; the concept of time had long since shattered for me. Then, breathless, he slumped onto me as if he'd just died. I was breathless too, though he had done all the work. I just lay there, looking up into the rafters of the cabin, glassy-eyed, content—and I had not even shot yet!

When he finally rose from atop me, he smiled. With only a slight adjustment of position—he let me lower my legs a bit—he took my right hand and wrapped the fingers around my still-hard, throbbing cock. Without words he told me it was my turn.

Though enough time had gone by for him to start growing soft inside my fuck hole, I discerned no noticeable change in the bulk of his organ. I started to stroke my own meat and again sank into the nether realms of passion. His mighty piece was pressing agonizingly against my prostate. I could feel the pressure, and two or three times I almost exploded without touching myself.

So it did not take too many strokes for me to send myself into the fiery cauldron of orgasm. The hot little droplets spilled over my chest, searing little globs, probably paltry in comparison to the amount this huge man had released into me, but I enjoyed my come as much as he did. As the monumental tickle overtook me, I threw my head about on the pillow and screamed, bucking my hips to exercise the organ that was still inside me, to press it ever closer against my twitching and draining prostate. Now it was my turn to collapse, incoherent, at peace, into the mattress beneath my back.

When I was still at last, he slowly withdrew and made very quick work of the mop-up: my chest, his dong, my crack. Then the towel went to the floor, and he came to my side and enfolded me in his huge arms once again, smiling into my face from mere inches away. I nuzzled my face into his hairy upper chest; he pulled the quilts up around us, and the whole cosmos suddenly became warm and womblike.

I usually thrash around a lot when I sleep, needing at least three quarters of the width of a bed for my restless nights. But now I sank almost immediately into a dreamless sleep and woke up in exactly the same position I last remembered the night before, in his arms with my face nestled into his hairy chest.

Darien yawned and rolled away, the back of his head in his folded palms, and looked up at the ceiling. The hair in his armpits was musty and pungent.

"When was the last time you had sex?" I inquired, still half convinced that the "pent-up desires" theory explained his ardor of the night before.

He looked at me and smiled through the shiny black beard surrounding his mouth. "Why is that important?"

"I was just wondering. You were pretty wild last night. I thought you might be a little on the hungry side."

Darien's only answer was a quiet snort. Then he went back to staring at the ceiling. Gray light was beginning to replace the blackness beyond the few curtainless windowpanes in the cabin. It was now chilly in the room.

There was something about this man that intrigued me. He was not being enigmatic just to impress someone. Sometimes people do that: purposely put on a cloak of mystery so others will try to pry and find out what is beneath the shroud. To these pseudosophisticates, mysteriousness is a contrived way of getting attention, and the surprise inside is hardly ever worth the effort to discover it.

Darien was definitely not trying to attract anyone's attention, not in the middle of nowhere. He was a real enigma, not seeming to care who figured him out or who didn't. I suddenly realized he might be with the most real person I'd ever encountered.

"Ever have anyone else live up here with you?" I inquired offhandedly.

"A boy. Once."

There was some sort of a spin on the word "boy" that led me to believe we were not talking about a child.

I frowned in a bit of confusion. "One small dresser," I stated, referencing the smallish, almost dollhouse-size bureau. "No closets. Only one easy chair…" I couldn't see two people living in the place, and I made my confusion known.

Darien snorted once again. "He didn't wear clothes, and he wasn't allowed to use the furniture."

My blood suddenly froze in my veins. "Come again?"

"You heard me. He was a boy. A dog boy really."

"You mean you lived here with a sort of slave-type person you humiliated on a daily basis?"

"No."

I raised myself up on one elbow to look at him directly. "Excuse me. Being kept naked and not being allowed to use the furniture is humiliation from where I sit."

"Fine," responded Darien. "It wasn't for him." He obviously didn't care what I thought on the matter.

I decided it was time for me to make some motion to leave this place. I slipped out of bed, and, rather than act rude, I went to the wood hod and opened the firebox in the stove. There was a layer of gray ash on the grate; I blew on it to reveal a thinner layer of live embers underneath. I carefully lowered a few small and medium chunks of split wood onto the glowing bed. It caught almost immediately, but it was a while before the room became comfortable again.

"Completely naked?" I inquired. "All the time?"

"Buck ass."

I didn't know exactly why at the time, but my dick started getting hard. The thought of a man submitting to this woodsman was doing something to me. I remembered certain scenes from movies that involved a power shift, sometimes bondage and seminudity…

I decided not to fret about the matter. I didn't feel in any danger; if Darien had wanted to do me harm, he could have done so long before this.

I grabbed the bucket with the dishes in it and went out the front door into the chilly dawn. I quickly emptied the dirty water, scrubbed its interior and all the dishes with snow, and filled the bucket with new snow, packing it down hard. Then I took a leak and scurried back into the relative warmth of the cabin.

Darien was still in bed. I warmed up the biscuits left over from the night before, whipped up a large batch of oatmeal, and, when the snow was melted in the bucket and the water was hot, made a pot of tea.

I could feel Darien watching me as I worked—I actually stayed busy so I could escape noticing how intimately he was studying me. Yet—and don't ask me why—I didn't bother to put any clothes on. The thick walls of the cabin held the heat very well, and soon it was warm inside once again.

Darien got up for breakfast; he didn't bother to put any clothes on either. And as I suspected, he consumed enough for any three of us. How he kept trim was anyone's guess. But then I suppose tramping around the wilderness in below-freezing conditions eats up a lot of calories.

He stood up from the breakfast table and took a long, careful look at me, his arms folded across his massive hairy chest. Then with new purpose he went to the top dresser drawer and drew out something black made of leather with a chain attached to it. It was a heavily studded collar, which he instantly snapped round my neck.

"Uh...Darien..." I stammered. "Uh..."

He gently pushed down on one of my shoulders, indicating I was to go to the floor. I was not afraid, just totally confused. I had not indicated I was submitting to this—well, maybe I had with a hard dick as we were talking about it earlier. But that wasn't exactly consent.

He wrapped the chain around one of the stove legs and slipped the snap hook at the end into one of the links. Without a word he dressed quickly in his briefs, socks, jeans, blue flannel shirt, and hiking boots. Still without a word he grabbed a thick parka from a peg next to the door and left.

I could barely believe what had just happened. I was crouched on the floor, completely naked, with a dog collar around my neck, my knees on the braided rug of a cabin, God only knew how many miles from the nearest neighbor, with my ass high in the air.

I don't know how long I stayed in that position. Perhaps I thought he might come back and do me harm if I was not in the same position he had left me in.

Harm?

What harm? What harm had he done me so far? None, pure and simple. When I did sit up, I realized there was enough slack in the chain to actually get comfortable, away from the searing front surface of the stove.

I suddenly burst into peals of uncontrollable laughter. Laughter at my own folly, laughter at my own foolishness.

There was no lock on the collar, nor on either end of the chain. The door was not bolted from the outside. My clothes were within easy reach. I could take the collar off, put my things on, walk to my car and the road beyond, hail a fellow motorist, and contract to have my car towed away and eventually repaired. I could report Darien to the authorities...

I started laughing louder than before. Report what?

The man had fed me the night before, let me sleep warm and safe in his bed, given me the best sex of my life, and shared his breakfast with me. "Oh, this is true dementia!" I screamed into the empty room. "The monster!"

Tears were springing into the corners of my eyes as the laughter went on undiminished. I pounded my fists into the braided carpeting in a vain attempt to bring the mirth under control. I would have a lot of trouble turning Darien in for anything illegal.

Then, as the laughter calmed and I could think a little more clearly, I began to chill myself with some thoughts and notions. The collar actually felt good around my neck, not cutting and chafing as one might think but substantial and comforting, like an old pair of shoes. When was the last time anyone thought enough of me to perform such a bold gesture?

After the last argument Greg and I had had as lovers, he smashed all my begonia pots and shredded the plants into practically powder. That was indeed a bold gesture, but it was meant to drive me away, to hurt me, to take something away from me, to vent blind rage on an innocent object. It was pettiness pure and simple, albeit bold.

The collar around my neck said exactly the opposite. It meant "Stay!" It meant "Learn!" It meant "See a new world with rules I did not make up." It meant "Dare to be adventurous, cut yourself loose from what you know, and see a new horizon—even if it is from the floor of a rude cabin in the wilderness." In short, the collar around my neck was, in some manner I could not fully understand yet, a way of giving me something.

Several times that morning I undid the chain and had my Jockey briefs poised to slip into, only to journey back to the stove leg and sit there thinking some more. Several times I looked up at the silver box housing the two-way radio, thinking I might figure out how to use it myself. Mostly I just sat and thought, occasionally shoving more wood into the fire to keep the place warm.

Since Darien hadn't taken any lunch with him and I didn't think there was a convenient diner nearby, I assumed he would come home around noon, hungry. I made some more biscuits, heated up a small tinned ham, and prepared some mixed veggies on the side.

I don't know exactly what time it was—there was no clock in the cabin, and my watch had stopped—when I heard Darien stomping up the steps and across the front porch. I reattached the chain around the stove leg and assumed the same position he had left me in: on my knees, upper chest on the floor, ass in the air, and legs spread wide. I think I was more interested in offering him a good noontime fuck than trying to impress him with how obedient I could be.

Without a word he sat down to his meal. After two bites he tossed a few things onto a plate and lowered it to the floor next to his boot, snapping his fingers to indicate that this was my share.

I ate silently with my fingers. I was really hoping he didn't want me to gobble it up with my mouth on the plate. Mercifully he let me sit and pick things up.

When he finished he left the dirty dishes on the table and retired to his easy chair. There had still not been a single word passed between us.

I was growing uneasy because there were some things I wanted to clarify, some detailing I needed to understand, and two or three items on a list I needed done for me.

"Can we talk?" I ventured at length.

I had obviously interrupted some sort of postlunch quiet time, a private reverie he did not appreciate having broken, but he did not explode with anger. He stood up calmly from the chair and reached for a flat riding crop that had been hanging by the door. Slowly and quietly he unhooked the chain from the stove leg and bent me over the captain's chair.

I received a smart slap on each cheek; neither hurt all that much, but I took this to mean that if I broke rules in the future, he might not be so lenient. I would like to have seen or at least heard a list of the rules, but because of his silence, I figured that would not be forthcoming. I had my choice: Accept the situation as it was presented or leave.

I have to be very honest: At this point I was so curious about Darien and the life he was offering me, I would not have left even if his punishment with the crop had left me black-and-blue. He replaced the crop on its hook next to the door, pulled on his parka, and left.

I sat in a quiet quandary for several minutes: naked, chained in a warm cabin, with a benefactor I was at a loss to figure out. But then as I pondered, I realized there was very little to figure out. He had not punished me for releasing my chain in order to cook for him. I figured housekeeping and tending to my natural functions would come under the same blanket dispensation. He just didn't want to talk. The "why" would take me a while to figure out, but for the time being I decided to go along with this weird scenario. I did not feel in danger in any way.

I found a broom and dustpan and gave the cabin a fluffing. I made the bed and tended the dirty dishes. Something was nagging at me, though, something I had to communicate with him even if it meant punishment.

While I was dusting around the base of the bureau, I noticed that the bottom drawer was open a few inches. I wondered at the time if that had been done on purpose. The corner of something complicated and metallic caught my eye.

I pulled the drawer open and found an ancient black Underwood typewriter. Next to it, nestled in the bottom of the drawer, was a thick stack of blank paper and two spare ribbons still sealed in their cellophane.

I'd never done any commercial writing. I'd spent some time as a secretary, writing business letters—which my peers told me were quite effective—and correcting a middle-level management executive's corrupt English to make him look good to his superiors, for which I was never thanked.

Writing...writing.

Surely the duties of taking care of this household would not take up much of a day's time. I had already pondered what life would be like here as Darien presented it to me, and the notion of sitting chained to a stove or bureau all day was nothing short of abhorrent because of the boredom.

Writing...writing.

When Darien came home late in the afternoon, I was ready for him. Not only was there a meal on the table, but I also had the typewriter set up beside his place with a sheet of paper in its carriage. I also had my clothing stacked neatly next to the stove.

When I heard him stomping across the porch, I attached my chain to the bureau leg—I wanted to see just how much flexibility I had with the way I presented myself to him as he came through the door. And I assumed my ass-in-the-air position, still hoping for a good fuck. I waited.

He was obviously reading my note before he reacted to anything else.

I had written:

Sir,

I'm not sure why yet, but I would like to stay with you for a time. I will learn your rules in whatever way you wish to teach them to me, and I will obey those rules to the best of my humbled ability.

There are some people in L.A. who will miss me if I do not return in a few days, and so I will beg you to communicate to Greg Rafferty at (310) 555-1918 that I will not be coming home and for all I care he can go fuck himself. He may have all my possessions in the apartment, and it is my sincere hope that he meet and fall in love with someone who will bash his face in if he does the cruel and dastardly things he did to me. Ask him please to call my place of employment and tell them they can take their job and shove it.

I will never again intrude on your privacy by addressing communications to you, sir. We will communicate with each other your way. And if this note offends you, I am prepared to suffer your punishment.

Your obedient servant,
Oscar

I had my face to the floor so I couldn't see the expression on his features. He took an agonizingly long time to move. At length he walked across the room to me. I wasn't sure he had the riding crop in his hand; I braced myself for stinging slaps on my upturned and waiting ass. Instead he reached down and unhooked the chain. He spoke not a word.

Once released, I went directly to my pile of clothing, which included my shoes. I opened the firebox door on the stove, and, one item at a time, I tossed them into the blaze within. Then I assumed my position next to his dining table chair. Still without a word he sat down to his meal, and we ate as we had eaten lunch.

After dinner he turned the chair around and activated the two-way radio. He did an accurate job of relaying my message, except he cleaned up the expletives.

It was almost eerie to hear his voice, knowing I would never hear actual words directed to me. Communicating with him on baser and simpler levels would be not only challenging but also intriguing. I would try to work things in the future so that I was out of the cabin when he checked in for the evening. I did not want the crutch of hearing his voice.

That night he set the tone for our evening time together. He sat in his easy chair and patted his thigh for me to join him. It was like curling up with Grampa for story time. He opened *Lady Chatterley's Lover* and began to read. I simply read along with him. I read a little faster than he did, so I was always ready when he turned the page.

He absently stroked my hair as if I were a favorite spaniel. And I think for the first time in my life, I was totally comfortable being near another human being. I did not feel threatened by human contact, perhaps because it was dawning on me exactly where I stood with Darien. No pretenses, no chance for lies.

Was it that my new friend was shy around strangers? I think not. A man of his stature need not fear what others think or do. Was it that he hated humankind in general? I doubted he could really hate anything or anyone. Perhaps he just wanted to be alone. It would be a while before I figured him out; but that was not high on my list of priorities. Being his proper pet and silent companion, learning and fine-tuning exactly what he expected of me—that was on my list.

Someday I would seek a broader cosmos. I was certain I would not stay with Darien forever; there would be a calling that would tell me that my new lessons had all been learned and that it was time to seek a greater place in the world. Perhaps I found comfort in Darien's tiny cabin now because I wasn't finished yet and needed a little more gestation time in a womb.

Lying next to this man at night, my sphincter throbbing from his penetrations, I would have multitudes of hours to give the matter careful, sublime thought.

He did communicate one thing to me that first night—silently yet in terms totally understandable: He did not put the typewriter away.

Writing…writing.

Toddy's Twick
by Lew Dwight

The summer before I go away to college is the final summer of the
Wicked Four. Henry, Joey, Bobby, and I have raised hell all
through high school and beyond, but once I leave the country to
go live in the city, the group will collapse, the rest of the boys van-
ishing into staid adult lives.

We don't go gently, however. We don't end with a whimper. We
end with a bang, being the troublemakers that we are.

We steal the porch swing from Mrs. Barrett's house and hang it
up in Mrs. Thompson's horse-chestnut tree.

We torch one of Suzy Smith's bras on the clothesline.

We wait for Mr. Trent to paint his chain-link fence with the
umpteenth coat of silver paint, then that night open bags of grass
clippings and throw them over the fresh paint.

We coax our neighbor Todd into Joey's dad's barn and have him
pull his pants down. Joey objects the entire time, but he never
leaves. (Joey will turn out to be an evangelist.)

Earlier, as we're coming out of the market in the village, we
pass Todd coming toward us, pulling his wagon behind him. His
jaw is bulging with chew, and his coppery Mohawk stands up on
end like a shoe brush. I remember when he used to go to school,
he'd sit there for hours, ignoring the lesson, pulling his red hairs
out one by one and laying the strands out side by side on his
desk. Now Todd's dad keeps Todd's hair cut real short so he can't
pluck it out.

Henry, always the inciter (though he's since become a drunk), says, "Hey, Toddy. I hear you have a high IQ."

Todd goes, "Uh-huh-huh-huh!"

Joey says, "Leave him alone, Henry."

Henry ignores him. "Tell us what it is, Toddy," Henry says. "What's your IQ?"

Bobby, the quiet one, just stands there rubbing his skinny belly under his T-shirt.

Todd drops the handle of his wagon and begins to count off on his big red hands, the fingers like carrots. When he runs out of carrots, he just shrugs.

Todd is older than we are but was always far behind us in school. One day he just dropped out.

He's just big and red and simple, and he wouldn't hurt a fly.

"You have toes, don't you, Toddy?" Henry says.

Joey shakes his head in disgust and turns away, but, like I said, he never leaves. Secretly he's having too much fun. Joey likes to pretend he's more virtuous than the rest of us.

Todd sits on the sidewalk, pulls off one of his size-13 high-top sneakers, and finishes counting on his huge toes.

"Twelf!"

"Wow, Toddy. That's quite an IQ. More than anyone else I know." Henry laughs and slaps Toddy on his meaty shoulder.

Bobby, taking his hand out of his T-shirt, looks from Henry to Todd, from Todd to Henry.

Todd gets his shoe back on and laughs along with Henry. His teeth are brown with tobacco stains. He laughs until he just about gags, then spits a big brown-red missile onto the sidewalk and wipes his mouth on the back of his hand. He picks up his wagon handle and takes off down the sidewalk toward the store, still laughing like a fiend: "Uh-huh-huh-huh!"

"Why do you always mess with him?" Joey says to Henry.

"Man, he enjoys it," Henry says. "Can't you tell he loves all the attention?"

"It's embarrassing."

"Maybe embarrassing to you," Henry says, "but I get a kick out of it. No harm done. What do you guys think?"

Bobby and I just shrug.

"Assholes," Henry says. "I know what'll get you going."

We walk up the road a ways and wait for Todd to come out of the store with his wagon full of grocery bags.

"Hey, Toddy," Henry says, popping out from behind a tree when Todd's red Mohawk comes up even to us. "These guys don't believe it."

"Huh?"

Todd's broad face, outlined with a red shadow of whiskers, crinkles up in puzzlement, as if Henry has just spoken in a foreign language or something. His shoulders bulge out of his ill-fitting T-shirt, and the seams have begun to burst from the pressure of his expanding lats. His jeans come way up above his ankles. He's like a baby in outgrown clothing.

"They said they don't believe your IQ is 12. What do you think about that?"

Todd drops his wagon handle and scratches his Mohawk. With his arm over his head, you can see the red armpit hairs pouring out of his sleeve. He gets this amused look on his face, as if re-membering something funny.

"Henry," Joey starts in, but Bobby thumps him on the back of the head to shut him up. Bobby wants to see what Henry is up to, but he won't say much.

"I tried to tell them, but they don't believe me. Any way you could prove it to these clowns, Toddy?"

Todd smiles broadly, meaningfully, then picks up the handle of his wagon. He starts up the road, all the while swinging his chin over his shoulder to look back at us.

"Let's follow him," Henry says.

"Let's not," Joey says. Bobby pushes Joey forward till he almost trips over his own feet.

We hide out in the woods near Todd's house and watch him take the groceries in to his father. He looks back over his shoulder several times from the porch before stooping to fit his Mohawk through the doorway.

He disappears into the house for a while, and we almost give up and leave, but then the red Mohawk appears in the door again. Todd looks around for a moment, then bounds down the stairs and runs toward the woods.

"Here he comes!" Henry says.

Soon Toddy, massive and sweating in his too-small shirt and drawers, is standing before us, smiling and panting. He laughs. "Uh-huh-huh!" and rubs his massive red hands together. They look like they could kill somebody easily.

"You'll show these guys, right, Toddy?" Henry says. "You'll make believers out of them. First, we gotta find a place... This way." He heads up the trail toward Joey's farm.

"No way," Joey says.

"Yes way," Henry says. "Everyone knows how Toddy likes animals. If anyone finds us there, we'll tell them he just wanted to see the cows."

Henry keeps to the trail, Todd following behind. Bobby and I pace behind Todd. I'm amazed at how big Todd is. Bulky but solid as a brick wall. The shirt, being two sizes too small, clings to his body and telegraphs only muscle, no fat. He grunts as he stumbles along the trail, neck hunched over. It's like following a pack animal.

Behind Bobby and me a ways is Joey. He's taking his time, kicking stones while he walks. He's good at making like he's not part of what's happening, like he has nothing to do with us.

Soon enough we come out of the woods and into the sumacs that encroach right up to the back of Joey's dad's dilapidated barn, out of sight of the house. We pick our way among rusted farm implements and an old truck chassis to come up to the broken sheathing board at one corner of the barn. Henry slips through the jagged hole easily, but Todd nearly becomes stuck, even turned sideways, one thick thigh in, one long leg out, and he has to scoot his huge torso through the hole with a grunt.

"Quiet!" Henry says within the barn.

Bobby and I turn sideways and slip through the gap. Inside, animals are thumping around and blowing. I look back through the gap to see if Joey's coming. He's still in the sumacs, looking around to see if anyone has seen us. Then he presses forward and comes into the gloomy barn with us.

We all stand around in the toolroom, where we barely have enough space to breathe. It's musty and smelly, and we have to wait for our eyes to adjust to the gloom.

"All right, Toddy," Henry says. "This is your chance. What's your IQ again?"

"Twelf."

"You all know what *IQ* stands for, don't you?"

"Intelligence quotient," I say.

"Show them, Toddy," Henry says.

Toddy holds his T-shirt up under his chin, revealing an absolute pasture of a stomach. He grabs fast on to the top of his drawers with both hands, then eases open the top button. The zipper peels open of its own accord, like it's under a lot of strain. The outline of a huge sex organ presents itself in the gloom, wedged up sideways under the waistband of his briefs.

"*IQ* means 'inch quotient,'" Henry says. He takes Todd by the waist and turns him toward the dirty window. "Move toward the light so they can see it better."

Todd turns so that the light coming through the cobwebby window falls on his bloated briefs. Henry tries to strip the briefs off Todd, but the huge cock, wedged under Todd's waistband, comes with them and nearly bends in half as Henry pulls the briefs down.

"A-a-ah!"

Everyone goes, "Shh!"

Henry carefully stretches out the waistband this time, pulls Todd's briefs down, and pushes them and the pants down around Todd's knees.

It gets very quiet in the cramped toolroom of Joey's dad's dilapidated barn as the magnitude of Todd's meat becomes clear to us all.

Todd grins stupidly and glances at each of us in turn as we take in the spectacle of his big erect dick.

It stands up straight, like a branch, so that we can see only the underside. Below it big testicles hang heavily in their sac, like cue balls. The foreskin, drawn up and puckered over the head in spite of the hugeness of the erection, gives the cock the appearance of being still in its wrapper. This makes it seem a mystery even when exposed.

"Twelf!" Todd gives a tobacco-stained grin, his forehead wrinkling up, Mohawk shifting forward on his scalp.

"So who's going to touch it?" Henry says right at Joey. Bobby is already on his knees, levering Todd's cock down with two hands to get a better look at it. It dwarfs Bobby's hands. It seems even longer when it's pointing forward, 12 inches easily, the balls in proportion too. It's a natural wonder, like one of those zucchini that have been hiding under leaves all summer, and when you finally come upon it, you startle, thinking it's some animal at first.

Bobby hooks his left hand around the base of Todd's cock, not even close to making a fist; then he gets his right hand around the middle of the shaft above his left. There are still several inches of uncut cock standing out. He lets go with his left hand and clamps that around the cock yet again above his right hand, the tip of the foreskin still showing above this third fistful of meat. Todd hums a little.

"All right, so it's big," Joey says. "Can we get out of here now before my dad comes?"

"Twick!" Todd says.

Bobby lets go and sits back on his heels.

Todd squats a little and moves his torso side to side so that his well-weighted scrotum swings like a bell clapper. "Twick!" he repeats. "Twick!"

"OK, Toddy," Henry says. "Let me look around a minute."

Henry bumps around the toolroom in search of something in answer to Todd's unintelligible (to us) request.

"What the hell now?" Joey says.

"Toddy wants to show you all something," Henry says. "I just need to find the right... Here we go."

Henry drags a cinder block forward to Todd's feet. Then he gets out his pocketknife and cuts a length of baling twine from a snarl of it shoved in an old grain bag.

"Take off your pants, Toddy."

Todd has to take off his size 13s first. Then he pulls his drawers inside out over his big feet and stands there before us, naked from the waist down. We can't take our eyes off his genitals. It's like when you see someone with a physical deformity in public for the first time—it grabs your interest. His cock seems to salute us in the musty room. His thighs are furred over with coppery red hair, and his balls sway like sailors in a hammock.

Henry loops one end of the baling twine through the open hole of the cinder block and ties it off tightly. He coils the rest of the twine around his fist and attempts to lift the block off the floor; it sways a little before he sets it back down.

"This is a hefty one, Toddy," Henry says. "Are you sure you can handle it?"

Todd just grins and looks around cockily.

Henry says, "OK, squat."

Todd spreads his thighs and makes to sit over the cinder block, his testicles hanging low and heavy. Henry grabs hold of Todd's balls as if they're fruit to be plucked from a tree, wraps the twine several times around the scrotum, and ties it off. A little more than a foot of twine now connects Todd's big balls to the heavy cinder block.

"OK. Show them your little trick," Henry says.

Todd bounces up and down on his toes a couple of times to test the weight of the block; then all the slack goes out of the twine. Todd's sac stretches out, and his balls seem to merge together and turn purple.

"What the hell are you—?" Joey begins.

Todd gives a cry like a weight lifter; he very carefully straightens his powerfully built legs.

Joey's jaw is still open in mid sentence. Bobby sits back and grabs his head in alarm.

The cinder block sways above the floor like that dangerous safe on a rope you see in early-morning cartoons.

The weight of the block pulls the still-sheathed erect cock down from its upright position so that it points away from Todd's body like a gangplank. Todd, quaking from the weight of the cinder block suspended from his balls, grabs Henry and me on either side of him for support. Once he steadies himself he waits for the block to stop swaying, then lets out a gasp of genuine relief.

"Un-fucking-believable," Bobby says, his only word of the day.

Breathing like a draft horse in front of a plow, Todd manages to flash us a quick grin—until that cinder block begins to twist slightly on its twine. For a moment Todd becomes as immobile as a statue.

"He'd really like it if someone got down there and sucked it for him now," Henry says.

"How do you know that?" Joey says.

Henry smiles.

Bobby gets back on his knees in front of Todd, answering the call. First he encircles the thick dick with both hands; then, with a hand-over-hand motion, he strips back the white foreskin until the magnificent head is bared, large and pink and as shiny as some live organ. You expect steam to rise from it.

Todd licks his lips and holds steady, watching Bobby examine his dick. The cinder block doesn't move.

Bobby leans forward and feeds Todd's now-naked cock head into his open mouth. Barely a third of the dick disappears beyond his lips before he can take no more.

Todd grits his teeth, lifts his face toward the ceiling, and inhales until the sinews stand out on his neck.

"Oh, shit!" Joey whispers.

Bobby backs his lips off the cock, bites down a bit on the head, and lets it pop out of his mouth with a soft sucking sound. The cock slaps up against Todd's hairy belly, stirring the cinder block.

"Ah! Ah!" Todd goes.

"Careful!" Henry says. "We wouldn't want to hurt him now, would we?"

Todd holds stock-still until the block ceases moving.

Again, but more gently this time, Bobby sucks the fat dick into his mouth as far as it will go.

Todd grimaces and bares his teeth, looking down at the top of Bobby's head in amazement. He digs his strong fingers into my shoulder until it hurts. *"E-e-e!"* Todd goes.

When Bobby lets the fat dick pop out of his mouth again, a loose strand of jizz spins end over end in midair for a moment, then plops down onto Bobby's ready tongue.

"Sensitive today, huh, Toddy?"

Immediately second and third strands of come leap out, both about a yard long, and attach themselves to Bobby's face and forehead like squiggles of hot glue.

The rest of Todd's load runs in a lumpy stream down the length of his thighs and balls, some of it dripping off and splashing against the dirty floor.

"My God!" Joey says.

"Way to go, Toddy boy!" Henry says.

We're all gawking at the mess dripping off Todd's alarmingly distended balls, that block still hanging there, twisting slowly on the twine cinched around his scrotum—when the door of the toolroom swings open.

Still breathing heavily, Todd lifts his Mohawked head and slowly turns his face toward the door.

Joey's father is standing there with a .38 in his hand.

"I thought I heard—"

Henry and Bobby are through that broken barn door like jackrabbits.

I'm right behind them, but as I step through the hole, I can't help glancing back.

Joey has fallen back against the wall with his hands splayed over his face.

His father is wiping the back of his gun hand across his forehead and grinning oddly. "What the—?"

And poor Todd, squatting there like an exhausted sumo wrestler, is carefully lowering that cinder block to the floor.

So ends the last great adventure of the Wicked Four.

Pinch
by R.J. March

Will Feezer looked down. The man's mouth seemed very much like a small dark hole far, far away. He could see the ridged edges of teeth and then the quick pink flicker of his tongue, catching the end of Will's erection, the honeyed drop that had collected in the piss slit like nectar or dew. He leaned forward then, committing himself, allowing his prick to enter the hot cave of the man's mouth. *Nothing is ever going to be the same again,* he thought.

When Will walked into the Montrose Café, he hadn't been thinking of blow jobs, certainly not from another man. He stepped into the air-conditioned cool and sighed, ready for a beer, two beers, as many as he had money for—it had been that kind of day. He got himself a stool at the end of the bar, glancing down at the bartender, who stood watching television with another man. Will looked at his hands, the grease still under his nails. He was still in his work clothes, the blue mechanic's uniform he wore every day. *Pants are getting a little tight,* he told himself. *Should order some bigger ones tomorrow.* If he still had a job tomorrow.

The bartender walked down to Will's end of the bar, a look of plain disinterest on his face. Will ordered a lager and felt his pockets in search of the cigarettes he quit smoking half a year ago. There was a cigarette machine behind him that sold his brand, and he sat counting change and coming up short. "Willpower," he muttered to himself, trying to be unwilling to break a dollar for the extra change he needed. He caught sight of himself in the mirror behind the bar. He looked like a kid and still, he thought, felt like one too—a stupid, know-nothing, dumb fuck of a kid. That's what his boss, Pete Cameron, had said at the garage that day when Will accidentally dropped the Cummins engine he was working on. It wasn't his fault the arm of the hoist had snapped, but Cameron was pissed and had to take it out on somebody, and since Will was the one pulling the engine, it was up to him to bear the man's wrath.

One more bit of bad luck, like a broken mirror, each shard promising new shit coming your way. He drained the glass and pushed it forward. Like Kirsten, his girlfriend, who decided last week to quit Will like cigarettes.

"Jimmy," Will half heard, concentrating on his low-grade, B-movie misery. He pulled the front of his pants away from his crotch because his cock and balls were pinched. He'd run out of clean shorts and went without and chafed all day long against the rough insides of his work pants. "That boy's looking for a refill—does he need a fucking bell?"

Will looked down to the other end of the bar and saw the man who had roused the bartender from his open-eyed nap. He was big—or at least gave the impression of being big. He carried his chest high, and it seemed three feet wide, his arms folded across it, the sleeves of his sweatshirt hacked off, showing off the size of his biceps. He didn't look at Will, didn't take his eyes off the TV screen, but Will was grateful that someone was looking out for him anyway. *Must be the owner,* Will was thinking, sipping the froth of the fresh beer in front of him. Maybe 40, maybe not, he reminded Will of a favorite uncle, one he hadn't thought about in years. Back when he was a boy, he'd had a strange fascination with his uncle's bare feet and would sit on the couch with him whenever he visited and take off the man's socks and pet his feet like dogs until his father decided it was something bad and put a stop to it.

The bartender walked up to Will with a shot glass, setting it next to his beer glass, saying, "Next one's on the house, Dink says." The man at the end of the bar, this "Dink," stared at the television—ESPN without sound. Will raised a hand and said thanks, and he thought he saw the man nod a little.

"Who's playing?" Will asked, his voice sounding dumb in all the quiet.

The man looked over at him. "Just scores," he said quietly. His eyes, Will saw, were light-colored, and he kept his arms folded over his chest, his pecs peeking up like cleavage. He tore himself away from the screen and walked the length of the bar, behind Will, and stood at the front door. Will watched him in the mirror. He wore tight jeans and had thick, squat legs and hard-looking fuzzy forearms. He stood for a while at the door, looking through the plate glass.

"Where the fuck are they, Jimmy?" he asked. Will continued to watch him in the mirror.

"The Valencia probably," the bartender answered from Dink's spot in front of the television. "Staring at Nikki's big tits."

"Fucking bitch," Dink muttered. "I hate that cunt. Shoulda killed her when I had the chance."

"I told you, leave her alone," Jimmy said. He was in his 60s, had been doing this all his life, would do it probably until he died, Will mused. Jimmy glanced down, not at Will but at his glass. He settled against the inside edge of the bar.

Will counted the bills in front of him. He had enough for a good buzz and then some. *Might as well make a night of it,* he thought.

"Damn right," Dink said, suddenly beside him, putting his big pink elbows on the bar. "Might as well. You always talk to yourself in bars? Quickest way to lose your stool, you know."

Will wasn't sure how to react, so he smiled and shrugged and looked down at his beer.

"You look like you got stepped on," Dink said. "You ought to sit up, put your shoulders back. Never let them think they got to you." And Will broke out of the hunch his body had taken on, taking a deep breath and feeling, if only for the moment, fortified. He looked at Dink, whose gaze had dropped to Will's tightly wrapped crotch. Then he looked away.

Dink wasn't tall, but you didn't think short when you saw him. Everything on him was thick, Will noticed—his lips, his fingers, his earlobes even.

"I was at the Valencia last week," Will said. Dink faced the mirror, the sparkle of the bottles reflected in his eyes. "Didn't like it there—bartender was a real bitch."

"Nikki." Dink nodded. "My ex. Fucked me big-time—left me for a fucking beer distributor and opened her own goddamn bar with the money she got from the settlement. Just about broke me." He shook his head with a tight smile on his face, a dimple developing in the cheek turned toward Will.

"Funny world, ain't it?" Dink said, and Will agreed.

"Small too," Will added.

"Yeah," Dink said, smiling still. "It's a funny, small world."

The lager flowed freely as Dink and Will rubbed elbows and knocked shoulders and commiserated. Will was always catching his new friend's downward glance, as if something interesting was between Will's legs. Maybe he was looking at a loose tile on the floor or wondering if he should have the foot rail polished. *Or maybe,* he thought, *he's checking me out.* Dink didn't seem even remotely queer, but you never knew, Will guessed. Kirsten had a friend, this really cool gay guy, who was always checking Will out when he thought Will wasn't looking. Will hadn't cared much—in fact, he found it almost flattering. And he always thought the hottest thing in the world would be to share a girl with another guy. Not that he'd do anything with the guy, but once he saw a movie at a stupid bachelor party in which this chick blew two guys standing on either side of her and then let them fuck her one after the other, the guys sandwiching her, their legs all knotted up, touching each other. Will had sauced his pants without even trying—nothing to be proud of at a party with a bunch of stupid drunk guys he didn't like very much. It had seemed to him, though, that the guys were trying to fuck her out of the way—what was she between them but a wet slide?

Then Dink said, "You know, I live upstairs."

"Doesn't it get loud?" Will asked. The place had started filling up and was getting smoky. Jimmy was replaced by a shaved-head guy with a goatee, looking to Will like someone in a porn film. *Must be horny,* Will thought, *because that's all I'm thinking of tonight.* He surveyed the bar for anyone single, but all the women were paired up or butt-ugly, and he wasn't really into one-nighters. Still, his dick was beginning to wake up from its nap. Dink leaned into him.

"Smoke's killing me," he said. "Want to see my place?"

"See?" Dink said, waving a hand around the place. "Can't hear a thing."

Will shook his head. The place was much nicer-looking than he'd anticipated, like something out of an interior-design maga-zine. He sat down in the nearest chair, feeling the effects of all the beer he'd had.

"Get up," Dink barked. "You haven't had the tour yet."

Other than the kitchen and the bathroom, there wasn't much that Will hadn't seen upon walking in the front door, save for Dink's bedroom, but Will followed, a docile, drunken puppy. He looked at Dink's behind as though he didn't have a choice. When-ever he got drunk, he checked out guys, letting his mind wander. He didn't consider himself bisexual or anything—maybe just a lit-tle curious, though. Or maybe a little more than curious. His dick, he noticed, was stiffer than set concrete. He put his hands in his pockets.

Dink's bedroom was as big as the rest of the apartment, bed in the center of the room with an oddly shaped headboard, flanked by two cubes that were stacked with books and magazines. The walls seemed far away to Will, and they were hung with black-framed art that was impossible to see in the dim light.

"The weight room's in the attic," Dink said, as if he had to explain its absence. He sat down on the bed. By the window were two chairs facing each other, separated by a small wooden stool. Will wanted badly to sit down, to get his crotch out of eyeshot before Dink noticed.

"What's up there, little fella?" Dink said, his eyebrows going up, his eyes on the big sorry lump in Will's blue pants.

"Just kinda—" Will started, not knowing how to finish. Horny? Couldn't actually say it, could you? He felt a little like he had earlier that afternoon when Cameron came running out of the office to find the Cummins lying on the floor, oil running out of it like blood.

Dink shook his head, smiling. "You like guys?"

"No, thank you," Will mumbled.

"I wasn't offering," he said, his face changing. He lost his grin, and he sat up a little straighter. "But in a pinch," he added.

Will blinked. "I don't get you," he said, and Dink laughed.

"But in a pinch one'll do—get what I'm saying?"

Will shook his head slowly. Suddenly he wasn't as drunk as he wanted to be. "I didn't say that," he said.

"No," Dink said evenly, "I did. And this is looking to me like a pinch, don't you think?"

Will shrugged.

"You look like you lift," Dink said.

"Some," Will admitted.

"When's the last time you got laid?"

"Christ," Will sighed, looking around him. He could leave if he wanted. He wasn't being held against his will or anything. Dink sat on the edge of the bed, his arms hanging between his legs. He looked at Will and squinted, like he was something he couldn't quite figure out.

"How old are you?"

Will said 23.

"I'm pretty close to your dad's age, I bet."

"My dad's dead," Will said.

"Hey, Will," Dink said.

Will lifted his chin, straightened his back.

"Will," Dink said, "I'm going to take my clothes off now." He took off his sweatshirt, nudging out of it with his elbows. Dink's chest was huge and smooth, and his nipples, nearly the same color as his skin, hung off his tits like grapes, swollen and pinkish and pinchable. His jeans were tight, and sitting gave him a gut. He sucked it in to undo his button and zipper, and suddenly there was all this hair. He stopped and put his hands on his thighs, looking down at his open jeans and the mass of pubic hair. He looked up at Will, who felt paralyzed, although there was plenty of movement in his pants, his cock twitching and bubbling over, a life of its own, a life that suddenly seemed counter to Will's own. He couldn't wait, though, for Dink to take off his pants.

Dink stood slowly. "Here we go," he said, as though he were attempting a high dive for the first time in his life. He pushed his jeans down, and his thick rod did a bobbing dance. Half hard, it had the dimensions of a summer sausage, thick and fat-headed. He knocked it around like a lazy stepson, and it inched upward, enjoying the beating. When it was fully engorged, Dink gave Will the eye, waiting, it seemed, for some feedback.

It was beautiful, but Will couldn't say it. His mouth filled with saliva. He watched Dink lie back on the bed and spread his legs. His nuts, a big bald bag of skin filled with two rocks the size of a fist, drooped down between his thighs. Will took a step forward, then a step back. "Ain't right," he said quietly.

"You don't think so?" he heard from the bed. "You know, your dick don't care one way or the other. It'll break off if you don't do something quick, though."

They stared at each other's crotch for a moment, and a tacit agreement was made. Will moved closer to the bed, and Dink sat up, reaching out for him, getting his fingers into the gaps of Will's work shirt and pulling it open. The metal snaps popped, and the shirt opened to bare the man's chest, covered with a light dusting of dark hair. He thumbed one of Will's nipples and with his other hand groped the front of his blue trousers, feeling up the firm hose that ran from fly to hip. Dink lifted his eyebrows and praised the piece, and Will's face flushed.

When his pants fell to the floor and his unimpeded cock bridged the gap between them, Dink opened his mouth and tasted the red-tipped thing, and it was like looking down over the side of a cliff for Will, like he was looking down from a great height.

"Never been with a guy?" Dink asked.

Will shook his head.

"Never been blown in a toilet or anything?"

Will shook his head again, wondering if it was that easy. He felt Dink's hands on the sides of his thighs, and his whole cock was engulfed by the warm, wet slide of Dink's mouth, and he wondered if his girlfriend's mouth had ever felt so nice, so accommodating. Dink's mouth was a hot bath and a rubdown all at the same time, and Will put his hands on Dink's ears, holding him by his fleshy lobes and watching his dick get worked over.

"I think you get the idea," Dink said, taking a break after nearly choking on Will's long and narrow prick. "Little out of practice," he said, spitting out a pubic hair.

Will couldn't imagine it getting any better, but he just said, "Cool." His dick, though, was bouncing around like a horny cheerleader, dripping precome and Dink's spit.

Dink lay back again, his own cock like a spire rising up out of a forest of darkish pubes. "You up to a little reciprocation?" he asked. He hand-jobbed himself, giving Will a long look. It didn't seem a likely endeavor to Will, who stared at the thick tower. He knelt on the mattress beside the man and took the cock in his hand. It filled his grasp and then some, reminding Will of taking up a baseball bat by the wrong end. Dink sighed and brought his arms up over his head. "Just kiss it," he said, exhaling loudly. "That's all it wants, some kissing." And Will ducked his blushing face, pressing his lips against the moist, rubbery head. He kissed Dink's burning shaft and the musky bag of balls and the very tip that oozed from its split and tasted both salty and sweet. He stroked the man's pecker with a shaking hand, his own cock chafing between his legs, fucking the hairy press of them.

"Put it in your mouth," Dink breathed, his voice almost gone, and Will covered the shining head with his mouth, enclosing the red rim.

"You like sucking cock, don't you, baby?" he heard through the crazy air he felt he was swimming in. "You're gonna be my cocksucker, right?"

He tried to nod, and he looked over Dink's torso, between the peaks of his tits, into Dink's eyes.

"Don't look at me," Dink whispered, his mouth hanging open, his tongue running along his lips. His eyes were closed, and his head was tipped back, and Will felt the rumble of Dink's cock and caught the hot flow from it with his mouth.

"Aw, shit," Dink said, his body twisting under Will's mouth as he swallowed up the copious flow. Dink sucked one of his own fingers and pushed it between Will's legs, finding his soft spot and pushing into it, and Will squeezed out three flying blasts of white, which sailed over Dink's belly and landed on the other side of the bed.

"That was some fine shooting," Dink said appreciatively, uncorking the boy's bottom.

Will didn't go back to the Montrose Café. He tried like hell to put that night out of his head. Pretending it never happened, he fueled his normal fantasies with a stack of *Hustler* magazines. He was even tempted to call Kirsten, but that seemed as bad an idea as popping in at the Montrose for a beer. He considered picking up a whore—good enough for Hugh Grant, but no better an idea.

He was constantly horny, though; it was beginning to feel more and more like an affliction. Sliding under a truck chassis made him hard. Rebuilding carburetors had him dripping. He'd look across the bay to where Kenny Meyers was leaning over a Mustang, his jeans hanging low and his shirt riding high, laying bare a fish-white stretch of naked skin and the shadowed crack of his ass. Or he'd look at Skippy, their parts runner, washing gaskets in a tub of diesel fuel, his curling hair hanging in his eyes, arms busting out of his shorn-sleeved work shirt. Even his boss, Pete Cameron, standing in the doorway of his office, stretching, with his long pecker pressed up against the inside of his pants, plain as day. Will would get so agitated that he'd have to lock himself in the men's room for a few minutes, struggling out of his coveralls to beat off into the shitter, getting grease all over his pecker, all over his shorts.

He was doing a brake job one day when he heard Dink's voice. He looked up to see Dink and Cameron shaking hands, then grabbing each other in a manly back-beating embrace. Loud and jocular, they feigned punches, poked bellies. Will watched them, hiding behind the fender of the Explorer he was working on. He needed to have the rotors turned and had been about to send Skippy out with them because the boy was wearing tight jeans and a flannel shirt practically all undone and was a particular distraction for Will. Up until now.

He heard his name hollered from the office. *Oh, Jesus, no,* flashed through his mind, and a cold breeze from nowhere blew inside his coveralls and chilled his genitals. He unsquatted and walked slowly to the office just as Cameron stuck his head out and yelled again.

"Coming," Will mumbled, pulling up the zipper of his uniform a little higher. He'd opted recently for the coverall for its erection-hiding bagginess, which came in handy lately. Not that he was erect now—the opposite, actually. He couldn't imagine getting any smaller.

Dink was sitting at Cameron's desk, his face showing no recognition when he glanced up at Will. He seemed more interested in the box of cigars on the desk.

"Will, this is my old buddy Steve Montrose. We call him Dink, though," Cameron said.

"How come?" Will asked quietly, looking at Dink, who had picked up a cigar and was studying it.

"On account of his little pecker," Cameron laughed.

"Where'd you get these shit sticks?" Dink asked, holding the cigar as if it were indeed covered with feces.

"They're Cubans, you dumb fuck," Cameron said. He turned to Will, saying, "No class, that one. Never had none, never will."

"Cubans, my ass," Dink said. "These are fucking Amish stogies, you stupid son of a bitch."

"Fuck they are," Cameron countered. He put his arm around Will, an odd gesture coming from a man who usually didn't say shit to Will. "My idiot friend here needs his car inspected, only he can't get it in until 7 tonight. Would you do me a favor and help the dumb fuck out?"

"Sure," Will said. "I don't have plans. I can work on getting that stockroom in order until then."

"Good man," Cameron said.

"I appreciate it," Dink said, not looking up.

I bet you do, Will thought.

He waited until 9, pissed off and dejected, and was about to leave when he saw the flash of headlights and heard the crunch of gravel out in the lot. He walked to the first bay and threw open the door. He had the zipper of his coveralls down as far as he'd dare; he could look down and see his bristly patch of pubic hairs. He squinted through the glare on the windshield from the floodlights outside and could make out Cameron in the passenger seat, waving a cigar and passing a bagged bottle. The Mercedes rolled in, its diesel engine chiming. The doors opened, and smoke billowed out with a cackle of raucous laughter—Cameron was drunk, and Dink wasn't feeling any pain, either.

"Sorry we're late," Dink said, straightening himself up.

"My fault," Cameron said, coming around the car. He put his arm around Will, his hand going into the open V of Will's coveralls. "Dink here was telling me a little story about someone we know—surprised the hell out of me."

Will's eyes flicked to Dink, who stood with his chest out. He dropped a hand to the front of his jeans and gave himself a good squeeze.

"Your inspection's not due for another six months," Will said numbly, and the two men laughed. Cameron's hand went deeper into Will's uniform, cupping the man's pec, his fingers stroking the soft underside of it. Dink stepped up and took hold of the already-lowered zipper, taking it all the way down.

"Would you look at that," Cameron said, peering down into Will's opened suit. He brought his face close to Will's. "That's a nice one." Dink brought it out, and the touch of his hand made it stiffen quickly. He pulled on it, playing with the skin just under the flanged head, stroking it with his fingers, undoing his own jeans with his free hand, bringing out his own massive pecker.

"Ooh-whee," Cameron said, turning to Will again. "What do you think of that? Ain't that the biggest dick you ever seen?" And then he bobbed his head and put his mouth on Will's tit.

The mechanic was in something like a state of shock. He leaned against the waxed fender of the Mercedes, sliding down until Dink made them all stop and strip, and then his bare ass stuck to the cold gray metal. Will watched Dink and Cameron undress, Cameron bowing down to chew Dink's red-ended big-swinging club, his ass directed at Will, white and smooth. Will stared at it as Cameron sucked down the whole of Dink's cock. His ass cheeks spread a little more, his dark crack fuzzy.

"Go ahead," Dink said. "He's given you the shaft often enough."

Will shook his head. The thought of sticking it to Pete Cameron made his knees weak. Cameron pushed his johnson between his legs, and it stuck out behind him like a short, stiff tail.

"He wants you to, you know," Dink said, leaning over to spread Cameron's ass cheeks more, letting the light hit the pink rosebud of Cameron's hole. "Tell him, Cam."

Cameron grunted and wiggled his fanny.

"I want to watch you fuck him—damn! Watch the teeth, Cam." Dink spat onto his fingers and smeared them over his buddy's cunt, pushing into it, causing Cameron to grunt and wiggle some more.

"Go for it," Dink said, grinning.

Will hadn't expected the heat. His dick felt as though it were being dipped into something thick and recently boiled. He held on to Cameron's hips and worked himself in and out slowly, staring at Dink, who whispered things and tried to get a good look at Will's fucking while trying not to break the connection he had with Cameron. Cameron groaned and pushed his butt against Will's hips, pinning the boy against the Mercedes, fucking himself on Will's long, straight rod until he was about to squirt. He straightened and leaned against Will, burying the bone deep inside him. He put his bourbon mouth near Will's, lips shining with drool.

"Harder," he said, as if Will had anything to do with the fucking anymore. "Yeah, slam it in me," he was saying, banging his butt against the boy and pulling on his pecker, hosing a spray of sperm all over Dink's thighs.

"Move it," Dink said, shoving Cameron aside. He laid himself out on the car hood. He lifted his big legs and opened them for Will, whose cock still buzzed from Cameron's tight pussy. He leaned into the pulsating hole Dink proffered, wondering how long he'd last. Dink's hole was different, not as tight, more like a mouth. Dink reached up and played with the boy's tits, pinching them hard, causing Will to moan and shake his head.

"I'm a goner," he tried to explain, his dick driving into the warm, moist bung.

"Just do it hard and don't fucking stop until I tell you to," Dink said. He called for Cameron's cock. "Put it in my mouth, you useless old lady." He yanked on Will's nipples, hurting him, and Will retaliated with fiercer strokes, a relentless fucking of Dink's buttery pussy.

"Oh, fuck, yeah!" Dink bellowed, his voice echoing through the garage. "Fuck me with that pole!" He pressed his enormous pecker against Will's belly, where it erupted a hot spew of milky come. Will jammed himself one more time into the man and felt himself coming undone, semen gushing from his quivering cock like a broken water main.

Dink hobbled to the men's room to unload Will's load, and Cameron lazily dressed. "I'd appreciate your discretion," he said, not looking at Will's face but at his cock, still hard, ready for another go. "You should wash that thing."

They stumbled up from the café to Dink's apartment, all of them drunk as priests. Dink tripped, and Cameron started singing, and Will wondered who would be the first to fuck him. They burst into Dink's apartment in search of more alcohol, and Will took a long piss.

"If not for me, you'd have never known," Dink said.

"If not for me, you'd have never met his ass," Cam countered.

"We'll flip for him," Dink suggested. "You first."

Will came out of the bathroom, undressed and ready for action, finding the two of them naked and snoring, sprawled all over the bed. Will yawned himself, getting between the two men and pulling a blanket over them all, snuggling down and looking forward to the morning and laughing a little at the pinch he had gotten himself in.

Jock Talk
by Leo Cardini

Every time I feel his huge balls pressing against me, sweaty from the strain of his morning workout, an indescribable thrill runs through every fiber of my elasticized cotton pouch. And if that's not enough to satisfy my lustful cravings, there's that big dick of his, all snuggled up inside me, taking up more space than we medium-size Bike jockstraps were ever made to hold.

But don't get me wrong; I'm not complaining. How could I? Every time I hold my master's substantial equipment in my embrace, I'm at complete liberty to examine that thick, rubbery shaft and that enormous mushroom of a cock head, which begins to ooze precome every time he steps into the locker room after his workout and strips down for the adventures that await him down the hall, where the showers, sauna, and steam room are located.

Not that he would ever think of wearing me into that backroom paradise. There are men who do, you know. I can't tell you how much I envy those privileged pouches when I watch them returning to the locker room soaking wet and proudly clinging to their masters' cocks and balls, flaunting their ability to contain all that meat. Though you do see a waistband now and then that, whether from too many washings or supporting too large a load, sags so far below its master's navel that his pubic bush spills out in exhibitionistic display.

Anyhow, here I am, once more shucked off and abandoned on the narrow bench that runs the length of the lockers, king of the hill atop my master's other gym wear: his tank top, stretch shorts, and white cotton socks. All of them are as limp and sweaty as I am, and all of them are envious of me for my intimate grasp of him. Besides that, I'm always the first one on, his cock and balls lovingly scooped up inside me, and the last one off when he liberates them again to swing freely in the open air as he struts into that intriguing back room.

Well, this morning I find the usual ache I feel during this cruel abandonment upstaged by my interest in the broad-chested hunk who follows my master out of the gym and into the locker room. Yes, I know he's deliberately trailed him in. When you serve a master like mine, you get to know these things. I don't mean to brag, but after all, he is a soap-opera star. Tall, with drop-dead good looks, he's got long blond hair, gentle blue eyes, straight white teeth that gleam through his rakish smile, and a dimpled chin. Add this to his wide shoulders, narrow waist, tight buns, and, of course, that provocative bulge that's my special responsibility, and it's no wonder that all eyes turn to follow him wherever he goes.

Well, this guy who's followed him in is no slouch either. In fact, he reminds me of Rocky Angel—you know, that Italian heartthrob who costarred with my master for several months. Anyhow, he pulls his gym bag out of a locker several down from my master's and proceeds to strip, tossing his workout clothes into it.

Not bad at all. Mounds of sleek muscle, washboard abs, and—oh, my God!—an immense brute of a dick with thick blue veins and a deeply furrowed nut sac the size of a baseball hugging the underside.

Of course, he's checking out my master with sly sidelong glances. But he's more than just checking him out. I don't know why, but I get a funny feeling about him. True, one hand reaches up to his chest to tug on a nipple, like I've seen countless other men do when they gaze upon my master. And true, no sooner has he tweaked it into its own miniature erection then he takes his free hand and reaches into his crotch to give his dick a long, slow tug, which is also expected behavior under the circumstances. But he keeps shifting his eyes, looking down at me, then up at my master, back and forth, until my master heads toward the back facilities.

That's when this guy steps over to me, reaches down, and picks me up, pressing the inside of my pouch against his nose and sniffing. One dose of my master's crotch sweat inspires him to inhale again, this time more deeply. Then he lowers me across his open mouth, pressing me against his tongue, a thin coat of saliva spreading over the damp traces of my master's workout.

Next he lowers me onto his muscular chest, drawing me across to his right pec. His nipple's still hard from the tweaking, and he pinches it with his thumb and forefinger right through the fabric of my pouch.

I've never before been sexually assaulted by a complete stranger. I know about the terrible misfortunes that can befall a jockstrap, and I know I should be outraged and distressed.

But frankly, I'm beginning to like this. Especially when he slides me across to his other pec for another bout of tit play, then lowers me down along the hard, hairy terrain of his chest and the bumpy badlands of his washboard abs, plunging me deep into the rampant overgrowth of his pubic bush, fragrant with the aroma of his own workout. Then, before I have time to recover from this eventful downward trek, he moves me along the wide, rugged top of his half-hard dick until he captures his cock head in my pouch and begins masturbating.

Now, this is the first time I've ever touched another man's dick, and the feeling is, well, exhilarating. His oversize cock head is so velvety smooth, his thickening dick shaft so responsive, growing inch by inch into what promises to be a truly magnificent erection, that I just let him have his way with me.

Shit! Just when things are beginning to get really good, we hear the approach of someone else entering the locker room, and I'm hastily thrown into his gym bag, landing on top of his sweaty workout gear, and zipped into darkness. His sweat socks, tank top, and gym shorts, damp and disheveled below me, seethe with resentment at my intrusion, and his jockstrap exudes downright hostility at my trespassing onto his turf.

Well, I can't tell you how relieved I am when, some minutes later, the zipper flies open, the light of overhead fluorescence comes flooding in, and I'm yanked out of this humid pit of hostility. I'm not prepared, however, to be hauled upward to his crotch, my straps stretched as he maneuvers one foot and then the other between my straps and pouch, sliding me up his muscular legs and depositing his cock and balls into me, drawing my straps across his firm ass cheeks with a snap, and adjusting my waistband along his solid, compact waist. His crotch is damp, smelling faintly of soap, so I know he's been off luxuriating in the shower room.

I've never housed another man's crotch before, so as I struggle to accommodate new needs, I feel invigorated with the novelty of discovery. For one thing, he has bigger balls than I'm used to, but since his snug sac imprisons his huge nuts close to his body, it's easier for me to hold them. This gives me freedom to examine his hairy sac, which intrigues me, since my master shaves his. And for another thing, my new wearer positions his dick up against his abdomen, not down over his balls. It's so fat and heavy, I really have to struggle to hold it in place. And even then it lists slightly to the right, his piss slit pressed against my pouch in a prolonged kiss.

Before I've had a chance to acclimate myself, up come his jeans, button after button, enclosing me in darkness, pressing me tightly against him as we make our way out of the health club and into the street.

Fortunately, it's an old, well-worn pair of 501s, so two of the buttons make their way out of their buttonholes, affording me a view of the way home. Turns out he lives barely a block away from my master.

Once we're inside his apartment, he strips off all his other clothes and begins tidying up. Every chance he gets, his right hand is kneading my pouch, encouraging his dick to swell up inside me. But to my frustration, it never grows beyond a rubbery half-hard before he has to pull out his hand again to attend to some chore. And then his intercom buzzes, drawing his attention away from me completely.

"Hello," he says into the speaker.

"Lou?"

"Yeah. Hi, Danny. Happy birthday. The door'll be unlocked, so just come on in." And with that he buzzes in this Danny and dashes into his bedroom. He flings himself onto the bed, spreads his legs, and adjusts my pouch to show himself off to full advantage. Then he lies back with his hands behind his head.

I feel his crotch heating up as his dick begins to stir. Let me tell you, there's nothing like the thrill of a man getting a hard-on inside you. But this time the thrill's increased with the excitement of fresh discovery. A fatter, more deeply veined dick grows inside me, placing greater demands on me than have ever been made before.

Just as my waistband's about to be pried away from his abdomen, I hear the front door to his apartment open.

"Lou?"

"In here," he yells out.

In walks Danny. He's lean and smooth-skinned, with long blond hair spilling over his forehead. The loose, low-hanging jeans and oversize T-shirt he's wearing emphasize his boyish good looks. "So what'd you get me for my birthday?" he asks, leaning over to kiss Lou.

"Greedy little bugger, aren't you?"

"Yeah. So what'd you get me?"

"This," he says, cupping my pouch.

"That worn-out piece of meat? Hell, I've had that. Like half of everyone else in the Village."

"You fuck! The jockstrap, stupid."

"Oh?" He leans over and sniffs me. "What makes you think I'd want a smelly old jockstrap?"

Hey, now! I might be smelly, but old? You can feel for yourself: My elastic is as springy as the day I was pulled out of my plastic wrapper.

"Because it's not just any smelly old jockstrap."

"Yeah?" Intrigued, he runs his palm across my pouch. "What makes it so special?"

"I'll give you a hint: Channel Q. Weekdays."

"Huh?"

"At 2 P.M."

"*The Gays of Our Lives.* Never miss it."

"I know."

"So?"

"So who's that actor you always cream over? The one who plays Broadway choreographer Tom D'Aria?"

"Lance Longfellow?"

"That's the one. What if I told you this is his jock?"

"It is?" Danny practically whispers.

"Yeah."

"Awesome! You're the best boyfriend a guy ever had." Worshipfully he strokes my pouch. "But wait a minute. If it's his jockstrap, how'd you get it?"

"Oh. Well...I asked him."

"Yeah, sure! Like you saw him on the street, walked up to him, and tapped him on the shoulder with, 'Uh, excuse me, but could I have your jockstrap?'"

"Well, not in so many words. And it wasn't on the street. He's been working out at the club every morning around the same time I do. So we're in the locker room, I ask him, and he says, 'Sure.' But then he says he's kinda horny from watching me work out, so would I mind sucking him off. So—"

"You blew Lance Longfellow? You actually took his dick in your mouth and—"

"Nah. The truth of the matter is, I stole the damn thing when he wasn't looking."

"You stole it? Wow! But what if he ever caught me wearing it at the club? He'd think I was the one who stole it from him." Danny pauses, pondering the possibilities, and then he resumes running his palm up and down my pouch against the swollen underside of Lou's dick.

"Danny, it's not like you have to wear it there. Besides, even if you did, you work out in the afternoon, and he works out in the morning."

"But suppose I just happen to work out some morning and just happen to be wearing it."

"Assuming he recognizes it's his jockstrap. I mean, how many Bikes do you think there are in the world?"

"But suppose he does recognize it, and suppose he doesn't like the fact that someone else is wearing his very own jockstrap. God knows what he might do to me! Or force me to do to him!"

Now, with Danny's hand sliding up and down my pouch, Lou's dick has risen to full erection, his insistent cock head relentlessly stretching my pouch up above my waistband. Danny grabs my waistband with both hands to lower me off Lou, but Lou intercepts, restraining him with, "So how do you say thank you?"

"Uh…thank you?" But you can tell from Danny's smile that he knows more's expected of him.

"That's all I get for stealing Lance Longfellow's jockstrap for you? Well, maybe I won't give it to you after all. No, I think I'll just lie right here"—he slowly reaches into me, wrapping his fingers around the fat shaft of his dick and pressing his bulbous cock head out against me—"and jack myself off, thinking about how Lance looked in the locker room, totally nude, totally gorgeous, his big piece of meat just dangling there… But you don't want to hear about that, do you?"

"You cockteaser," Danny says with clear delight. Taking Lou by surprise, he pulls his hand out of me, pushes both of Lou's hands up over his head, and falls on top of him, forcing his tongue into Lou's mouth.

And while Lou yields to this assault, the soft, worn denim of Danny's jeans rubs against me as he begins hunching his hips into Lou's crotch. Lou responds by hunching back, pressing his hard-on against Danny's, treating me to a delicious double dose of hard cock as the animal inside each of them begins to take over.

Finally Danny jumps off Lou. Standing next to the bed, his eyes wild, he kicks off his sneakers and tears off his socks, T-shirt, and Levi's, carelessly tossing them onto the floor. Standing there in just his briefs, he pauses to admire his boyfriend with a ferocious intensity.

I, in turn, take advantage of the moment to savor the sight of his youthful features. Such a lean, tight body. And such an outrageous hard-on, barely constrained by those poor, put-upon briefs of his, the broad expanse of its underside pressing outward, his enormous cock head resting against his hip.

When he pulls down his briefs and kicks them off, his truly monumental erection drops down heavily between his legs, a victim of its own weight. His pale brown shaft ends in a neat cut, below which hangs a purple-red cock head the size of a plum. Behind, two big balls are suspended in a low-hanging, nearly hairless sac.

As he jumps back onto the bed and straddles Lou, his balls brush lightly against my pouch as his huge dick flops forward onto Lou's belly.

All that marvelous meat! It nearly drives me crazy. You see, Lance always tossed me onto the floor beside the bed before things got good, so I was always on the sidelines of his sexual exploits, never up close like this.

Danny leans forward, and the underside of his dick presses roughly against my waistband as he grips Lou's nipples, gently twisting them.

"Oh!" Lou moans.

Danny leans farther forward. He falls onto his hands, more of his dick slides down across my pouch, and he bites into Lou's left nipple. He gives it a gentle tug. Lou moans again and suddenly thrusts upward.

Aw, shit! Do you know what it's like to have two big, stiff dicks rubbing against you at the same time? You do? Then you can just imagine how overwhelmed with passion I feel right now.

Well, Danny tugs and tugs, first on Lou's left nipple, then on his right. Then he abandons his tit play and kisses his way down Lou's chest, following the same route I'd been forced to follow earlier when I was abducted.

By the time Danny reaches Lou's navel, Lou's cock head is once more pushing my sorely stretched pouch up over my waistband, impatiently lunging toward Danny's mouth, begging for the touch of Danny's lips. But instead Danny reaches for my waistband to lower me once again. Rather than rejoicing in this liberation, I feel an intense pang of loss. Fortunately, Lou restrains Danny, and Danny instead repositions himself flat on his stomach between the V of Lou's spread legs and sticks out his tongue, slithering the tip of it under my pouch where my straps meet. Lou moans again, and Danny's tongue probes the swollen, tender territory below his nuts.

Then I feel Danny's tongue against the rough mesh of my pouch, licking Lou's balls right through me, drenching me in his saliva until Lou's warm nuts cling to me, sticky and wet. Next he moves up to lick the throbbing underside of Lou's cock shaft. By now Lou's oozed out so much precome, his cock head has managed to nose its way under my waistband, his piss slit dribbling as it takes a peek at the outside world.

Danny reaches up to take it into his mouth, but my waistband holds it flat against Lou's taut belly, so he contents himself with flicking his tongue across Lou's piss slit. Lou's dick insistently throbs against my restraining waistband. Once more Danny goes to slide me off Lou, and once more Lou's quick to restrain him.

"Fuck me first, OK?" Lou begs, raising up on his bent legs, his butt hole coming into view.

"Christ, that's still the most beautiful hole I've ever seen!" It's pink and puckered, with a halo of sparse hair surrounding it, and Lou repeatedly clenches it until Danny succumbs to its allure and plunges his tongue deep inside, his forehead pressing against my pouch.

"Oh!" Lou groans as Danny feasts on his hole. I'm spellbound, since I've never seen anyone get rimmed before. You see, Lance was heavy into sucking cock and having his sucked. And on those few occasions when he allowed someone to rim him, I was already tossed onto the floor by the bed, my view obstructed. And now here I am, as Danny presses his hot palms against Lou's butt cheeks, pulls them as far apart as they'll go, and greedily plunges his tongue in and out of Lou's sensitive hole.

"Oh!" Lou moans again and again, wriggling his ass until Danny finally slides out his tongue and reaches under the bed, pulling out a plastic bottle of Vaseline. Squeezing some onto his hand, he slathers it across Lou's hole. Then he works one finger inside. Lou responds by squirming and moaning all over again. A second finger joins the first, and a third joins the second, and Lou's screaming and writhing out of control.

Once Danny's got Lou fully lubricated, he applies some to his own cock. Then, raising himself up onto his knees, he presses his greased-up member against Lou's rear entrance. When I see this union of cock head and butt hole, I begin to grow a bit concerned for Lou because, after all, his hole is only so big and Danny's dick is fucking enormous. I mean, just the head alone is fat enough to stretch him well beyond the dimensions of three little fingers.

But when Danny slips his fat cock head into Lou's hole and Lou lets out with a prolonged "O-o-oh," I realize I'm concerned over nothing at all.

Well, inch after amazing inch of Danny's dick makes its way inside Lou, whose cock grows into a rock-hard nine-incher as he strokes it. Because his hand (as well as his dick) is still inside my pouch, which is stretched beyond anything I've ever experienced before, I begin to understand what his fortunate butt hole must feel like.

Soon Danny's fucking Lou with an even rhythm, each thrust sending a shock wave through Lou's hard body, registering against my rear straps and in the constant jostling of his nuts inside my pouch. And all this time Lou's stroking his dick. My waistband gets stretched to the max as Lou's fist makes its way up and down his shaft, faster and faster until he forces his dick head right out into the open, hovering over his navel.

Suddenly Danny lets out with a loud "Ah, shit!" and, with the mightiest plunge of all, drives his cock all the way up Lou's ass, draining his nuts of the first outpouring of come and then proceeding to hammer the rest of his load into Lou. At this same time, Lou lets loose with "Oh! Oh! Oh!" as his own violent discharge of come lands all over his chest in long, ropy strands.

As they come to rest and catch their breath, Lou takes his softening dick and stuffs it back into my pouch. I willingly embrace it, appreciatively soaking up the last drops of come that seep out of his piss slit.

"Happy birthday, baby," he says, finally slipping me off. "Hope you like your present."

The way Danny takes me and rubs the inside of my pouch against his cheek, I know he does. And when he puts me on and I feel his mammoth equipment filling me up, I think he's as much a gift to me as I am to him.

You're probably not going to be surprised when I tell you that Danny jacked off several times without ever taking me off that night. The next morning, after a rejuvenating visit to those two great democratic institutions, the washer and the dryer (where brutes like me get to pal around with the likes of silk boxer shorts), he puts me on again and heads for the club.

Though I'd heard he worked out in the afternoon, I wasn't really surprised when he decided to alter his routine to get there before noon, especially since Lou mentioned that he wouldn't be there this morning.

Well, when Danny finally "just happens" to meet up with Lance, it's in the steam room. This is the first time I've been in the back. Let me tell you, it's like heaven: men in jockstraps, men with towels around their waists, men in the buff! Anyhow, he steps into the steam room, and there's Lance, alone, seated on the second tier.

Standing in front of him, Danny runs his hands across my pouch. "You're Lance Longfellow, aren't you?"

"Why, yes, I am," Lance says, his eyes making their way down Danny's sleek body, coming to rest on my pouch with a complete lack of recognition.

"I knew it! I'm one of your biggest fans!"

"Oh?" he says. "And just how big would that be?"

Danny grips me by the waistband on both sides of my pouch and slowly lowers me over his taut lower abs. His blond pubic hair spills out, and then the base of his cock comes into view.

"I see," Lance says, lowering himself down onto the bottom tier right in front of Danny. "Very big indeed."

Caught in the grip of my present master, I watch my former master's head come close, closer, and closer still as Danny's cock presses out against me. Sliding down onto his haunches, Lance opens his mouth, sticks out his tongue, and looks up at Danny's face with pleading eyes.

Danny continues to lower me until his dick flops out. From below Danny's thickening rod, I look up to see Lance wrap his lips around Danny's cock head, then proceed to take in inch after inch of his hardening shaft with an ease that exceeds even my expectations of his cocksucking abilities.

Danny issues a prolonged, impassioned moan. Lance's chin begins to press against me as Danny's dick reaches full erection, his cock head burrowing its way into Lance's throat. Then Lance proceeds to give Danny the blow job of his life.

But it's not until a few minutes later, when Lou steps into the steam room, that things *really* begin to get hot!

Fantasies
by Bob Vickery

The building's one of those converted Victorians, all the fancy woodwork stripped away, the facade covered with badly painted stucco. The steps are scattered with your standard-issue urban litter: fliers for pizza parlors and Chinese take-out joints, yellowing newspapers, that kind of thing. I take them two at a time, and when I get to the top, I pace up and down the stoop, breathing deeply. I'm getting an adrenaline rush like you wouldn't believe; my heart's pounding like a racing-car piston, and my brain's buzzing so much, I feel like I'm about to burst a blood vessel.

OK, focus, I tell myself. *Channel the energy.*

After I've calmed down a bit, I bend over and read the names on the strips of cardboard beneath each mailbox. VINNIE CASTELLONI is printed on the far right strip, VINNIE written in bold strokes, CASTELLONI all scrunched together. I push the doorbell and wait.

My hand begins to cramp, and I look down and see that I'm holding my Bible so tightly, my knuckles are white. I loosen my fingers.

Relax, I tell myself. *Get into this.*

I shut my eyes and take another deep breath. By the time the front door finally opens, I'm ready for bear.

The guy on the other side of the door eyes me suspiciously. He's in his mid to late 20s, too old for the street-punk attitude he's giving off. His black hair is greased back, there's two-day stubble on his face, and a cigarette dangles from his mouth. The tank top he wears hugs a well-muscled torso. There's a tear in it above his left pectoral, exposing a nipple the color and toughness of an old pencil eraser. His gaze flicks up and down my body and then settles on my face. He has the eyes of a fallen angel: dark and liquid but burning with a hard, cynical light. Mingled with the smell of old sweat is the unmistakable stench of a hell-bound sinner.

"Yeah?" he growls.

I clear my throat. I glance at the name card under the mailbox and then back at his face again. "Good morning, Vinnie," I say, making my voice as loud and hearty as I can. I raise my eyebrows and beam him my friendliest smile. "It is all right if I call you Vinnie, isn't it?"

Vinnie just glares at me with narrowed eyes, saying nothing.

"I'm here to share with you some wonderful news," I plunge on, "about how you can lay down the burden of life and let Jesus into your heart." I tug on the knot of my tie and inhale deeply. "I wonder if you'd be willing to give me a minute of your time?"

Vinnie just stands there in the doorway staring at me. He takes a deep drag from his cigarette and flicks the butt down the front steps. His full lips curl up into a nasty little smile. "Sure," he says, opening the door wider. "Come on in."

I push through before he has a chance to change his mind.

The apartment's small and dark: cheap thrift-store furniture, a threadbare rug, a beat-up old TV set. There are beer cans and newspapers scattered around the floor, and the kitchen sink is stacked with dirty dishes. A *Hustler* magazine lies open on the floor beside the couch, the centerfold model posed with her legs spread wide, showing pink (*Just what was Vinnie doing when I rang the bell?* I wonder).

I turn my head away and catch Vinnie watching me, smirking. He pulls a chair out from the table and straddles it, his forearms resting on its back. I sit down on the couch. I make a point of sliding my foot under the *Hustler* cover and flipping it shut.

"So what did you want to talk to me about?" he asks.

I run my tongue over my lips and put both hands on my knees. I'm feeling pumped. "Have you taken Jesus into your heart, Vinnie?" I ask.

Vinnie raises his arms above his head and stretches like some big jungle cat. The muscles of his torso ripple under his tight shirt. "No," he says calmly, "I can't say that I have."

I look directly into his beautiful dark eyes. "Did you ever stop to think that there may be a better way to live your life? Do you ever worry about your soul?" I raise my arm and shake my Bible at him. "The Bible says, 'Believe in the Lord, Jesus Christ, and thou shalt be saved.'" I realize I must look more like I'm trying to exorcise him than convert him, and I lower my arm.

Vinnie gives a little bark of laughter. He picks up a pack of cigarettes from the table next to him and shakes one loose. He looks at me over the flame of his match. "Do you really believe all that stuff?" he asks.

"Yes, I do. And it's worth your soul that you believe it too."

Vinnie looks amused. "What'll happen if I don't?"

I hold up my Bible. "It's all in here, Vinnie. If you don't believe, then you're just opening the door and letting Satan rule your life."

Vinnie seems to consider this. He takes a deep drag from his cigarette and exhales a stream of smoke. "Does Satan have a big dick?" he asks. "Do you ever wonder about things like that?"

"Well," I say, "if you're going to go on like that—"

"Does he?" Vinnie interrupts, his voice louder. He doesn't look amused now. His eyes drill into mine. "Is it thick and long? Do his balls hang low?" He stands up so abruptly, his chair topples back with a crash. He takes a step forward. "Do you ever wonder what it'd be like to suck it?"

I don't say anything for a while. "Is there a point you're trying to make?" I finally ask.

Vinnie's grin is boyish, but his eyes are two hard chips of stone. He walks over and stands before me, his crotch inches from my face. I can't help noticing the sizable bulge under the frayed denim of his jeans.

"Just answer the question," Vinnie says, his voice louder now. "Do you ever think about giving Satan head?"

There's nothing I can say to that. I close my eyes and start praying, the words spilling out in a steady stream.

"Do you wonder how Satan's cock would feel crammed down your throat?" Vinnie sneers. "Or shoved up your ass?" He's clenching and unclenching his fists now. "Is that what you want? To get fucked by Satan?"

"Sweet Jesus, but you've got a filthy mouth."

"I do, huh?" Vinnie growls. "Well, then, what about me? Maybe you'd like to chew on *my* dick for a while." With a quick movement he unzips his fly and yanks down his jeans. His hard dick springs out in front of him, inches from my face. "How about it?" he sneers. "How do I measure up?"

I stare at the thick shaft before me. "I've seen bigger," I lie.

"Bullshit!" Vinnie snarls. He grabs my shoulders and pins me down on the couch. I struggle, but I don't have enough purchase room to break free. Vinnie straddles my torso, his meaty red cock looming above my face. He grabs it by the base and slaps it against my left cheek. "Aren't you supposed to turn the other cheek now?" he jeers.

"Why are you doing this to me?" I cry out. "I only came here to help you!"

"Shut up!" Vinnie snaps. He glares down at me. "You Jesus boys make me want to puke! Damned hypocrites!"

He stands up and kicks off his sneakers and jeans. He pulls his tank top off last; I watch as it slides up over his body, revealing a hairless torso packed with muscles. I stare at his naked body: the sharp cut of the muscles; the smooth, chiseled abs; the dark, meaty cock jutting straight out before him.

"Now, I want you to get on your knees before me like you're going to pray," he says, "and lick my balls. Lick them for Jesus."

I don't move. I can't take my eyes off his body. With a snarl Vinnie pulls me off the couch and onto the floor. He yanks back my hair, and when I open my mouth to protest, he drops his balls in. The fleshy scrotum fills my mouth, and, as if it had a mind of its own, my tongue starts bathing it, rolling it around, savoring the taste and heft of his ball meat.

"Yeah," Vinnie growls. "Give those balls a good washing."

I burrow my nose into his crotch and inhale deeply, breathing in the ripe scent. The smell travels down into my lungs, intoxicating me. It has the stench of Satan: raw, animal, musky. I can't get enough of it!

I wrap my hand around his dick and begin stroking it, feeling the living tube of flesh throb in my palm. I look at it hungrily, tracing the veins up the shaft, noticing how the head flares out, red and angry. *This is what Satan's dick would look like,* I think. *Just as meaty. Just as dark and threatening.*

I slide my tongue up the fleshy shaft and swirl it around the engorged head. Vinnie grunts his approval. I squeeze his dick, and a clear drop of precome oozes out. I lap it up and then swoop down, taking Vinnie's dick deep in my throat. Vinnie gasps, and I feel a twinge of smugness that I've knocked him down a peg. I begin bobbing my head up and down, sliding my lips along the thick shaft.

Vinnie seizes my head with both hands and pumps his hips savagely. His cock rams against the back of my throat, slamming down it. I grab his ass cheeks with both hands and give them a good squeeze, feeling their hard muscularity. I tug down my zipper and pull out my own stiff dick. I start beating off furiously, timing my strokes to Vinnie's thrusting hips.

We quickly settle into a fast-paced rhythm of cock sucking and pud pounding. It's been too long since I've had a dick in my mouth, and the old hunger sweeps over me again.

Vinnie is relentless; he plows my face like there's hell to pay, but as brutal as he tries to be, I take it all eagerly. Old skills that I haven't used for some time come back now, and I give Vinnie what I'm willing to bet is a truly righteous blow job. Vinnie's breath comes in ragged grunts, then low whimpers.

I look up and see the sweat dripping down his face, his eyes glazed, his mouth open. My lips slide down his shaft, and I bury my nose in his pubes, keeping his dick deep inside my throat, working it with my tongue. I cup his fleshy balls in my hand and squeeze them. Vinnie groans, and his legs begin to tremble.

I take his dick out of my mouth and stroke it quickly. Vinnie's groans rise in volume; then he throws back his head and bellows as his jizz shoots out, splattering against my face, coating my cheeks, my mouth, my neck, my chest. His body shudders a few more times and then grows still.

A few quick strokes with my hand is all I need before I feel my own load pulsing out, oozing between my closed fingers. I groan loudly. Vinnie bends down and kisses me, pushing his tongue deep inside my mouth. He wraps his arms around me, holding me until the last of the spasms pass.

We lie like that for a few moments, Vinnie propped up against the couch, me cradled in his arms. I can feel his chest rise and fall as he breathes. He looks down, and our eyes meet. There's a moment of silence, and then we both laugh.

Vinnie runs his finger along my cheek, scooping up a dollop of his come. "Jeez, what a mess!" he grins.

I laugh again.

Vinnie disentangles himself and leaves the room. He comes back with a hand towel and tosses it to me. I wipe his load from my face.

"Well, did you enjoy yourself?" he asks.

"You have to ask?" I say, grinning. I toss him back the towel. "I think that was our best fantasy yet. Better than the TV repairman. Even better than the census taker."

Vinnie laughs again but says nothing. He picks up the fallen chair and puts it back by the table. I just lean back against the couch, watching his naked body. Even after just squirting a load, I feel myself getting turned on again, he's so handsome.

"You're a natural at this," I say, "playing out these little fantasies I set up. You should go into acting."

Vinnie shakes his head. "No, thanks. The escort business pays better."

Vinnie lets me use his shower. When I'm cleaned and dressed, I hand him the $100 I owe him.

"I'll give you a call in a couple of weeks," I say, "after I work out another fantasy. Maybe something involving a cop next time."

Vinnie shrugs. "Whatever you want, Gary." Now that he's out of character, he's amiable and relaxed. He's actually a sweet guy when he's not acting out some role.

He walks me to his door. Next to it stands a table cluttered with envelopes, notepads, an appointment calendar. There's also a framed photograph I hadn't noticed before. I look at it briefly. Vinnie and another man are standing on the deck of a cabin cruiser, the sea and a sunny sky behind them. Both men are laughing and have their arms around each other. Vinnie's friend has those all-American good looks found in milk commercials: wavy red hair; boyish face; compact, muscular body. The two of them make a very handsome couple, and I feel a pang of envy at how happy they look. I know nothing about Vinnie's personal life and have no idea what romances he's involved in when he isn't working.

I pick up the picture for a closer look. "Your friend's good-looking." I glance toward Vinnie. "Where was this taken?"

Vinnie gives me a polite smile, but there's a tightness to it that wasn't there before. "Cancún," he says. He takes the picture from me and puts it back on the table. "Well, good night."

I can take a hint. We shake hands, and I leave.

About a week later I run into Vinnie on Castro Street. Well, *run into* isn't exactly right. I see him on the other side of the street waiting in line in front of a theater. It's a little after 9 on a Saturday night, and the neighborhood is just beginning to come alive. The restaurants are full, and the music from the bars spills out onto the sidewalks. It's a warm evening, unusual for San Francisco, and the uniform of the night seems to be tank tops and shorts. Vinnie's no exception, and the gym shorts and T-shirt he's wearing show off his body to good effect. Vinnie's with someone; in fact, he has his arm draped around the guy's shoulder. The gesture is too casual to be erotic, but it's that very casualness that makes it look so intimate.

I'm in no rush, and because I'm a nosy little fucker, I stop and watch them from the doorway of a doughnut shop. There's something familiar about the guy with Vinnie, but I can't quite place him. I look at him closely and suddenly make the connection: He's the man I saw in the picture with Vinnie. Only I can see now that the photo was incredibly flattering; in real life he isn't nearly as good-looking. In fact, he's actually kind of scrawny and worn around the edges. This surprises me. A guy with Vinnie's looks could easily do better. Hell, he could get anybody he wanted.

Vinnie's friend says something to Vinnie, and Vinnie grins. Once again I'm struck by how fuckin' beautiful Vinnie is; it breaks my heart just to look at him. After a while I move on.

Later, in a bar, as I'm talking with friends, that scene with Vinnie and his friend flashes through my mind. *What does Vinnie see in that scrawny little fucker?* I think. But someone says something to me, and I let the thought drop.

The phone rings and rings, and I start to wonder if Vinnie's out. It's been more than two months since we acted out our little Jehovah's Witness fantasy, and my dick is hard and juicing with the thought of him naked in bed with me. I'm a regular client, and I usually don't let so much time go by between sessions, but with business trips and a two-week vacation to Hawaii, things just got in the way. But now I'm ready to make up for lost time. No fantasies, no role-playing, just down-home sweaty gruntin' sex.

Someone finally picks up the phone. "Hello?"

"Yo, Vinnie," I say. "It's Gary."

"Hi." Vinnie's voice sounds oddly flat.

"How have you been?" I ask.

"OK."

There's a long silence. I begin to wonder if Vinnie's put off with me for some reason. Last time, I told him that I'd call in a couple of weeks; is he pissed because I've taken so long?

"Is everything OK?" I ask. "You sound kind of funny."

"I'm fine." Another pause. "So what's up?"

I clear my throat. "I was wondering if we could get together tonight. Nothing fancy, no fantasies this time, just a regular roll in the hay."

There's a long silence on the other end of the line. For a moment I wonder if we've been disconnected. "All right," Vinnie says after another long pause. "What time?"

His tone is really putting me off. He sounds so remote. "Around 10 o'clock?" I say. I hear my own voice taking on a certain coolness, matching his.

"Yeah, that'll be fine," he says. He hangs up without saying good-bye.

I sit there with the phone still in my hand. *That was weird,* I think as I return it to its cradle. Vinnie's usually a friendly guy. I don't know what the hell is going on with him.

I go through the evening thinking about that conversation and getting more and more annoyed. A large part of Vinnie's charm as an escort comes from his being a down-to-earth guy, a rare trait for someone in his line, especially if they're as hot as he is. If he's going to suddenly start copping an attitude with me, that'll kill the mood for sure. I begin thinking about the possibility of canceling with Vinnie and finding someone else. God knows, the city's full of handsome guys willing to turn a trick if the price is right.

The latest issue of the local gay rag is on my coffee table. I pick it up and start flipping through the pages toward the back section where the escorts advertise. I find myself in the obituaries, and I'm about to turn the page again when one of the notices catches my eye.

I recognize the picture immediately: It's Vinnie's red-haired friend. In fact, it looks like the photo's been cropped from the framed photo I saw on Vinnie's table. I sit down and read the obituary all the way to the end. The man's name was Steve Benson, and he was 26 when he died, the cause of death "complications due to AIDS." The obituary ends by saying that Steve is survived by his mother, his father, a sister, and his loving partner, Vincent. I see that the funeral was today.

I look at the picture of the laughing man for a few seconds more and then close the paper.

Oh, shit! I think. *Poor Vinnie.*

Vinnie answers the door in his bathrobe. He smiles apologetically. "Hi, Gary," he says. "I'm running a little late. I just got out of the shower."

He stands aside and motions for me to enter. I walk in and sit on the couch.

"Do you want a beer or something?" he asks.

I shake my head, watching Vinnie closely. He seems pretty normal, maybe a little subdued. As always, I'm awed by his good looks. I think of the muscular body under that terry cloth robe and feel my dick begin to stiffen.

"It's been a while," I say.

Vinnie smiles. Some of his old charm returns. "Yeah, I've been wondering what happened to you. Everything OK?"

I nod. "Sure. Things are all right." I let a few seconds go by. "How about you?"

Vinnie shrugs. "Yeah, things are fine."

Both of us are silent for a few moments. Vinnie finally walks over to the couch and slips off his robe. It falls to the floor around his feet.

I sit back and look at him: the beautifully sculpted body, the thick dick hanging down between his thighs. "God, you're handsome," I say.

Vinnie gives a small smile. "Let's go back to the bedroom."

I undress by the night-light next to Vinnie's bed. Vinnie is already lying on top of his bedspread, legs splayed, hands behind his head.

Once I'm naked I slip in beside him, kissing him lightly on the lips. My mouth travels south, down his neck, stopping for a moment at each nipple, then down across the hard, rippled expanse of his belly. Vinnie lies motionless. I rest his dick in my hand and kiss it too; even soft it has an impressive thickness. I put it in my mouth and start sucking, twisting my head from side to side for maximum effect. Vinnie's dick stays limp. After a couple of minutes I give it up. I look up at Vinnie's face.

Vinnie's staring somewhere over my shoulder, his expression unreadable.

"Vinnie," I say softly.

He turns toward me. His eyes have the stunned, baffled look of a plane-crash victim's. Beneath the shock all I see is despair.

"Oh, Vinnie" is all I can say. I reach up and stroke his cheek. After a few seconds I add, "I saw his obituary."

Vinnie stares at me for a long time without saying anything. Suddenly his eyes brim with tears. He reaches down and pulls me up against him.

We lie in bed, our naked bodies pressed together, my face against Vinnie's neck. My hands stroke his back up and down, kneading the skin. There's nothing erotic in my intent; it's the only way I know to comfort him. I feel his hands rub against my back as well. We lie together like that for a long time, his heart beating against my chest.

I'm not quite sure exactly when it happens, but there's a subtle change now in the way Vinnie's holding me. He slowly lowers his head and kisses me, pressing his lips gently against mine. He does it again, more passionately, this time slipping his tongue inside my mouth. His pelvis starts grinding against mine, and I can feel his dick thickening, getting harder. He starts dry-humping my belly, pushing his now-erect cock against my body. My own dick is stiff and ready for action.

He breaks away and opens the drawer of the nightstand, pulling out a condom package. I take it from him, tear it open with my teeth, and roll it down his dick. Vinnie pulls a tube of lube out of the drawer and squirts a dollop onto his palm. He reaches down and massages my ass, probing into my crack, pushing a finger up my hole. I groan. When I'm nicely lubed, he wraps me in his arms again, rubbing his body against mine. He works his thick, hard dick between my legs, and I take over from there, holding it with my hand, guiding it in. I breathe deeply, letting myself relax, welcoming the sensations of Vinnie's dick pushing its way up inside me.

Vinnie wraps his arms around me again and begins to pump his hips. His hands travel over my torso, kneading my warming flesh. With his eyes closed he kisses my face, his lips gently pressing against my mouth, my eyes, my hair. He has never been this tender before.

His thrusts pick up speed, and I move my body in time to them. Vinnie sighs his gratitude. I squeeze my ass muscles hard around Vinnie's thick root, and he kisses me again, shoving his tongue once more down my throat. I push my tongue against his, holding his face between my hands. Vinnie's eyes are still closed, and it doesn't take a rocket scientist to figure out who he's pretending I am.

With a quick movement Vinnie flips me on my back and lies on top of me. His muscular torso, slippery with sweat, squirms against mine. He plows my ass with deep, quick thrusts now, his dick pulling almost completely out and then plunging all the way in. Vinnie grinds his hips against mine, his balls pressed against my ass, his thrusts pushing me hard against the headboard.

And yet, even with the increased tempo, the tenderness remains. His hand is wrapped around my dick, and he beats me off with long, slow strokes. I reach down and cup his balls in my hand. They're pulled up tight against his body, and I know it won't be long before he blows.

He pulls out again and then skewers me deeply, his hips churning. I feel his body shudder, and I pull his face down to mine, kissing him hard, biting his lips. Vinnie cries out as the first wave of jizz slams into the condom up my ass. His torso heaves and bucks against mine with each succeeding spasm. Vinnie's strokes take me closer and closer to climax, and then I'm shooting too, squirting my load into his hand, my groans muffled by Vinnie's mouth over mine. Our bodies strain and push against each other and then fall apart.

I glance over at Vinnie. He's lying on his back, staring up at the ceiling. I get up and pull my clothes on. Vinnie doesn't say a word. For a moment I think he's fallen asleep, but when I look at him, his eyes are still open.

When I've finished dressing, I pull my wallet out of my back pocket and fish out a wad of $20 bills. I sit on the edge of the bed and shake Vinnie's shoulder. He turns his head and looks at me, saying nothing. The misery in his eyes hasn't changed.

I never know what to say at moments like this. "Here's the money I owe you," I say, feeling very awkward.

Vinnie pushes my hand away. "Forget it." He manages a small laugh. "Tonight it's on the house."

I squeeze his arm, but I can't think of anything to say.

"Good night, Gary," Vinnie finally says.

I stand up. "Good night, Vinnie."

I walk out the bedroom door. When I'm in the living room, I glance at the picture of Vinnie and Steve laughing on the cabin cruiser. I slide the money under it and leave the apartment.

Outside I see that the fog has rolled in and the night has turned chilly. So much for our Indian summer. I zip up my coat and jam my hands in my pockets. It's late, and nobody else is out on the streets.

The last time I was with Vinnie, I think, *I was a Jehovah's Witness. Tonight I was his lover.*

I decide that I just might take a break from fantasies for a while. I climb into my car and drive down the deserted streets toward home.

The Innocent Predator
by Evan Robertson

As if to awaken sleepy passengers, the bus driver loudly announced, "Chicago! The Windy City! Those making transfers to Monmouth, La Grange, Danville…make 'em here. Rest rooms and coffee shop inside the station. Hope you enjoyed the ride."

I'd hated it. Every fucking minute of it. All the way from the correctional institute in Vacaville, California, mile after boring mile of gazing out the window at nothing, barely dozing at night, using public rest rooms at dreary stops, glancing through small-town newspapers.

I ran a hand over my chin stubble. I felt cramped, dirty, stiff, and lousy. But I was a free man. No more guards, fellow inmates, prison routine, cell doors clanging shut, sucking cigs in the yard, parole boards looking you over. Free!

I'd played their game carefully by keeping my nose out of trouble, being a good boy, doing my daily chores, acting polite always. Constantly in my mind was one ambition: to get out after years spent in the pen for car stealing, beating up people who annoyed me, and leaving a few gay inmates lying on their bunks with jaws needing to be wired.

When I got off the bus, I grabbed my sack of stuff, put it in a locker, and headed for the public toilet and pay showers.

Looking in the mirror there, I saw that I was a mess: bleary-eyed, needing a shave, mussed hair, wrinkled clothes. Chance to clean up now.

In the showers I casually glanced at the other guys soaping themselves, giving special priority to their genitals, scrubbing their heads, soaping their asses. Now and then I caught one or two of them looking me over. Not too surprising; still, I'll never get used to it. All my life I've been the focus of both men and women because of my looks; my powerful, muscled body; my height; and, in situations like this, my enormous equipment. Privately I get a kick out of being envied.

Newly clean and shaved, my hair neatly combed, I felt more human as I climbed on the connecting bus to Danville and took my assigned seat. This wouldn't be a long trip.

Settling down, I reached into my pocket for Jeremy's last letter, lit a cigarette, and formulated my plans. I kept telling myself to remember three rules: Never scare the boy, never threaten him, and never make him distrustful. Gay magazines were full of warnings for innocent guys like Jeremy. I was determined to gain his trust, to keep my meal ticket.

I also knew that I was expected to live up to what he expected, the anticipated sexual shit. Well, I could supply that.

For years around my various cell blocks, I'd heard whispers that I was "dangerous" and "brutal when angry," had "sinister, greedy eyes on a masklike face." I suppose that my menacing presence scared even some of the hardened inmates, who took care to avoid my outbursts. Were I to be sprung, I realized, I had to change that impression, so I worked at it: smiling in the mirror, trying to soften my glances, showing off my deep wrinkles, unclenching my fists during furies.

Also I kept my voice low, purring, and hoarse. Suited the image I wanted.

Switching on the overhead light, I examined Jeremy's long letter. I squirmed over the loving contents because, being normally a straight guy who used a cute boy's ass only for satisfaction in prison life, I rarely bothered with gay guys. They were an occasional healthy necessity.

Over time Jeremy's letters had grown into passionate pleas for love, dominance, and sex. I encouraged him in my responses, borrowing phrases from gay periodicals. Along the way I learned some useful information: He was wealthy, young, orphaned, lonely.

We began corresponding over an ad a cell mate had encouraged me to submit. There were hungry gay guys out there who could provide exactly what an ex-con needed, my cell mate had told me: three squares, room and board, company, probably money.

And I had hooked a live one.

However, through all of this I never begged and never claimed that I loved him. Otherwise, I was honest with him.

He would be mincemeat.

We pulled up to Danville's bus station. About three of us got off. Immediately I looked around for Jeremy. The station was practically empty. But then a flashy, expensive sports car pulled up, driven by a handsome red-haired guy who had to be Jeremy.

Piling my stuff into the backseat, I settled down comfortably, secretly watching the boy wheel the automobile easily along the highway, out of the burbs, past the farmhouses. As we chatted and got personally acquainted, the heat began to get to me. Casually I reached up and opened my shirt to cool off. The boy nearly drove off the road, staring at the expanse of my chest, my washboard stomach, and my huge pectorals, all covered with a mass of curling black hair.

Straightening out the car, he tried to concentrate on his driving. "Golly, Monty, you sure got a build on you! You weren't lying in those letters. You gonna let me see all of you soon?"

Suddenly I didn't like his familiarity, his sexual assumption. I let my smile drain into my customary impassive mask, and this instantly corrected his behavior.

He drove up a long private driveway and pulled up in front of an enormous residence. We got out, I picked up my stuff, and we went inside.

Jeremy watched me for some kind of reaction to the lavishness of the place, but I managed to look indifferent to it all.

"Not bad, not bad at all," I remarked. Shit—the joint certainly wasn't a prison cell!

He seemed determined to get one thing straight, hanging around and looking hopefully at my face. When would he receive my grateful, welcoming kiss?

But I was playing my cards carefully. *Keep the kid waiting, hoping for intimacy,* I told myself. *Fuck, that's what these relationships are supposed to be about.* Now that I was here, I was going to take my fucking time.

"You got a room for me somewhere? Place I can shower, clean up, dump my shit?"

Returning to reality, he snapped into action. He escorted me upstairs and presented first a spare room (small) and then his own room (large), a beautiful bedroom with view windows, plenty of furniture, and a private bath and deck.

"Well," he asked finally, smiling, "which bedroom do you like better, Monty?"

With as much indifference as I could muster, I replied, "Oh, this will do fine. Where do you sleep?"

He looked confused. "Why, here, naturally. I'd hoped that we'd share…everything, Monty."

"Oh, yeah," I said, lighting a cigarette. "I forgot. Look, why don't you make us a drink downstairs, and I'll join you as soon as I get my life in order up here?"

"Hey, great! See you in the living room." He turned and left.

That boy was hot to study my body, arouse some action. I'd kept him waiting through all those hot love letters of mine. *Gotta face the inevitable,* I resolved.

Fresh and smelling good again, I returned downstairs, found a drink waiting for me on the coffee table, and lounged back on the long sofa, my feet on the table. Jeremy sat opposite me, his face glowing.

For a minute I stared at him. Getting an impression of someone from intimate letters may be one thing; actually seeing the
guy was something else. He was pretty, nicely built, masculine,
and unaffected. And he was also rich.

Gradually, as we conversed, I found out that his dead folks had
left everything to him, that he was in college, that he had never
had a job (didn't need one), that he liked tennis, and that he'd
been gay all his life.

Deciding that I'd better get this show on the road, I casually
patted the space beside me, a gesture that suggested he join me on
the sofa. He complied, carrying over his drink and placing it next
to mine. Turning, he gazed silently into my eyes.

Slipping my muscled arm around his shoulders, I gently pulled
him to me. As I bent my lips over his, I wondered how much he
was worth.

Our sucking mouths got me going in the usual manner: My
rising erection was an iron crowbar in my pants. Our tongues
delved in and out, plowing into the depths of each other's
mouths. Without turning, I pulled his arm so that his hand flattened over my crotch, his fingers sliding over my rock-hard cock.
My intense kissing seemed to activate his hand, which explored
the boner hidden in my trousers.

"Oh, Monty," he breathed, "I've been waiting for this."

Spreading my legs, I encouraged his fumbling with my zipper.
It wasn't necessary to say anything. Men didn't have to.

My zipper now down, I urged him on, coaxing him to stroke
my dick, make it swell even harder, cup my testicles and stretch
them out. As his hips rose, I could see by the bulge in his pants
that he was totally ready, but again I let him wait. I had to keep
him dangling on my line before reeling him in. He was a catch I
fully intended to serve me seconds and thirds after I drained him
of all resistance. In such draining I would squeeze him dry.

Stroking his crotch a little, just to encourage him, I kept him
focused on mine. Playing the guest for whom Jeremy was sup-

posed to be grateful, I whispered gentle, urgent instructions. My boots felt heavy; would he pull them off? He would, and he wrestled with each one until they came off. I nodded then as he went for my sweaty socks.

"Slide my pants down, Jeremy. You've been wanting this for a while. Take your time. I know you're eager."

In his desire to please me, he seemed to forget his own "problem." All of his concentration was on my cock and balls. Now, with my shirt wide open, my pants nearly down over my knees, and my hairy legs spread open invitingly, I reached out to draw the boy up into position. He looked down, his tongue running over his lips hungrily. Again I made him wait.

"Think you can handle that? Stroke it; it gets bigger, you know. That's it, puppy. You want to lick that head, don't you? Make my cock bounce with your tongue? Slide your hungry mouth around it? Make your buddy feel good? Ah…bounce it, baby. I wanna see it flop up and down. You want it, I know. Got that from your hot letters."

Clearly he enjoyed dominance, obviously never having really had parental control. Well, I'd change his independence if I got lucky. Then I'd apply the sexual tourniquet, twisting slowly, relentlessly until he couldn't live without me.

My organ now waved like a giant fleshy tower, veined, throbbing, ripe with man aroma. He lapped at the head, making the purple mushroom moist. *We're getting off to a good beginning,* I thought. *My way.*

He attempted to swallow the meat whole, but I prevented such pleasure. "Take it easy, boy. Hungry boy. Gotta be fed and can't wait. Don't worry, you'll get it. I'll feed you. Eat those balls first. Pull up on 'em with your teeth. That's my boy. Swallow 'em all the way. Um…nice boy. Taste good?"

By now he had yanked off my pants. Not having worn shorts, I supplied him with a naked lunch. My powerful smell rose from my equipment, filling his nostrils.

"Love me, Jeremy? Think you'll want this frequently? I'll need a lot of it if we're staying together."

"*If?*" he sputtered, raising his head and staring at me. "I thought that our being together was the main idea, Monty! Sure, I'd do anything to stay with you! Please."

"Well," I said, looking serious, "that 'if' depends on a lot of things. I love what you're doing to me right now, but there is the future to think about. I ain't got no money, no car, and no way to pay you back for anything." There it was, out in the open.

Meanwhile, my erection was growing limp, so I stroked it, pointedly looking down woefully at what I was missing. And with that comment floating in the air between us, he wasted little time in enveloping the head with his thirsty mouth, sliding determinedly down to suck up the throbbing monster. His mouth, like a velvet glove, gripped my meat, his tongue whirling around the hard bony sides. Then he arrived at the thick hilt, his tongue now moistening the hairy black forest.

Raising my hips, I sank into his throat, his teeth gently raking my meat. It hurt a little, but I wallowed in the wetness and sexual expectations.

"Got a load to deliver, boy. Think you can take it? All of it? You gonna drain this pistol? Let me shoot you full of hot desire? Pump it down your thirsty throat?"

To each question he gagged out some response as he worked my cock over, his head nodding. I felt the come rising to the old boiling point. My hips, spasms shaking them along with my moans, bucked my cock into mighty ejections of flowing come. The stuff made him slobber, spilling down his throat and out over his lips, causing him to cough. Man, did I feed my puppy! His throat was working overtime. Eventually he drained me, his face caked with dried come.

As he wiped my cock, still dripping come on the carpet, and wiped his lips, my previous comments hit home, for he immediately took up the subject of keeping me around. At any price.

There would be, he explained during newly made drinks, no problem with anything. No job necessity, no concern about having money on me (he had plenty), no need to repay him anything—except, of course, giving him sex constantly. Meanwhile, the house would be ours.

I gazed around. Hadn't thought of going after the house! Maybe getting it in my name on some legal document or something? Start building my bank account? I grinned and kissed him, giving him plenty of tongue.

So our lives together commenced. I never had occasion to ask for a check; Jeremy would leave a large one on his desk each week (to cover personal expenses).

I bought, with his money, a used car to get around in. We bought me new outfits. We went to the theater, movies, musicals…and he, as expected, footed the bills.

When I grew bored with repeated sucking sessions, having conditioned him not to expect me to suck him (I might leave if bothered with obligations of any kind), I trained him to bring me my shoes, put on my pants and shirt and jacket, make me drinks, and lie back for fucking sessions, with me doing the fucking.

Jeremy had a nice, juicy asshole, which I used constantly, grinding into him with powerful thrusts, sometimes coming several times a day into that hungry receptacle. He couldn't get enough.

I made certain he felt he needed my sexual energy. And sometimes I gave him the best of both worlds. Fucking him with a heavy dildo, I'd slide under him, raising my erection for his mouth to suck. A little contortion here—but well worth it. Then I'd reverse the process, insisting he suck the dildo while being vigorously plowed by real meat.

When exactly one year had elapsed, I suddenly realized that my bank account was bulging. Shit, now I could pay my own way— unless, that is, I wanted to find another sucker.

I felt not one pang of guilt for what I had exacted from Jeremy; it had been a pay-for-play deal, and we both knew it.

But what I had failed to realize was that I had fallen in love with the man.

Apart from those penitentiary letters (scrawls on lined paper) to Jeremy, I'd never written letters to anyone, nor had I ever expected to receive any. So when I sauntered out to our mailbox one afternoon to pick up the mail, I idly sorted through the many letters, several from overseas, seeing what Jeremy was getting this time. God, he got mail from everywhere! No wonder he was constantly writing letters and notes!

I stopped short suddenly. Here was a return address from the Sonoma County Correctional Institute, Sonoma, California! Directed to #13558, Cell Block C. Now who the fuck was that?

I stormed back into the house and confronted a calm and placid Jeremy. Waving the letter in his face, I demanded to know what the hell was going on! Who was inmate #13558?

Jeremy merely smiled. "OK, Monty, I might as well tell you. You'd better sit down."

Making myself a drink, I sat impatiently. I wasn't accustomed to receiving orders from Jeremy, orders of any kind.

Lighting a cigarette, pushing back his red hair from his face, he ripped open the letter. Totally in command of the scene, he scanned the letter while a dead silence descended.

Without looking at me, Jeremy spoke to the wall, his words direct, metallic, decisive: "Monty, it's over for us. I've firmly decided. Our relationship was going nowhere anyway. Sure, I got what I wanted out of it, but so did you. Proof of the latter: I came across your bankbook—no, I wasn't prying—quite by accident. You've done awfully well with my 'loans.' Of course, I don't begrudge you anything; the money is yours, the car, the clothes, and so forth. But it is over. Over."

Crestfallen, shocked, I slumped in my chair. "But why? *Why?* What went wrong? I thought you were happy..."

He rose, strolling around the room. "Happy? You filled a void in my life. You supplied what I wanted. I suppose that is happiness for a while. But you see, now I've found a new source for my needs. Like you, he's an inmate, and he's being released this week. And I love him. I want him as I wanted you. And I can take him, keep him. You, Monty, became irrelevant in my life. I drained you of excitement and surprise. Now I don't need you any longer."

Going up to him, I grabbed him in a viselike hold, attempting to kiss him, but he turned away.

"But what about *me,* you bastard? What happens to *me* now? You can't just walk out of my life! Look, I'll give you back the money, everything! Stay with me. Let me make love to you. I love you, baby!"

Impassively he turned toward me. "You gave me what I needed. The house is being sold, so we are both leaving: I, for a life in California; you, for wherever you like." He sat down and scrawled out a check for $5,000. "Please, Monty, pack and leave now."

The tables were turned. I was the guy on my knees between his legs, trying to unzip his fly, nuzzling his crotch, about to suck his cock finally.

"Shit, I'll do anything!" I begged him, I pleaded with him. I think I started to cry.

He remained unmoved. "Now, Monty. Get your things together and leave. It's over."

Ranting, raving, swearing, and even threatening, I went upstairs, packed, and returned to the living room, where Jeremy was waiting for me.

"I'll get you! I'll slice you up! You won't get away with this, you little fucker!"

Calmly he ushered me though the front door.

Before slamming it behind me, he delivered threats of his own: "Never come near me again, or you'll be back where I found you!" And then, ever so coldly, he said the words I'll never forget: "I could never love someone so...so ordinary."

Later, sitting on the bus heading for New York, I scanned the personals column in a gay newspaper I'd remembered to pack. And there it was:

> "Young man willing to care for handsome, built ex-convict, give him a start in life, supply his sexual needs. Walks on the beach, wine in front of the fireplace, mutual comfort, pursuing the good life together. I'm honest. You be too. Write…"

After marking the item, I folded the newspaper and stuffed it into my back pocket. At our next rest stop, I'd post a card to this innocent.

About East Coast time, I'd be ready to get laid.

Souvenir
by Barry Alexander

R-i-i-ing!

Fuck! Why does the doorbell always ring when you're in the middle of sex?

"I've got to answer it," I say, even though I don't move. I feel too good lying here, spread out like a banquet on flaming peach silk sheets. One hand slowly strokes my shaft; the other is occupied with a more intimate exploration. But I think I know who's at the door. I've been expecting him. "I've got to answer it," I say again, with more conviction.

Warm fingers slide reluctantly from my hole. I shiver as Brock's shirt cuffs tickle the fine hairs lining my cleft as gently as a breath.

I smooth my hair and quickly make myself presentable. Sighing, I dig under the tangled sheets for my jeans and tug them over my softening erection.

We picked out the sheets together. Had a ball giving the sales-clerk a hard time. We were just killing time in the mall, waiting while I had my tires rotated. A saleswoman with an iron-gray frizzled perm latched on to us as soon as we wandered into her department.

"What can I help you boys with?" she asked, hovering at our sides and baring a perfect porcelain smile with just a touch of red lipstick on her teeth. You always told me I looked younger than 30, but I hadn't been called "boy" in a long time.

You nudged me before I could answer.

"We're looking for some sheets," you said with a secret wink.

"Bed linens make a wonderful wedding gift. We've just received a new shipment of percales in some lovely florals— Oh, it's not a wedding? Well, I'm sure we can find something that would make a lovely birthday gift. Your mother must be so proud of her sons. Most men aren't so thoughtful— You're not brothers? For you?" She looked puzzled for a moment, then redirected her sales pitch. "Well, let's see…we've got some nice abstracts and geometrics over here, perfect for the bachelor pad. Queen or king?"

"Queen definitely," you said.

"And what about you?"

"Queen," I said, stifling a giggle.

"These are excellent quality: permanent-press, carefree, very durable…"

You picked up a package of flaming peach silk sheets. "Oh, look, honey! These will be just perfect for our bed, don't you think?" You put your arm around me and nuzzled my ear, even though you knew I wasn't much for public displays of affection.

Her face turned purple, and her mouth dropped open so far, I could count her molars.

I saw you glance at the price tag. "Thank you so much, ma'am, but I think—"

"—these will be perfect," I finished. "We'll take them." I put them on my Visa.

We laughed all the way to the car.

"You're terrible," I said.

"Nonsense. You loved every minute of it."

I always wanted to do something like that, but I never had the nerve. I think that's when I knew I loved you.

Faded loafers. Mine.

Ragged Nikes. His. Clunk.

Kenny G. Mine.

Counting Crows. His. Clink.

In-line skates. Helmet. Kneepads. His. His. His. Clunk. Clunk. Clunk.

There was a certain satisfaction in watching the box fill. It felt good to be actually doing something. They were just things after all, and they no longer had a place in my life. I didn't want anything lying around to remind me of the creep.

I moved out of the bedroom and started searching, determined to root his things out of my apartment as completely as he'd removed himself from my life.

R-i-i-ing!

"Damn it, I'm coming!"

Just because he's gone doesn't mean my sex life is over, I think as I walk through the kitchen toward the door. *OK, so it's not the same, but sex is sex. I'll get by. There'll be others.*

There'll be others for him too. For a second I picture other men touching him, being touched by him. Hands moving over the golden perfection of his body. Hands cupping the smooth white boulders of his ass as his powerful hips drive his cock deep. His blunt-tipped fingers drawing patterns over another's body. His lips nestled in the hollow under someone else's throat as he drifts off to sleep. But it makes absolutely no difference to me. I don't care.

I.

Do.

Not.

Care.

If you knew for sure—I mean, absolutely for sure—how it was going to end, would you ever pick anyone up? I've often wondered. If you envisioned the bitter fights, the cold words, the gaping hole in the center of your life that not even the biggest cock can fill, would you be able to resist that first glimpse of golden skin inside an open col-

lar, the sweet promise of hard curved muscle, the mystery of dark-lashed eyes?

I've often wondered.

The rattle of pots woke me. I glanced at the clock: 3 A.M. *Who in the hell is in my kitchen?*

Not bothering to dress, I grabbed my tennis racket for protection and crept down the hall to the phone. Just as I started to dial, I heard a crash, followed by a string of profanity that would have made a trucker blush. I put down the phone and walked into the kitchen, smiling. No one else could swear like you.

Surrounded by an avalanche of kitchen utensils, you knelt on the floor, scraping up cookie dough. You looked up, and we both started laughing. Your nose was smudged with flour, and the backside of your jeans was stamped with two floury handprints.

"What's so funny?" I demanded. "You're the one who looks ridiculous."

"Right. And I suppose you always play tennis in the nude?"

I looked down at the tennis racket I was still clutching. "I thought you were a prowler," I said defensively. I didn't tell you that for a moment I'd forgotten I'd asked you to move in. "What are you doing?"

"I got hungry for chocolate. I thought I'd make a quick batch of chocolate chip cookies."

"It's 3 o'clock in the morning."

"I believe in instant gratification."

"Do you often get these sudden urges?"

"Yep, and I'm having one right now." You leered at me. "So which weapon were you planning to bludgeon me with? I'm afraid neither looks very dangerous."

Grinning wickedly, you wrapped your flour-dusted hand around my dick, tugged me closer, and kissed me. You looked totally absurd—floured head to toe, your hair sticking up in frosted tufts—and I never wanted anyone so much in my life.

Cookie sheets. His.

But where do you stop? When you live with someone for two years, they touch everything in your life. Even the most mundane objects become imbued with history.

The recliner that tipped over when we were making love.

The bottle of cold medicine he went out to buy when I had trouble getting to sleep.

The copies of *Island* he kept stacked under the bed. Neither of us had ever been sailing, but we were saving up. "Just imagine, Alex!" he said. "Two weeks of nothing but sun and sand and sex!"

My battered copy of *The Front Runner*. I couldn't believe he'd never heard of it. I read it to him in bed, and we both cried when Harlan lost Billy.

What about the condoms, half for him and half for me? He taught me to keep condoms in every room. I never knew where or when he would want to have me. I tossed half the strip in the box.

But what were a few books and magazines when almost everywhere I looked was a chair or a table we'd made love on? There was no getting rid of him.

Power crystal. His.

Steuben crystal. Mine.

First-Christmas-together ornament. Ours.

But there is no ours. Not now. Not ever.

I open the door.

He stands there, cradling a bouquet of flaming peach roses.

"Alex, I've been such a fool. Can you ever forgive me?" He looks at me with his deep brown eyes, silently pleading.

How can I resist? I open my arms, and he falls into them.

No! No! No! No! No!

~~Strike through!~~

Erase and rewind.

It's not going to be that easy for the bastard.

I know exactly what I'm going to say.
I've practiced for two weeks.
He deserves it.
He deserves every word of it.

Strange how when someone first moves in, everything seems so crowded. Shirts squashed in the closet. Not enough drawer space. His things cluttering the dresser, cramming the medicine cabinet. And he's always in the john when you have to go.

The apartment has really opened up now. My shirts have room to breathe. My underwear has a whole drawer to itself. Everything is back in its proper place. No dirty socks under the couch. No pop cans tiered on the coffee table. I can use the john whenever I want.

Your tongue tasted of dark chocolate as it searched the recesses of my mouth. I sucked the sweetness from it and mashed my lips against yours. We both came up panting.

"I've got to go to work in the morning," I protested.

"Me too," you said with a grin. You kissed the corner of my mouth, then trailed a line of kisses along my jaw and down my throat, licking at the stubble and sucking at my flesh.

You caught my cock in your doughy hands and squeezed it gently. It swelled and thickened, nudging at your hands like a puppy eager for attention. "Want me to stop so you can get your beauty rest?"

"Do you want to die? You woke it up; you damn well better take care of it."

"Sure you're not too sleepy?" Your finger rolled over the deep red glans of my cock.

I gasped and pressed closer. I loved the roughness of your jeans against my bare thighs. The metal of your zipper was cold against my skin, but I ground myself against you anyway, eager for the heat and fullness behind it. "Positive," I sighed.

Your lips nuzzled through my chest hair and brushed against my nipple. You touched the tip of your tongue against the tiny peak, flicking it with wetness, then blew a puff of cool air across it. The pink nub crinkled and hardened, aching for more attention. I pushed your head down, and you sucked my nipple hard. The exquisite sensations rushed straight to my cock, making it jump in your hands. "Oh, yeah! That's the way!"

But I had to touch you too, to feel that perfect golden skin under my fingers. I fumbled with your shirt buttons, my hands shaking with eagerness. Finally I just grabbed a handful of fabric and ripped. Buttons ricocheted around the kitchen, bouncing against the stove and the stack of unwashed dishes.

"Hey! You owe me a shirt, mister."

"Remind me. Tomorrow."

I bought you a blue one. Long-sleeved. Expensive.

You had to let go of me so I could drag your shirt off your body. My cock felt sticky from the cookie dough you left behind; I made you nibble it off later. I reached for your jeans, but you pushed me away.

"You just stand back and watch. You might break something."

I grumbled in feigned protest. I loved watching you strip. I never knew what you'd have on under your clothes: zebra-striped bikini, red silk thong, basic white jockstrap, studded leather cock ring. You were always coming up with something new.

You unpopped your jeans. The zipper slid halfway down, then hung up on the shiny black bulge pushing out against it. You turned around and teased me, letting the jeans dip below your cheeks for a moment.

What the hell were you wearing? Holy shit! Shiny black rubber hugged your butt, revealing the deep crevice between the twin globes. You yanked your jeans back up and spun around, grinning at the expression on my face.

Mesmerized, I watched you slip out of your tight jeans. I never tired of looking at your gorgeous body—lightly muscled chest with the small patch of red-gold hair, flat stomach, long runner's legs—but I couldn't take my eyes from that glistening black basket. The rubber molded itself to your body, covering you completely, revealing every bulge and vein in your fat cock. I'd never seen anything so erotic in my life. It seemed alive, clinging to you like a second skin, showing every twitch. I had to touch you.

I stroked the shaft, and it arched under my touch. I knelt down and mouthed it, the strange scent of rubber mingling with your own intimate musk. I gnawed at your rubber-shielded cock, worrying it like a bone. It throbbed and squirmed beneath my mouth, trapped beneath the rubber but trying to get free. It was a unique sensation, but I was eager to taste the real thing.

Wriggling my tongue under the leg band, I touched a hot, hairy ball. I peeled the briefs down your legs. Your cock sprang free, bouncing up and slapping your belly. I traced the thick veins twisted around the hard red shaft. I loved the feel of your cock in my mouth, the warm meatiness, the throbbing weight. It was just the right size—long enough to nudge at the back of my throat but not long enough to gag me, thick enough to fill my mouth or my ass completely but without pain, big enough that I knew a real man was inside me.

Your hips started a gentle rhythm as I sucked you. I ran my hands up and down your thighs, ruffling the fine coat of hair. I could have sucked you all night, but you held my shoulders and pushed me away. I opened my mouth, your cock throbbing on my tongue, as I looked up at you. You started to pull away, but I gobbled it back, sealing my lips around the thick shaft.

You traced your fingers over my lips and smiled. You let me have it for a while, then pushed me lower. I knew what you wanted. I licked your balls while you fisted your cock. I drew in one of the furry orbs and sucked it gently, slathering my tongue over the silky skin.

When I looked up you had that dreamy expression on your face, lashes lowered over eyes gone dark and sultry, lips half open as you slowly stroked your shaft. I knew you could come just from having your balls licked, but I wanted more.

I open the door.

He stands there, looking at the floor, shoulders slumped, not sure how to begin.

I can be cruel too.

I make him say it.

He looks up at me, and I can see his lips trembling. He tries to hold them still, but his lower lip is red and swollen, like it gets after I've been sucking on it. When he gets nervous, he bites his lips.

He has beautiful lips. I don't look at his lips.

He has been crying. Good—he deserves to cry. His river-brown eyes swim with tears.

He has beautiful eyes. I don't look at his eyes.

I stand rigidly, arms folded across my chest, waiting.

He looks up at me. "Alex," he says, his voice no more than a whisper.

"It was my fault," I blurt out helplessly. "Whatever it was, I'm sorry. Please come home."

No!

Cancel.

Rewrite scene.

I will not say that.

It's his fault.

I've done nothing to apologize for.

I'm not going to beg.

I wanted you inside me, filling me with your heat and vital juices. I let you slip out, your balls wet and shiny from the heavy coating of spit. I kissed the smooth skin joining your groin and thigh. "I want you," I begged.

"Hold still," you said as you turned me and pushed me roughly against the sink.

Something thick and cool trickled down my spine. I looked over my shoulder and saw the bottle of butter-flavored cooking oil in your hand.

Your fingers caught the golden puddle before it reached my ass and worked it back up, gliding over my back and chest. "Mmm, you smell like popcorn." Your tongue snaked into the hollow under my arm, lapping salty sweat and oil. "Taste like it too."

"Don't you ever think of anything but eating?" I groaned.

You licked down my side, across my hips, and up my spine. You nuzzled under my hair and sucked the back of my neck. "Got a problem with that?" you whispered in my ear.

I shuddered as your tongue plunged deep inside. "God, no, that feels wonderful!"

You leaned against me. I felt your hard pecs pressed against my back and the fierce heat of your cock burning into my skin. You rubbed yourself against me, coating your chest and stomach with oil so we could glide freely. Your oiled hands slipped down to my buttocks, kneading and cupping my cheeks.

"Oh, yeah! Slide a finger in."

"Can't. Oil and latex don't mix. Of course, if all you want is a finger…"

"That'll do for an opener, but I want the real thing."

You grabbed your shirt to wipe your hands and scrub any lingering oil out of my crack. "Here, get these slicked up."

I licked your fingers until there was no oil left, then coated them heavily with my saliva.

"Good enough," you said.

One finger worked around my tight bud, teasing it and easing it open. I pushed against it, and you slipped inside so smoothly. Your finger worked in and out, circling and twisting until I was fully open.

You rubbed and rolled your body against mine as you probed my ass. My wanton hole accepted a second finger as easily as the first. I moaned as your fingers brushed over my prostate.

"Don't make me wait. I have to have you now."

"Now who's hungry?" you teased, but you slid your fingers free. I leaned over the mess of unwashed supper dishes and spread my legs, quivering in anticipation as I heard you open the cupboard and take out a condom from our kitchen stash. Strange how I never found that a disruption. The sound of plastic ripping can be as erotic as the sound of a zipper unzipping, but you put the packet in my hand instead of opening it. You knew I loved any excuse to get my hands on your dick.

I wanted you so much that even with just spit, your cock slid right in. You were so hard, you never even had to touch your dick. You waited, letting me get used to the swollen crown cramming my portal, then gave a gentle nudge. Inch by exquisite inch you filled me.

I loved that final moment when the coarseness of your pubes pricked my butt cheeks. It meant I had all of you, every bit of you inside me. Still, I couldn't resist wriggling backward to see if I could capture another fraction of your fullness.

"You feel so good," you said. "So hot and silky."

You lay against my back and wrapped your arms around me, your cheek resting against my shoulder. For a few minutes neither of us moved. We just savored the closeness. I could feel your cock throbbing inside me, matching time with the beat of your heart against my back. I squeezed down on your dick a couple of times to show my appreciation and to hear the deep grunt of pleasure you made.

Your hips went into a slow fuck as you rocked against me. You grabbed the bottle of oil off the counter and dumped half of it down my chest. The golden liquid dripped down my stomach and thighs and puddled on the floor.

"Hey, you're making a mess!" I protested.

"Don't worry about it. I'll get it later."

You always said that, but I knew I'd be the one cleaning it up in the morning. You started finger painting in the oil slick spreading across my body, circling my nipples and trailing down my sternum, and I forgot about such mundane chores. My cock was dripping with oil and precome when your fingers wrapped around it. There was absolutely no friction, just pure sensation as your hand glided up and down. You always knew just the right places, the touches and strokes that sent tingles down my spine.

By the time you got down to some serious fucking, I was ready. You grabbed my hips and started pumping harder. I braced myself against the sink, eager to take everything you had to give. Your thighs smacked against my buttocks, slopping oil everywhere. I was getting off on the smell of butter and sweat and sex. Hell, even the sound was exciting.

My cock was doing a frantic dance of pleasure, leaping and swaying without even being touched. You filled me again and again. Pounding. Pumping. Pistoning. I couldn't get enough of you. Each time you pulled back, I followed, reluctant to lose even an inch of contact.

I tried to hold back, but you were too good. I cried out as waves of pleasure coursed through me, spraying white streams of come in all directions. I was still shooting when I felt you come seconds later, your body rigid as you filled me with hot cream. You collapsed against me, gasping and trembling, and said, "That was awesome! There's never been anyone like you."

I turned around and kissed you. We were a mess—oil and come and cookie dough. "I love you too. Now, how about helping me clean up?"

You started laughing. "I think you look perfect just like this."

If I were younger—
    I would smash everything into pieces and gift wrap the box.
    I'd burn it to ashes.
    I'd seed his clothes with Limburger.
    Instead I buy a roll of strapping tape and carefully seal the box.
I wait for him to pick up the last of his things.

If he were older—
Would he understand what this is doing to me?

At first I left the carton just sitting by the door. Convenient. Waiting. But I didn't like seeing it every day. He was gone, but the damn box was still here.

When my folks had my dog cremated, the ground was frozen, so they couldn't bury the ashes right away. I kept running into that little plastic box tucked away into odd corners. Sealed inside were the broken bits and pieces of my dog, ashes and charred bone. I didn't like touching it, but I couldn't stop looking for it.

I shoved the sealed carton in the back of the closet—I didn't want to see it—but I kept checking to make sure it was still there. I couldn't wait for him to get it out of my house.

He was gone.

It was time to bury the ashes.

I open the door.

Brock stands there looking like...Brock.

If I knew...if I knew everything... I'd still have picked him up.

I wouldn't have been able to resist those eyes.

I'm suddenly overwhelmed by a jumble of images: the way he looks fresh from the shower, fine hair feathered over his damp body like the delicate shadings of a pen-and-ink sketch; the way his penis contracts from the cold, huddled into itself, small and soft, waiting to be coaxed back to life—nothing like the fierce weapon that batters my body and my soul, leaving me wanting nothing more than to be its sheath and acolyte.

I struggle to shake the images, to keep from throwing myself at him. I wait for him to say it.

"Hi. I came for the rest of my stuff."

For a moment we stare at each other. It's OK. There is still time. He could apologize. I could apologize. There are a thousand things I want to say to him, but they all sound stupid and melodramatic and futile.

Come back and love me forever.

Don't do this to us.

"It's over here," I say to him. *Please don't go.* "I've already got it packed up."

"Thanks. That'll save me some time."

God, why was I so stupid? It would have taken him an hour or two to find everything. I'd spent days packing and unpacking the box. Reliving memories, scraps of conversation.

"Hey, you didn't find my blue shirt, did ya? I thought maybe I'd left it in the dirty clothes."

"No," I lie, "but maybe you should check just to make sure you've got everything? I might have missed some stuff."

He hesitates. Maybe he'll open the box and be overwhelmed by memories. Maybe he'll realize what a mistake he's making. Maybe...maybe what? Just maybe...

"No, that's OK. I already got the important stuff." And then, "Well, I'd better be going." He casually picks up the cardboard box that contains the broken shards of our broken relationship. Some dark and bitter. Some bright and shiny. All still sharp enough to hurt. He stands there awkwardly for a moment.

Say it! I scream at him, at me. *Say it!* I can feel my throat closing and the start of tears stinging my eyes.

"See ya."

The door shuts behind you.

I walk back into the bedroom and put your blue shirt back on. Your arms wrap around me, holding me close.

I tuck my nose into the crook of my arm, breathing in your fading scent.

"Why?" I ask the empty room. "Why?"

Fever
by R.J. March

He grabbed me when I was walking by, saying, "Where you been, Carson?" I ain't small, but he is fast and strong, the strongest man I know of, and he got my arm twisted up behind my back. I thought he would bust it off, only I acted as though I didn't feel a thing. But he knew. He always knows.

He was stripped down to his shorts, and I could see he was getting uppity. He had a horse piece that he could swing around like an elephant's trunk, a circus piece, the hurting kind, and I watched it climb the front of his shorts and could see some of it through the fly along with the bunch of black hair he had down there. I heard him laugh at me for looking or for the dumb look on my face, maybe, or maybe because he was a little embarrassed, but I heard him laugh, and I looked up at him.

"Hey, pussy boy," he said, giving me that pickax grin, showing off his gap by sticking his tongue into it for me.

I got myself out from under him; I could do that much, but I didn't know what to do next. He stood there waiting, nostrils flaring, looking peeved. His hair shot off his forehead in a spiky rooster tail greased up with pomade, the same pomade I'd used as dick grease to dick Exton last month. He'd kill me if he ever found out, both about Exton and about my using his pomade for fucking.

"Darvis," I said to him, but nothing else came, no other words, just his stupid-ass name, and he looked at me, disarmed, and I grabbed his forearm—thighlike—and somehow got him into a jury-rigged half nelson, hopping around with him. He kept trying to throw me, but we were locked together like lovers, and I wanted to stay that way forever.

Finally he slicked his way out, and we stood facing each other again. I could see his pride, the way it stood so stiffly in his shorts, and I wondered what he had in mind for us to do this time. The last time, I got my hair all cut down to silvery little bristles, and he held me down and dragged his bare ass across my scalp, rasping his bung against my skull and squeezing out his goo all over me. He looked at me now as though he wanted me dead.

Swatting my head with his big hands, he called me "pussy boy" again and again. I held my tongue and watched his eyes and shoulders, which seemed to signal everything a split second before it happened, every movement of his arms, every hand lunge. I stayed back, playing him, watching him. I dreamed about him straddling the stick shift of the Mustang he said he used to have, the blunt, dull-angled head of it buried deep inside his ass. Crazy stuff. What was I to do? I watched his eyes and shoulders for the quick darts that muscles about to be moved make. He'd dance on the end of a pin with a billion other angels—rough-mouthed, dirty-handed.

"Carson," he said.

"It's Dow," I said, disappointment pulling at my mouth; he didn't even know my name. "Carson's gone."

"I know that," he barked, his hands coming at me. He'd throw me to the ground if he could, I knew. I felt the concrete under my bare feet, cold and smooth, waxed by me or Exton Jones or Muhammed. Never Darvis, though. Darvis waxes nothing but bananas, we all said. Never so he could hear us, though.

Darvis was getting peevish, and his initial interest was waning. I could see by the floppy swing in his shorts, the soft head peeking out of the hem. His eyes went dull, lids dropping, and his hands unclenched, and he straightened his body, his torso a mosaic of muscle, veins coursing down his arms. I saw him breathe and took a breath myself, and it was over, it wasn't fun anymore, there wasn't any more sport to it.

He pulled on the front of his shorts, glancing downward at my crotch. I had yet to lose my interest, my excitement. I was still ready. I stepped up, suddenly unchallenged. It wasn't that he wouldn't whip my ass; I could get him to beat me to death—that's the easy thing for Darvis. I wanted to confuse him, and I could see that I had. His eyes shifted; he looked away and back again and said something, reminding me of a little boy.

I put a hand inside my shirt and touched my chest, the hard dot of a nipple, teasing him. He wanted none of it now, not if he couldn't feel he was stealing or hurting. He went back to his corner, to his lumpy cot and faded girlies.

Exton and Muhammed were outside recreating. They'd be back in an hour or so, depending on the weather. It was Sunday, and we didn't have to do anything. Monday through Saturday we were up and cutting down trees, part of the deforestation crew.

Darvis laid himself down and covered his eyes with his big arm. Strange to see someone here without any body art, no inky home-made tats—no girls' names, no swastikas, no burning demons.

"You all right?" I asked, because he'd been sick, although he'd never said. I could tell, saw the headache reshape his eyes, heard his teeth chattering at night when we were all sweating hot. "Did you take your quinine?" I asked him.

"Ain't none left," he replied, his lips barely moving.

"I got some still," I told him. "You can have it."

"Keep it," he said. "I'm all right."

His knees were up and bent, legs falling to the sides, and I could see everything falling out. He didn't care; he liked the way we looked at him, mouths open like baby birds. He'd fed us all at one time or another. He had a girl's name for each of us: I was his Connie, Muhammed was Keisha, and Exton was Baby Girl on account of his pouty mouth and blond hair. I'd seen him mouth-fuck Exton, holding him by his golden ponytail. And I'd seen Muhammed spread his ass cheeks and offer his black hole to Darvis and his horse piece and regret it later on.

Darvis wasn't so rough-and-ready now. His limp dick leaked out of his shorts and touched the mattress, so much thick cable, sleek, like an anaconda or whatever the hell kind of snake we saw just this past week hanging from a tree branch, tongue flickering. Exton had pointed to it and said, "Hey, Darvis, put it back in your pants," and we all laughed, even Darvis, who axed the snake's head off as it swung to lick Muhammed's ear.

"I thank you for that," Muhammed said to Darvis, his eyes wide, a bulging artery in his throat throbbing with pulse.

I could feel my own heart beating now up around my ears. The front of my pants showed where I'd leaked, a big wet spot. I pushed the ball of my hand against the hard-headed poke and shuddered.

I sat on the edge of his cot, causing him to lift his arm and squint at me. He looked at me for a while, his eyes glassy. I touched his shin, his skin greasy with sweat. He covered his eyes again, granting permission, legs going wider, offering me his piece. I picked it up with my fingers, leaning down between his thighs, elbows making room on the thin mattress. His crotch stank of sweat and three days without a bath, making my mouth water. It was Thanksgiving Day for me, and I was about to eat a turkey dinner.

I licked the salty tip of him, wishing he still had his skin like Muhammed did, a soft sliding sheath for my tongue to play with. I filled my mouth with him easily, snorting through my nostrils. I swallowed what I could, feeling the soft slide down my throat, rubbery, pliable. Hard, it was like swallowing a stick. I liked him best like this—flaccid.

I tickled his nuts, pulling the long hairs, and twisted the bag, making him moan a little. I drew my head back, using my teeth to scrape the underside of his shaft, wanting to excite him, to make him hard, but he stayed the way he was. I used my hand, tonguing the fat opening, rubbing my lips hard around the outer edge of his head. There wasn't anything I could do, though, to bring him up, to arouse him.

I dug around in my own pants then and brought out my cock. Dribbling precome, it was slicked enough to jack, making wet, sticky noises. Darvis's foot moved and came to rest on my exposed balls, and I pushed my pants down, wanting him to put his foot between my legs, to bugger his toe up my ass, which I'd seen him do to Exton once. He kept his toes on my nuts, though, playing against the taut skin.

I groaned on his piece, taking as much as I could into my mouth, stopping my throat and my breath, and I felt the fiery rumble of orgasm on the edge of my palm. I said something un-intelligible, that I loved him, and he pressed the ball of his foot firmly just under my balls, and I lost my head, screaming silently, hosing his ankle with my streaming juices.

"Dow," he said, and I dropped his pecker, all sticky with saliva, thicker now, harder. He said I had to clean him up, so I went to get a rag to wipe my spunk from his ankle.

I was wetting it when he came up behind me. His piece was all up now, redheaded. I hadn't pulled up my pants yet, and my ass was there for him to take. He spit in the general direction of my hole, missing wide, and slapped my cheeks. He pinched out some of his leakage, smearing it over the head, lubing himself up for my tightness.

His first stab tore me open, it seemed, and he pinned my screaming head against the dirty porcelain of the sink. He fucked my ass with long, deep strokes, his hips slapping my behind, his big, swinging balls knocking against mine. He fucked me as though he had two feet of cock, and that's what it felt like root-ing around in my insides. His thickness stretched my anus, his rocky shaft burning my ass lips. I squeezed out tears, trying not to cry. I wanted him like this, always did, wanted to be his bitch, his hole, and I told him so as he ripped me up, racing in and out of me, setting my cunt on fire.

He started calling me Connie, gripping my shoulders and forcing me back against his hips. "Connie, Connie, Connie," he whispered, breathing hard, spittle raining on my back. I wanted him to flip me over so I could see him, his wet chest and little red nipples, the hair on him in smooth, straight lines. I wanted to see the converging lines on either side of his muscled gut meet at his crotch, and I wanted to see his piece, the fat end of it pulling out of my gut and pouring buckets of hot come all over my stomach.

This wasn't for my benefit, though, and he was doing me his way, ruthlessly skewering me, pleasuring himself angrily, hollering at me for going loose on him, pounding my back and stinging my ass with sharp slaps until he couldn't keep it back any longer and threw himself all the way into me. It felt like he was trying to take a step inside of me, one foot and then the other, putting me on like a pair of pants, and I felt his cheek on my back, then his drool, and he whimpered, trying to hold still as his piece erupted, planting his seed in the hot, spaceless gullet he'd made inside me.

He let me up and said, "I'm ready," and he turned and walked over to where the shower was. I joined him, turning on the water, rubbing my face, waiting for the hot water to come, and he stood beside me, his piece still big, still stiff, stinking of my ass.

I saw him with Exton Jones, pulling on his work pants, making a nuisance of himself. He didn't seem to me to be as mean with Exton as he was with me, but Exton was smaller. He was wiry, scrappy, but he didn't have the muscle or the power. We were all three giants compared to Exton, and maybe that's why he got it so much, but we were all of us kind to him, even Darvis, and I was always making sure he was taken care of. Whenever I fucked him I fucked him on his back and played with his pecker, bringing him off, and once I sucked him off, but only once, maybe twice, and he said, "Dow, I like you best," but you can't ever believe anything you hear. Nothing is ever the truth.

We were in the jungle working on a tree as big as a building. Taking it down would bring down four or five other trees as well, we figured, depending on the direction it decided to take. It would take the four of us to do it, all working together. Darvis and Muhammed worked the saws, and Exton and I roped the tree to guide it down the way we wanted. It was a crapshoot, though, and we all knew it, and at midday the tree was still standing. Darvis called for a break, staring at Exton, who was holding the thick rope in his gloveless hands.

I wanted to be the one catching Darvis's favor. I always had a 25% chance, I figured—it was myself or Exton Jones or Muhammed or Darvis by himself—but the odds were against me this day, and he winked at Exton, and they went off together into the jungle. I looked at Muhammed, who didn't care; he wasn't really like me or Exton, didn't relish the thought of Darvis's rough hands on him the way we did, didn't crave his big piece or his bad mouth, his hands or his hard fuckings. He whistled up at a queer-colored bird in the tree overhead and said to it, "Sing while you can. You're losing your home soon."

I went into the jungle, following them. I wanted to watch them. I wanted to see what Exton Jones was willing to do for him and see how I could outdistance him, better him. It was crazy, I guess, but I had decided ever since that day we were together that I was in love with Darvis, and I wanted him to be in love with me.

We shaved once a week—Sundays—and all had beards come Fridays save for Exton, who couldn't grow one. With his blond hair, long and silky, he was most like a girl, I guess, and maybe that's what made Darvis so crazy for him. I wasn't much interested in having a girl of my own or in being Darvis's girl either, but I would have been his man in a heartbeat.

"You're my man" is what I wanted to hear from him, beating on my chest like a drum, thumping on the thick pad of muscle I had there from secret push-ups. I wanted him to roll over grudg-ingly, saying something like "OK, but this ain't going to become a habit." I wanted him to reach back behind himself and pull open those fleshy globes, open those great muscled doors and show me his other door, the one he'd kept hidden, his little pink portal. Oh, man, can you imagine that? Him looking over his shoulder, saying, "Come on in, Dow. Dip your stick, buddy."

What I liked about Exton Jones—what I suspect we all liked about him—was his accommodating manner. He'd do whatever you told him, like he was simple or you had a gun to his head.

I liked him because I could say my ass needed cleaning and he'd take my ankles and lift them high and get in between my butt cheeks and lick me clean. I loved to hear him snort around down there, loved the drag of his tongue across my bung, and I'd play with myself, bringing myself up to the very edge of coming, then stopping, over and over until all it would take was a long lick up my shaft and a finger tickling my cunt to make my dick explode.

And then I'd say, "Bring it here, Exton," and he'd bring me his cock, his short, thick plug, sticking it in my mouth, and I'd get him to fuck me that way until he'd start whimpering and touch-ing my face and telling me how I was his favorite, his jizz jetti-soning down my gulping throat.

I stayed behind them a good distance, not wanting to inhibit them—not that you could, not Darvis. I could see that they'd stopped and Exton was already on his knees. I could see the thick tube of flesh he was trying to swallow, and I was reminded of snakes and how they'll eat something so much larger than them-selves. My throat ached for days last time I blew Darvis.

I saw that Exton could put a good amount of it away. He was getting better—*Practice makes perfect,* I said to myself—his head bobbing back and forth, going sideways, loving the shaft with his tongue and teeth. Watching them gave me a hard-on, and I pulled it out to play with, kneeling on the jungle floor like Exton, wishing my mouth was as full as his.

I closed my eyes and pictured the man's ass and my mouth kissing it, his balls draped over my face, each orb resting on one of my eyes, the big thing smothering me, making me hungry, hungry enough to take big, toothy bites of his cheeks and tongue-fuck his muddy run.

I opened my eyes again. Exton's shirt was off, and he looked so boyish kneeling in front of Darvis. His pants were undone, and I could see his white behind and wondered how long it would be before Darvis was standing behind him and pile-driving our little Billy Budd.

I felt the weight of it, but it didn't register right away, not until it shifted and continued to slide over my calves, and I was paralyzed. It turned the corner of my knee and wound itself around my thighs, going between my legs, moving sensually, dragging itself around me like a lover, its tongue flickering against my balls. It brought more and more of itself around me, tightening its embrace. It coiled around the base of my cock, hiding most of it, squeezing it tightly, keeping it engorged. Its undulations made my cock quiver and leak. It looked to me like I was going to die, but I was going to come first.

"Looks like you've found the dreaded faggot snake," Darvis said, his voice nearly causing my heart to stop.

"Do something, Darvis," Exton whispered like a girl, his belly, I noted, awash with glistening come.

Darvis laughed, and I felt tears come to rest in the corners of my eyes. The snake courted with the head of my dick, which had turned a sickly purple. Its tongue licked me. I looked up at Darvis, begging him softly.

"You're always on your knees begging me for something, ain't you, Dow?" he said. And then he grabbed the snake's head, his hand moving like lightning, getting it just behind the jaws. Its body contorted, flexing its wrap around my cock and torso and legs. It tightened, and I saw stars, feeling as though my middle would bust, and Darvis unsheathed his knife and cut the head off with a simple flick of his wrist. The rest of the snake stayed around me, but it slackened its hold little by little, and I was able to breathe, and it uncoiled off my dick, which was no longer hard but very small and very soft. I stood and pushed the snake body off of me and got my dick back in my pants.

"Thanks," I said to Darvis, eyeing Exton too to make sure I didn't see any smirks, because I would have pounded his face off in a second.

I went back to our still-standing tree and wiped my face on a wet rag, and we got together again, Muhammed and Darvis with the saw and me and Exton with the ropes, and we brought down the fucker by nightfall but lost Muhammed doing it.

They sent us another one who wasn't anything like Muhammed. He wasn't much impressed with Darvis's antics and seemed very unlikely to ever join in on the showers we took together, Darvis telling Exton and me what to do to each other, then doing to us whatever he had in mind, calling out to the new one, "Hey, Mr. High-'n'-Mighty, you don't know what you're missing!" dipping into me and then into Exton, telling the two of us to kiss or suck each other.

Mr. High-'n'-Mighty's name was Deloff, first name Christopher, and he looked as mean as Darvis. He could take down trees single-handed and could clear an acre in half the time it took Exton and me. He worked and worked and ignored us for the most part, but sometimes he watched us, a look of distilled disgust on his face.

There was one Saturday night, though, when we were all wiped out from the day's work but itching to drink some of the grain they sent us as appeasement for lack of decent food. Alcohol tended not to spoil or attract vermin, and they sent us plenty. We all sat around on our beds with our bottles, Darvis setting up a good

array of empties beside his cot. We talked about the dreaded fag-
got snake and good old Muhammed, and I noticed Darvis and
Deloff glancing at each other with much less malice than usual.
Darvis was stripped to his shorts, his legs spread wide, enticing.

Deloff had taken off his shirt, the grime of the day browning
his skin. We hadn't any of us seen him with his trousers off. Exton
and me had been discussing this fact earlier that day when we'd
slipped off together to swallow each other's come. (I'd convinced
him the protein of it kept the mosquitoes off us.) Despite getting
off already that day, I was ready for another dose of medicine, and
I could see that Exton was too, looking at all of us and putting his
hands down his pants to squeeze his stuff.

"Exton," Darvis laughed, "you feeling randy again, boy?"

Exton went red on his cot and gave Darvis the finger, but you
could see his boner plain as day. It seemed to catch Deloff's eye, I
noticed.

Darvis lifted his hips and pushed his shorts off. His mighty
pecker rose like one of the trees we hacked at all day long. "Here's
something for you," he said nicely, and Exton eased himself off his
cot and joined Darvis on his and started lapping the fat red head
of the man's horselike piece.

Whenever Darvis was like this, Deloff was gone—he'd leave the
bunkhouse without so much as a word. He stayed put this time,
scrutinizing the coupled men. His hands went between his legs,
touching the crotch of his trousers.

I remember Muhammed saying to me once, his big black cock
pumping between my legs, "You do what you can out here. Pleasure so simple can't be no sin. It's like having a sweet every once
in a while or drinking a beer on a hot Sabbath day. Jesus turns his
head, I bet. Maybe he don't even do that. Maybe he watches."

Seeing Deloff stand up and drop his trousers reminded me of
that. His prick was fat and came to a point. It almost looked like
a beet, the way it was shaped. He fingered the pointed end, the
sleeve of skin there, and bared his white little head. His balls were

large and covered with kinky fuzz, his thighs packed and cut with muscle. He was a little unsteady, a little drunk, and mesmerized by Darvis and Exton going at it, Darvis sticking his fingers into Exton's behind, causing Exton to suck faster and harder.

I wasn't sure what was going to happen. It looked to me like I was about to witness a threesome, the way he stared at them with such longing, but he turned his look my way, his other hand going to his right nipple. A huge, snaking vein pulsed across his biceps, and I felt pulled to him, only I wasn't moving. He came to me, though, offering his crotch to me, and I accepted it, tonguing the little head. I took it in my hand, and it filled my palm like a grenade, and I slurped my tongue over it and made him bigger and harder, and he groaned over me, undoing my pants.

It seemed almost to become a contest then, Darvis and Deloff competing to see which one was going to fuck his partner first, then to see who was going to fuck his partner hardest, then who was going to make his partner scream the loudest, come the hardest, come the most.

He plugged my hole with his thing, stretching me, hitting up inside me just right and taking my breath away. He pushed my face against the dirty mattress and beat my ass with his pecker, knocking against my prostate and giving me the shakes. I heard Exton wail, and I felt my heart in my throat, and I begged for his cock. I begged good and hard for him to fuck my ass and make me his bitch, his pussy, and he slapped my fanny and called me a whore, and I heard Darvis growl and looked up to see him watching us, his lips wet with spit as he hurried his huge tree trunk into poor Exton's rear end.

I couldn't say who came first. I think we all came together or just seconds apart, all connected to one another by our cocks and our gazes. When he was finished Deloff wiped himself on my sheets and touched my shoulders sweetly, and I leaned back against his hot, wet cock. Darvis collapsed on his fuck, and they cuddled like brothers.

We drank some more, Deloff and I, and watched the flickering shadows the moonlit trees made outside our window. He told me he had a wife in Florida.

"We all got wives," I told him, and he nodded, and I said to him what Muhammed said to me, that nothing could be bad about a pleasure so simple, and he nodded again and touched the lip of his bottle against mine, our bottles making a ringing kiss.

The Man at the Gym
by Derek Adams

At first glance the place was far from promising. There was noth-ing high-tech about it except the boom box on the shelf behind the counter. A young woman was poised between the speakers, her smile unnaturally bright. I scanned the room: Three women in warm-up socks and leotards were standing in front of a bank of mirrors that could have done with a polishing. They didn't look like they'd been doing much in the way of stretching. Beyond that, nothing. There wasn't a barbell in sight—or a man to pump it.

"Can I help you?" The young woman bounced out at me, clutching a fan of tapes in her right hand.

"Is this Grayson's Family Health Center?"

She nodded eagerly.

"You do have a weight room, don't you?"

"Oh, that." Her smile sagged a bit. "You're not another one of those 'Gotta pump iron, don't have time for aerobics class' guys, are you?"

"I'm afraid so," I replied, shrugging my shoulders. "I've got no sense of rhythm. Sorry."

"Yeah. Me too." She jerked her thumb over her right shoulder. "Over there, handsome. Through those double doors at the back. You go down the hall, then up the stairs. You can't miss it. Smells like old socks."

I thanked her and skirted the trio by the mirror. The skinny one wearing the red thong over her gray sweat suit smiled toothily.

I scanned her fingers: no significant rings. Single female, small town, slim matrimonial pickings. I could smell danger on the horizon. I picked up the pace, eyes firmly on those double doors.

I hadn't expected to end up here, in the middle of nowhere, which just goes to show how little a man can depend on life working out as planned. Short version: Hotshot from prestigious school dazzles recruiters, rockets through ranks to become number two man in four years, falls for number one man's much younger lover, gets discovered in flagrante delicto, and ends up heading the start-up team for the most rural plant in the universe. It was clear to me that I was no longer on the fast track. On the bright side, I still had a job that paid in the low six figures.

I climbed the long, uncarpeted stairs two at a time and pushed open the door at the top. The door shut behind me with a very loud smack.

The place reminded me of the family garage where I had first pumped iron as a teenager. There were a couple of racks with barbells, a disorganized pile of weights, a few tattered mats, and an adjustable bench. The floor-to-ceiling windows across the back had been whitewashed, casting a golden gloom across the exercise area.

I know there were several people there that day because I heard snippets of conversation, strained grunts, and the clink of weights, but I saw only him. At first I told myself I noticed him because there was nothing else to look at, but I knew that wasn't true. At any time, in any place this one would've been special.

The guy—Dan, as I soon learned—was wearing a pair of faded Levi's cut off at the knee and a baggy white T-shirt soaked with enough sweat to cling to an eye-catching torso. Details were scarce, but I thought I detected big nipples and a hint of fleece between the pecs. The biceps were crowding the stretched-out sleeves of the shirt, and his forearms were beyond reproach. His ears stuck out just a bit more than perfection dictated, but the effect was to make his clean-cut, boyishly handsome face even sexier. Our eyes locked briefly, then he diverted his gaze into space as he counted off the reps.

He was curling a bar loaded with a lot of weight. I stepped farther into the room and stopped to watch him. I counted 20 myself and knew that the veins in his neck had been distended when I walked in. Sweat popped out on his brow, and his right arm quivered slightly.

"Come on!" I encouraged, dropping my bag and stepping up in front of him, extending my hands. His eyes flashed up briefly, then locked back down on my palms. I pushed air under the bar, never touching it, willing him to raise it alone.

"Shit!" he gasped, sucking air, the bar clutched to his chest. His biceps were beyond flexed.

"Again!" I urged.

He shook his head but slowly began to lower the bar anyway. When it rested against his thighs, he inhaled deeply and began to curl the bar back up to his thick chest.

"You can do it!" I hissed at him, watching the veins that snaked over the bulbous expanse of his biceps bulge dangerously. My fingertips brushed against the back of his hands, and the bar rose three inches. "Come on, man. Do it!" I took a deep breath.

"That's all! Help me put it down."

I grabbed the bar and helped him lower it to the floor. He stood—he was half a head taller than I—shook my hand, and smiled at me.

"You OK?"

"Man, I got a terrific burn. My arms are like spaghetti." He held them high above his head, stretching. They didn't look much like any type of pasta I'd ever run across. "Who can I thank?"

"Joe Leighton. You?"

"Dan Sullivan." He bent down, picked up a towel, and wiped his face and neck. "You look like you know your way around a gym." He glanced around, then leaned close. "Which leads me to ask you what the hell you're doing here."

"Following a paycheck, Dan. I'm working to get Peyton Industries up and running."

"You don't say. I've been hired on as a section head. I'll probably be seeing you around, Joe. However, work is work, and this is the gym. I was thinking about calling it quits, but I'd be more than happy to hang around and spot you."

"If you're serious, you're on."

Dan flashed me a grin, and we got down to business.

Two hours later I had a great pump and felt I had laid the groundwork for a new friendship. Dan was bright and funny— and getting sexier by the minute. On more than one occasion while he was spotting me, he made lingering body contact. The hottest thing about it was, he wasn't coming on to me, not consciously in any case. He was just a guy touching another guy while he helped him work out. I was the one who was fighting back a hard-on that felt like it could've stretched all the way to the city limits.

By the time our workout was over, I was starting to give serious thought to how I might be able to seduce my new buddy.

"Lead me to the showers," I gasped, hooking the barbell back onto the rack with a clatter. "I am totally pitted out."

"I got bad news for you, Joe. Pipes blew out in this dive over two months ago. Not a drop of water since then."

"Swell."

We got out to the parking lot, and I disarmed the alarm on my sporty little BMW. I eyed the seats ruefully. I was literally soaked and didn't figure all that sweat was going to do the soft, pale leather any good at all.

"That your car?"

I nodded my head, and Dan shook his.

"Damn, Joe, you can't go and ruin that upholstery. Listen, why don't you come on out to my place? You can get cleaned up, then I'll drive you back to pick up your baby here. Sound like a plan?" He smiled at me, the problem obviously solved to his satisfaction.

I followed him over to his pickup. The thought of spending a couple of more hours in his company suited me just fine.

When we got out to his place, he parked under a tree, and we stepped out of the truck into a yipping melee of dogs. Dan got them calmed down, and then they all sniffed my ankles and shoes and slobbered on my hands before they went back to resting in the shade.

I checked the place out: a house, small but tidy; a red barn and several other outbuildings; rolling fields as far as the eye could see; a big tree-fringed lake sparkling in the near distance.

"This is nice, Dan," I remarked, breathing deep of the fresh, clean air.

"Thanks. I grew up here. I can't make a go of it farming, but I can't bear to get rid of the place. I lease fields to a couple of the neighboring farmers and let a gal in town stable her horses here."

"That your lake?"

"Sure is, Joe. Tell you what: I figured we might grab a couple of beers, then wander down there for a swim. Afterward you can come up to the house for a real shower. The water's real nice this time of year."

"You're on, Dan." I could think of nothing more pleasant than skinny-dipping with this man—for starters, at least.

He ducked into the house, returning a few moments later with a small cooler and a couple of old towels. I fell in beside him, and we walked across the fields together.

When we arrived at the grassy shore of the lake, I peeled out of my sodden tank top and knelt to untie my shoes. The socks followed, and then I stood and pushed my shorts down and kicked them aside.

"Nobody can see us, right?"

He shook his head.

"Good." I peeled off my jock and stood there naked, savoring the breeze that caressed my bare skin.

Dan was doing his best not to stare at me, but he wasn't having much luck. I couldn't help feeling good about that. I had spent the first 18 years of my life as a tall, skinny kid. When I got to college, I discovered the weight room at the intramural building and never turned back. Now, almost ten years later, I was still slender, but every muscle in my body was developed to the max. My pecs were pumped to obscene dimensions—at least according to my personal trainer back in the city—my biceps were pushing 18 inches, my thighs were rock-hard, and my calves bulged with solid, knotted muscle. If I do say so myself, I also had a bubble butt that was as close to perfect as I could make it and a belly you could wash clothes on.

I stretched, just to show off a little bit, then waded out into the cool, clear water.

When I was in up to about mid-thigh, I turned to watch Joe strip. The shirt went first, revealing a stunning torso. His pecs were flattish, beautifully squared, dusted with dark glossy fur. His nipples jutted through the fine short hairs, thick and pink. His waist was narrow, and the concave wall of his belly was ridged with a perfect six-pack of abs. A fine line of hair split the washboarded plane down the center.

Joe smiled nervously, then bent to untie his shoes. When his feet were bare, he stood, took a few steps toward the water, and paused, his hands hovering around the fly of his old cutoffs. He touched the waistband, then let his hands drop to his sides. He looked up, down, side to side. His face was scarlet.

"Better hurry, man. Don't be shy. Hell, I'm naked as the day I was born. You said nobody could see us."

"Yeah, I know. You look great, Joe. I'm not so sure about me."

"*I'm* sure, Dan. You look fucking terrific. Now get naked and come on in."

"I...uh, I got...I got this control problem." He blurted it out, his face getting redder by the second.

"What? You piss in your pants?"

"No!" he yelped, looking mortally offended. "I...uh, I just get, you know, excited sometimes."

"Hey, buddy, hard-ons aren't a crime. Not in my book anyhow. Tell you what: You get one, I'll do my best to get one too. Hell, we can practice digging holes in the mud."

That got a laugh out of him. He took a deep breath and dropped his shorts.

As he waded out to where I stood, I took in the whole package, doing my best not to slobber all over myself. His legs lived up to the promise of the rest of his body: his thighs, thick, hard, defined, and hairy; his calves, massed with muscle that flexed and shifted sexily as he moved. His fat balls drooped low, smacking gently against his inner thighs as he walked. His cock, tightly clipped, curved down over his furry orbs, pointing off to the left. His glans was a pale pink in color, tapering to where his piss slit puckered temptingly at the tip. The very thought of helping to take the wrinkles out of that veiny stalk of flesh sent a shiver of lust through my groin. Dan wasn't the only one in danger of losing control.

As it turned out, fate—or clumsiness—took over, and control quickly became a moot point.

Dan was about three feet away when I took a step to the side. I lost my footing and started to fall forward. The next thing I knew, my hard body smacked solidly against his hard body, and his strong thigh wedged between my muscular legs and mashed against my dick. My hands clamped on his swollen biceps, and his big callused hands ended up encircling my waist. I felt his succulent nipples against my bare skin, felt the pounding of his heart, the tickle of his body hair, the rapidly swelling shaft of his cock against my hip.

I slowly raised my eyes to his, saw how the blue of the irises was flecked with green, noticed how thick his lashes were, caught the pulsing of his pupils as fear and desire fought for dominance of his big body.

I did my part to carry the day—hell, I had a vested interest here! I winked, then kissed him, a firm, chaste kiss, lips only, no hint of tongue.

Dan groaned, but he didn't push me away. His fingers squirmed, curling down over the swell of my ass cheeks, his heart beat faster, and his cock quickly pumped up to full fucking size.

Somehow that chaste kiss ended up full of tongue—maybe it was him, maybe me. Whoever was responsible, we stood there in the water, lips locked, tongues thrashing. Then he took a deep breath without breaking the lip lock and sucked the wind right out of me and into him. It was the sexiest fucking thing imaginable. I held him tighter, rubbed my prick against his hard sweat-wet belly, and sucked the air back out of him while I probed his throat with my tongue. We kept it up till we started getting dizzy, then broke the kiss and gasped for air in each other's arms.

My heart was still pounding and my belly full of butterflies when Dan dropped to his knees. The water splashed up around us as the waves lapped against his beautifully sculpted pecs. He pressed his lips to my belly, just above the pale gold curls of my bush, and let them slide down to my prick, out along the steely hard shaft to my knob. He looked up at me through his long lashes, his expression almost angelic. Then he lunged forward and swallowed me to the balls, literally taking my breath away.

I cried out my pleasure and slumped over him, my belly against his forehead, my cheek pressed against his shoulder. I stroked his sides, following the line of his lats from armpit to waist. From there I felt even lower, my arms in the water up to my elbows, my hands parting the cool liquid to trace the submerged shape of his hard, fuzzy ass. I let my fingers slide forward along the lower curve of his thighs to tickle his dangling balls, and then I reached up and gripped his prick.

I gave his dick a squeeze, and he squeezed back, tightening the muscles of his throat around my meat. I retraced my route, down the shaft, over the firm round nuts, and across the hard ridge of his perineum to his tightly puckered ass lips. Short hairs floated around the little slot like water grass, waving in the current.

I parted his ass and touched the silky soft pucker of its lips. Dan grunted, and his pecs flexed against my thighs. I pushed gently, felt resistance, and pushed again. On the third try I breached the defenses and slipped up inside the silken heat. I stirred my finger around in him and felt his sphincter grab my knuckle, flex, and then relax, allowing a little of the cool lake water to flow up into his steamy man channel.

I straightened up and pushed Dan away from my twitching prick. The blow job was too much, too intense, too likely to make me come now, not later. I wanted to wait for later.

I pulled him to his feet, kissed him, stepped behind him, and knelt. I kissed his ass cheeks and tailbone and moved down the deep cleft of his crack. As I went lower Dan bent forward, hands on knees, spreading his cheeks wide. I saw the hair-ringed pucker of his hole, licked it, kissed it, probed it gently with my tongue, and saw the lake water dribble out and run down onto his nuts.

I took my sweet time licking all the hairs away from the ruddy pucker of flesh. When I had every single one plastered flat against his cheeks, he was panting, his cock drawn up tight against his muscled gut. I drew back, blew gently on him, and watched him tighten and then relax. I blew again, watching his hole dilate until I could see the rich pink inside of him, the sweet secret region where I wanted to plant my seed. I tongued him, savoring the heady funk of his ass juices, the musky smell that rose from his cock and balls.

Standing behind him, I rubbed his back, his broad shoulders, and his tightly muscled sides. My cock was so hard, it arced, the head pointing slightly up, making it the perfect weapon for a full-fledged anal assault. I humped his crack, rubbed his belly, and jacked his prick. He braced his hands on his knees, flexed his cheeks, and groaned his willingness to be ridden to the edge and over into bliss.

I spit on my cock and rubbed my bloated knob along his crack to the superheated pucker that offered entry into his strong, hard body. I thrust forward, sank in deep, drove my hips forward, and impaled him to the hilt. The muscles danced across his broad back, and his breathing grew ragged, irregular. I waited, stroking his ass, rubbing his taut belly, anticipating a sign. It came: He reached back, gripped my hips, and began pushing me back and then drawing me deep inside of him. I clamped my hands on his broad shoulders and started driving, pumping in and out of him, sinking deep into the heat, then withdrawing every gleaming, veiny, bloated inch of my cock so that I could see the fuck as well as feel it.

I pulled him back against my body with a loud smack and began nibbling the solid ridge of his shoulder. I reached down, grabbing his prick in one hand and one of his nipples in the other. I twisted his tit and jerked on his cock, making him writhe and dance there in the water, bouncing up and down, riding on my prick. The heat grew, intensified, became unbearable.

I screamed out my orgasm, pounding the rhythm of it deep up his butt, spewing my jizz, all thick and creamy, into his clutching chute. He howled his release as I was ending, pushed back against me, flexed, and writhed as I jacked the come out of him. It rose up in thick arcs that cut through the evening air and landed on the surface of the water. The strings of white floated back to us, caught in the hairs on our legs.

I held Dan tightly around the waist and fell slowly backward into the cooling waters.

"We had quite a workout today, huh, Joe?"

We were standing beside my BMW, all showered and clean after our aquatic tangle.

"The best," I assured him, grazing his knuckles with my fingertips. A woman in leotards walked out of the gym and glanced our way. I touched him again, then dropped my hand to my side.

"It isn't a bad gym for such a small town. Best showers I've ever experienced."

"That could be a regular part of the workout," Dan replied, winking at me. "I thought it was the best part." He grabbed at his crotch. "I'm still pumped from it."

"You aren't the only one," I assured him.

"Same time tomorrow?"

"Wouldn't miss it."

I drove back to my new apartment, ready to unpack. All of a sudden country life was looking a hell of a lot less grim.

Blind Date
by Bob Vickery

He's standing in the theater lobby, leaning against the wall by the entrance. I do a classic double take as I push through the door, first a quick glance and then a longer look. He's younger and much better-looking than the average clientele here, and I find myself wondering if he's here to audition for a job as a dancer. Guys drift in and out of here so often. I take in the bomber jacket, the tight chinos, the T-shirt one size too small stretching across his tight torso, and I think, *This guy is hot.* The dark glasses, though, are a bit much; the lobby is dimly lit, and it's hard enough to see in it with normal eyesight. *Terminator chic,* I think, until I notice the folded white cane in his right hand. With a start I realize he's blind.

Rusty's in the ticket booth counting out $1 bills for the till. It's all part of a closed loop. The customers get the singles as change for larger bills, they stuff them in the dancers' socks for a little extra attention, and the dancers exchange them for larger bills after their shows. Rusty has told me that he's getting to know each dollar intimately now, he's been handling the same ones over and over for so long.

I go and lean against the door that separates the booth from the lobby. "Hi," I say.

Rusty glances up. "How ya doin', Mike?" He speaks in the barest Alabama drawl.

I shoot a look up the stairs that lead to the dressing room. "Is Kevin here yet?"

Rusty nods. "He came in about ten minutes ago."

Kevin and I are tonight's two-man show. He's easily my favorite dancer to work with: a nicely muscled body the color of dark mocha; an easy, sexy smile; and that thick, fleshy dick of his that just begs to be sucked. I never have to fake arousal when I'm on-stage with him.

I glance at the clock in Rusty's booth: five minutes till show time. Plenty of time to get ready. I turn my head and stare at the blind guy. He's only a few feet away, and his head is tilted as if he's straining to listen to us. "Are you tonight's entertainment?" he suddenly asks.

"Half of it," I answer carefully. "At least for the 8 o'clock show."

"Good," he says, nodding. "I like your voice. You sound sexy." Stretching his arm before him, he makes his way across the lobby and opens the theater door. Music spills out into the lobby, the standard bass beat of your generic suck-and-fuck flick. The door swings closed behind him.

I look at Rusty. "What the hell is a blind man doing in a movie theater?"

Rusty shrugs. "I don't think he's here for the movie."

Kevin and I have performed together often enough to have the routine down cold. We wait until the music begins. Tonight it's a tape of Gregorian chants revved up to a disco beat. We both amble out onto the dark stage and strike our usual poses, Kevin with his arms crossed over his chest and his legs apart, me with my back to the audience, fists on hips. The lights come up slowly. After a few beats we turn toward each other and kiss, softly at first, then more passionately, pressing our bodies together, grinding our pelvises against each other in a slow, circular movement. I slide my hands over Kevin's firm ass and squeeze his cheeks as my jock-encased dick rubs back and forth against his. I don't *see* the audience out there as much as *feel* it, this presence in the darkness watching us.

I slip my thumbs under the elastic band of Kevin's jockstrap and yank it down. Kevin's meaty dick spills out, half hard, and sways heavily against his thigh. Always the pro, he turns so that everyone out there can get a good look at what he's got. I kiss his neck, flick his nipples with my tongue, then drop to my knees and take his dick in my mouth, nibbling down the thick shaft. I feel it stir and grow hard in my mouth. I never lose the buzz I get sucking cock in front of an audience, the brassiness of it, the knowledge that all those guys out there have paid money to watch me do this.

I whip out my own dick and start stroking it slowly, easily, teasing it into hardness. My other hand kneads the tight muscles of Kevin's torso, playing across the ridged abs, the hard pecs. I cup Kevin's balls, tugging on them gently as he pumps his dick in and out of my mouth. The stage lights prevent me from seeing beyond the first couple of rows, but the guys up front all have their dicks out and are pounding their puds like there's hell to pay.

After about a minute of this, Kevin hooks his hands under my armpits and pulls me up. We kiss again and then kick ourselves free of the jockstraps dangling below our knees. We walk to the front of the stage. We're both jerking off now, not seriously, just enough light strokes to keep our boners hard.

I give Kevin's firm rump another hard squeeze, and he flashes me a grin. He really is a sweet, sexy guy. I'd love to throw him onto a bed someday and have some real, honest-to-goodness sex with him. *Yeah,* I think, *me and every other guy.* The only action I ever get off of him is here onstage in front of an audience. Kevin has a boyfriend and limits his extracurricular sex to his performances. This is how he defines monogamy.

It's time to work the audience. Kevin and I step down off the stage and into the central aisle that runs down the length of the theater. I go left, and Kevin goes right.

The first row is filled with what looks like Japanese businessmen, all neatly dressed in suits and ties. These guys just love us decadent Americans, and they tip big. I stand in front of the first one, stroking my dick, giving him my friendliest smile. He bends down and stuffs a dollar bill in my sock. Madonna is on the sound system now, and her high voice pours down over me as the man's hands travel over my body, massaging my flesh, his fingers flicking my nipples. One hand drops back to his cock; the other wraps around mine. He strokes both dicks with a quick, excited tempo. After a few seconds of this, I squeeze his arm and move on to the next one.

By the time I've worked the row, my socks are bulging with bills. I glance over Kevin's way. He's climbed up onto the armrests of two seats, hands behind his head, his dick swaying heavily as he swings his hips in time to the music. The man in front of him stares up, mouth open, eyes glassy. He's stuffing bills in Kevin's socks, buying time, urging Kevin to stay a few seconds longer so that he can continue to drink in the sight of that black cock swaying inches from his mouth. He takes a hit of poppers and stuffs another bill in Kevin's sock. Kevin smiles benignly at him and squats down low, dropping his balls into the man's eager mouth. Technically we're not supposed to let the patrons take such liberties with us, but every now and then, when we're feeling generous, we bend the rules a little.

It's not until I work my way back to the fifth row that I spot the blind guy again. I had forgotten all about him. He's sitting in the middle seat, his head cocked. I touch his cheek with my hand, and he jerks his face toward me.

"Howdy," I say above the din of the music.

He doesn't say anything, just reaches up and touches my torso with his fingers. His touch is light, not so much a grope as a fixing of my position. I swing my leg over, straddling him. His fingers are less tentative now. They knead my flesh, explore my upper body and arms.

"You have a great body," he says. He pulls a bill out of his pocket and holds it out to me.

"That's a $20 bill," I tell him, figuring he's made a mistake. I mean, hell, I don't want to take advantage of the guy.

"I know," he says. "How about giving me $20 worth of your attention?"

I stuff the bill into my sock and then take his hands and place them back on my torso. His fingers slide over me quickly, lightly tugging and massaging me. There's something hesitant about his touch, as if he doesn't know how far he's allowed to go. I help him out by grasping his wrist and dragging his hand down to my cock. His fingers play up and down the shaft, exploring it, gauging its size. They wrap around it and start stroking. His other hand cups my balls.

"Your cock feels really big!" he says enthusiastically. "What are you, nine inches?"

"Eight, actually," I say. "It's the thickness that makes it seem bigger."

He lets go of my balls and pulls down his zipper. He fishes out his own dick and begins pumping it with his fist.

"Let me help you out," I say, replacing his hand with mine. His dick has a good heft to it and fills my hand nicely. He leans back against the chair, mouth open, hips thrust forward as I beat him off. He's breathing heavily now, his chest rising and falling rapidly. I spit in my hand and slick his dick up good. He gives a loud groan.

He keeps stroking my dick while his other hand explores the rest of my body. His fingers squeeze my nipples and then slide up to my face, lightly pushing against my chin, my cheeks, my eyes and forehead.

"I bet you're a hot-looking stud," he pants.

"Yeah," I grunt. "I'm a fuckin' heartbreaker." Actually, I'm only average. My eyes are too close together, and my nose is too big. I got this gig because of my muscles and my big dick. But if it turns this guy on to think I'm drop-dead gorgeous, I'm willing to play out the fantasy.

I quicken the pace of my strokes and tweak his left nipple. That does the trick. A shudder runs through his body, and he begins to moan. He arches his back, and jizz squirts out of his dick, splattering against my chest and belly. He thrashes around for a few seconds and then collapses back into his chair, panting, his shades tilting at an angle on his nose.

I squeeze his arm. "See you around, buddy," I say.

He holds on to my wrist. "What's your name?"

I look around. The other patrons in the theater are looking at me, waiting for me to continue my rounds. I've spent more time with this guy than I should have. Kevin has already worked his way to the rear of the theater. "Mike," I say a little abruptly.

"I'm Carl," the guy says. "Thanks, Mike."

He lets go of my hand, and I move on to the next guy.

A few minutes later I join Kevin back on the stage. We face the audience, pounding our puds to the beat of the music coming over the sound system. Kevin's dark skin gleams with sweat under the spotlight, and I reach over and gently squeeze his balls. He flashes me a big grin as his load squirts out over the front row. I follow quickly after him, thrusting my hips out, shooting my wad as I give a loud, theatrical groan.

When my dick's done squirting, I shake the excess come off my hand and wave at the audience. Everyone breaks into applause. The spotlight's in my face, and I can't make out Carl. I can only assume he's clapping too. I find myself hoping that the fucker had a good time.

I run into Carl a week later in the Safeway where I have my daytime job. I'm in the dairy section putting in a fresh supply of milk. Out of the corner of my eye, I see someone standing to my left, hovering over me. I turn my head and see that it's Carl. I almost didn't recognize him; he's dressed casually in jeans and a blue flannel shirt, a far cry from the look he was sporting in the theater. Only the shades are the same.

"Excuse me," he says. "Can you hand me a gallon of nonfat milk, please?" His head is turned at a slight angle, his blind eyes trained over my left shoulder.

I pull out a carton and hand it to him.

"Thanks" he says.

"No problem, Carl," I answer.

That stops him in his tracks. He turns back to me. "Uh, do I know you?"

I look around to make sure no one is in earshot. "We met last week. At the porn theater. I was one of the dancers."

Carl tilts his head, taking this in. "Mike?"

I place the last carton of milk on the shelf and stand up. "In the flesh."

"Not as much as when we last met," Carl says, grinning. He shifts his basket to his other arm. "You shopping here too?"

I clear my throat. "Well, actually, I work here. I stock the shelves."

"Hot damn!" Carl laughs. "I don't fuckin' believe it."

I laugh too. "It doesn't exactly conform to the fantasy, does it?"

I check Carl out again: the tight, compact body; the dark curly hair; the strong jaw and wide mouth. The memory of his thick dick in my hand flashes through my mind, and I find myself wondering what he would look like naked. The blindness doesn't detract from the images playing in my head; it just gives them an exotic touch.

"It's too bad you're working," he says. "Otherwise, I'd offer to buy you a beer."

I push a stray strand out of my face. "I get off in fifteen minutes. You feel like waiting?"

"Hell yeah!"

We go to a beat-up neighborhood bar around the corner from the store. I order a pitcher of beer and fill both our glasses. We clink them together, Carl spilling some of his beer on the table. He doesn't seem to mind. "Here's to chance encounters," I say.

"A-fucking-men," Carl replies.

I take a pull from my beer. "So was that your first time in a porn theater?"

Carl shrugs. "Yeah." He grins. "My little walk on the wild side. A friend told me about the live dancers that worked the audience. I was feeling horny, so I decided to give it a shot." He holds his hands out, palms up. "For once the reality outstripped the fantasy. I've been beating off all week thinking about you."

"Oh, yeah?" I say. I finish off my glass and pour another one. I see that Carl's is almost empty, and I refill his as well. "It's nice to know my work is appreciated."

He shakes his head. "It blows my mind that I just ran into you like this." He takes a pull from his glass. "It's kind of hard picturing you stocking shelves."

I give a little laugh. "Well, we nude dancers have to live too, you know. We certainly can't make it on what they pay us at the theater. Even with tips."

Carl sits back. "It's a hot fantasy, thinking about dancing naked in front of an audience, jerking off while everyone is watching. What's it like to do something like that?"

I shrug, a gesture wasted on Carl. "After a while it's just another day at the office."

We sit in silence for a few seconds. I look at the hairs peeking out above the top button of Carl's shirt and think about slowly unsnapping the buttons, one by one. It's a lazy summer afternoon, the type of day that feels so nice when you're in bed naked with another man. Unexpectedly I feel lonely, even a little sad.

"Would you like to go up to my place?" Carl suddenly asks. "I live just a couple of blocks away."

"Yeah," I say slowly. "I'd like that a lot."

Carl lives in a small one-bedroom apartment that overlooks a back alley. The place is sparsely furnished and excruciatingly tidy. There's a weight bench over in the corner of the living room, the weights neatly stacked in piles around it. A few chairs, a table, a couch, and that's about it. One of the walls is lined with shelves filled with audiocassettes. Photographs are mounted on the wall above the sofa: Carl blowing out the candles of a birthday cake; shots of what looks like a family reunion; Carl on a beach blanket with three other guys, all laughing. I wonder who looks at these pictures. Certainly not Carl.

By the window there's a small end table bathed in a shaft of sunlight. Something on it gleams, catching my eye. I look more closely and see a syringe laid neatly along the table's edge.

Carl goes over to a box of CDs and runs his fingers along their spines until he stops and pulls one out. He pops it into a CD player, and the Talking Heads start singing "Take Me to the River."

"You want some unsolicited advice?" I ask him.

Carl turns and faces me. "Yeah?"

"You shouldn't leave your works out for anyone to see. It might get you into a shitload of trouble."

Carl cocks his head. "My works?"

I clear my throat. "Your syringe, I mean."

Carl gives a thin smile. "I don't do drugs, Mike, if that's what you're thinking. At least not illegal ones. I use that syringe for my insulin shots. I'm a diabetic." He pauses. "That's how come I'm blind."

"Oh," I say, totally embarrassed. "Sorry."

Carl walks cautiously toward me. "Don't be."

I hold out my hand and touch him lightly on the shoulder. He takes off his shades and places them on the end table next to us. I notice with relief that his eyes are normal-looking: gray, fringed by long lashes. I don't know what I was expecting—something scarred and disfigured, perhaps.

He reaches out and lightly runs his hands over my torso, anchoring down my coordinates just the way he did in the theater. I pull him toward me, and we kiss, gently at first and then not so gently, our tongues pushing into each other's mouths.

Carl's hands slip under my T-shirt and slide over my torso, pulling on my flesh, kneading the muscles. His fingers find my nipples, and he pinches them. I cup his ass with my hands and pull him hard against me, rubbing my crotch against his. We kiss again, and then Carl pulls back.

"Just stand there," he says. "I want to take your clothes off."

I'm more than willing to oblige him. Carl pulls my T-shirt over my head and tosses it to the floor. He runs his hands again over my naked torso, gently this time, his head tilted as if in concentration. His fingers feel like feathers; they barely touch my skin.

Carl kneels down and pulls off my sneakers, then my socks. Still on his knees, he rubs his face against my jeans like some great cat. I run my fingers through his hair as he presses his mouth against the bulge of my hardening cock, his tongue licking the denim, leaving a dark smear across my crotch. He reaches up, unbuckles my belt, and pulls down my zipper. His fingers hook into my waistband, and with killing slowness he tugs down my jeans and briefs. I kick them off when they're around my ankles and stand naked in the middle of the room. A slight breeze comes in from the half-open window and plays across my skin.

I bend down to kiss him, but Carl gently pushes me away. "Don't do anything," he says. "Just stand still."

I oblige him, my feet slightly apart and my arms at my sides. I'm used to performing when I'm naked; it feels strange to just stand here so passively.

Carl reaches out and wraps his hand around my cock. He doesn't stroke it, just squeezes and touches it, his fingers exploring the shaft. His other hand cups my balls gently, cradling them in his palm, the fingers massaging them.

He looks up at me with his unseeing eyes. "Tell me about your dick and balls," he says. "What color are they? What do they look like? Give me a full description."

I stare back down at him. "They're dark," I say. "I'm half Italian, and I have some Puerto Rican blood in me too. My dick's the color of old oak. The head flares out and is even darker. My balls are almost black. As you can probably tell, they tend to hang low, the right ball more than the left. My nut sac is pretty fleshy. My pubes are black."

Carl listens with his head cocked attentively, as if he's expecting to be quizzed on this later. His hand strokes the shaft of my cock. I can feel it start to swell, grow hard under his touch.

"Is your dick as beautiful as it feels?" he asks.

"Yeah," I answer truthfully. "I'd say so. I get a lot of compliments on it."

"I don't doubt it," Carl says. He buries his nose in the flesh of my nut sac and sniffs. "I love the smell of your balls," he says.

Holding my dick in his hand, he sniffs along the shaft. He bends his head and presses his lips against my dick with a pressure that's not quite a kiss, then drags his tongue slowly up the shaft and swirls it around the head. My body tingles with sensation.

Carl suddenly plunges down and takes my whole dick in his mouth, his nose pushed up hard against my pubes. I groan and start pumping my hips, fucking his face with hard, quick thrusts. Carl spits in his hand and slicks my dick up good. I groan again, louder this time. He reaches behind me and grabs my ass, squeezing each cheek.

I bend over and pull him up by the armpits. "It's time you got naked," I say.

I pull off his clothes, kissing each patch of bare skin revealed. Carl's skin is smooth and pale, the torso nicely defined, the nipples wide and pink. It's clear that he uses his weight set often. His pecs are hard, his abs are cut beautifully, and his biceps bulge impressively. I put my mouth over his left nipple and kiss it.

Carl bends down and presses his face in my hair. "Let's go to bed," he murmurs.

Back in Carl's bedroom I suck his cock as he lies on his back, face turned to the ceiling. His dick is pink and fat and fills my mouth nicely. I work my way down the shaft, sliding my tongue over it with great slurping noises. I squeeze his nipples with one hand, alternating from right to left to right again.

My other hand slides under his firm, tight ass, kneading the cheeks, exploring the crack. I feel the pucker of his asshole, and I brush my index finger against it. Carl sighs deeply. I worm the finger in knuckle by knuckle, twisting it inside. Carl's sighs get deeper and turn into moans.

"Turn your body around," he growls. "I want to suck on your dick while you do that to me."

I pivot and straddle Carl, and we fuck each other's faces as I continue to work his ass. Carl's hands are all over me, sliding up and down my back, tugging on my skin, stroking, kneading. He twists his head from side to side as he bobs it up and down, and the sensations this produces on my dick radiate out through my body like electricity. I push my finger against his prostate, and Carl groans mightily.

"I want you to fuck me," he says. "Plow my ass really good."

The drawer in Carl's nightstand is fully stocked with condoms and lube. I sheathe up and grease up and drag Carl's legs over my shoulders. Carl reaches down and guides my dick to the pucker of his asshole.

I carefully impale him, working each inch in with painstaking attention. I start pumping my hips, first slowly, then with increasing tempo. My face hovers inches above Carl's, and I stare down into his blind eyes. His eyelids are pulled back, and his wide, blank stare gives him a look of amazement, even shock, as if he can't quite believe this is happening to him. His forehead is dotted with perspiration, and his lips are parted, increasing the illusion. This both unsettles me and excites me. I shove my dick hard up his ass and churn my hips against his. He begins to pant loudly, and I put my mouth over his, biting his lips.

Carl wraps his arms tightly around me and rolls us both over. He sits on my dick now, leaning forward, working his ass, his mouth still glued to mine. I reach down with a lube-smeared hand and begin jacking him off, sliding my fingers up and down his grease-slicked dick. Carl goes wild, bucking and snorting like a bull in heat. The bedsprings creak under the combined weight of our thrashing bodies.

Carl reaches back behind him and tugs on my balls. He squeezes and relaxes his ass muscles as he rides up and down my dick, winding me up like a clock. With each slide down my dick, he ratchets me up another level of pleasure.

I stare at him, astonished. "Where the hell did you learn to fuck like that?" I gasp.

Carl gives me a wide smile, his face turned to the wall behind the bed. He has the happy expression of a kid riding a roller coaster. "I'm just playing this by ear, man," he says, laughing.

He bends down, and we kiss again, Carl thrusting his tongue deep into my mouth. I suck on his tongue like I did his dick a few minutes ago. I feel myself getting close, the climax building up to the trigger point.

I pull my dick almost out of his ass and then thrust it in all the way, going for broke. That does the trick for me. The orgasm sweeps over me, and my load squirts out into the condom up Carl's ass. I cry out as I ride out the waves, one after another, my body jerking as each one crashes over me.

When the last spasm subsides, I wrap my palm around Carl's dick and start stroking. Carl slides up my chest until his balls are right above my mouth. I run my tongue over them eagerly, sucking on them, giving them a good washing. With my other hand I reach up and squeeze one of his nipples. Carl groans, and his body trembles. The first shot of his load splatters over my head, followed by others, all raining down on my cheeks, my mouth, my neck. I close my eyes and let the come squirt down in hot, sticky drops.

Carl rolls over and collapses onto the bed. "Damn!" he sighs.

I slide my arm around his shoulders and pull him to me. We lie together in silence for what seems a long time, our bodies pressed together. I can feel the pounding of Carl's heart against my chest.

"You know what I miss most?" Carl says suddenly. "I mean, about being blind?"

"What?" I ask, stroking his back. Sunlight slants through the bedroom window, lighting up the dust motes in the air.

"It's not the sunsets or the movies or some damn view on a mountain." Carl's face is turned to the ceiling, his voice matter-of-fact. "It's men's bodies. Their faces. Their fat, hard dicks. Jesus, I would love to take a long, hard look at your long, hard dick!"

"It's not so hard right now," I say kiddingly. "You definitely took care of that."

Carl doesn't say anything. The room is getting dark.

After a couple of minutes, I prop myself on my elbow. "I gotta go, Carl," I say. "Show time's in an hour."

Carl shrugs.

When I'm dressed he walks me to the door. We kiss, and he puts a piece of paper in my hand. "My phone number," he says. "In case you feel like calling."

"I will," I say, meaning it.

We kiss again, and I walk out the door.

That evening as I work the audience, I watch the men watching my naked body, their faces hungry, their eyes bright. Their hands wander over my torso, pull on my dick. I close my eyes and remember the feel of Carl's hands just an hour ago.

When I'm back onstage, stroking my dick along with Kevin, I shoot a load that makes it to the second row. *For you, Carl,* I think. The audience claps loudly as I grin and bow.

"You're feeling frisky tonight," Kevin whispers, grinning.

I grin back, my eyes sweeping over his naked body, a drop of jizz dangling from his still-stiff cock.

"Did I ever tell you how much I enjoy looking at your body?" I say. I pick up my jockstrap and walk off the stage, the audience still clapping and whistling.

Checkmate
by Todd McGuire

"You wanna grab some Chinese tonight?"

"Sure," Jim agreed, studying the chessboard for his next move. "Do you mind if we go across town?"

"Why?" I inquired. "You're always talking about the Red Dragon, and it's only a few blocks away."

"I know." He slowly moved his black rook across the board. "But Jessica and I always go there together."

I was puzzled. "So?"

"She doesn't know about us."

My brows rose. "What's to know?"

I'd been honest a few weeks back, when Jim and I first started hanging out together, telling him in confidence about a few gay encounters I'd had with a couple of former buddies. He said it was cool with him, even asking for a few explicit details, which I'd intentionally omitted.

But nothing had happened. And my hanging out with Jim didn't *mean* anything. Sure, he was a good-looking guy, with a muscularly lean build and an alluringly boyish appearance. But anyone, straight or gay, would have noticed a hunk like Jim.

"Jessica doesn't know I'm hanging out with a bisexual."

Me...a bisexual?

But I didn't respond immediately. Instead I halfheartedly snatched one of his pawns with my white knight, finally asking, "Is that what you think I am now, a bisexual?"

"That or a closet fag." The black rook took my white knight and formed a direct path down my open flanks, straight to the white king. "Checkmate!"

Fuck it! Instead of looking for a way out, I started to collect my pieces from the board.

"Ready to eat?"

I shook my head. "We'd better call it a night. You should be going."

"Don't be like this," Jim pleaded.

"Like what?" I rose from the kitchen table and, without waiting for a reply, walked straight to the back door. Jim hesitantly followed. "You should probably find another guy to hang with," I said. "Maybe you could find a gorgeous jock like yourself. The two of you could hit the bars…pick up broads…and all the other stuff you can't do with a guy like me!"

Jim stopped directly before me. My back straightened against the wall, but at six foot three, he still stood half a head taller. It was all I could do to look up and meet his piercingly honest gaze.

"For the record, I happen to like you a lot," he admitted without hesitation. "You're a lot cooler than my other buddies. I can drink a few beers with them, but that's about it."

Staring deep into his soul, I'd never seen a truer shade of blue. "Really?"

"Yeah," Jim said, cracking half a smile. "I certainly couldn't get a good game of chess out of any of them. And there's no way any of them would ever admit to having a homoerotic crush on another guy. Compared to you, they're total bores."

My head shook in disbelief.

"It's true," Jim swore. "I never know what you're going to do from day to day. And I've gotta admit, I like the uncertainty of never knowing what to expect."

The time seemed right, so I went with my instinct and reached my hands around his waist. When he didn't protest, I pushed on, raising my head to his as I initiated a kiss. Again he didn't resist.

Instead he backed me tighter against the wall until every muscle of his form pressed tightly into my own. His hardened prick pounded against my own throbbing rod.

That was when he went on the offensive by slipping me the tongue. Jim was all over me, exploring every detail of my mouth, kissing with an intensity most guys reserve for the actual sex act itself; foreplay couldn't have been more arousing. None of my previous buddy-fucking experience had prepared me for a jock as demanding as Jim.

And when his lips finally pulled from mine, my body was pleading for more tongue action from head to toe. Jim had to know it. An amused grin swept across his perfectly full lips.

"What?" I asked.

"It's nothing." After a minute he continued. "I just didn't think you were ever going to make a move; I was beginning to doubt my masculine appeal."

My eyes widened. "How long have you been waiting?"

"The truth?" Jim hesitated, though his boyish grin never vanished. "I've stained my briefs every night since finding out you were into guys."

"No way!"

"Wanna bet?" Without waiting he unzipped his fly and slid his jeans all the way down his legs. The fresh stains of precome were as apparent as the heavy equipment he was packing beneath his plain white Fruit of the Looms. "As you can see, I've got it hard for you."

I couldn't help smiling. Even the straightest guy would admire a bulge like that.

"So?" Jim questioned while slowly pulling my T-shirt up over my head. His rough fingertips explored the soft texture of my bare flesh with precise detail. It took little to leave both my nipples hard as steel. "What do you say? You wanna make my day?"

"You really want to do this here and now?" There was no denying how hot he was getting me—and with so little effort. Yet as he ventured farther down my stomach, my fire was just starting to burn. "Do you have some…?"

Jim finished my sentence by producing five packages of assorted condoms from the front pocket of his shirt, placing them on the edge of the counter. "Two for you, three for me."

"Aren't you being a little presumptuous?"

His grin grew from cheek to cheek. "Ask me that in the morning, bud."

Then, without wasting another moment, he unbuckled my fly and slid my zipper all the way down. Almost immediately my front came way out to greet him as he tugged my jeans down.

Jim dropped to his knees, exploring my seven cut inches through my briefs with his open lips. Dampness from his tongue wet both my briefs and the growing erection beneath. I was swelling to record length from his foreplay long before he finally lowered the elastic of my underwear with his clenched teeth. My prick immediately stabbed him in the cheek.

"Oh, God!" Amazement filled his features; he couldn't believe the state of my prick. For me, precome had been a long time coming. But now it was oozing all over my dick head.

Jim reached across to the condoms, selecting a minted one. He couldn't break into the package fast enough, and I couldn't wait as he hastily unwrapped it all the way down my shaft.

It seemed as though nothing could have stopped him from devouring me. Starting at the tip, he worked his way inch by inch all the way down my hard prick.

All I could do was lean back against the wall and rub my hands through Jim's thick brown hair as he went at it with no mercy. He was all over my joystick, racing back and forth, and once he got into the groove, nothing stopped him from getting a little wild with it. He jacked me with his right hand while teasing my crown with his lips and playing with both my balls.

I felt I was very close to losing my wad. My prick was getting heavier by the second. "Please stop," I begged.

But Jim didn't listen. Instead he took me deep down his throat. "I don't want to..."

But it was too late. I came in a long, hot blast of jism that seemed to erupt from my very soul. Jim pulled off me in an instant and ripped the rubber off my prick as wave after wave of fresh come burst from my piss hole. He wasted no time, taking my deflating prick in both hands and jacking every drop of remaining jism from my head. My once-solid masculinity turned to Jell-O beneath his touch. I was spent.

Luckily, that wasn't a problem Jim was suffering from, and I couldn't wait to wrap my lips around every hard inch of him.

First things first. I literally ripped the shirt from his back and flung it across the room. I was on him in record time, exploring his perfectly toned pecs with my hands, lips, and tongue. I drenched both of his hard nipples with my wet tongue, playing with the small forests of hair around them.

But Jim had had enough foreplay. He kept urging me down his abs and beneath his navel. He wasn't happy until I sat on my knees before the bulge of his briefs. Carefully he pulled his dick through the flap. And what a dick it was!

The word *long* doesn't begin to describe it. The shaft alone was well over ten inches in length. And chubby. He had one hell of a fat prick, which ended with a pink head barely visible beneath a thick layer of foreskin.

I was in love—but not with Jim. I'd had a love affair with foreskins ever since my first fuck buddy taught me how to drive him absolutely wild with delight. And now it was Jim's turn to be driven over the edge by my oral technique.

"What are you waiting for?" he demanded, reaching for another rubber.

"Relax." Instead of applying immediate protection, I pulled back the skin and finger-teased his prick head. A sigh that could only have been from delight escaped his lips as I mastered his foreskin. "We've got plenty of time."

"Do we?"

Suddenly more than a little uncertain, I gave in and centered the protection over his come hole. While holding back his foreskin, I pulled the rubber all the way down his prick.

"Open your mouth...wider!"

I obliged.

The next thing I knew, Jim was forcing himself between my lips. There was nothing polite about it. He got straight down to business, hammering his prick back and forth deep down my throat. The first couple of times almost gagged me; he went farther than any guy ever had. But nothing broke his concentration as he fucked me deep down the throat.

It was all I could do to not be slammed backward against the wall. The force of each thrust was undeniable. It left me gasping for air as he continued his oral assault.

We went at it for a good 15 minutes of intense head. But Jim didn't want to come with a rubber on, so he pulled out of my mouth, tossing the rubber to the side. He finished by jacking himself with both hands. Pointing his loaded weapon against my chin, he gave the trigger a final squeeze. And before my eyes it exploded. The initial blast of jism hit me square in the chin, covering my flesh in his sticky white sperm. The second and third eruptions weren't much farther off target. But he kept jacking himself, tossing jism all over both of us.

Jim wasn't finished yet, however. In fact, his prick was still harder than the average hard-on. And he took advantage of it by laying me, back first, across the kitchen table. Standing between my open legs, he spread my rear cheeks with both his hands. The next thing I knew, his tongue was wetting my ass. Then his finger dipped into the pool of spit and wriggled into my tight pucker. It was incredible.

Jim eagerly yanked another rubber, this one lubricated, over his still-hard prick and forced his cock about half an inch up my ass. I flinched, but it was nothing. I knew much more was coming.

And it was. It took him maybe a minute or more to force his dick all the way up my ass. He went deep, but it wasn't that bad. I just relaxed and let him plunge on in.

Soon we were fucking like a well-oiled machine, and Jim had worked my prick into a second erection. Though weaker than my first, it was slowly building in intensity.

So was Jim. This orgasm was coming a lot faster than his last. It was no surprise when he finally pulled out and tossed his rubber aside. With only a few strokes, he shot his wad across my stomach. It was only a few waves of jism, but I was no less impressed.

Without catching his breath he unwrapped his fourth rubber over my prick and bent down to ravish me with his lips and tongue. His last excursion into giving head had been nothing compared with the tenderness of his newfound passion. It wasn't wildly hot and totally unrestricted. Instead his second attempt was calm and controlled, but it was no less erotic.

I lasted a little while, allowing both of us to savor the experience. But Jim could tell I was getting close to reaching my second orgasm, so he ripped off my rubber and started giving me a two-handed jack-off.

It was ecstasy, but it ended way too soon.

I exploded in a weak blast of semen. This climax wasn't earth-shattering, but it left us both gasping for air as another wave of jism came running down my prick head.

"One to go," Jim reminded me.

I shook my head. "Save it for next time," I said. "The Red Dragon delivers."

"What? You want Chinese food and fortune cookies now?" he teased, jacking the last of my seed from my piss hole. "I've got a fortune right here for you," Jim said, stroking his own spent prick. From its limp state, it slowly came back to life. Its red head was pointed straight back at me. "You're going to get fucked every night for the foreseeable future by a big fat prick that'll go deep up your tight ass."

"What about Jessica?"

He climbed all the way up my body until we saw each other eye to eye. That same sincerity I'd noticed earlier was still there. And so was the electricity. Sparks flew as his lips found mine and we shared another lingering, wet kiss.

For one brief moment fortune smiled down upon the two of us. And I was grateful.

Boystown
by R.J. March

Maybe we weren't getting a lot of studying done; maybe we were always this close to academic probation. "But maybe ass really is more important than the social structure of England in the 16th century," McFeeley said in all earnestness, burning his fingers on what was left of a big fat joint.

McFeeley and I got together at orientation. We were standing in line to register for freshman comp. He stood behind me. I'd seen him all weekend—he looked like a man to me and not at all like some prefrosh 18-year-old. He'd worn the same clothes all weekend: a scruffy yellow Polo button-down oxford-cloth shirt and a pair of chinos with a tear in the ass that hung open like a toothless grin, exposing a variety of boxers throughout the three days. On this particular day I noticed tattersall, which tugged at me somewhere inside, becoming meaningful for no apparent reason. I had, I guessed, a tattersall fetish.

I straightened my shoulders and pushed out my chest when he came up behind me. I glanced back casually—you know, checking out the lines and shit, and mumbled a "How ya doin'?" He smiled, his green eyes on me, and nodded. He chewed gum, his dimples working in his cheeks.

It was a slow-moving line, inching up a little at a time. McFeeley was moving a little faster, though, and I felt the wind of his spearminty breath against the top of my head. I was afraid to move—I didn't want to turn and bump into him, and I didn't want to get any closer to the girl in front of me, and I didn't want to stop feeling the heat his body generated radiating toward me.

I got up to the table to register, my hands shaking, my cock just about hard. After a few moments of floundering, I found a class that sort of fit my schedule. I put the pencil down and turned, McFeeley having pressed up against me the whole time I was bent over the table.

"Wait for me," he said uncoyly. I nodded, a sudden slave to his whim and my boner.

I went with him to his room. His roommate for the weekend, an Asian he called Duck Soup, was at the getting-to-know-you party in the quad. McFeeley unbuttoned his shirt, his chest thick with hair and muscle.

"You gonna wrestle?" he asked, stretching out on the bed, his chino pants going taut over his crotch and accentuating the McFeeley log.

"Now?" I asked. "Oh, for school." I shrugged, feeling more than stupid. "Thinking of it, I guess."

"Me too," he said, his hand going behind the curtain of his shirt.

I still don't remember exactly how he got me on his lap. I recall his scratching an itch on his back and then having taken off his shirt. "Is this a fleabite?" he asked me, wanting me to come closer so I could inspect the thing. The next thing I knew, his big black-haired chest was tickling my ear, and his hand rumbled over my hard-on.

"You suck dick?" he asked. "You've got pretty lips. Pretty eyes too. Don't look like a cocksucker, that's why I didn't bust a move the first night at that asshole dance." We'd pissed together at the dance, wordlessly, shyly. I didn't look at him or anything. *A feat in itself,* I thought at the time.

His voice lulled me but not my cock. He played with it to distraction.

He had me stand for him, undoing my pants. My dick poked up stiffly in my briefs. He slid them down. My pointer vibrated as he regarded the pouting snout of my foreskin. "Cool," he said, leaning forward and taking the frilly end into his mouth, teething on it, pulling it, tonguing into the turtleneck of it. His hands circled my waist, fingers resting in the crack of my behind. He pressed his cheek against my prong, inviting me to hump his face, and I did for a while, but I had to pull back. "I'll shoot," I said, and he looked up at me, his face all serious.

"Oh, no," he said. "Don't do that yet."

He had me sit down to watch him strip off his pants. He was solid, already a man, and I felt so fucking pubescent looking up at him, with my boner all sticky between my thighs. He stood before me in his tattersall boxers, the front dotted with leakage. He was prickly with hair, his legs carved columns, slightly bowed. His toes lay on the linoleum like fingers, his feet wide and white.

He stepped up to me, pushing me backward, crawling over me, straddling my middle. He bent over and pushed his mouth against mine, the stubble of his face burning mine. He licked around my lips and into each nostril and then across my eyelids. I could feel the big press of him against my chest, still wrapped in tattersall. I wanted to haul it out and feel its hot skin and slimy leak; I wanted to taste it.

"Never sucked dick?" He pulled my arms up over my head, tipping his hips forward, butting the soft underside of my chin with his cock. I shook my head slowly to feel the head of it down there.

"You picked a roommate yet?" I had: Kevin Stein, bright and innocuous and unattractive—but only because he asked me.

"You wanna room with me?"

I nodded slowly, his huge dick restricting the full movement of my head. "OK," I said quietly, my spit thick and making it hard to speak. I wanted him fiercely, pointedly. All the things I'd ever wanted to do rushed through my head like a porn flick on fast-forward as his cock rested against my throat.

He rolled off and lay beside me.

"Go to it," he said.

McFeeley's log was thick and long and straight. It did not taper to a point like mine; instead it stayed the same circumference from base to head, a frigging telephone pole of a dick. I held it in my fist, impressed with its being there. I'd always wanted to suck dick, forever and ever—I just hadn't had the opportunity. There had been a couple of close calls, I guess—jacking off with a buddy, trying to pretend it was a matter of course, meaningless. Cases like that, you just jack, come, and act like nothing ever happened.

But this time there was no pretending, no need to pretend. It pulsed in my hand, wanting my mouth. I pressed my lips against its flat red-rimmed head. I took it into my mouth and tried to swirl my tongue around it. His fingers played over my shoulders, and I laid a hand on his thigh, stroking the fur on it. His nuts, two racquetballs in a bushy bag, bobbed as I ran my bottom teeth along the tender front of his cock. There was no way I could take half of it in my mouth, but I was satisfied, and I think he was too. I used my hand to take care of the rest, a firm sliding grip that banged against his pubes.

"Oh, my God," McFeeley said, an arm slung over his face. "That's a sweet fucking mouth."

He rolled me over, his dick planted in my mouth, and began to fuck me that way. He screwed my face gently, taking care not to choke me. I gripped his fleecy ass, fingering into his crack, loving the feel of him in my hands. His bung hole pushed out like lips waiting to be kissed. I poked around it, the hairs there coarse, thick. "Touch it," I heard him say, and I fingered the plushness, the wrinkled, winking gash turning hard and tight. I pushed in and found him wet as a whore. He fed me a little more dick. He throbbed on my flattened, useless tongue; he throbbed into the aching cave of my throat. He stopped breathing, and his whole body tightened. He brought his fanny down hard on my finger.

"Oh, fuck," he whispered as his cock chugged in and out of my mouth, its split opening and hosing my tonsils with the warm pudding from his balls. His thighs tensed against my cheeks, and he pulled out to finish the job by hand, gushing sweetly over my lips and chin.

He turned around and grabbed my pecker. "Never played with one like this before," he said, fisting it, exposing the head. I shot up into the air between us, splashing us both.

"Jesus," McFeeley said, wiping his eyes. "You could have warned me."

McFeeley liked games. His favorite was "I'll Get Him First." I guess he made it up. I mean, it doesn't exactly sound like the kind of game you'd play in the backseat of a car, your miserable parents up front trying to get you to Disney World.

When we moved off campus from the room we shared in Boynton Hall—*Boystown* Hall, we used to call it—we realized the freedoms we just didn't have on campus. McFeeley liked loud sex, a lot of loud sex—something that living in the dorms didn't foster. And I liked screwing the swim team, but discretion made up a small part of their valor, and smuggling the breaststroker Dickerson into my twin bed (with McFeeley feigning some pretty awesome snoring and drunken mumblings, all the while jacking off and watching us have at it) was no small feat. "No more mower sheds for us!" we rejoiced, toasting ourselves with shots of beer our first night, trying to get a quick buzz before Dickerson came by to our private housewarming party.

There was this new guy—Val Palmer was his name—a transfer from the Midwest. Mack and I spotted him at the student union. "Mine," I said, as though calling him first would give me dibs on this blondie with the falling-down socks and big switching ass, his homemade tank top riding his little pink nipples into some kind of hardness.

"To the victor go the spoils," McFeeley said with some smugness, and a week later I came home from biology and walked in on the two of them, McFeeley naked on his knees, his big dick disappearing into the fat-lipped mouth of Mr. Palmer, who lay spread-legged on the floor, his little flopper hanging out of his undone jeans.

I stayed where I was. Mack liked an audience anyway, although he didn't see me at first. He was too busy staring lovingly at Palmer's widened mouth. Val hummed and kissed the red end of McFeeley's joint and licked the thick shaft and slack-skinned balls that swung mid-thigh. He took them into his mouth, and McFeeley lowered himself onto Val's face. He unbuttoned the boy's shirt, uncovering those now-famous—with me, at least—nipples, firmly puckered, like his lips.

His chest was free of hair except for a pretty feathering of the stuff narrowing up from the big blond bush that surrounded his impossibly white, nicely thick, and strangely soft cock. He moaned under the touch of Mack's fingers.

Mack was a big-ass monster. His beefed-up arms were leglike in their girth, and he was more interested in the gym than the gridiron for a couple of fairly obvious reasons I don't feel it necessary to go into. But he didn't mind making the occasional tackle, throwing himself headlong at one of those big, sweating guards from Penn State.

Unlike Palmer, McFeeley was all haired-up with black curlies, but under it all his skin was as white as a salt lick. He was as pretty as a picture—to me, at least—his face nicely sculpted, his cheek and chin always carrying a shadow of beard no matter when or how often he'd shave, his mouth full and always smiling, reminding me of kissing. His green eyes were closed as he squatted himself on Val's face.

The boy under him squirmed and scrambled, his hands impotent weapons against McFeeley's sequoia thighs and boulderlike glutes. I noticed Val's prick twitching to life.

It was then that I also noticed that I'd been noticed, McFeeley blinking up at me with a shit-eating grin. He reached down and swung Palmer's little bat at me. "You snooze, you lose," he said.

"Hmm?" Val mumbled with a mouthful.

I gave Mack the finger.

"Feels awesome, baby," he said, his voice dripping with sex. "C'mon, buddy, clean me up."

I left them alone, myself in some sore need of attention. I drove fast to the bookstore on Route 222, where'd I'd stop every now and then after class. I walked sheepishly past the attendant, trying to look like I wasn't here for a blow job. My dick felt as obvious as a shoe in my pants, though. I got some quarters and roamed the place—it was a big room lined with stalls, featured movies posted outside each door. My peers today were familiar faces: two old men sucking Luckys and giving me the glad eye. "Cold enough for you?" they both asked as I walked past.

Out of a booth fell a thin boy wearing sad bicycle pants, wiping his lips with the edge of his T-shirt. He looked up at me like I was his next meal. From the same booth exited Monty Viceroy, patting the wet spots on his crotch and checking his zipper, his car keys already in hand. He saw me and glanced away quickly, but he knew he was busted, so he gave me a little nod. I'd seen him here before and in the library john at school, so I was not surprised to see the president of the student council looking so post-coital. He ducked his red head and did some fancy stepping around his trick and the two smoking fogies.

Present company did not present any likely or likable suck candidates save for Viceroy, him only for the sheer pleasure of doing someone in politics. I viewed some video sex and yanked on my pud. McFeeley and Val were probably covered with goo and in each other's arms right now, I was thinking. McFeeley had probably already turned on *Mighty Morphin Power Rangers,* which he never missed, his dick soft and heavy and sticky and reeking of Palmer's ass.

I sighed, feeling lonely. I heard someone getting change and checked my watch. The screen went blank. My Sambas smacked on the sticky floor, sounding as though I'd walked in wet paint. I wondered why there weren't any good fuck films about hockey players. I tucked my rock away, the stubby, flat-ended thing with its frill of skin. I sniffed my fingers.

Standing to the left of my door, wearing a tank top and warm-ups and startling me when I emerged, was someone who looked vaguely familiar. I was pretty sure I hadn't boothed it with him before, though. His hair was flattopped, and he had the long, stretched-out muscles of a basketball player. He looked at me, then away, his hands restless in his pockets—I could hear them rustling in the nylon. What I could see of his chest was free of hair; there was a russet peek of titty when he worked his shoulders into a purposeless shrug.

I left him standing there. As eager as I was to see him with his filmy pants about his ankles, he didn't seem the type to suck or be sucked. There were a lot of players who just liked to garner some attention, showing off their tent poles before secreting themselves and their cocks away in a video closet and adding to the sticky mess on the floor, going home chaste to the wife or girlfriend. I walked away from this one, trusting my judgment.

Sometimes I'm wrong, though, and so when this one turned and followed me, staying a few doors behind me, I figured I was going to have to reconsider my initial impression.

He mumbled a greeting, and I said hey, and he leaned toward me and said he felt here the same way he felt in church when he was a boy. "You know—a lot of whispering and thinking bad thoughts when you're supposed to be praying," he said, his voice barely above a whisper. He had long white teeth and was clean-shaven. He looked to be about 30.

"You go to Kutztown," he said, and I looked at him a little more closely, wondering if I should know him. Had we already boothed it?

"I was coaching tennis there," he said. "Name's Nicholson. I remember seeing you around. You're what's-his-name's roommate."

And Nicholson was the one what's-his-name told me about, the coach let go when rumors of sexual impropriety started circulating. "He was probably screwing Velakos," McFeeley speculated. "But fucking Velakos is fucking with fate, man, 'cause the fucker's nuts. Probably went to the dean with a butt full of the coach's come." McFeeley had a good eye for such things—Palmer, for instance, who was probably walking back to his dormitory room with a butt full of McFeeley's man juice. Good fucking eye, Mack.

I didn't feel right about this one, though, not trusting my own eye. He was nice to look at—very nice—with his short brown hair and his heavy brow and his pants rustling like a flag in the wind. I caught sight then of someone familiar, a black man whose dick never seemed fully engaged, who took a long time to come. We nodded—it was nice to be remembered. The huge vegetablelike curve of his dick was apparent through his zebra-stripe workout pants. I looked over at Nicholson. He scratched his bared tit.

The two old guys shuffled off, giving us whippersnappers dirty looks, and Bicycle Shorts left, miffed at being so completely ignored. It was just the three of us then, circling the outer walls, every now and then popping individually into a booth to freshen our tumescences.

There was an alcove out of sight of the security cameras, which hovered and flashed little red lights over our heads. It was a favorite resting area for me when I felt like loitering outside a booth, and it was also a handy place to gather a small group of daring pud-pullers. I'd seen as many as seven guys in the tight little space doing all sorts of shit. I stood and waited. It was a proving ground—I figured if Coach came around and stopped too, it was a done deal.

He came around, parking himself in a doorway, gripping the front of his pants. He stepped into the booth and looked at me, but I stayed where I was. I fingered the outline of my dick, making it hard. He kneaded himself through the blue nylon, producing a sizable erection. He pulled it out and shook it at me, the second time I'd been wagged at like that today. *Second time's the charm,* I told myself and undid my jeans. My cock hit the air running, thrusting up with a snap. I did not have the coach's length or girth, but I made up for it with a wealth of foreskin. I could see his lips wet with drool, and I figured I knew what his favorite food was.

I pinched the end of my pecker and twirled it around for him like a bag of Shake 'n Bake. I skinned the head back and fingered the hard bluish head. I pushed my jeans down my hard-muscled quads and lifted my shirt. My chest and stomach were covered with a fine stubble of see-through hairs. I pinched my right tit and rolled it under my thumb, circling it, feeling the rasp of mowed-down hairs all around it.

Nicholson's prick was monolithic. His grip failed to cover half of it, and his fingers could not close around it. It was by far the longest johnson I'd ever seen. He worked it in his fist and squeezed out a ladle's worth of juice, leaking as much as I ejaculate. He wiped his sticky hand on his stomach as though the stuff were offensive, while I was thirsty for some of that.

There was the sound of someone getting change, $5 in quarters falling and reminding me of Atlantic City. Nicholson's cock was gone in a flash. I peered around the corner. Another old shuffler, probably a retired trucker, got himself into a booth and stayed there.

I gave Coach the all-clear. I still had mine out; it was buzzing in my hand. I watched the slow unveiling of Nicholson's member and decided then and there to bend at the waist and have a taste. I was not normally inclined to the act, though certainly no stranger to it. The fat gusher appealed to me—its fat knob, the trim and taut shaft that looked suntanned, a brown ring running around the middle of it, marking the beginning of the deep end.

"We could watch a movie," he said.

"I'm claustrophobic," I told him. "It's all right here; nobody can see." I liked it outside the narrow, coffinlike cubbies. I liked the chance of an audience, the dangerous thrill of being caught by the club-armed attendant.

The black guy pulled up like a shadow, soundlessly. Nicholson quickly turned shy, but I kept playing with mine. The man stepped into the alcove with us, between the coach and me, his back against the wall, and let out his hose. It was similar to Nicholson's in size and shape, and it was the color, almost, of an eggplant. He kept his eyes on my prong, which seemed hardy and useful and insistently hard. His head was shaved, and he wore a Tommy Hilfiger T-shirt through which he rubbed his rubbery tits. Coach eyed us both, shrugging his shoulders and dropping his pants, and we were all unimpeded. I reached out and plucked at one of Coach's rusty nipples—it shrank up and pointed at me. I twisted until I heard him sigh.

I wanted them side by side, their similar, contrasting bangers swinging toward my mouth. Tommy's curved downward as though tugged by gravity and its heavy purple knob. He smacked it against his thigh until it left wet marks. Coach's cock was bone-hard and ruler-straight. I decided then and there to blow them both. I wasn't much of a cocksucker—not much!—but when would this ebony-and-ivory opportunity present itself again? I went to my knees in the alcove between them, and they both stepped up.

I licked Tommy's salty tip and held on to Coach's staff, jacking the rocky thing as I nosed under the plummy hang of Tommy's balls. I looked up to see the two of them fiddling with one another's pecs, their hands pawing, their faces coming closer and closer. I switched to the concrete head of Nicholson's dick, forcing it to the back of my throat. I heard his sigh and the smack of lips, and I squinted up to see Tommy's snaking tongue bathing the stubble of Nicholson's chin. I felt my own leaky piece twitch.

Tommy thrust his dick in my face, and someone's fingers tangled in my hair.

I sucked one and then the other, switching back and forth. I was pretty pleased with my performance, and my cock was feeling as though the head would come off in a gooey blast. I pulled on it until I felt my nuts suck up into my insides, and my pecker vibrated over and over again.

Coach was close too, I could tell, but there was no telling when Tommy would get off. I decided to concentrate on Nicholson's sticky knob, using my hand to get to where my mouth couldn't. His hands cradled my head, holding it still, and he fucked into me, and I swallowed an amazing amount of dick. He made a noise, something between a moan and a growl, and he pulled out, swearing and panting, looking down at his pipe. He aimed for my mouth, his own gaping, and shot five or six blasts into me, thick and stringy.

Tommy grunted with approval and lust and turned my head with a finger and added his own deposit of come, adding to my already sizable postnasal drip.

"Ah, shit," I said, feeling like a cat stretching in the sun. I tossed a big load onto the gray linoleum, getting a little on Tommy's Filas.

I got home after dark, and McFeeley was on the couch watching *The Ren & Stimpy Show.* He was wearing a pair of boxers and some dark-heeled socks. He lifted his hand in greeting.

His boxers were the tattersall ones, my favorites, and I found myself wishing I hadn't just wasted my time and come at the 222 Adulte Shoppe. I could see the warm, soft, fuzzy sac that leaked out of the leg of Mack's shorts. I felt a little wistful.

I went into the bathroom, ready for a shower. Mack followed me. I turned on the water and started undressing. Mack sat on the lidded toilet watching me. "What?" I said, getting down to my shorts and finding my dick glued to the inside of my briefs. I gave a little yank and felt as though I had ripped off a chunk of skin. I checked for bleeding. McFeeley snorted.

"Where were you?" he asked, smirking. "Who was sucking your dick?"

"Sex, sex, sex, McFeeley—is that all you think of?" I said, my cock pulsing upward.

Gaijin
by Ron Templeton

I had done these kinds of negotiations in the past, sitting in on the board meeting of the Kojintestu company as my company's representative. My bosses would request a translator to be present for the entire negotiations, despite the fact that I speak fluent Japanese. The reason, of course, is oftentimes men speak among themselves more freely if they feel I don't understand what they are saying. I stare at them with a blank expression and bewildered smile, waiting for the translations to be completed. You get only one shot at this kind of ploy, because when the cards are laid on the table and they see my offer is a perfect match for their lowest bid, they catch on pretty fast.

Toshiro smiled at me when the contracts were signed. "You know, they are going to be upset for weeks over what you have done," he said.

I returned the smile, and in Japanese I replied, "We tend to watch our backs ever since the IBM fiasco. You remember those contracts and promises…voided for the greater good of Japan. We aren't going to let that happen with our chip technologies. That's why Kojintestu will manufacture only one part of the entire chip. The brains of the unit are staying stateside forever."

"You gaijin are inscrutable," he laughed. "But enough of this. The negotiations are over, and the contracts are signed. Both our companies will benefit, and a little healthy skepticism is a good thing." He pushed his *o-bento* away from him. "Where would you like to go for entertainment? We have many bars and nightclubs that cater to gaijin."

"You know, if I had the option, I would love to go see a sumo match. I know they're in Tokyo for another two nights. I thought maybe I could find a spare seat somewhere up in the nosebleed section."

"You like sumo?" Toshiro asked, finally switching from English to Japanese.

"I love it," I said.

"Well, you are full of interesting surprises, Mr. Richardson. If you can wait until tomorrow, I will get you seats for the final tournament." Toshiro stood up. "However, tonight is still open. What would you like to do?"

I sighed and stretched. "Tonight I would like to sit back in a hot tub and enjoy a little R and R. After today's negotiations I think I've earned a quiet evening."

"So be it," Toshiro said. "I will come to pick you up tomorrow. We can catch the train to Tokyo and enjoy a day in the big city. I'm sure you have some shopping to do. And I believe I can offer *you* a few surprises that will rival even your expertise in the Japanese language." He laughed out loud. "Thank goodness I was only the translator. I have a feeling your performance today will have some entertaining repercussions all their own."

"None that will be serious, I hope," I replied.

"No, not at all. But fodder for a number of contract-negotiation seminars, I am sure. Our men fell for a very old trick today. That approach has been anticipated and countered for so long, we couldn't imagine anyone being crazy enough to try it." He stood up from the table. "I will need to be going if I am to inquire about seats for tomorrow's bout. You will please excuse me."

We bowed, and he pushed aside the shoji doors and stepped into his shoes.

I headed to my room. While relaxing in the warm waters of the *o-furo*, I imagined what the day would be like tomorrow. My mind watched the parade of huge *sumotori* as they came into the ring. I could see their hard, firm bodies slamming into each other as they struggled to unseat their opponents. I could hear their loud groaning as hands grappled around bellies and pulled flesh to flesh in a moment of sheer energy for them and pure eroticism for me.

Looking down, I watched my hard-on bobbing happily in the water.

The next day Toshiro was waiting outside the inn for me with his perpetual smile. He held up an envelope, which I knew held tickets to the tournament.

"These are some of the finest seats in the entire Kuramae Kokugikan," he enthusiastically said. "Like you, I am a great fan. And I felt that my company should spare no expense to show you a good time. Besides, what I have saved on not buying you a prostitute last night should be spent on something that you will truly enjoy."

"Then you have made the best decision I could hope for," I replied. "How long will it take us to get into Tokyo?"

"Less than an hour by train. But today timing is everything. We will eat on the train. I have something very special planned for you, and we must be at the Kuramae Kokugikan by 10."

When we arrived at the Kuramae Kokugikan, we were shown to our booth, which we would be allowed to enter and exit throughout the day.

The early hours are filled with younger *sumotori* trying to work their way up to the *maku uchi*, the highest-ranking sumo wrestlers.

We had scarcely put down our belongings when Toshiro eagerly grabbed my arm and began dragging me away from the booth. "We must hurry. Our audience is in just a few minutes."

"Our audience?"

"You will see. But you must promise never to tell anyone that I have gone to these lengths."

Toshiro ushered me back up the walkway and around some corridors. Before I knew what was happening, we stepped into a large room full of naked and nearly naked *sumotori* preparing for their bouts. In one corner a long *mawashi* that would be wrapped around a wrestler's waist was being carefully stretched and folded by some younger men. I knew that at the appropriate time, the higher-ranking sumo wrestler would allow the *mawashi* to be wrapped around him in the centuries-old traditional fashion.

The first thing I realized was that despite my six-foot two-inch frame, I felt dwarfed by many of these men. Not only were they impressively large with full guts and rounded chests, but many were taller than I. I watched transfixed as the men went about their dressing rituals.

It wasn't until Toshiro laughed that I realized the effect the men were having on me. "You gaijin have such huge cocks," he said, grinning. "It would appear you enjoy the sport of sumo for more than just the aesthetics."

I hastily tried to readjust the large shaft jutting down my leg, but placing it upright along the zipper line of my pants did little to hide the obvious erection.

"Don't worry," Toshiro said. "You're not the first man to ever have a love affair for the *sumotori*."

"Perhaps not," I groaned. "But as you said, we gaijin have big cocks, and our excitement tends to show."

At that moment I felt two large, firm hands press into my shoulders. In broken English I heard, "Toshiro, is this the big fan you tell me about?"

I turned to see the round face of one of the top-ranking *sekiwake*. He was smiling broadly. "My English is no very good."

"Don't worry," Toshiro said in Japanese. "He speaks Japanese fluently. You can talk to him without any problems."

"I am..." the mountainous man began.

"I know who you are," I said, staring into his face. "I've followed your career since you entered the *maku uchi*. Toshiro is right: I am one of your biggest fans. I have no doubt that one day the name of Umimatsu will be ranked with the great Yokozuna."

"Ha!" the wrestler laughed. "This is indeed a fan. Not even the press thinks I have that in me. But I will show them a thing or two before I am done." He gently brushed my shoulders and continued. "Kojintestu is one of my sponsors. When Toshiro called and told me of you, I thought you would enjoy a brief visit. I have to get dressed soon, but I did want to say hello."

It was in that moment that I realized I had been so transfixed by his smooth face and bulging chest that I hadn't even noticed he was completely naked.

"Rub his belly, Mr. Richardson," Toshiro encouraged.

"I couldn't possibly," I protested, praying all the while I might.

"Of course you can," the wrestler said. He took my hands and placed them on his belly. From a distance the belly of a sumo looks like any other large man's, but when you rub your hands across the smooth hairless flesh, you realize that it is rock-solid.

"I never expected it to be so firm," I gushed.

Umimatsu smiled at me. "You look very firm yourself," he said. "Is your belly button turned inside out?"

I thought through my translation and came up with the same obtuse question. "Uh, I'm not sure I understand. My belly button sticks inside me, if that's what you mean."

The behemoth laughed out loud. "No...no! I mean, are you gay? I guess you don't understand all the slang we have in Japan."

Totally confused, I looked to Toshiro.

Toshiro smiled. "You can tell him the truth, Mr. Richardson. Being gay in Japan is no more notorious than being left-handed in America."

"Well, then, the answer is yes," I responded. "But I assure you that I wouldn't think of hitting on a man who could squash me like a bug."

Umimatsu grinned and leaned toward my ear. "It might be worth your while to take the chance," he said softly. He took my hand and pulled it down below his belly. I felt the thick, short shaft of his dick pushing straight out from his groin. "You can never be a champion if you don't take some risks," he whispered.

But suddenly he changed his tone, releasing my hand and pivoting. "Now I have a match to win," he said. "Mr. Richardson, if I am victorious tonight, I will advance in the rankings, and my sponsors will wish to celebrate. Would you like to join us in a celebration dinner?"

I looked at him, and my eyes traveled down to his firm round butt. "I would...be...honored," I stammered in awe.

"Then I must win at any and all cost," he said, turning to smile back at me.

When the senior wrestlers entered the ring in the brightly ornate ceremonial robes for the *dohyo-iri*, or ring-entry ceremony, I watched carefully to catch a glimpse of the firm rounded belly now adorned in an apron of an ocean wave cresting behind a stand of windswept pines. Toshiro pointed Umimatsu out as he walked into the ring.

He handily defeated his opponent in under 20 seconds, grabbing him by the *mawashi* and walking out of the ring while his opponent's feet dangled helplessly off the ground.

The celebration party was a wild, raucous affair. The sake and food were plentiful, but as I watched Umimatsu move in and out of the party, I noticed he snacked but never drank.

Toward the end of the evening we found ourselves alone in a corner of the room.

"We of the *sumotori* are a very pampered group. In exchange for our hard work and constant training, we are rewarded with a life many envy. But like so much in Japan, there are expectations that must be met. A life that must be led." Umimatsu cleared his throat as if he were choking on something. "In time I will take my place in that life. I will leave the ring. I hope I will leave as a great champion, but undoubtedly before then, I will marry, most likely have children, and prepare for a life outside the ring."

"How will you deal with that?" I asked.

"Very well, I imagine. I am Japanese. I have been trained since birth to accept my responsibilities, and I embrace each one as I should. I am 32 now, which means in just a few years I will leave sumo. We seem to gravitate toward restaurant and bar ownership—places where our fans can come and remind us of how great we once were." He paused, his hand tracing over the carved lines of a tanuki statue sitting beside us. "As for the love I have for men, from time to time I will meet with them and quickly deal with the need. As long as I am discreet, my wife, my children, and all of Japan will look the other way. You see, they too are trained from birth in what is expected of them."

"I wish for you the best then," I said. "I can't say I understand it, but then I'm not here to judge the culture that you grew up in. God only knows that my own culture has more than enough problems."

"How true!" Umimatsu smiled. "But you will return home, and in time you will find another man to share your life. I envy that part of what you will have. I will only dangle my feet in the lake of life you will swim in."

He looked at me quietly for a moment and then brushed his hand lightly across my beard.

"In each of our lives we should have one great regret," he continued, "one moment when we wonder forever if the path we chose was the right one. One path leads to our desires, the other to our destiny. My destiny is already decided by my birth and by my status as *sumotori*. But the other path has not yet been opened to me. I would like you to be my one great regret. The one thing in my life I willingly let slip through my fingers when I know that it is the most foolish thing I will ever do."

He gestured to the party going on around us. "My name outside the ring and away from all this noise is Yoiichi. And that man, Yoiichi, would very much like to spend the night with you. If the answer is yes, ask Toshiro to take you back to the inn, and I'll join you in two hours."

Two hours later the shoji doors of my room slid open, and Yoiichi, clad in a dark kimono, stepped into my room. His hair was let down and flowed thickly down his back. He was as strikingly handsome as ever, and in the soft candlelight of my room, he looked for the first time oddly vulnerable.

He walked over to me and pulled me into a warm hug. "I ask only one thing of you, tonight, Mr. Richardson. Tonight please don't look at me as *sumotori*. I do not want to spend the evening with my biggest fan. I want to spend the night with a man who wants to be with Yoiichi, not an aspiring *sekiwake* by the name of Umimatsu. I didn't drink tonight because I wanted you to know that my whole heart and body were in this, that I would not wake up tomorrow and blame the sake. I want to believe you feel the same way about me, Mr. Richardson."

"My name is Ken," I said.

I let my hand slip into his kimono and felt the warmth of his hairless flesh. My fingers smoothed over the large nipples that were already growing tighter.

"Out of that kimono you will no longer be Umimatsu. You will only be Yoiichi, and I will only be Ken."

His hands reached down and pulled at his obi. In a few short motions Yoiichi had stepped out of his kimono and was standing naked before me. I had to restrain myself from grabbing him then and there. I removed my robe and invited him to lie down with me on the futon that lay across the tatami.

Yoiichi's massive bulk never hindered him from moving easily about. His firm pawlike hands explored my hairy chest while I watched the fascination in his eyes.

"Look how different we are," he said, smiling. Grasping my hardened cock, he pushed up to his knees and jutted his belly out, allowing his crotch to come into view. I saw his own swollen prick pressing outward from his body. "And look," he said, hefting both erections in one hand, "how much alike we are."

I rose up to embrace him and let my lips linger on the firm, rounded nipples of his chest. The massive circles of darkened flesh filled my whole mouth. I could feel them tighten even more firmly as I tongued them lightly. He groaned happily and let his arms wrap around my shoulders, pulling me in closer to his chest. I sucked all the more eagerly, and by the way he rubbed his hands through my hair, I could tell he approved.

His round face lowered to my chest as he sucked my furred nipples into his mouth. He laughed as he backed off and pulled out a hair from his mouth. "What a wonderful thing to have so much hair," he said, smiling.

I kissed his lips and added, "What a wonderful thing to be so smooth."

My hand had played with his crotch for some time. I knew now I craved more. I turned around and lay down on the ground with my head buried in his crotch. I took each pendulous ball into my mouth one at a time. The precome leaked from his uncut prick and spilled into my beard. When I finally sucked his dick into my mouth, it was fully lubricated by the slick, clear liquid of his own making.

He sighed contentedly as I sucked on his hardened flesh. The single patch of thick black hair curling around his dick pushed up against my face, and occasionally I felt the push of his body into mine as he thrust his hips forward into me. He encouraged me with whispered words I didn't understand. But it didn't matter. We both understood the need, and the need drove us toward fulfillment.

His bulky body fell on top of mine in a wall of flesh, and I felt my cock engulfed by his mouth. He sucked like a starving child at a mother's tit and all too soon was rewarded by a surge of warm come flowing out of me into his mouth. Nearly suffocating under the weight of his flesh, I gulped quickly when his dick began to spill its creamy liquid into me.

He rolled off of me and smiled. "Are you going to be able to do that again?" he asked.

Oh, yes," I said, breathing heavily. "Just give me a moment."

"A moment is all I'll give you," he said, leaning over and gently taking my cock back into his mouth. "You taste sweet," he mumbled.

He reached over toward his kimono. In a quick series of motions, he did something that I couldn't quite see because his large shoulders blocked the view. He turned around with a broad, closed smile. Taking my still-firm manhood into his hand, he stroked it gently. Then leaning over, he placed his lips onto the cock head and moved slowly down the shaft until nearly the entire eight inches was embedded in his mouth. When he rose up I saw that a bright red condom had been slipped over my engorged flesh.

"Tonight Yoiichi and Ken will be one," he whispered. "You in me…and forever me a part of you."

He deftly slipped his entire body on top of me. His huge, firm belly slammed into mine, and I felt his hand reach around and grab my dick. He shifted slightly, and I felt the latex-lined shaft push into his ass. His legs pumped up and down like pistons. His body totally enveloped me in warm, heavy flesh, and his expert working of my cock deep into his ass drove me to the edge of another orgasm. But each time my dick hardened to shoot the white liquid, Yoiichi skillfully relaxed his muscles and let the mountain of pleasure begin to build all over again.

When at last he let me come, I knew without a doubt that a bottom is in total control of a top.

With far more awkwardness than he had done with me, I lubed myself and placed a condom over his stout pillar of flesh.

"You in me," I said, looking into his smiling face, "and forever me a part of you."

I lay down on the futon and spread my legs wide. I felt his weight slide on top of me, his belly moving up along my back. And then I felt the cool latex-covered shaft push between the crack of my butt, eager to find my ass.

Little more than his cock head slipped into my hole before his own bulk kept him from pushing in farther, but it was more than enough for both of us. His labored breathing told me all I needed to know.

In a Japanese inn, where the walls are literally paper-thin, the loud primal screams of men together are forcibly controlled. I had been muffling my pleasure by shoving my face into the futon, but as Yoiichi neared his orgasm, he grabbed my shoulders and pulled me up toward him as if I were a small rag doll. His mouth gently bit into my neck as his body shook in uncontrolled ecstasy. His muffled cries against my neck sounded almost like a child crying in the distance.

Sometime near daybreak I gently soaped down his sweaty body and washed him clean. In turn his soapy paws lovingly explored every inch of my body. He rinsed us, and the two of us climbed into the hot water of the *o-furo*. I lay in his arms until dawn streamed its light into the room through the white paper windows of the shoji doors.

The greatest difficulty I had was letting him put on his kimono and head into Tokyo for a scheduled press conference.

As I waited for my plane, I watched the TV news. I saw a jubilant Umimatsu thronged by fans drawing him away from the camera, away from me, and toward his destiny.

Now, a year later, I remember that night. Yoiichi said we should all have one great regret in our lives. In becoming his that night, he became mine. Since that night I have never spoken the name he uses as a sumo wrestler. For one night he made me promise to see him not as *sumotori* but as a man. In that single night Yoiichi became a man in my eyes forever.

Liberation!
by Cain Berlinger

Uncle Ted loosened his collar while unbuttoning the stiff white shirt of his butler's uniform. His muscled chest heaved beneath the finery and ruffles. In the humid heat of a hot Southern afternoon, his body glistened with the sweat of a day's labor, making him as pungent as the hardest-working field slave.

It could be worse, he thought. *Being a house nigger has its privileges.* Among those privileges: He could unbutton his uniform and raid the master's liquor cabinet in the shade of the house patio whenever he found himself alone in the great white plantation mansion. *Yes,* he thought, *it could be a whole lot worse. Thank God for the county fair, where the whole family could disappear for a whole afternoon.*

He rolled the tall, cool glass of Southern Comfort across his forehead as he plunked himself down into the large white wicker chair and rested his tall boots on the glass table. For the moment the world was his.

He avoided glancing toward the fields where his brothers toiled in the hot sun. He reveled in his own superiority, grateful that he had been born a lighter shade of darkness that set him above his people at birth.

All his life had been spent in the white mansion. His only duties had been to be companion to the young master, Beau Tarleton, who was his own age, and to do odd jobs around the huge house. Eventually he had risen in ranks to be the head of the household staff. He had been dubbed "Uncle" at the drunken whimsy of the elder Tarleton, and the name had stuck.

And now Beau was a young man finding companions of his own among the white aristocracy. Ted thought this was the reason that talk among the gentlemen quieted whenever he entered a room lately carrying drinks. No one joked or laughed with him as much as they had before. He feared that he was about to be reassigned because of Lincoln's damn fool policies. He shuddered at the thought of being sent to work in the fields. His world was the mansion, and nothing beyond that mattered to him at all.

A familiar laugh filled the silence of the patio, snapping Ted to attention.

"Ha, ha, ha! The family goes away, and the servants come out to play! Weren't you paying attention, you stupid slave? I feigned headache and stayed behind to keep an eye on dear Daddy upstairs, sleeping off his latest drunk!"

Beau Tarleton moved toward Ted, clutching a riding crop in one hand. His tight pants caressed his butt like a second skin as he strode quietly across the floor in his fine leather boots. Blond chest hairs cascaded over the collar of his tailored shirt.

Within moments he was kneeling at Ted's feet. "I waited so long to be alone with you," he said. "We can make this our morning!" Beau began to kiss Ted's chest, licking at the salty sweat while his hands groped frantically at Ted's codpiece. "We haven't much time. They'll be back from the fair soon. Daddy's asleep, so you can fuck my ass..."

Beau pulled his pants down to his knees and grasped Ted's thick shaft in his hands, as he had done so many times since they were children. He squealed as Ted's prick grew harder and the coffee-colored rod began to pulse. He spit into his hands and rubbed the spittle over his butt hole, then covered Ted's shaft with a gleaming river of saliva.

Ted slapped the rounded pink cheeks before him, his fingers dancing in and out of Beau's furry butt hole. Quickly stepping behind Beau, he aimed his cock head like a missile and, with a deep intake of breath, plunged the elongated and swollen shaft in to the hilt.

Beau's impassioned cries, punctuated with moans bouncing between pain and pleasure, did little to slow Ted's violent attack upon the man he had to call "Master" in public. The solid slapping of flesh against flesh filled his ears with echoes, and he continued to plow into Beau as the young blond held his butt cheeks apart.

When the abruptness of change came over Beau, Ted was too involved to notice. Suddenly there was a struggle, and Beau made a mad attempt to extricate himself from the familiar attack upon his butt hole. His words took on a different tone—one of desperation, pain, and betrayal.

"Please, please stop doing this to me!" Beau cried. "I can't stand it anymore! I don't want this! I promise I won't tell! I won't betray you—just don't make me do this anymore! I won't be a woman to you. Please stop—my daddy will kill you!"

Beau's pleas were expressions of real fear, for his daddy was standing in the doorway of the patio, immobilized with anger, eyes blazing with drunken fury.

Before Ted knew what was happening, the swift blows of a riding crop rained down upon him with a fury he had seen only in the fields.

"After all we done for you, you ungrateful bastard nigger! Raping my son is the way you repay us? You'll hear his cries in your sleep, but they'll be nothing compared to the screams you'll be makin' before I'm through!"

Ted fell off to the side, attempting to shield himself from the fury of a humiliated father, an enraged slave owner.

Frantic whispers, like the buzzing of so many flies, assailed Ted's ears as he struggled to regain consciousness. His eyes felt swollen, and his entire body ached as it had never ached before. He tried to move, but every motion sent waves of pain through him.

What is this pain? What's happened to me? Where am I? Where are those voices coming from?

Ted lifted his head for a moment before drifting once more into a state of unconsciousness.

"I tell ya, there's rumors all over the South…they says we's free men! Free, I tell you!"

"And I says you just better swallow that kinda talk. I'm tellin' ya, Blue. If'n we's free, what exactly is it we's free to do?"

"We don't have to be here anymore…all this time we been workin' for free…"

"We gots room and board and work. What do you think we'll have if we go north?"

"We'll have freedom, that's what we'll have. Wait a minute, I think ol' Ted's tryin' to wake up. Shush up now, we'll talk about this later. You go on home. I've got some body-mendin' work to do here."

"I'll bet. That Ted, he's a pretty big buck for a house nigger. We'll talk later."

Ted listened to the sound of the closing door and tried to understand the conversation he'd heard. Free? What did that mean?

Ted moaned. His mouth was bone-dry, and his lungs felt as though they would burst. He felt the strong arms of the man called Blue lifting his head and placing a cool glass of water against his lips.

"Take it real slow, Ted…you been out for a few days. You received quite a beating from ol' Mr. Tarleton. Don't know what you did, but I understand that once you're patched up, you'll be a field hand from now on."

Ted's arms flailed out in anger. Work the fields? Never! He was better'n "them"—better'n the rest. He struggled to sit upright before collapsing back onto the blanket.

Blue stood up abruptly, disgusted by the display. "All my life I heard stories about you, livin' in the big house among the white rich. Hearin' how you looked down your nose on us 'cause we works the fields. You better get used to this, Uncle Ted, 'cause down here you're just Ted, the ex-boss at the house. There's no frills here, and the only white butt you'll be screwin' is in your head." He turned away and walked over to the window, where he began soaking a bandage in witch hazel.

Ted moved slowly. He was tired, hungry, thirsty, and confused. His whole world had been turned upside down because of bad judgment and a scared white boy who had used him for years. Now he had been thrown back into the mix among his people, who most likely would despise him, he imagined. They were as alien to him as he was to them.

He had heard them talking about freedom. What would he do with this newfound freedom? Plantation life was all he'd ever known. The very concept was as frightening to him as the physical pain he was currently enduring.

"How...how long have I been here?" His voice was low and controlled. He didn't want to anger this man with classic African features, whose skin was almost blue-black, the texture of which appeared to be of the finest velvet.

"A couple of days. Tarleton just dropped you at my doorstep sayin', 'Blue, clean this nigger up, then put him inta the fields.' See, I'm kinda the overseer here." Blue grinned proudly at this, his perfect white teeth glistening like ivory against his skin. His eyes were clear and knowing, his pupils deeply black.

He bent over Ted to apply witch hazel to the cuts crisscrossing his chest and arms. To Ted the touch was cool and healing, brushing across his heated and bruised flesh.

"Did I...did I have any visitors?" Ted asked.

"You mean Beau Tarleton? I heard he was sent to visit family in Augusta. They say he was packing for a *long* stay. I think you had better forget about him and concentrate on getting better. This is gonna sting a bit." Blue placed more of the witch hazel on the open wounds. Ted grimaced but held still.

"I'm gonna fill the tub with some hot water and strong soap. You got beautiful coffee skin, my brother, but you stink a bit. You get out of them clothes, and I'll help you into the tub."

After assisting Ted to his feet, Blue grabbed a couple of oversize buckets and headed out the door.

Ted was a little unsteady but managed to pull the tattered remnants of clothing from his body. Sweat seeped into the open wounds, stinging him slightly, but he ignored these new sensations and let his clothes fall easily from his body. His back ached, and his legs had never felt so numb, but they supported him as he pulled his boots off.

He stood before the mirror, pleased with his body but depressed by the drabness of the cabin. He hadn't heard the door open behind him, but he heard the sound of the water-filled bucket hitting the floor. He turned to see Blue staring at him.

"Damnation!" Blue uttered. He hadn't been prepared to be greeted by the naked man standing still and silent in the smallness of the cabin. His presence dominated the room; his aura was almost palpable.

Blue ached to touch Ted, and he felt the hardness of his cock straining against the cheap cotton of his trousers. His eyes traveled the length of Ted's body and settled on the thickness and curve of his cock over heavy, pendulous balls hanging casually against his thigh. Pouring the buckets into the tub, Blue wished he were not wearing trousers and could impress Ted with his own endowment and obvious excitement.

"I...I'll go get a couple more buckets," Blue said as he hurriedly left the room, his bare feet hardly making a sound.

Ted walked around the cabin, examining its contents: nothing of real value except maybe to their owner.

Then he saw a newspaper hidden under the bed. He had seen plenty of them in the mansion, but he couldn't read, could only study the pictures, mostly of white folks having fun and older white men looking important. He ran his fingers across the bold black type. There was a picture of Lincoln on the front page. Beau had shown him pictures of Lincoln. All he knew about the man was that he led the country and was not popular among the men who ruled the South since they depended on slavery to spur the economy.

"I guess they taught you to read up there," Blue said, stepping behind Ted and taking the paper from him.

Ted didn't respond. He just nodded and walked toward the tub.

"I kinda taught myself...it took some time," said Blue. "A while back there was a missionary who tried to teach some of us to read, but Master Tarleton bounced him out of here so fast... what with the war on and all. He found no reason to be wastin' our time with learnin'!" Blue laughed at the memory of the missionary, who had all these strange ideas about something he called equality. Blue had managed to hide a few of the books and other written material he had left behind. The newspaper was one of those cherished items.

"I was always taught not to believe anything I heard from any white man," Blue continued. "But this...this is different." He held the newspaper up and pointed to the headlines. "Do you believe this?"

Ted turned away from him. "I'm in too much pain to read now. Is there more water coming? I think I'll need more," he said as he eased his body into the tub.

"Oh, yeah, sure. I'll get some more." Blue smiled and left the cabin, returning shortly with two more huge buckets of water, his muscles straining as he easily lifted the giant buckets in his arms.

He poured some water into the tub and stirred his hands through the hot liquid. Bubbles began to grow and float across the tub. Ted looked on in wonder. He had seen this in the mansion. He didn't think that field slaves had these luxuries.

"I tell you, that freckled little missionary brought all kinds of joys to us out here. But I guess it's old hat to someone who's lived all his life on the hill."

Ted turned away from the accusatory gaze of the handsome caregiver. He was unfamiliar with the guilt that seemed to wash over him. In an attempt to cover his discomfort, he angrily pushed Blue away from him.

"I am not a slave! I am a house man! I am the companion to the master's son!" His eyes blazed with anger.

Blue held on to the sponge as he pushed past Ted's hand and continued squeezing hot soapy water across Ted's chest. Ted once again pushed the man's hand away.

Blue sat back, his eyes matching Ted's in their intensity. Neither man backed down from the challenge of the other, both feeling rage and passion.

"Look around you, man. We's all slaves. You ain't no companion to no one now except maybe the rats that infest these cabins in the summer. You'd better get used to it, my brother, 'cause for you the dream life is over! Unless what I read is true." Blue began rubbing the sponge again against Ted's chest.

Again, that veiled reference to the newspaper. Ted's curiosity was piqued, but how could he find out what was in the paper without revealing his ignorance?

Blue exhaled. It had been a long time since he had rubbed his hands against the body of such a strong and handsome man. Mending the field hands daily was part of his job; they were a complacent, quiet lot, resigned to their fate, confident in the promise of a better life after death. Ted was different, though. Even as a member of the privileged class, he nurtured a seething anger just boiling beneath the surface, and his flesh was hot to the touch.

Blue felt the subtle pounding of Ted's heart beneath his fingers, and a shudder went through him. He longed to look into the man's eyes but feared what he would find there. He could sense the arrogance, the haughtiness, the distance created between brothers simply because one had been born with a lighter skin color.

It would be up to Blue to bridge the gap. He slowly lifted his eyes to Ted's, and, as he feared, he found hostility, a challenge. But it was the challenge that intrigued Blue.

He began to rub the sponge in broader strokes, brushing against the raised nipples of Ted's chest. He moved it over Ted's broad shoulders, and the touch of Ted's biceps made his cock start to throb. Taking Ted's hands in his own, Blue held his fingers to his lips, and one kiss became many.

As he held Ted's hand, he felt his returning the passion with a strong grasp of his own. Ted's cock bobbed above the surface of the water, its shiny brown head gasping for attention.

Blue looked into Ted's eyes again, and now there was a softness, a sort of resignation. Ted was prepared to give in to Blue and his own desires. Blue barely heard the plea.

"Touch me," Ted whispered, his lips parting slightly. His breath was a soothing breeze that caressed Blue's face.

Blue inhaled deeply, and it was ambrosia to him. He leaned forward and tasted the bitter dryness of Ted's mouth. Ted opened his lips and waited until Blue's tongue invaded his mouth; together their tongues searched each other out until saliva dripped down their chins.

Ted realized now that his times with Beau were not lovemaking—they were nothing more than violent expressions. The thing he felt with Blue was sweet, gentle, long-awaited. And he was hungry to experience more.

He felt his arms lifting of their own accord, seeking out the strong musculature of Blue's body as he encircled the man, drawing him closer. Blue responded sweetly to Ted's embrace, and the distance that had previously existed between them gradually fell away like a dissolving wall.

Ted rose up from the tub, and Blue's kisses nurtured him, caressed and nibbled every inch of him. When Blue's lips brushed against his cock, Ted shivered uncontrollably. Here was a man who wanted to make love to him, suck his cock, love his flesh, salute his color, savor his texture, relish his taste. Ted surrendered willingly. There would be no need to establish dominance or fulfill a fantasy. He would just let whatever was going to happen, happen. It was Ted's first time making love to an equal as an equal, and his head spun with the drunkenness of discovery.

Ted stepped out of the tub as Blue kissed his feet, kneeling forward, the round curvature of his butt raised high. Ted leaned over and traced the fullness of his brother's butt and mentally noted the difference in how he felt, what he needed, and how he would accept it when it finally came to him.

Ted pushed Blue's trousers down around his thighs. Moments later Ted leaned forward, licking his fingers before inserting two of them, saliva-coated, into Blue's tight butt hole, stretching the hairline crack until his fingers felt comfortably buried inside. Blue's arms held on tightly to Ted's strong legs while he pushed his ass higher, and his hole opened to the playfulness of thick black fingers massaging his prostate. His moans filled the room as his butt gave in to the most delicious foreplay he had ever known.

When Ted stood up, Blue moved quickly to engulf his cock in his mouth, then surged forward for a massive shove into his throat.

Ted accepted Blue's worship of his cock. The smooth wetness of Blue's tongue slipped over the shaft of Ted's cock, swallowing the head effortlessly and then releasing it as he sucked the egg-shaped testicles into his mouth, savoring each as a fruit never before tasted. Blue once again sucked the precome juice from Ted's dripping piss slit. Hot blood made the veins on Ted's cock stand out like rivers traveling down the mountain of his rock-hard cock. Blue took his fingers and inserted them alongside the head of Ted's dick, pulling the foreskin away, his tongue surrounding the head, and then he sucked on the foreskin until there was no distinction between the dripping precome and his spit.

Ted held Blue's head while he dropped to his knees. He pulled Blue to him and cradled the man's head as they began to suck and lick at each other. With his face pressed to the cold hardwood floor, Blue pulled his cheeks apart while Ted covered him with kisses. He kissed across Blue's back, down the curvature of his spine, across the full roundness of his butt until, leaning forward, he tasted the sweetness of Blue's crack with his tongue.

Ted positioned himself above him, rubbing his fully engorged cock up and down the heated darkness of Blue's ass, the wet trails of his precome cool on hot skin. The head of his cock popped in almost effortlessly before the frenzied madness of his full-powered thrusts began.

Like an ocean, the passion between the men ebbed and flowed, their fucking going from mad frenzy to gentle, love-inspired strokes. By the time the heat had cooled in both of their bodies, Ted had pumped as long and slow as he could—and the night moon had completed its journey across the sky.

"This paper says that we were freed a long time ago. What with the war raging and all and most of us bein' not able to read…well, it says here it happened almost two years ago. Ted, we been locked here by our own ignorance. But I tell you—I don't know how— I'm goin' up north. And I want you to come with me."

Ted was silent. He knew what Blue was asking.

"Up north?" He looked away from Blue. "I don't know. So much has happened in the last few days."

Blue knew that Ted was talking about them now. Something had passed between them, and neither was eager to let go of the connection. Blue could sense the apprehension, the fear, and the confusion that Ted felt.

"I don't know," Ted continued. "I just don't know. Could we make it? I don't think Tarleton would let us go without a fight." He pressed closer to Blue, relying on the stronger, older man for support.

"There's a war, and it's the law. We can make it, Ted. We just have to trust in ourselves!" Blue nestled his face against Ted's chest, sucking Ted's nipples until he heard the now-familiar moans and groans that accompanied his resurgent passion.

"I guess if I was so wrong before..." Ted began and then lifted Blue's face to his. They kissed sweetly. But then he pushed Blue gently away from him. "I...I just need time to think. This is too much to take in all at once."

Ted kissed the wetness of Blue's lips and then sighed to himself as he exited the cabin, closing the door behind him.

The star-filled skies rushed to greet him, familiar smells assailed his senses, and in an instant he was home again. He was raised on this land, grew up in the white mansion. How could he live anywhere but here? Life in the fields would be different, but it would at least be familiar. Life in the north with this man he barely knew...this change was alien to him, and he wasn't sure how adaptable he could be.

When Ted finally returned, Blue knew that anxiety was masking the fear on his face.

Ted took him in his arms, his strong hands grasping the firmness of Blue's muscled butt cheeks. "It ain't easy for me to just up and leave," he began. "I don't know what I got here, but it's all I know. You're askin' me to go with you to somewhere I know nuthin' about." He paused and then continued, painfully. "I...I can't read. All I know is how to take care of other people."

Blue touched his fingers to Ted's tears and tasted them on his tongue.

"I'm gonna need a hell of a lot of convincin' to help me do what's right," Ted whispered, aware of the growing warmth spreading below his waist.

"Ain't no big deal convincin' you that what we want is right. Hell, no way I can lose this argument." Blue smiled and pressed his warm body against the former house slave.

Taking Out the Trash
by Michael Boyd

Life in Summerfield can get pretty damned dreary for a queer boy with an overactive libido.

Summerfield is a gradually deteriorating, strictly working-class suburb—a shit hole, if you will. OK, I'm being a little hard on the place. Summerfield is full of good salt-of-the-earth people who breed screaming snotty-nosed kids and shop at Wal-Mart and suppress their desires to be tied up and pissed on. Satisfied?

Summerfield is very straight—violently straight. Factory workers, road builders, ditch diggers, guys who would rip a fag's head off in a second...these are the men of Summerfield. Fuck, there's some serious repressing going on in my neighborhood.

I spill my seed a good deal around here. What's to do but jack off? I fantasize a lot about some of the guys in the neighborhood—young, gorgeous ultrabutch types who in the next ten years will have 20 extra pounds in the belly and an even more fucked-up perspective on life. No, I'm not proud of the fact that I have visions of these guys fucking the shit out of me when I whack off. These are the guys good queers are supposed to hate, right? Dumb-ass fag bashers.

Yeah, I hate them...until my dick gets hard. Then I conjure up images of sweat-soaked construction workers driving in pickups, wet T-shirts clinging to their muscles. Yeah, I guess I feel a little guilty after I spray myself with come and squeeze the oversize dildo from my asshole, but Christ, to see some of those guys mowing their lawns and washing their cars wearing only cutoffs, pecs glistening in the sun, faded denim bulging with dick meat… you get the picture. I'm only human. My sex drive is much stronger than my capacity to hate.

I try to lay low in Summerfield. I don't bring many guys home; I don't hang around outside much; I definitely don't have a pink-triangle bumper sticker on my car.

I guess I'm the type of queer who can be spotted from a mile off. I look queer without trying, which is fine by me. Queer is sexy…but dangerous in some parts.

I just quietly reside in my side of the duplex. But there have been a few occasions when things have…well, sometimes things just happen when you least expect them. OK, that's pretty vague. Let's see, where should I begin…

I think it was a Tuesday night. Yeah, yeah, Tuesday, that's right. It had to have been a Tuesday night, because Wednesday is garbage day.

I got a hard-on during *The Mary Tyler Moore Show.* No, Mary didn't cause it. Purely spontaneous.

I popped a porno in the VCR. Three guys fucking. Yeah, they were hot, but I was bored with them. I had tired of all of my little smut collection. Overexposure.

I clicked the VCR off and closed my eyes, flashing images through my brain of the young, hunky, straight married guys who lived on my street. They too had been played too many times.

I couldn't find a fantasy to satisfy me.

I felt my balls. They were prickly. Time to shave again. Shaving…maybe that's what I needed. I always get off feeling my crotch so baby-smooth, thinking how shocked my neighbors would be if they knew there was a queer among them who shaved his cock, who removed a sign of masculine maturity on purpose.

I went to the bathroom and readied myself for a trim, lathering my chest, my pits, my ass, my cock, and my balls. My legs would take too long. Screw the legs. Another time.

I started with the pits. I like to work downward, saving the best for last. Just a few strokes of the razor, that's all it took. It had been only a few days since my last shaving.

I had made it to my balls when I heard a hissing noise. No, a pissing noise. It was coming from next door. Thin walls. It was Hal…or maybe it was his wife or one of his kids. No, women and children can't piss like what I was hearing. Loud, forceful, urgent. Yep, I heard the pissing of a young roughneck construction worker who'd had a few beers. It had to have been Hal.

My cock had softened somewhat while I shaved, but now it throbbed again. I had flashed Hal through my brain just moments before and rejected him, but hearing him piss made me interested.

Flush. Footsteps. He was gone. But he was stuck in my mind. Hal was the focus. His cock had been just feet away, and, oh, how I wanted to see it! Only a thin wall separated me from a brute who pissed beer. Only a thin wall separated him from a fag who shaved his pubes.

I finished shaving my cock and wiped myself clean. Beautifully smooth. Painfully hard.

I went back to my bedroom and opened the window. Hal's bedroom was right next to mine. I hoped to hear something, but there was nothing. I wanted to hear him fucking his wife. She must have been asleep. Hal fucked her often, and he fucked her hard. I could hear them.

Poor woman! She didn't look like the type who wanted to be fucked hard and rough. Mercifully, for her sake anyway, it never lasted that long. Ten minutes tops. It was always over too soon for me. By the time I would get good and horny, ready for a long jack-off session, Hal would have already shot his wad, and I had no more aural stimulation. I wondered if he made her swallow, if he came on her tits.

Poor woman! I could tell by listening that she hated it. I would have gladly taken her place.

No more sounds from Hal. I lay back on my bed and stroked my hairless prick. The sound of his pissing was stuck in my mind. My cock was hard. My asshole needed to be filled.

I grabbed the seven-inch rubber dildo from my nightstand and squirted lube from my economy-size dispenser all up and down the makeshift cock. I pushed the dildo against my ass and slowly forced it all the way inside. Easy. Minimal pain. I had become accustomed to fucking myself.

God, it felt good to have a cock in my ass! OK, so it wasn't real, but I have a vivid imagination. Jacking off feels so much more intense when I'm squeezing my ass around a rigid shaft. I closed my eyes and let the pleasure that I felt in my ass spread over every inch of my body.

Hal was still there. I envisioned him standing over the toilet in his frayed, dirty jeans and sweaty T-shirt, his leather boots and hard hat, with a great big uncut cock in one hand spewing yellow piss. I kept him standing there forever, taking the world's longest piss, as I squeezed my ass around the dildo and pulled on my dick. The piss kept gushing harder and harder and harder as I stroked, until finally I saw streams of thick cream spurt from the big uncut cock, a projectile of white interrupted by the raised toilet seat.

I opened my eyes. My chest was drenched with come. I felt so good. I closed my eyes again, relieved, and squeezed the lubed dildo from my ass onto the sheets. I would just go to sleep, letting my come dry on my smooth, freshly shaved skin.

A sudden thought jarred me awake just as I was about to drift off to sleep. Tomorrow was trash day. I had forgotten to put out the trash. The garbage collectors came early. I had forgotten the last week too, and the garbage was piling up and beginning to smell. As much as I deplored getting out of bed after such a delicious orgasm, I knew I couldn't let the trash stand in the kitchen for another week.

I got up. I wiped my chest with the much-used come rag I keep by the bed. I looked for something to put on. I opened my dresser to get a pair of shorts and was struck by a wicked idea.

It was late. Everyone was in bed, and it was dark out. I would just stay naked. Yep, I would just add taking out the trash to the list of activities I had done in the nude.

My cock began to swell just a little at the idea. I thought it had had enough gratification for the night, but my cock was telling me otherwise.

I went to the kitchen and rounded up two plastic bags of garbage and headed out. I opened the front door. The street was dark. There was no sign of life.

I walked out on the front porch without a stitch covering my soft skin, clutching a trash bag in each hand. My heart raced. The cool night air awakened every nerve in my body. I slowly crept down the steps and walked down the short gravel driveway to the edge of the street where I set the bags. I stood there and looked around, running my hands up and down from my thighs to my chest. Naked, hairless, queer…and exposed in the middle of Summerfield. God, what a rush!

I reached around to feel my smooth buttocks and squeezed them hard. I fingered my asshole. It was still sticky with lube. I felt for hairs. None. Slowly I wiggled my middle finger inside. Jesus, I had never done anything so bold! I stood next to my mailbox and finger-fucked myself. I looked back toward my house and remembered Hal. Then I looked down the street and thought of other guys whose names I did not know. I wanted one of them, any of them, to come out there and fuck me senseless.

I heard the hum of a motor. Headlights in the distance. I thought of just standing there. No, no way. I was horny but not stupid. I walked back toward the door, but I took my time.

I was safely inside when the car passed. I started to go back out…but then I remembered: more trash. I figured I might as well get it.

I went back into the kitchen and hoisted up the recycle bin of beer bottles and aluminum cans.

Slowly I eased down the steps, across the gravel. I walked carefully so the bottles would not clatter. I was almost there...

Ouch! I felt sharpness beneath my bare foot. I lost control. The bottles shattered loudly.

Quickly I examined my foot. No blood. I had just stepped on a sharp rock, that's all. Damn! I should have known better than to walk barefoot on gravel.

I looked at the bin. The glass was shattered, but nothing had spilled. Thank God. No mess.

Never mind that. The bottles were the least of my worries. I remembered my predicament: naked, hairless, queer...and very noisy—not a good combination when you're standing in the middle of my neighborhood.

Another rush: fear. I looked all around frantically. No lights came on. No voices.

I left the bin in the driveway and walked briskly toward the porch steps. I thought I was home free...but then a light came on in Hal's side of the duplex. I prayed that no one would look out the window before I was safely inside.

I made it to the bottom of the steps that I share with Hal. The porch light flashed on, and Hal's front door swung open all at once. I froze. I knew I couldn't make it. Paralyzed, I made no effort to cover myself. I stood there at the bottom of the steps, my naked body quivering, my denuded cock in clear view. I looked toward the opened door, awaiting my fate.

Hal stood there. He too was naked.

I stared. I could not help myself. His nakedness was just as I had imagined it.

He seemed extraordinarily tall. I don't know how tall. I've never been good at estimates, but the top of his head couldn't have been more than a few inches from the top of the doorway. Dark hair, dark eyes, thick stubble. He had probably shaved just the morning before; I have to go a week to get stubble like that. Rock-hard muscles, powerful shoulders, massive thighs, and then his cock…just as perfect as I had imagined it when I heard him pissing. Uncut. Somehow I knew it would be. Long. So very long…like I said, I'm not much good at estimates. Thick, ungodly thick. Foreskin covering half the head. I stared at his cock and wanted it. I wanted it so very badly in spite of my fear of being crushed and ripped to shreds.

He returned the stare…directly to my cock. I looked down as if I didn't know what he was staring at. I was hard. Fully hard. I sure as hell didn't mean to be…but I was. My cock pointed straight at him.

I looked up. His gaze had turned toward my face. He wore a scowling expression—one of pure contempt. *Surely he's going to kill me,* I thought.

But then I looked at his cock again. He had pinned his right thumb on the base of his cock and brushed his balls with the other fingers. He was half hard! I looked back to his face and hoped to see some sign of an invitation…but the scowl remained: icy, contemptuous.

I didn't know what to do…so I just watched. The foreskin retracted, the beautiful cock head appeared, the shaft grew fully hard. I wanted it so badly.

I looked at his face again and licked my lips slowly. Still no sign of invitation. I glanced back at his cock again and licked my lips more deliberately. No change.

I was beginning to feel like a complete fool. I couldn't just stand there forever licking my fucking lips.

I climbed the steps ever so slowly and stood on the same plane as Hal. No change. I crept forward, halfway across the porch. No change. I stood just a few feet from him, coming up to only his shoulders. I looked up. Finally a change. He smiled.

No, not a warm smile. An evil smile…one that conveyed contempt just as forcefully as his stare.

I bowed my head in shame. I don't know why I was ashamed. Fear I could live with but not shame. I grew angry with myself for feeling ashamed...but I blocked everything out.

Hal's cock was right there in full focus. It had swollen to full erection. He kept his thumb firmly on the base of his shaft. I looked back up at him, trying my best to conceal my emotions. Still the evil smile. I figured his hard-on was the only invitation to suck that I was going to get.

I sunk down to my knees and looked directly at his cock. It was so beautiful up close. I looked back up at him for some sign of approval. His smile had disappeared. The icy stare had returned.

I kept my eyes focused upward as I opened my mouth. God, I know I must have looked like some pathetic puppy dog! My tongue touched his cock head. I immediately tasted a trace of bitter piss. I kissed the cock head gently, over and over again. I wanted to feel his hand lightly stroking my head—but nothing. I wanted to see him smile, to sigh, to show some sign that he liked what I was doing—but nothing.

I swallowed his cock head and sucked gently, savoring his soft skin. My tongue could feel his tightened foreskin, which had stretched behind his head. I intended to kiss every inch of his shaft, to show him what it felt like to have a queer boy make love to his cock...but suddenly I felt the hair on my head being tightly clenched...a thick rod shoved down my throat...my face in a thick black pubic bush. I gagged and struggled. He did not let go. My heart raced. I tried to pull back but to no avail. No, there would be no tender cock sucking with this man. Hal didn't know how to respond to tenderness. I would get my faced fucked...and on his terms.

Hal held my head firmly in place and thrust his hips forward over and over again. It hurt. He gave me a brutal, unsympathetic face fucking. I prayed it would never end.

As much as the reality of having an uncut blue-collar cock in my mouth thrilled and scared me, I was not satisfied. Cocksucker is a title I wear proudly, and I would not deem myself worthy of the name if I wasn't thoroughly versed in the art of drawing forth the juices of a man's loins.

But Hal didn't give me the chance to suck his cock. I could not show him just how wonderful I was at it. There's a big difference between cock sucking and face fucking, you know. Hal fucked my face. He held me firmly in place and let me have it.

Yes, face fucking has its merits, and I love to take it rough sometimes, but any dumb-ass faggot can sit back and get his face fucked. Cock sucking—or at least good cock sucking—requires skill. I wanted to show Hal just how good I was.

Oh, I would have shown him what a good blow job was all about...ever so slow and then suddenly hard...intense and then gentle...never, ever predictable. Christ, I bet he had never even had a proper blow job! I knew no woman could suck like I could. But no. I was completely powerless. He denied me the privilege of sucking.

Goddamn it! Cocksucker is part of my fucking identity. I wanted Hal to know who I was. I wanted to make him weak in the knees like I had done to so many other men. I wanted to make it so good for him that he would thank me for it and beg me to do it every fucking night! I had the most beautiful cock imaginable in my mouth. I wanted to give the performance of a lifetime...but Hal fucked my face more and more vigorously, rendering me powerless to move.

I saw that Hal had no intention of letting up. He was rapidly building toward climax.

Once I had adjusted to his forceful rhythm, I constrained my frustrations and contented myself with getting my face fucked. My cock throbbed and leaked precome, begging to be touched. I stroked it urgently with one hand, hoping to catch up with Hal's imminent orgasm. With the other hand I fingered my asshole, inserting two fingers as far as they would go. I was still loose and slippery.

I was beginning to lose myself in complete sex mania, preparing myself to swallow Hal's load, when once again I heard the hum of a distant motor. I feared we would be seen. Even more, though, I feared Hal would stop and leave me. I gazed upward, my mouth stuffed with cock.

Hal slowed down abruptly, releasing my head from his brutal grasp and reaching inside the door to click off the porch light.

Yes! I finally had my chance. I began to suck him to the base of his cock and then back down. Oh, yes! I know it felt good for him. I knew he would love it. I sucked him again and again...but three strokes was all I managed. Hal grasped my head again and resumed his ruthless fucking.

I grew anxious as I heard the car approaching. The noisy motor clamored in my brain as the vehicle passed directly in front of the house. The noise faded in the distance without incident. I can only assume we were not seen. I had no power to turn around and look.

I knew then that Hal would not let me give him a blow job—not like I wanted to. I began to grow fearful. If I sucked him, he would want more. My skill would be my assurance of safety. If he just fucked my face, if he just used me like some kind of sex toy, he would have no appreciation for what I could do. He might well beat the shit out of me when he blew his load. I didn't want him to stop fucking my face but not just because I loved having his cock in my mouth.

I didn't know how he would react when he came, but he was coming...soon. I could tell by his movements, by his breathing. I knew he would come in my mouth. I knew he would not warn me when he was ready to shoot.

I stroked my cock and prayed that his fucking would never end...but then my mouth grew hot. With a final thrust Hal buried his cock all the way in my throat and relieved himself of the jizz that had built up in his ample balls...those beautiful balls that I hadn't been given the chance to suck and lick. I gagged. Hal had forced himself too far down. I thought I would suffocate with my head buried in his thick black pubic bush.

At last he released me. I couldn't help but heave. Hal's come dripped out of my mouth, a few drops falling on his left foot. I swallowed hard as soon as I gained control of my breathing. His come was bitter and salty, more salty I think than any other come I've ever swallowed. I wanted more.

Hal didn't move. He still stared at me with evil eyes. I knelt all the way down and licked the droplets of come from his foot. Slowly I continued to lick and gently kiss his ankles and his massive leg.

I moved upward until my face was again level with his cock. Hal did not move. He held his hands to his side. His cock was only half hard by then. The foreskin covered half the cock head. I wrapped my lips around his come-soaked cock and savored the salty flavor. I sucked gently until I had cleaned his cock of all the sticky fluids.

I released his cock from my mouth and looked up for a sign of approval. We stared into one another's eyes for a brief moment. There was no connection.

When I leaned forward to resume, Hal thrust his hand in my face and pushed me back hard. I wanted to cry. He stepped back, withdrawing into the house. I couldn't stand it.

"Please, please! Don't go. I want to suck you. I want your cock." Those were the first words I spoke to Hal...ever. We had never so much as said hello in the two years that we had been neighbors. "Let me suck it. I'll do anything...I need it."

Hal looked at me. The stare was not as intense as his earlier ones. No, he was thinking. He was considering what I had said.

What kind of man is going to turn down an offer to have his cock drooled over and worshiped? Hal's cock slowly grew harder.

That was all I needed. I crept forward on my knees so that I was just inside the doorway. Hal didn't bother to close the door. We were still visible from the street. I wrapped my lips around his cock. He did not protest. He let me suck him. He let me make love to his beautiful cock.

Hal let his hands dangle at his side. He did not touch me. Any sign of affection would have compromised his machismo. No, as long as he did not touch me, he could be the horny straight guy just getting some relief. He did not move. He did not thrust...not at first. He just stood there and let me suck him.

Yes! Finally I could savor every inch of his cock. I clasped my hands on Hal's thighs for support. He showed no sign of objection. I closed my eyes to lose myself in the feeling of warm flesh enveloped in my mouth...but I could not help opening them often.

We were inside his house, after all—just inside the living room. What about Hal's wife and kids? Maybe they weren't home. No, they had to be there. I had heard them clamoring around earlier that night. Good God, what if one of them woke up and got out of bed? A lamp in the corner illuminated the room. They could see everything if they walked in: Hal and the queer-boy neighbor bare-assed naked having sex in the living room. The danger scared me and thrilled me at the same time.

I sucked and sucked and sucked. Hal grew hard in my mouth. I released his cock and moved down to his balls. He had big, sweaty, hairy balls. I ran my tongue all over them, and then I sucked them one by one into my mouth. I chewed them hard and heard Hal start to moan again. Yeah, I could tell by looking at him that he was the type of guy who liked rough ball play.

Hal became urgently hard while I sucked his balls. I wanted to taste his rigid shaft again. I swallowed him and sucked gently. He begin to thrust, slowly at first, then gradually faster and harder. He was ready to get off again. I felt his hand on the back of my head. I knew what was coming. I pulled away quickly before he had a good grasp.

"Fuck me, man. Fuck my ass." I said it without even thinking. I didn't have to think. That's what I wanted more than anything, although I knew he would be rough.

I stood up and boldly walked to the sofa. I knelt on the middle cushion with my ass thrust outward and balanced myself on the back. I wiggled my ass invitingly.

Hal followed me and stroked his cock. Yeah, he wanted my ass. Hal liked to fuck, and men who really like to fuck aren't gender-specific. I felt sure that my nice, tight asshole would suit him fine.

Hal came up behind me. He didn't bother to lube me up. Christ, what nerve! Thankfully, my ass was still loose and sticky from the dildo I used earlier.

I felt his cock head press against my asshole. I closed my eyes. I knew this was going to be rough. I had heard Hal's poor wife enough to know that he was a ruthless fucker.

He slid all the way in with one thrust. Yeah, I was lubed but not enough. The stuff had begun to dry. It still hurt like a mother-fucker when he penetrated me. I bit my lower lip. I could not scream; after all…his wife and kids. I began to think about them again. Man, we were both incredibly daring or stupid…or extra-ordinarily horny.

I couldn't help opening my eyes and looking around. No one woke up and walked into the room…but still, we were being watched. There were pictures on the wall. One was Jesus, I guess. It was a cheap black felt painting of a long-haired bearded guy with a sad expression on his face. Sad because of my sin? Nah. I figured he was sad because he was up on the wall instead of bent over the couch like me.

There were other paintings: the Virgin Mary and some other Bible folks. Then there were photos of stern-looking old people. Parents? Grandparents? Curmudgeons. They all stared at me. They all watched me get the hardest fucking of my life.

Yes, Hal's ass fucking proved to be just as violent as his mouth fucking. I experienced firsthand why his wife made those pathet-ic noises…but I liked it. *Yeah, I'll show him,* I thought. I would take it just as hard as he could give it to me and love every fuck-ing second of it.

I did. I loved it. I had to bite my lip again and again to keep from vocalizing my agonizing pleasure.

I stroked my cock rapidly. I wanted to come, and I wanted it to happen before Hal came. I figured he would kick me out when he was done. I wanted to get off first. I stroked my cock and squeezed my ass as tightly around Hal's cock as I could manage with his moving in and out so rapidly. Stroke and squeeze, stroke and squeeze, again and again and again. Oh, fuck, he felt good! No more pain. Just pure pleasure.

Every ounce of pleasure that my asshole absorbed filtered straight to my cock. I couldn't stand it anymore. I wanted to scream out...but I held it in so that only muffled groans and grunts escaped my lips.

My breath quickened. The room spun around. Jesus and Mary and the old guys danced in a circle around my head. I came. I let my semen spurt onto the couch, staining the gaudy flowered fabric...and just in time. With a final inward thrust, Hal pulled his rigid cock out of my ass. I felt warm liquid hit my back...a long string of come. God, I wish I could have seen it!

Hal stepped back, breathing heavily.

I tried to stand up, but my knees were too weak. I sunk to the floor and leaned against the couch, panting like a dog.

Hal looked at the sofa cushion that was stained with my come. His eyes grew narrow and mean. Without a word he grabbed me by the hairs on my head and forced my face into the small puddle of my own come. I licked every drop off the couch obediently as Hal held me down. When he was satisfied that I had cleaned up the mess I had made, he pulled me up.

"Get out, faggot."

Those were the only words he spoke that night. Those were the only words he had ever uttered to me.

I looked at him briefly. I was not afraid anymore. I was not insulted or ashamed. I was satisfied that I had gotten him off... twice. He could have called me anything he wanted, but he could not deny what had just happened: A queer boy made his dick hard with lust. I knew I was the best he had ever had.

I quietly strolled toward the door, which was still wide open. When I was in the doorway, I turned around and looked at Hal across the living room. With one hand I reached back and felt inside my come-soaked ass crack. I smeared Hal's come on all my fingers and brought my hand up to my lips. Slowly I licked every finger, one by one, savoring every drop of his come while he stared at me with his intense, angry stare. I swallowed the come and smiled at Hal...the biggest sunshine smile I could muster. I puckered my lips into a kiss and smacked loudly.

I left him standing there, fuming in anger.

I walked back into my side of the duplex, just as naked as when I walked out. I didn't realize how completely exhausted I was until I was safely inside with the door bolted.

I stumbled into my bedroom and fell naked across the bed next to the dildo I had left there. I didn't have the energy to clean myself up. I just lay there with my abused ass upturned, vulnerable and exposed. I felt a rivulet of Hal's come stream down my ass crack and around my tortured asshole, forming droplets that gently tickled my hairless balls. Savoring the feeling, I drifted into sleep.

The Canadian Censor
by Bob Vickery

The alarm wakes me up at 7 o'clock, and I can tell right away that it's going to be a good day. An overall feeling of well-being pulses through me. Sunlight is streaming through the window, and I can smell the coffee from the breakfast Anne is fixing for me. God bless her. Who could ask for a better wife?

I get up, shower and shave, and dress carefully. My appearance is important; as an employee of the Canadian Department of Decency, I have to set a good example.

While reading the paper I eat my breakfast of bacon and pancakes with lots of maple syrup. For the moment my good mood clouds. All these muggings, murders, and rapes—this country is getting more like its neighbor to the south every day. It's sad, but at least I can console myself with the fact that in my own small way, I'm in the trenches, fighting the good fight for the forces of decency.

When I'm done eating breakfast, I kiss Anne good-bye; she tries to slip her tongue in, but I keep my lips firmly pressed together.

Outside I see Timmy working on his hot rod next door. I chuckle to myself. That kid! He's always bent over that engine, covered with grease. Timmy's family has lived next to us for as long as I can remember, and I've seen Timmy grow up over the years from a freckle-faced, pug-nosed kid to the strapping teenager he is today.

Timmy sees me walking out the door, and he straightens up and waves. "Good morning, Mr. Robinson!" he calls out.

I walk over to him. "Good morning, Timmy," I say, smiling. "Still working on that bucket of bolts, I see."

"Bucket of bolts, my foot!" Timmy says indignantly. "I can out-race any car in this neighborhood, including that overpriced heap you drive!" We both have a little laugh. "By the way, aren't you going to congratulate me?"

"Congratulate you? What for?"

Timmy rolls his eyes. "Gosh, Mr. Robinson, you mean you forgot? Today's my 18th birthday!"

I stare at him. "Let me get this straight. You're 18 today?"

Timmy gives an exasperated sigh. "Didn't I just tell you?"

"You're absolutely sure about this?" I say. "You are 18 years old as of today?"

Timmy nods. "Uh-huh." He gives an impish grin. "It's still not too late for you to give me a present."

I give Timmy a long, hard look. With a shock I realize what a handsome young man he's grown into. His torn, greasy T-shirt fits his muscular torso like a second skin, and I can see the swell of his pecs pushing against the thin fabric, how his biceps bunch up and ripple with each movement of his arms. He's wearing cutoffs that he's clearly outgrown; his taut young ass strains against the confining denim, and the bulge of his crotch threatens to split the zipper of his fly wide open. I think of all the hormones and juices surging through his tight, muscled young body, and I feel my throat constrict and my dick stir to hardness.

I reach over and squeeze Timmy's crotch. "I'll give you a present, you sexy little bastard," I growl. "Just follow me into the garage and close the door behind you."

Timmy's mouth curls up into a sly smile. "Sure thing, Mr. Robinson," he says.

Timmy stands in the shaft of sunlight that comes streaming in through the garage's one window. Dust motes drift lazily around him. I look at him, taking in the firm, muscular body, beautifully proportioned but with just the slightest padding of baby fat; the smooth face; the wide, vacant eyes. *Young, dumb, and full of come,* I think as I sink to my knees in front of him and slowly pull down the zipper to his fly.

Timmy's dick meat spills out, already half hard: thick, veined, cut, a good eight inches long at least. I reach inside his fly and pull out his balls as well; they fill my hand nicely—candy-pink, plump, furred by light blond hair. Squeezing them, I look up into Timmy's sky-blue eyes.

"You got a load in there for me, Timmy?" I croon. "Some nice, sticky jizz you can splatter against my face?"

"You betcha!" Timmy says.

I open wide and slide my lips down Timmy's dick. Timmy groans, and his dick immediately swells to full hardness. Eight inches, my ass! That sucker's got to be at least nine, maybe more! Timmy lays his hands on both sides of my head and begins pumping his hips, fucking my face with slow, lazy thrusts.

My hands slide under his T-shirt, kneading the flesh of his young torso. I find his nipples and give them a good squeeze. Timmy groans loudly.

"Gee, that feels good, Mr. Robinson!" he sighs. "Really good!"

I lightly slide my hands down Timmy's back and across his tight young ass, feeling the play of muscles under my fingers. His ass cheeks feel smooth and warm, like sunbathed stone. I burrow my fingers into his crack until I find his hole. I push lightly against it.

"Oh, yeah!" Timmy says. His dick is deep down my throat now, his balls pressed against my chin, and he grinds his hips against my face. I work my finger into his ass and push, sliding up the warm, velvety chute. I massage Timmy's prostate, and he groans loudly. His body shudders violently.

"Oh, jeez, Mr. Robinson, I'm going to shoot!" he gasps. He pulls his dick out of my mouth just as a creamy load of jizz spurts out. It splatters against my face, coating my cheeks, my mouth, and my chin. I close my eyes and feel the warm, sticky drops sliding down.

I look up, and my gaze meets Timmy's. "Happy birthday, Timmy," I say smiling.

Timmy just gives me a shy, boyish grin, his face turning red. What a nice kid. A nice *18-year-old* kid, that is.

Later, while driving to work, I realize that my encounter with Timmy has whetted my appetite for more. After all, it was Timmy who shot his load, not me. I know just the place to go. There's a run-down old gas station on the corner of Main and Elm. I pull into the vacant lot next to it and walk over to the men's room at the back of the building.

If the timing's right, this place can be a hotbed of activity. No one is at the urinals, but I see a man's legs under the partition of one of the stalls, his jeans and briefs down around his ankles.

As I walk into the dank, pissy-smelling room, the stall door slowly swings open. The man sitting on the toilet is sporting a hard-on, stroking it slowly with a greasy hand. I recognize him immediately as Jake, the garage mechanic.

Jake has an unpleasant face, his mouth loose and moist, his eyes shrewdly piglike, his nose broken, his chin stubbled with a two-day beard. A scar beginning at his left ear zigzags down across his cheek like frozen lightning. Yep, that face of his could stop a clock, all right.

But his body is quite another story. Jake works out, as he'll be the first to tell you. Every time I stop for gas or take my car in for maintenance, I have to listen to him go on in detail about his lats, abs, delts, pecs, quads, biceps—you get the picture. He's a jerk, but the payoff is clearly there.

Underneath his matted black chest hair, his pectoral muscles are thickly developed and beautifully defined, his belly cut like Baccarat crystal. Tattoos work their way up his arms and spill over onto his shoulders: snakes, dragons, skulls, bloody knives, tits, leering demon faces. The man has to be seriously depraved. His nipples are set wide apart and stand out like little fireplugs, begging for a good chewing.

And that dick of his! Dark, swollen, and evil, gnarled with veins, the head flaring out like a cobra's. His balls hang down obscenely in their fleshy sac, swaying heavily to every stroke of his hand, his nuts like meaty little eggs.

"How ya doin', Mr. Robinson?" he growls. "You want your dick sucked?"

I shudder with revulsion, remembering Timmy's clean-cut wholesomeness and now having to interact with this, this...pig. But my dick has another take on the situation. It springs to life, pushing hard against the fabric of my slacks. Oh, well.

I yank down my zipper and pull it out. "Sure, Jake," I smile. "Be my guest."

Jake gives me a loutish grin and wraps his greasy fingers around my dick. He bends forward and slides his wet lips down the shaft, long ropes of saliva drooling from his mouth. I lean back and start pumping my hips, fucking Jake's face with determined abandon. Then I remember: Jeez, I can't have two oral scenes in a row!

I clear my throat. "'Er, Jake," I say. "Do you mind if I fuck your ass instead?"

"Sure, Mr. Robinson," Jake sneers. "I was hoping you'd ask."

He lumbers over to the condom machine on the wall and smashes it hard with his fist. A condom package falls out of the slot and into Jake's meaty paw. He hands it to me and then leans against the wall, his arms outstretched, his palms flat, his hairy ass exposed and waiting. The pose definitely shows Jake to his best advantage; I can drink in his beautifully toned body without looking at his butt-ugly face.

I slide the condom down the shaft of my dick and lube it up as best I can with my spit. I pull apart the fleshy cheeks of Jake's ass, exposing the pucker of his hole. I push my dick against it. Jake groans with anticipation. The head of my dick slides in, and then, inch by inch, I slowly skewer Jake until my balls are pressed against him.

Jake groans again. "Fuck, that feels good!" he moans.

I start pumping my hips, sliding my dick in and out of the grease monkey's asshole, my hands kneading the flesh of his torso, slick with grime and sweat. I seize Jake's nipples and twist them viciously. Jake whimpers, and his body convulses with pleasure.

I shove my dick in as far as it'll go and grind my hips against him. His whimper escalates into a full-fledged groan. I proceed to truly trash his ass, fucking him with hard, savage strokes that make him cry out with each plunge of my dick.

"*This* is for charging me $127 for changing my spark plugs!" I grunt, slamming into his ass viciously. "And *this* is for the $213 to reline my brakes!"

Jake whimpers pitifully.

Finally, when I'm ready to shoot, I pull out to the point where my dick head is just inside his sphincter. "And *this* is for the $84 to rotate my fuckin' tires!" I snarl.

I hold firmly to Jake's hips and plunge in hard. The orgasm sweeps through me like an electric shock, my body shaking as my dick pumps what feels like several quarts of jizz into the condom up Jake's ass. I cry out.

"Yeah," Jake growls. "Shoot that load!"

When I'm finally done I pull out, my dick still half hard. Jake turns around and drops to his knees before me, stroking his dick furiously. "How about pissing in my face while I drop a load, Mr. Robinson?" he growls, his mouth twisted in a salacious leer.

I pull myself up to my full height and stare down at him. "Jake," I say to him sternly, "we don't do that kind of thing here in Canada."

The color drains out of Jake's face and then rushes back in, turning it bright red. "I-I'm sorry, Mr. Robinson," he stammers. "I didn't mean that the way it sounded." He gives me a sickly smile. "Honest!"

I pull up my pants and zip my fly. "Well, I certainly hope not!" I give him a hard look. "The body's excretory functions are *not* a proper venue for sexual expression!"

Jake flinches.

I walk out of the tearoom with what I trust is the proper amount of dignity and skewer him one last look. "Save that kind of depravity for south of the border."

Jake looks like he's going to cry.

I make it to the office just barely on time. It's a good thing I left home a little early this morning.

The receptionist smiles at me as I walk in. "Good morning, Mr. Robinson," she says brightly.

I smile back at her. "Good morning, Lynn."

There's a pile of magazines on my desk—the usual filth. I sit down and pick up the first one, opening to one of the stories inside. Christ, another one about a humpy telephone installer; can't these writers ever come up with an original plotline?

I read it carefully, red-ink pen in hand. In the middle of the story, the installer lashes down the apartment tenant with a telephone cord and rapes him. My dick springs to hardness, but I ignore it. I slash a giant red *X* across the cover of the magazine and drop it into the reject bin. I reach for the next magazine.

Tony sticks his head into my cubicle. "Good morning, Dan," he says. "You got a second?"

I swing my chair around to face him. "Sure, Tony," I say, smiling. "Come on in."

Tony sits in my one free chair. "My kid's selling tickets for his school raffle. To help pay for wrestling mats for the gym." He looks at me with raised eyebrows. "You interested in buying one for a dollar? First prize is a color TV."

I take out my wallet and pull out a $5 bill. "Hell, give me five, Tony," I say. "It sounds like a good cause."

Tony flashes me a bright smile. His teeth gleam white in his dark face. He really is a good-looking guy. "Thanks, Dan," he says. He hands me five tickets. "You want to do Mexican today for lunch?"

"Let's do sushi," I say. I pat my belly. "My pants have been getting a little tight lately. I have to start eating lighter."

Tony laughs. "Sushi it is. I'll see you at noon." He glances at his watch. "I gotta go. I have a meeting with the boss." He ducks out of the cubicle.

I have a productive morning poring over the cheap, sleazy porn that crosses my desk, making sure anything that strays from vanilla winds up in the reject bin. God, I love this job! It gives me such a glow of...well, purpose. Today I feel particularly driven, and it doesn't take long before I work my way to the bottom of the stack. I glance at my watch: It's nearly 11 o'clock. Too early for lunch.

I stand up and stretch, then walk across the hall to Mr. Willoughby's office.

Lynn stops me at the door. "Mr. Willoughby is in a conference now," she says. "He told me specifically that he didn't want to be interrupted."

"Now, Lynn," I say, smiling. "I believe he has a shipment of magazines from Los Angeles that needs to be checked. I just want to run in and grab it." I give her a conspiratorial wink. "It'll just take me a second." Before she can protest I open the door to his office and walk in.

I'm not prepared for the scene that greets me. Tony is kneeling on the conference table, his shirt unbuttoned and his fly open. Mr. Willoughby is crouched before him on his knees. Their heads jerk up when they hear me enter.

"I'm terribly sorry," I say, blushing. "I'll come back later."

Mr. Willoughby straightens up. "No, no, Dan, it's quite all right." He smiles. "As a matter of fact, I was thinking about calling you in to join us."

Mr. Willoughby is stripped down to his boxer shorts, and I take in his solid, muscled body. I see Mr. Willoughby often at the company fitness center, so it's no surprise to me that he's in the shape he's in: the broad shoulders, the nicely swelled pecs, the powerful arms. His chest is covered with a light dusting of grayish brown hair that trails down across his flat belly and disappears tantalizingly beneath the elastic waistband of his shorts.

Tony's lithe brown body is a nice contrast to Mr. Willoughby's. He's more of a cheetah to Mr. Willoughby's bull: hairless, tight, compact, each muscle defined but not overdeveloped. His dick juts straight out from his open fly, gleaming with Mr. Willoughby's saliva. For some reason the necktie that hangs against his bare chest strikes a note I find almost unbearably erotic. He looks at me with his warm brown eyes and smiles. "Yeah, Dan," he says. "The party's just begun. Come on in!"

Well, who am I to resist an invitation like that? I close the door behind me and join the other two men.

Tony and Mr. Willoughby start pulling off my clothes, unbuttoning my shirt, unzipping my slacks. It's only a matter of seconds before I'm naked.

Tony pulls me toward him and kisses me, his tongue pushing deep into my mouth, and Mr. Willoughby starts sucking on my dick. His lips slide up and down the shaft, and he twists his head from side to side, creating sensations in me that make my knees tremble violently.

"Jeez, Mr. Willoughby," I gasp. "I had no idea you could give such great head!"

Mr. Willoughby looks up at me and grins, his hand wrapped around my dick. "How the hell do you think I got to be the boss?" He stands up and pulls off his underwear. "OK, boys," he says, "it's time we shift this party into higher gear." Naked, he walks over to his desk and opens the top drawer. "Let's play out a little fantasy here. Dan, I want you and Tony to tie me down to the conference table."

Tony and I exchange startled glances. "Wait just a minute, Mr. Willoughby," I say. "You know very well that we can't do that kind of thing here in Canada."

"Yeah," pipes up Tony, his face showing genuine concern. "We don't believe in bondage here—not even safe, sane, consensual bondage."

A smile creases Mr. Willoughby's handsome face. "But you see, boys," he says, reaching into the open drawer, "these aren't just *any* ropes. These are very *special* ropes." He withdraws his hand from the drawer and holds it up. It's clenched as though holding something, but there's nothing in it. "These," he says, "are my special *Canadian-bondage* ropes. You can't see them because they're invisible. I want you to tie me up with these. This way we can enjoy the concept of restraint without actually engaging in any of the decadent habits practiced in other places."

Tony and I look at each other in amazement. "What I hear you telling me," I say cautiously, "is that you willingly want to participate in a completely consensual sexual act involving being 'tied down' with these special invisible Canadian-bondage ropes. And that anytime you want the fantasy to stop, all you have to do is say so, and we'll immediately 'untie' you. Is that right, Mr. Willoughby?"

"Of course," Mr. Willoughby says, frowning. "You surely don't think I was suggesting a sexual act that involved even the slightest degree of coercion, do you?"

"No, no, of course not," I say hurriedly. I make the motion of tossing a length of rope to Tony as Mr. Willoughby climbs onto the table.

Mr. Willoughby lies down on his back, his arms and legs dangling over the edges. Tony immediately starts pretending to tie down his ankles as I work on his wrists. It doesn't take long before we announce to Mr. Willoughby that he's securely lashed to the conference table.

"Remember, Mr. Willoughby," I say, starting to get into the fantasy, "just give us the word, and we'll untie you in a jiffy. Anytime you want. This is all just voluntary role-playing."

"Totally consensual," Tony says, backing me up.

Mr. Willoughby nods his head. He looks at the two of us, his arms and legs splayed across the table, his thick dick hard and twitching, his balls hanging low between his legs. "Let's start by the two of you coming over here and fucking my face good," he growls. "Just cram both your dicks in my mouth at the same time."

A look of distress passes over Tony's face, no doubt mirroring mine. I clear my throat. "Um, Mr. Willoughby, I'm sure I must have heard you wrong," I say, keeping my tone respectful. "I know you would never consent to an act as degrading as having two penises in your mouth at the very same time." I smile helpfully. "Perhaps what you really want is for Tony to fuck your face while I plow your ass?"

Mr. Willoughby looks embarrassed. "Yes, yes," he says hurriedly. "You're right, Dan. That's exactly what I want." He nods toward his desk. "You'll find condoms and lube in the top drawer."

It takes me a moment to get tubed and lubed, and I climb up onto the table between Mr. Willoughby's legs. Tony is situated on the other end, squatting down, his balls swinging just above the boss's face. Tony is now wearing nothing except the tie around his neck. He starts loosening it.

"No, Tony," I say. "Why don't you leave it on?"

Tony gives me a sly grin. "Jeez, Dan, you're such a fetishist."

But he humors me and lets the tie alone. Christ, he looks sexy!

He squats a little lower. "All right, boss," he growls. "Why don't we start with your giving my balls a nice bath?"

Mr. Willoughby cranes his neck up and sucks Tony's balls into his mouth. Tony pulls back his head and closes his eyes as Mr. Willoughby tongues his sac. I pry apart Mr. Willoughby's ass cheeks and generously lube up his hole, inserting a couple of fingers. Mr. Willoughby groans, his voice muffled by Tony's balls. I rub my dick head around his sphincter, poking against it without penetrating, teasing him. Mr. Willoughby squirms his hips, squeezing and relaxing his ass in anticipation. His arms and legs strain as if they were restrained by ropes.

"Oh, my God," he whimpers. "You're not going to fuck my virgin ass with that...that battering ram, are you?"

Oh, puhl-e-e-eze, I think. *Somebody get this guy a ghostwriter.* I put on my fiercest frown. "Shut up!" I snarl. "You'll take whatever I give you!"

Grasping his hips with both hands, I proceed to impale Mr. Willoughby, pushing my dick in inch by inch. Mr. Willoughby moans piteously. I start pumping my hips.

"Yeah," Tony growls. "Plow his ass good!" Tony shifts his position so that he's got his dick crammed into Mr. Willoughby's mouth. Mr. Willoughby sucks on it noisily, and Tony plunges deep down Mr. Willoughby's throat. He reaches over and tugs on the boss's nipples, squeezing them hard between his thumbs and forefingers. Meanwhile, I have a lube-slicked hand around Mr. Willoughby's dick, and I'm stroking it hard, sliding up and down the thick shaft. Between the two of us, we're working the boss over but good.

Tony's face is just inches from mine, and I lean forward and kiss him, pushing my tongue between his lips and into his mouth. Tony returns my kiss with equal enthusiasm.

We settle into a rather intricate choreography of sex: me plowing Mr. Willoughby's ass while stroking his dick; Tony fucking Mr. Willoughby's face while working his nipples; the two of us heavily tonguing each other above Mr. Willoughby's body. After a while we match our rhythms and fall into sync, moving our bodies in unison like the parts of a well-oiled sex machine. Each thrust, suck, and stroke pushes us all closer to the edge. The room is filled with our grunts, groans, and sighs.

Perspiration beads on Tony's forehead and begins to trickle down his face. I can taste it as I slide my tongue over his cheeks, his nose, his chin.

I pull back to get a better view of Tony, drinking him in with my eyes. His body is truly beautiful—dark, muscled, and lithe, gleaming now with a sheen of sweat. We hold each other's gazes as we plow Mr. Willoughby's respective orifices, and it's as if I can feel each of Tony's thrusts myself, actually tasting that magnificent thick dick of his as it's shoved down Mr. Willoughby's throat.

Tony grins at me and winks, and the joy in his face is enough to break my heart. I make a mental note to set up something with Tony sometime in the future.

Tony pulls his dick out of Mr. Willoughby's mouth and squats over his face. I watch as Mr. Willoughby enthusiastically eats Tony's ass while Tony beats off, fucking his fist with quick, short strokes. Tony's eyes are glazed with pleasure, his balls are pulled up tight, and I know it won't be long before he starts shooting.

I reach over and twist Tony's nipple, and that does the trick. With a loud groan he comes, his load gushing out and splattering against Mr. Willoughby's chest. Squirt by squirt it shoots out, and every time I think I've seen the end of it, damned if more doesn't ooze out. Tony's body is racked with spasms, and his mouth is pulled back into a grimace of pleasure.

When he's finally done, Tony grabs me by the back of the neck and pulls my mouth against his. I kiss him tenderly, my lips working against his.

Mr. Willoughby is groaning louder with each thrust of my dick up his ass. His body is drenched with sweat, and his dick throbs in my hand with the hardness of a steel bar. I think about the promotion I'm up for and decide to give him an orgasm he won't easily forget.

His body begins to tremble, and I immediately press down hard between his balls. Mr. Willoughby arches his back and cries out as the first load of spunk spews out of his dick. I shove my dick hard up his ass, grinding my hips, and Mr. Willoughby cries out again, even louder. I imagine the office outside is getting quite an earful.

Mr. Willoughby is spewing a veritable geyser of jizz, splattering it against his chest and belly, his body still writhing as if his wrists and ankles were tied to the legs of the conference table. I give another savage thrust up his ass, and that's all it takes to push me over the edge.

I quickly pull out and whip the condom off, and my own load spews out. Tony is watching all of this with bright, appreciative eyes. My cries mingle with Mr. Willoughby's, my tenor to his bass, as we shoot our loads in unison.

When we're finally done, Mr. Willoughby is a dripping, oozing swamp of spunk, the combined loads of all three of us puddled together in all their spermy glory.

There's a moment of silence. The three of us exchange glances and then burst out laughing.

"Damn!" Mr. Willoughby says, shaking his head and grinning broadly. "Sex just doesn't get any better than that!"

Just remember that when we discuss my promotion next week, I think as I act out untying the ropes around his ankles.

Tony and I finish "freeing" Mr. Willoughby, and the three of us get dressed. Mr. Willoughby smears our jizz into his chest, making no effort to clean it off. "I have a budgetary meeting with the division head this afternoon," he says. "I want to feel your dried, caking loads on me while I'm discussing material acquisitions."

Tony and I exchange looks. He slaps me on the back. "I think we have a date for some sushi," he says.

"You boys just get out of here then," Mr. Willoughby says, chuckling. "Let the old man get back to his work."

When I get home again, I give Anne a big kiss at the door.

"How was your day today, dear?" she asks, smiling.

"Just great!" I say. "I had three different sexual encounters. All partners were 18 or older, all sex acts were entirely consensual, no excretory bodily functions were involved, and at no time did more than one penis ever wind up in anyone's mouth!"

"That's just wonderful," Anne says, beaming. She helps me take off my coat. "I made a special treat for dinner tonight. We're having sushi."

Oh, well, I think. *No day can be completely perfect.* "Swell!" I manage to say.

While washing my hands in the upstairs bathroom, I look out the window at Timmy's house. His bedroom light is on. Probably doing his homework.

Timmy confessed recently that he's having a little trouble with algebra; maybe after dinner I can offer to help him.

I make a mental note to bring along plenty of condoms. I dry my hands and start whistling a cheerful tune as I head on down to dinner.

Bringing Up Robbie
by Mark Caldwell

Robbie is my boy. Well, actually he's 28, and we are not related at all, but he is still my boy. And like a good boy, he calls me Daddy.

Today Robbie called me from the studio and said he had been a bad boy. I said nothing. I smoked the last few puffs of my cigarette and waited. I could hear Robbie squirm.

Robbie is a local newscaster in our palm tree–lined town. His job involves lots of public exposure and high pressure. In difficult situations with his fellow workers, Robbie often becomes cross or peevish. I don't care for this sort of attitude, and Robbie knows it. He also knows that he'd better call me right away and tell his daddy all about it.

So now I am waiting and smoking my cigarette. I don't need to ask Robbie what happened. Robbie will tell me. And as his words stutter and fall over each other, I can feel his blush heat up the wires between us. His voice is hushed and muffled as he explains some flippant abuse he perpetrated on a hapless PA.

He stops for long pauses, and I know it is because he is in a crowded room and cannot speak frankly or else the humiliating nature of his phone call will be disclosed. It's about 5:30, and he knows that he must be already made-up and dressed for the 6 P.M. live broadcast.

As Robbie's confession sighs to a finish, I stub out my cigarette in the black marble ashtray next to Robbie's bed and sit up slightly. "Robbie, you make people very unhappy and tense when you behave like a spoiled child."

Silence.

"There must be some way that I can firmly impress upon you how inappropriate your actions are."

Silence.

"Robbie, I want you to go to your office and open the third drawer down."

A strangled whimper.

"I want you to wear Jeffy tonight for the broadcast."

"No!" he blurts defiantly. It is the daring taunt of a young man vainly trying to usurp his father's power. All cocky and brave in the face of unbeatable odds.

I can feel the silence now between us as it erodes his nerves. I wait till I can hear the sweat form on his brow, and I burst into laughter.

"Robbie, I'm very comfortable here, and my dinner is almost ready, but don't think for even a moment that I wouldn't hesitate to put my clothes on and get in that BMW of yours—which, by the way, you still haven't put the plates on—and drive down to the studio to deal with you in person."

"No!"

The same word but as if from another language. A pleading, hoarse whine instead of a defiant bleat.

"Well, then, as I said, I want you to wear Jeffy tonight to help you remember to be a little more considerate of other people's feelings."

A wet sigh bubbles through the wires.

"And besides, Robbie, Daddy wants that little hole opened wide by the time you come home, so please don't take it out before you get here. I've got to go now. Terrence just called up that dinner is ready. Good-bye, Robbie."

I hang up without waiting for a response. He'd just be wasting my time anyway. He'd snivel and beg and use up all his time be-

fore the broadcast to evade his responsibilities. He's tried it before.
A father has to be cleverer than his son at times. Brute force alone
will not transform an errant lad into a fine young man.

As I sit in bed with my dinner tray, I reach for the remote control to the television. Fifteen minutes until the news. I picture
Robbie hurrying down the tiled hallway to his office and rushing
to lock the office door behind him. I wish I could see the look
on his face. I called the maintenance department earlier today to
have them remove the lock, "per Robert's orders." He must be
panicked by now, knowing that he's got to be back upstairs in
moments.

The phone rings. The house phone is on speed dial.

"Hello," I answer in a calm, measured voice.

Rather than words, an exasperated whimper bursts my ear.
Then, "God, oh, God, I've only got... How could you do this?
How am I supposed to—"

I can't help but laugh. Then I remind Robbie that he'd better
not waste his time sputtering as he has only seven minutes. Then
I hang up.

I picture my boy now, sweat building on his handsome brow. I
picture him stripping his pants down over his globular smooth
cheeks—underwear and all in one swoop—and then yanking the
third drawer open and pulling out the Jeff Stryker dildo and a
large jar of Albolene. I can see him placing the dildo on the chair
and then slathering his perfectly formed asshole with the goo.

Robbie must be checking his Raymond Weil watch now. But
there's no time to get used to the imposing thickness. I see his
classic good-looking Italian face contort as he squeezes himself
down on it as fast as he can. I can hear the deep groan as he hits
Jeffy's balls.

Normally my boy can take bigger and thicker than the Jeff
Stryker dildo. Especially if he is at home with his dad and we're
just having a little father-and-son roughhousing. But now, as his
intercom comes on and the assistant director is yelling for him to

come to the set right away, my boy is ripping off a length of gaffer's tape to secure the dildo and painfully pulling up his crisp white Jockey shorts and his navy gabardine slacks from Polo/Ralph Lauren.

Grunting from the pain of adjusting to the intruder inside him, Robbie quickly and carefully tucks his shirt back into his slacks and straightens his navy, yellow, and maroon brocade tie. I bought him that tie at Selfridge's when we were in London last year. On his charge.

I smile as I imagine him having to run upstairs now to the soundstage, almost waddling with discomfort. I see him whisking past the crew, carefully tugging at the back of his navy blazer so that the bulge of Jeffy's balls doesn't show behind him.

One or two may raise a knowing eyebrow to each other. A couple of them have witnessed my chastisement of Robbie at the station. But Robbie is so good-looking and so good at delivering the news and his ratings are so high that the powers that be have chosen to ignore his little "family problems," as they are referred to.

I turn up the sound on the remote control just as the commercial is ending and the titles start for Robbie's show. And there he is. My boy. A son any father could be proud of. Robbie has the perfect white teeth and regular features of a classic news broadcaster. A masculine authority radiates from his warm brown eyes as he informs us of the day's events.

His well-timed responses and perfect pacing are absolutely irreproachable, very much in keeping with a confident, intelligent, and imperturbable man on his way to the top of his field. As the camera pulls back to include video graphics illustrating a rise in summer vandalism, one's eyes tend to stray from the graphics to Robbie's broad shoulders filling more than his fair share of the wood-toned desk space for the three newspeople.

One would hardly guess that a man so utterly masculine and self-assured had only moments before been ordered to stuff his ass with a grossly large dildo by someone he called Daddy.

But a good father knows what a boy needs, and Robbie needs to be reminded all the time that Daddy loves him and is thinking about him. And only a daddy can tell by the slight twitching movement in Robbie's right temple that the stuffed-full pain of the dildo is stripping his veneer.

A sleepy haze takes over after my dinner. The ringing phone wakes me, and I see that *Entertainment Tonight* is already on.

"Hello," I yawn into the phone.

Robbie groans. I hear static and street noises, which indicate he is on the car phone.

"Oh, Daddy, please let me take it out. It's been in too long. My ass is cramping. Oh, God, please—"

"Robbie, if you come home and that dildo is not in place, there will be hell to pay. Now stop wasting time blabbing to me about your troubles and get your ass back here. The sooner you get that sorry excuse for an ass home, the sooner Daddy can take Jeffy out."

I slam down the receiver.

God, I hate being awakened by the phone!

Over the years I've had to punish Robbie for a number of reasons. But Robbie is not being punished tonight. He is merely being disciplined. I believe in discipline.

Discipline is often loving but always firm. Punishment is very loving but quite a bit more serious.

Robbie knows that if he doesn't follow my orders, he will be punished, and so he always submits to my discipline. Well, most of the time anyway. Sometimes Robbie tests my limits. He tried tonight earlier with that defiant little "No."

Just as I light another cigarette, I hear the door bang open downstairs. I sip the coffee that Terrence has brought up to me as I hear Robbie bounding up the steps.

And indeed he's panting now and sweating like a horse. He practically backs into the room as he yanks his pants down around his tan thighs. Offering his ass to me, he whimpers, "Please, Daddy, please take it out!"

I puff on my cigarette and flip through the *TV Guide.* "No," I say in a deliberate imitation of his earlier refusal.

"Oh, God, Daddy, I'm sorry I said that earlier. Please, I'll do anything. Just take it out for a few minutes at least!"

Absentmindedly I pick at an edge of the gaffer's tape and rip it off his ass, pulling the dildo out with what must be for Robbie an embarrassing plop. Five pounds of lifelike latex bounces off the berber carpeting as Robbie yelps from the pain and pleasure of release and topples facedown on the bed in front of me.

"Hard day at the office, honey?"

I take in his form stretching before me. Long, well-built limbs and the spinal curve of a pubescent. His ass, even in its relaxed state, arches up into the air. I can still see the rosier pink stripes where the tape took off a light layer of skin. His very elastic asshole has already contracted but not exactly to its original pucker.

Robbie is finally able to relax now and remains stretched out like an offering. He is fully clothed with his torso bared. His face is turned toward me, and his eyes are closed. There is still a little glow of sweat on his forehead and upper lip, and his mouth is open. He is breathing deeply in preparation for sleep.

But my son will not sleep for a while yet. He still needs to be bathed, powdered, and tucked in. I smack him hard enough on his ass that a large red handprint appears immediately. Robbie is up like a shot, startled out of his near-sleep state.

"Into the bathroom, young man!"

Robbie is already clean as a whistle inside. I make sure of that each afternoon before he leaves for the studio. After all, the last thing you want to see when you watch the 6 o'clock news is an anchorman full of shit.

So now I have my baby boy in a tub full of bubbles with all his favorite toys: his rubber duck, of course; his styrofoam tugboat; his Nerf football; and my favorite, the panda scrub mitt. I like to sit on the edge of the tub and have a smoke while Robbie bathes, just to see that he doesn't get carried away while cleaning his genital area and to make sure that he thoroughly cleans the bathroom when he is finished.

Robbie is in a happy little mood now as he lies back in the tub, bubbles breaking cutely under his chin while he babbles on about his day at the studio. As he talks he is bouncing his Nerf football higher and higher off the tiled wall.

"Young man, watch it! We don't want any accidents in the bathroom, now, do we?"

Robbie uncharacteristically ignores me and continues talking about himself in the manner that young boys are wont to do, bouncing the ball higher and higher until he finally misses his catch and the ball splashes soundly in the tub, splattering water all over my silk pajamas.

One can hear a pin drop.

"Uh, I'm sorry. I didn't mean to—"

As I grab Robbie by the hair on his head and lift him up out of the tub to flop him on his hands and knees, the water lapping at his balls, he continues to sputter his pointless apology. But Robbie knows how I feel when he has purposely ignored my warnings. He has to pay the price.

His ass is raised out of the bubbles, and soapy water drips down his hairless crack. I still have a hold of his hair, and as I wind up for the pitch, I dunk his head under the water.

Spank, spank, spank, spank.

Glub, glub, glub, glub.

Then I let go of Robbie's head, and he comes up coughing and gasping for air. I let him get enough in his lungs for another round, then redunk him as I haul off and whack his upturned butt repeatedly. Water is splashing all around us, and my pj's are soaked.

There will be hell to pay.

His ass is good and red now, and he is flailing in the tub, trying to come up for air and avoid the connection of my hand to his ass at the same time. When I let him up this time, he is not only coughing and gasping for air, I'm afraid, he's also crying. Little Robbie was scared that Daddy wasn't going to let him up.

I am a strict father, but when my boy cries, I lose my resolve. I grab my boy to my chest even though he is all wet and hug him tightly to me. My cock is hard immediately in my wet silk pj's, and it bumps around between us.

"Daddy is sorry he had to be so mean, baby, but I told you to stop, and you didn't. Now, let's get you scrubbed up real good. Daddy will help."

Robbie sniffles and coos as I pull my pj's off and toss them into the corner. My cock stands up straight as I get into the warm soapy water and put on the panda scrub mitt.

Robbie's face starts to beam at me as I work up a lather. The combination of Robbie's neon smile, his black curly hair, his cheeks all pink from the hot water, and his eyes still brimming with tears is enough to melt the heart of Attila the Hun. As I scrub him all over briskly with the mitt, he holds on to my cock. His hands are slippery with soap, and he slides his fists up and down slightly, making it fairly hard to concentrate on my task.

All pink and scrubbed now.

I turn on the showerhead to rinse us both off as the tub water drains. Robbie is on his knees before me. The burst of water rains down on his head, and the suds rush off of my cock. Robbie leans forward slowly, as if waiting for my approval before his head glides in a swift motion to engulf my cock. As I wash the suds from my hair, then his, Robbie's head bobs up and down, his eyes tightly shut so as not to get water in them.

Robbie stands obediently with his arms raised, passively watching me as I dry him off, getting the towel into every little nook and cranny. A light dusting of baby powder, then a sparklingly white pair of Calvin Kleins and a white T-shirt finish the job.

I let Robbie off the hook tonight about cleaning up the bathroom, mostly because I still feel bad about scaring him. So when Terrence brings Robbie's dinner up on a tray, I ask him to attend to it. Terrence is a rather avuncular old man and has warmly ful-filled his duties for us for several years now. He is used to clean-ing up the little messes we make and sometimes has had to assist me when Robbie's treatment has required punishment rather than simply discipline.

For instance, the time I came home and found Robbie blowing our gardener, Louis, in the foyer. Terrence was only too happy to take pictures of Robbie sucking Louis's hugely engorged cock as I whipped my boy's ass with a wet belt. Robbie, of course, thought that I would send the gardener away.

But I knew that Robbie had planned for me to catch him. So instead of blaming the gardener (and who could really blame him? Robbie has a mouth like an angel), I made Robbie continue and finish Louis off with a good hand job, spraying his load in Rob-bie's camera-perfect face.

Terrence took a great picture of it that I keep in an envelope ad-dressed to the TV station as another means of discipline.

But there have been no major crimes tonight. Simply the naughty misdemeanors of a young boy who needs to know the boundaries of his father's patience. So we sit happily on the bed, Robbie tucked in and me spoon-feeding him supper.

When Terrence finishes in the bathroom, he stops by the bed and daintily suspends the Jeff Stryker dildo by his forefinger and thumb.

"Will you be wanting me to have this cleaned yet, sir?"

"No, Terrence, I don't think we are finished with that yet tonight. Please leave it here next to the bed."

I hand him Robbie's cleaned plate on the tray, and Terrence thanks me as he backs out of the room.

Robbie has a dumbfounded look on his face. He had forgotten completely about Jeffy, and I am sure that he thought he was mo-ments away from being tucked in, all warm and snuggly. Robbie nervously reaches for his glass of milk on the table next to the bed, and as he jerks it to his face to drink, some spills down his front.

He looks down at the white drops on his tan chest and then suddenly up at me to see if I will laugh or be angry.

I'm angry. I hate spilled milk in the bed, and Robbie is very aware of that.

"All right, young man, we have a method for dealing with boys who can't hold their milk."

Before he can react I have the dildo in one hand and Robbie dangling by his upper arm in the other.

Robbie is already yelping a little when I throw him down on the fluffy white rug in the bathroom. Out of the cabinet I grab a small white towel, two very large safety pins with blue plastic tops, and a tube of K-Y jelly. Robbie is watching this all through puppy eyes and a pouty mouth. He knows what is going to happen, so he just lies back on the rug and waits for Daddy to do it.

The full-length mirror on the bathroom wall reflects everything as I pull Robbie's pristine white shorts down and drag them over his puffy white socks. Robbie had already removed his white T-shirt after dinner, so all he has on is his great tan and a little chest hair.

I keep Robbie cleanly shaven so that I can see everything that goes on down there. A growing boy must be closely observed for any irregularities. And besides, the curve of his taut little stomach above his rather thick cock is so cute. It just makes me want to hug him and kiss him all over.

Robbie is lying on his back, staring up at the ceiling in a dream world, as I fold the towel carefully, then lift him by his legs to place the towel beneath him. I squeeze a large gob of K-Y into my hand and pack it up into his ass, slathering the rest around the general area of his pert hole. Then I put some more on the entire length of Jeffy, and as I place it at Robbie's hole, he closes his eyes, and his thumb distractedly grazes its way to his mouth.

I hardly notice my own cock stretched out in front of me as I concentrate on working the dildo up into my little newscaster's asshole. Robbie is panting and sucking at his thumb furiously, and his eyes are squinched shut. His free hand has strayed to his nipples, and it plucks and pulls on them alternately. Robbie's thick cock is rock-hard and bouncing on his stomach, and his shaved balls have tightened up to his body.

Once the dildo is in place, Robbie relaxes a bit, and I pull the flap end of the towel up tightly between his legs and secure the safety pins with the large baby-blue plastic heads at each side. Our diaper performs the task of holding Jeffy snuggly up my little boy's bottom. I can see the bulge of Robbie's cock throb in its confines.

"Robbie, into the bedroom."

As I stand in front of the deco armoire, I see Robbie crawling on all fours out of the bathroom, his right sock starting to slip off his foot. He stops in front of me and looks up into my eyes from his position on the floor. In the mirror on the armoire, I can see his diapered butt, the bulge of the dildo sticking out obscenely.

"Make your old man feel good, Robbie."

Robbie crawls up my legs with his wide hands, and on his knees in front of me he begins to lick my cock, which is arched out in front of him like a toy. In the mirror I see the back of his head perched on his long thick neck as it bends and swivels so he can lick all around my crotch.

I am much taller than Robbie, so even on his knees he has to reach up to tongue my balls.

As Robbie impales his head on my shaft, his hands busy themselves elsewhere: One is jammed down the front of his diaper, and the other alternates between his nipples and tugging and pushing at the large object lodged in his tight rectum.

I lean over and unpin the sides of Robbie's diaper, and it flops down at his strained flanks. Since he is in a squatting position in front of me, it naturally forces the thick dildo out, and as he sucks fast and wet on my cock, spit drooling from his lower lip, the plastic cock slips out of him until just the head is still in and the balls and base rest on the cream-colored carpet.

Putting my hands on his shoulders, I push firmly, grinding him back down onto it, and then I let go again to watch him rise up off of it.

Watching the impossibly thick shaft squeeze in and out of Robbie's hole turns me on so much, I have to jam my cock as far back as it will go in Robbie's clutching throat. He gags and sputters but makes no move to stop me.

The thought of his perfect white teeth raking over the head of my dick is too much, and I rest hard on his shoulders, pushing him all the way down to Jeffy's balls. I hear a muffled yelp from him, and that sends me over the top. Yanking my cock out, I squirt long streams of clotted white over his perfectly cut hair and watch in the armoire mirror as it drips down the hollow formed by the strong muscles on either side of his spine.

Robbie has to watch the 11 o'clock news. It's part of his job.

Tonight Robbie is watching it with Jeffy strapped into his mouth by his own diaper. He is facedown on the bed with his head propped up on a pillow so that he can see the news team on the TV. Robbie is snuffling air through his nose as fast as he can, and sometimes he tries to open his mouth around Jeffy and gasp for more.

He needs a lot of air because the pounding I'm giving his ass is using up a lot of energy. The whole bed is shaking and rocking.

Robbie's ass is twitching fast around my cock, and the way it looks, his strong thighs spread wide and the thick column of my cock sliding in and out, is hypnotic.

I haven't shaved for several days, and I can see red marks around Robbie's neck, and the tops of his shoulders have been rubbed raw. He's my boy, and I can mark him up any way I want to.

That thought alone is enough to send me over, and as the female news anchor signs off for the night, I slam home and feel jet after jet as it fills the condom around my cock. Robbie moans as he feels each throbbing salvo in his rectum.

Terrence turns off the bedroom light as he removes our dessert dishes.

I'm not quite asleep, but Robbie has just turned the TV off, and he gives his old man a long, wet tongue kiss before he pads off into the kitchen to get himself another glass of milk.

I struggle deliciously against sleep for a while, waiting for Robbie to come back to the warm bed so I can wrap my strong arms around him.

That's the only way I can really sleep, with my son safe and tucked in place.

In the darkened room I stare out the window next to my bed and see the moon reflected in the swimming pool. The garage and the gardener's apartment are both dark across the patio, but it seems there is a fleeting shadow out there.

Suddenly I see the lights come on in Louis's apartment and two silhouettes in his window.

There will be hell to pay for this. Robbie knows how I hate his blowing the gardener when he is supposed to be in bed with me.

The Golden Boys
by R.J. March

He'd been living in the rented cabin for a week when it was put
up for sale. There was something about this place—the cabin and
the little town—that suited him, and the asking price for the
cabin was ridiculously low, even considering the money it was
going to take to refurbish the place and turn it into a year-round
residence. So he bought the little cabin and had the contents of
his apartment in Rochester moved to Cross Lake.

It wasn't much of a town, really—just a concentration of cabins like his own plus a few newer, sturdier brick homes built in the
'50s. There was a square of sorts, around which sat a convenience
store, a diner, a drugstore, and two bait shops. The village of Cross
Lake sat on the shore of the lake itself, and while fishing wasn't
considered an economic concern for the town, it probably was the
most popular pastime for its older inhabitants.

Mike Polsen bought himself a little boat. It looked like the ones
you see in paintings you can buy at Kmart—an old man and a little girl sitting together, rowing sweetly. It was wide and sun-
bleached white with huge long-handled oars. "You could put a little trolling motor on the back of that—anything bigger'd sink ya,"
said the old man who'd sold him the boat. "Got one the missus
bought me for Christmas some years back. Ain't worth a damn to
me, so's you can have it with the boat here. How's that?"

Mike had the summer free for the first time in years. He got
himself into a routine of having breakfast at the diner and then

going down to the stone beach to read the nearest local paper. There was a small island in the center of the lake, a green float that obscured the view of the other side. Boys went out there, the same pack he always saw floating around town, aimless, handsome. They all looked alike, like brothers, but they weren't, he figured, hearing them call each other by their last names, jostling one another outside the convenience store, leaning against the shining fenders of their cars. There were five or six of them, all roughly the same age, just out of high school, a couple of older ones, and two of the group actually were brothers, he gathered. Mike got them mixed up until one of them showed up on his doorstep with the trolling motor.

"I'm Kyle Briggs," the boy said, holding the motor and twirling it on the porch like a cane. "My grandfather said he was giving this to you." He eyed Mike suspiciously, as if Mike had connived the motor away from the old man. The boy peered through the screen into Mike's living room, which he'd outfitted with two linen-covered sofas and a coffee table made out of the door to an outhouse. The apricot-colored walls gave him away, he supposed, but the reflected light was lovely, coming from the candles he had lit as though awaiting a lover. The boy stood and stared, squinting.

"Looks like a magazine," Kyle said. He leaned the motor against the wall beside the door. "You fixed the dump up nice. Shoulda seen what it used to look like." He stopped and looked at Mike, smiling. "Well, I guess you kinda did," he finished.

Mike asked the boy in—being hospitable, he wondered, or testing the lake's waters? The boy was of medium height and had sand-colored hair. He had the thick, freckled arms of a baseball player, but he wasn't a big boy, so to speak. He shoved his hands into the pockets of his denim shorts, long and baggy, the tail end of his braided leather belt pointing in the direction of his groin. He sort of smiled, dallying on the porch until the screen door opened and he stepped inside. Kyle looked around himself before entering, as if being seen were not in his best interests. Mike noted all of this with a small amount of satisfaction.

He showed the boy around the house, reveling in Kyle's exclamations over the changes he'd produced in the shambled cottage.

"The upstairs is next," Mike said with a sigh, the task of it a burden he'd been putting off for a while. "I've got to get it insulated up there."

"My brother'd help you," Kyle said. "He does that kind of stuff. He works with my uncle. You should talk to him. He'd help you."

"Send him over," Mike said. They passed a side table covered with trophies, old ones that Mike had collected, all topped with male figures with wreathed heads, arms upheld in victory. Behind them on the wall was a black-and-white photograph of an old beau, naked and resplendent on a zebra skin, ass up, dark-cracked. The boy looked closely, then away, his face a mortified blank.

"Well, I ought to get g-going," Kyle said, taking on a bit of a stutter. He hurried to the door and stopped short. "Place looks cool," he said, turning to face Mike. "I like your things."

Oh, you do? Mike thought, standing at the door, watching the boy disappear into the dark beyond the light of the porch lamp.

Kyle Briggs lay on his back on Davis's bed, listening to his friend complain the way he always did about the lack of local pussy. The only babes, he said, were on the other side of the lake, like Jenna Krupp. Kyle was only half listening, mesmerized while watching Davis change clothes. Bill Davis had a man's body, more so even than Kyle's brother, Kevin. He stared at the easy hugeness of Davis's biceps, round and smooth as softballs, and his thighs, covered with dark and curling fuzz, the rest of him hairless and white so that he looked almost like a satyr. Down to dingy white briefs and talking about busting his nut, Davis had the swagger and appeal of an older boy.

Kyle was thinking of Mr. Polsen in his candlelit living room. He didn't look like a fag—more like a gym teacher, with those big tree-trunk legs and furred forearms, short-cropped dark hair silvering a little on the sides, standing at the door in a pair of shorts as tight as briefs and showing everything. Kyle had gone home that night, gotten himself into bed, and fallen asleep, only to dream about the guy, waking up with a boner he could not ignore.

"Pussy," Davis chanted. "Pussy, pussy, pussy."

"Pussy," Kyle rejoined, thinking, *Dick—big, thick, fat dick.* He could see Davis's cock in the yellowed front of his briefs, thumb-size, its covered head inching upward. Davis was a grower; his little uncut wiener grew as fat as a sausage at the state fair. He watched the boy brush at his future hard-on, pushing it down. It would eventually curl down the curve of his tight-bagged balls, trapped in the tightening cotton pouch.

"What do you know about pussy?" Davis said.

"Just your mom's," Kyle returned.

Davis jumped him, getting his armpit over Kyle's face. The boy resisted the strong urge to lick his friend there, the black and stinking beard that lined Davis's underarms. Davis didn't go for that kind of shit, though; none of that ass-grabbing stuff the other guys did so easily, without thinking, it seemed, as if it were all in-nocent and beyond implication. Davis was always the first to bust on the queer kid at school and on fags they saw on television.

But Kyle also felt the bone Davis sported and remembered a time when they'd jerked off together looking at a *Playboy* Kyle had stolen from his brother's room. He liked thinking about the awesomely high arc of Davis's spew, how droplets of it landed on Kyle's forearm, droplets he'd discreetly licked off when the other wasn't looking.

And he thought about other times, recent times: Davis's com-plaining about the pain of his hard-ons, the pain of needing to get off so bad, and then doing it as if it were a necessary course of na-ture, allowing, if only for a moment or two, Kyle to put his mouth on the cowled head and tongue into the sleeve of skin and taste the sweetness of his best friend.

"Shit," Davis muttered, rolling off of Kyle, hiding his erection against the mattress. Kyle wanted nothing more than to reach under his friend and squeeze the hell out of the big thing—he would have been entirely happy to jerk Davis off, just to see the thing shoot again. His own come spurted out in thick clots onto his belly, seeping into his bush; it didn't propel itself the way Davis's would. *He must get a face full every time he whacks,* Kyle thought.

Thinking about touching his friend's prick got his own going so that it started leaking, leaving dark, wet spots on the front of his shorts, ones he used to wear in gym class. He hated the way his cock dripped and made a mess of his underwear, betraying any excitement he tried to hide (though there were times when all that extra lube came in handy—like the night before, when he'd had his prong in his hand and Mr. Polsen on his mind).

Davis's white-clothed butt shone in a rectangle of sun that came in from the window beside his bed. Kyle watched the danc-ing dust motes over it, the suddenly interesting intricate weave of the cloth, the small flexes of Davis's butt muscles—glutes, he re-called his gym teacher calling them—as Davis did a little mattress humping. He had his arms up under his head, and Kyle saw him facing him, closed-eyed.

He wants it, Kyle realized. *He's all horned up, and he wants it. All I have to do is make the first move, so he doesn't feel like he's beg-ging for it.*

He put his hand on his friend's cotton-covered butt.

"Cut it out," Davis complained, making his glutes jump under Kyle's moist palm.

"One more time," Kyle said. "You aren't any closer to the inside of Jenna Krupp's pants," he added meanly.

"You're not a faggot, are you?" Davis asked, opening his eyes and looking into Kyle's.

"Are you?" Kyle asked back.

"Yeah, right," Davis snorted, rolling over and presenting Kyle with his briefs-encased throb.

Kyle moved himself up so that his head was within range of Davis's sweet-smelling crotch. Davis thumbed his waistband down so that his cock fell out, hard and bareheaded. It landed quite nearly in Kyle's mouth. All he had to do was stick his short stub of a tongue out to touch it, and he did, and Davis put his hand on the back of Kyle's head and drew his mouth down the thick stalk, pressing Kyle's nose into that lush black bush.

"Easy," Davis said, and Kyle raised his eyebrows in surprise— who needed to go easy here? Davis's hand on the back of his head was insistent. It drew Kyle down into that silky, wiry pad of hair again and again.

"Oh, man," Davis breathed, and his fingers went slack and curled against Kyle's scalp, almost a caress. His nuts had tightened even more than they had to begin with, hairy little walnuts that Kyle stroked with his fingers, rolling them around, pressing beyond them toward the soft, furry rut of Davis's ass crack, to lips that went rigid, as hard as a kiss from a maiden aunt.

He took his mouth off of Davis's thrusting bone. "I want to see it," he whispered, taking it in his fist, jacking the slack-skinned thing. He wished for his own forsaken foreskin; the sight of Davis's slipping back and forth over his purple dick head was enough to unleash a flow from his own untouched cock. He rode the mattress, anticipating Davis's blast, and came himself when Davis bulleted a rope of come that fell heavily into Kyle's hair from a thin slit of a piss hole.

Davis got himself up quickly—no lingering for him. "The guys are waiting," he said, not looking at Kyle, who wanted to lie about and enjoy what had just happened between them. But for Davis it had never happened. He started in about pussy again, looking for something to wipe the spit and come from the end of his dick with, and he talked about Jenna Krupp and how hot she was, and Kyle watched the dust dancing in the beam of sunlight falling uninvited through the window.

He was sitting on his porch, combating mosquitoes, wishing he had gone ahead and screened himself in when he'd had the opportunity earlier that year. There were a couple of citronella candles on either side of him and a book on his lap, but he wasn't reading, couldn't read. The darkness surrounded him. He had his bare feet up on the porch rail, flexing his toes until they cracked. Crickets chirruped. His balls dangled, spiked with stiff, straight hairs. He was just about ready to go inside and yank out a fuck film to masturbate with.

Fucking boonies, he complained to himself, regretting just now his exile in Virginville. *Sure, there are good-looking guys floating around, riding by. Stopping by, even, bearing gifts,* he thought, recalling the boy with the trolling motor. But where was he now, this Briggs boy? He recalled the boy saying, "I like your things." Not, apparently, "I like your thing." More's the pity. Mike sighed.

There was some rustling in the distance, some panting. *The boys playing a prank?* he wondered. Then there was some faint whistling, something nameless and tuneless that stopped short, and the rattle of keys, or something like it, and then the quick steps of something on four legs. It turned out to be a dog, a golden Lab striding toward him as if it had finally found home.

"Blanket!" he heard whispered sharply. The dog trotted up the steps and pushed its cold nose into Mike's crotch and bared balls.

"*Oof!*" he said, closing his legs fast.

"Blanket!" someone called, a man, a boy. Mike stood up and tried not to squint into the darkness that edged the dim light of his lamps.

"It's Kevin Briggs, Mr. Polsen," he heard. "Kyle's brother. Dan Briggs's grandson."

This Briggs boy was an older twin of his brother. His hair was only slightly darker, impossibly shorter, his frame slightly larger. He was wearing jeans and a shirt shorn of its sleeves, left open and untucked, revealing the soft gold of his torso. He had his brother's stubby freckled nose and light-colored eyes. Green? Blue?

Polsen couldn't tell from this distance. His hands in his pockets lowered his jeans so that his pubes were evident, as were the dipping lines that dropped from the boy's hips down to his crotch. He looked at Mike, who got up out of his chair, pulling at the crotch of his shorts to cover himself thoroughly.

"My brother said you needed some help."

Help? Mike thought. "Oh, yeah, the attic," he said, crossing his arms over his chest, squeezing his pecs together and giving himself some awesome cleavage. "There's next to nothing for insulation up there, and I wanted to get things squared away before the cold sets in."

"You planning on making this your home year-round?" the boy asked, making a face.

"I do," Mike answered. "I think it's nice here."

"I guess," Kevin Briggs said.

"Not enough action, huh?" Mike asked.

"Not nearly enough," Kevin affirmed, shaking his head. He drew his hands out of his pockets. Crickets came up singing, and the dog fell to the floor at Mike's feet in a tired heap. "Ain't much to do out here," Kevin said, rolling his shoulder like a pitcher doing seven innings. "No girls to speak of," he added quietly.

"I hadn't really noticed," Mike replied, getting a quick grin from the boy.

Getting the boy into bed was the easy part; getting him to do something there was a different matter. Kevin lay on his back, naked and hard, with his hands behind his head as though ready to take a nap. Mike heard the dog sniffing around the living room. The boy's cock was thick and not very long; sparse blond hairs grew on the shaft, which tapered sharply at its end, taking a left turn. His balls hung low in the V of his legs, resting on the sheets. He seemed very comfortable, looking at Mike through half-closed eyes. There was a shining thread of precome hanging from his dick.

Mike put his hand on Kevin's stomach. It was hard and hot and quivered under his touch.

"I ain't queer, you know," Kevin said. "There just aren't enough girls around."

"You do what you can," Mike said agreeably.

"I got this guy who sucks my dick. Friend of my brother's." He looked at Mike as if awaiting judgment or congratulations. "I want to fuck him, but he won't let me—says it's too big. Is my dick too big for fucking?"

Mike looked at it, thinking nothing was too big for fucking. He took it in his hand, squeezing the shaft, turning the pointed head purple.

"This," he said, "is perfectly suitable for fucking."

"You like getting it up the ass?" Kevin asked.

"Not too much," Mike admitted.

"Does it hurt?"

Mike shook his head. "Depends. You want to find out?"

"Fuck, no," the boy said, almost laughing.

Mike pinched out a droplet of dick honey and licked his sticky fingers. Kevin's eyes slitted. He bent his toes back and cracked them and spread his legs a little.

"When was the last time your little buddy sucked you off?" Mike asked.

"Oh," the boy said, "not too long ago. Sometime last week, I guess it was."

"You horny now?"

"Dude, I'm always horny."

Still spread-eagled on his back on the too-soft mattress, Kevin looked up at Mike with a mixture of manly lust and boyish impatience clouding his eyes. "I've got an idea. Why don't you just jerk me off?" the boy suggested.

"Are you sure that's that all you want?" Mike asked. "You could do that yourself."

"Feels good anyway," Kevin said, lifting his head a little. "Spit on it and jerk it off, man."

He did not mind doing the boy's dirty work. He'd gone long enough with his own in his hand, and Kevin's shaft fit in the curling cup of his palm the way Mike's own couldn't. At its base it had the circumference of a zucchini, narrowing to a gumdrop-size head that made Mike salivate. Perfect for fucking, he was thinking, if he were the one to be fucked. It had happened only a few times, countable on one hand, and that was by a Greek monk-to-be with similar-size equipment, though not so anus-stretching, its girth more evenly distributed from top to bottom.

He slid his slippery hand over the boy's little head and watched Kevin's legs twitch as he leaked a gob of lube from his tiny piss hole. Mike's grip was good and wet, sloppy-sounding, the noise turning up his own horniness a notch.

"Lick that shit up," Kevin said, his voice deep and manly, dirty and sexy.

If the boy ever learned what to do with his hands, he'd be one hell of a lay, Mike was thinking, lapping up the salty-sweet seepage from Kevin's tightened nuts. Kevin put his hand on the back of Mike's shaved neck and pressed the man's mouth down the long and thickening pole.

"Suck it, man," Kevin whispered, pumping himself down Mike's constricting throat. Mike's cock was trapped in his pants, aching for some kind of manipulation. He twisted his hips and managed to press himself against Kevin's naked shin, riding the hard bone of it.

He reached both hands under the boy's butt and spread his ass cheeks wide, stretching the hole open and causing the boy to yelp like a puppy lifted by its ears. Mike pressed on and fingered the gulping hole, moist already, as if lubed. He knuckled into the boy, making him squirm, taking the quivering stick into his hot mouth, imagining himself on his feet, dipping into the ankle-grabbing wiseass, fucking the daylights out of the Briggs boy. He found the boy's prostate hardening and felt his ass lips tightening. He finger-fucked Kevin the way he wanted to dick-fuck him: fast and hard.

"I'm gonna shoot!" Kevin shouted suddenly, filling Mike's mouth full of warm, creamy come. Mike got up on his knees, wobbling on the spongy bed, and pulled his cock out of his shorts. He spat out a little of Kevin's jizz onto his buzzing dick head and swallowed the rest, jacking hard on his long pole, thumbing the sensitive head. The boy stared—curious, smug—as Mike pulled on his fat-headed prong. He straddled the boy's thigh and rubbed his balls against it. The boy fingered his own still-hard pecker, pinching out the last drops from his nuts, offering the juice to Mike, who leaned over and took the come-covered fingers into his mouth.

"Oh," he said, squirting a thick, flying line of white all over the surprised boy. His body shook with the last few strokes, and Kevin wiped the come from himself with the corner of the nearest pillowcase.

"Sorry," Mike said.

"S'cool," Kevin said. "I just wasn't expecting it. You always shoot like that?"

"It's been a while," Mike shrugged.

The boy looked up at the ceiling. "We can get on that when the weather breaks." Mike looked up. The attic. He nodded, his dick dripping onto the boy's blond-furred thigh.

Kyle went out to the island by himself. He was supposed to meet Tim and Hal at Bill's house at 10 but came here instead. He felt weird about being with Davis and the other guys, like what they'd done that afternoon was all over his face—he always felt like that after they did stuff together. His penis rolled in his shorts. He sat down on the cool, damp sand, lay back, and looked at the stars. He couldn't get the thought of Bill Davis's prick out of his mind or get the feel and taste of it out of his mouth.

He stood and undid his shorts, letting them fall, feeling the night air between his legs like a caress. He was erect as he stepped into the water, treading carefully over the slippery rocks, small waves licking at his ankles, his shins, and his calves. He brought Bill and Mr. Polsen together in his mind, the two of them making love on Bill's twin bed, fucking and fucking, Polsen sticking his cock deep inside Bill and making the boy wail, Bill choking Polsen with his fat little pud.

The lake covered his cock like a warm mouth, and he felt the suck of it, the flow of it, and he came underwater without touching himself at all. On the shore, toward home, he heard the hoots and hollers of the guys. They were coming looking for him. He dived in and stroked through the black water, out to where he couldn't feel the bottom without going under, and he waited for his friends to come.

A Queer Turn
by R.J. March

I'd told this one to stay away. I didn't want him coming around anymore. He stood by the door, naked, his cock erect, defiant.

"You shouldn't be here," I told him, ignoring the hard-on, gathering all my resolve. Truth was, I loved his dick, worshiped it, even. It had a fat beginning and slimmed a bit, topped with a little cherry of a head, this little bullet not much bigger than, say, my thumb to the first knuckle, long like that and snake-headed. He could slip that thing up my ass with a little spit and ingenuity, and I'd be none the wiser until he'd push in and surprise me with his sudden width. He could wrestle me around until he had me topped, skewering me with his backward baseball bat, swearing and sputtering over my chest. He wasn't much more than five foot six, but he was a wiry little scrapper, and I did love the way he fucked me.

But no more. I had my reasons.

"Why you got to be this way?" he said with a smile, his voice soft from beer. He had his hands behind his back, one naked foot on top of the other, this little brown spray of hair at the center of his chest, nipples the color of dried blood. His torso was lean, white. I liked his hipbones, how they jutted out like a girl's. He made me feel like an old man, my soft beginnings of a beer gut, soft all over, it seemed, except down there. I saw him looking there. He liked that too, that he could do that to me. Simply watching him bend over to untie his boots could make me hard.

"Come away from the door like that," I told him, because it was open, and I didn't want anybody seeing him like that. Wasn't I in enough trouble already with this boy? He did not know the trouble he caused me, but he probably wouldn't have cared much even if he did.

He didn't move, so I turned off the lights. Then I went up to him and grabbed his arm and pulled him away from the door. I led him to one of the sofas and pushed him down onto it. I had a fire going and could see by the light of it his amusement at being pulled around.

"Why you got to act all mad? Tough guy," he said, tossing his chin my way, stretching himself out. He spread his legs so that I could see between them the little dark knot of his asshole, which he must have just shaved around, clearing the brush of curling dark hair that used to keep it hidden. His balls were tight, no slack-skinned low-hangers, and they were clean and pink. I'd never seen such hairy balls, and now it was all gone, and they were as bright and bare as billiard balls, his fingers playing over their new smoothness, stopping at a bit of stubble where he'd not gotten close enough.

"I told you to keep your mouth shut," I said, standing over him, my pecker making a sorry jut in my pants. I regretted my excitement and the control this boy had over me. Twenty years old, he hadn't any right to control me the way he did.

"Mike," he said. "Michael." His voice was smooth and easy; it wrapped around my prick and squeezed and pulled me to him. I fell over him, humping his crotch with my covered cock. I pushed at my jeans, freeing up my dick. I knew he liked the feel of it there, and I liked the drag of fuzz on his hard, channeled belly.

I got my hand down between us, feeling up that new baby skin, smearing his gut with my first batch of precome. He must have felt the wetness of it, because he pushed his hand between us too, then brought it back up to his mouth, licking his fingers noisily.

"More," he said when he was done, digging his hands into my armpits and trying to pull me up, wanting my leaking prick in his mouth. I straddled his head and felt his hands on my butt cheeks and let him suckle the fat end of my boner, siphoning the sticky self-lube my big bag of nuts produced, groaning with each salty taste of the stuff. I squeezed his face with the sides of my knees; I fucked into his mean little mouth. He started fingering my hole, getting all fidgety back there, and I turned to see him humping the air, his torpedo aimed for my ass crack. Slightly curved, the creamy white of old alabaster, its little arrowhead caused my butt hole to gape with want. I dragged my pecker out of his mouth, trailing a slimy line of spit and jizz down his chest until I felt the point of his banger just under my balls.

"You old pig," he said, his lips disappearing, his teeth showing. "Dirty old fucking pig."

I stopped dead, and he thrust into me.

"You fucking love my cock, don't you, Mike?" he said, grabbing the knobs of my nipples, twisting them. I sat back and felt the stretch my hole did, gobbling up the thick-based pole.

"I like it fine," I said, bouncing on it, feeling the pointed end going to work on my prostate. I tightened the grip I had on myself, the hard handful I was jacking. I stared at the fine hairs between his small, flat pecs. I put my hands there to steady myself and felt his chest give, and his face softened the way it always did when he was about to come. He'd get all clingy and push his face up into me and wrap his arms around me and tell me he loved me.

I was all set to gush on him and for him to get sweet on me, but neither happened. He whipped out of me and left my hole blowing smoke rings of wanting. He slipped out from under me, leaving me on wobbling knees. Suddenly he was in front of me, on his knees too, his little white ass in his hands as he spread his cheeks and showed me his newly bald cunt.

"You've had a change of heart," I said, the first thing that popped into my head.

"Shut up and pop me," he said, not looking back.

I got hold of his hips and pulled him back. My dick was wet enough to slip into his little pussy, but the rest was slow and painstaking, the boy gasping every now and then, grunting with every half inch. The light from the fire made our shadows flicker on the walls like dark flames, and the boy's back was wet, his knobby spine trail a little crooked, his shoulder blades jutting. I licked his back and listened to the sloppy handwork he did on himself as I pushed in and out of him with my man's dick, thick from bottom to top, as big around as a church candle, which was why he'd sworn off fucking with me and always wrestled for tops. "Horse dick," he'd said once. "Go find yourself another horse."

But now he was making amends. He straightened, pressing his back against my chest, his shoulder blades rubbing against my chewed-up nipples. I looked over his shoulder and watched my little man taking aim.

"Not on the slipcover!" I warned, sounding like the queen I never wanted to be.

"Oh, shit," he said, paying no attention to me. His little ass wriggled, impaled, as he worked his little butt button to hardness and jet-streamed an arc of come that cleared the sofa and landed with a splat on the floor. The next blasts lacked the force and speed of the first and fell in clotted clumps on the sofa's arm, and he slumped over the mess he'd made.

I pulled out and slid my hot, wet dick along the crack of his skinny ass, squeezing his little cheeks together for some friction. I lofted a shot of jizz that fell on the back of the boy's buzzed head, making him curse, and grunted the rest out on his wet, bony back.

I didn't see him for a while. His brother and his friends came around, though. I liked the quiet one, the one named Hal. There was something about the way he sat with his shoes off, his fingers woven between his toes, listening to his buddies' bullshit, staring at one and then another with a fascination that was not idle. He seemed to love them all: Kyle; cocky Bill Davis; the dark, mean-mouthed Tim. His light eyes would focus on Davis's brown ankles and then shift to the plaid hem of Kyle Briggs's showing boxers and then to Tim's hand going up under his shirt to scratch his muscled gut, his dark happy trail fanning out and spreading across his torso.

Now that it was getting colder, the boys started coming by more often, my little cabin becoming something of a clubhouse for them. I did not mind much, but it seemed to keep Kevin from coming over. Wasn't that what I wanted, though? Still, I could not say that I didn't miss his tapered boner and grunted curses.

His brother, Kyle, was looking at me and then at Hal and then at the fire. He lay back on the carpet, bending his legs at the knees. I could see into his shorts, dark with shadow. Tim raised his arms over his head, pulling up his T-shirt and baring his belly, its furred, hollow concavity. I'd seen him earlier in the summer wearing next to nothing and wanted to see him that way again. He grabbed another beer from the bag he kept between his feet. I'd offered to keep them in the refrigerator when he arrived. "Too far to walk," he'd said, half his mouth curling up with a grin. His eyes were chocolate-brown, dark-rimmed, with thick lashes. He was the least intelligent of the three but sometimes the most attractive.

He said: "You win all them trophies yourself, Mike?" He was referring to the table by the door to the kitchen, laden with trophies, men and boys with laurel-wreathed heads and upheld arms.

"It's decoration," Kyle said. "You wouldn't understand."

"And you do?" Tim laughed back.

"They look cool," Kyle said. The golden boys glistened as the real boys spoke, and I remembered a dream I had a couple of nights ago in which all these boys and Kevin too held me aloft in their arms, carrying me down to the lake and down the Briggs's long dock to throw me off at the end, only there wasn't any lake—

it had gone dry, nothing but a huge gape of a hole lined with the stink of dead fish and seaweed, buzzing with flies. They counted off, bellowing like Marines: "One! Two! Three!" On "Three" I felt their hands leave me, and I was airborne, falling, falling. I awoke before hitting bottom.

Tim stretched out his legs. He was wearing boots without any socks, reminding me of Kevin, and I wondered if Tim was the one Kevin told me about, the one he would go to whenever he needed to get sucked—the other sucker besides me, that is. I eyed the soft roll of denim that covered his crotch, worn white from touching, the way our pockets show the outlines of our wallets. His showed the two-by-four outline of his pecker. I was wondering when I was going to see the uncovered version.

When the beer was gone, the boys left. I went around blowing out candles, stoking the fire for the night, feeling a little heavy in the crotch. I stripped and turned on the shower. There was a knock on the door. I smiled to myself, thinking, *Kevin.* I wrapped a towel around myself and went to the door.

"Mr. Polsen?" I heard through the screen.

It was Hal.

"I think I dropped my wallet here," he said, glancing over his shoulder. He looked as though he was afraid he'd be seen. I stepped back and let the boy in.

"I was sitting over here," he was saying, walking over to the front of the sofa he'd leaned against earlier, playing with his toes. The living room was dark save for the light of the fire; the wallet lay just under the dust ruffle, easily found. He put it back in his pocket and stayed where he was, waiting.

I walked up to him, standing close. I could hear the rush of his breathing, the fear he had in him. His hands moved slowly toward the knot of my towel, and it fell to the floor.

"Well," I said, unable to come up with anything more worthy.

There was then a knock at the door that made me jump. The boy said easily, "That's Kyle. Let him in."

I went to the door, naked and swinging.

"Hey, Mr. Polsen," he said, sounding nothing like his brother. He was looking past me at Hal, who was taking off his denim jacket and elbowing out of his T-shirt, standing in the firelight like some golden boy. Kyle stepped in, mesmerized. He walked slowly to one of the sofas and sat down hard as Hal unbuttoned his jeans and let them fall down his slim hips.

I found myself with a dripping boner as hard as a candle in a cold, empty church. Hal knelt on the carpet. Kyle looked away from his friend, at me, his hands still on his lap.

"He wants to watch," Hal said. "Come on, Kyle."

Hal was in command. I stepped up to him and felt his hot breath all over my prick, his snaky tongue flicking at the buttery head. He hummed, taking me into his mouth. "Shit," I heard the Briggs boy breathe, and I leaned into Hal, filling him with my horse dick. He coughed and swallowed, and spit spilled out of his mouth in shiny ropes that fell on the carpet, his thighs, and my feet. He tongued into my piss slit and then let his lips stretch wide as I pushed myself down his throat.

The Briggs boy hauled out his cock and was stroking it, watching us. Again and again he'd lick his palm and jack his tiny-headed prick, an exact replica of his brother's. Had either of them any idea they had twin boners? Seeing it made me miss the older Briggs, and my ass felt empty. I peeked at Hal's crotch; it looked like a perfect fit. I turned around then, offering the boy my ass. He paused as if unsure of what to do next, and then I felt a few tentative licks and then his rooting nose burrowing into the fur of my crack. I looked over my shoulder at Kyle, who was staring intently at his friend's behind, working his fingers along the underside of his own tapering shaft, tickling himself just under the head.

"My dick's all lonely, Kyle," I said. "You want to come over here and keep it company?"

Hal unplugged his face from my ass long enough to explain that Kyle wasn't queer.

"And you are?" I asked the hungry-mouthed boy over my shoulder. All he did was nod.

"And you just like to watch?" I asked Kyle. He nodded too before clearing his throat and saying, "Just checking shit out. Somebody taking a shower?"

"That was supposed to be me," I said, distracted by Hal's deft tongue.

I made Hal stand up, and I lowered my ass and invited him in. I felt his slippery knob bump around blindly between my legs. When he found a soft spot, he pushed in, and I let out a yell.

"Does it hurt?" he asked. "Am I too big?"

"You're a regular giant," I told him. "Just take it easy at first."

He slowed his manic thrustings, rising up on his toes and gripping my hips, attempting some technique. Kyle spread across the couch, opening his legs. I told him he ought to take off his jeans, and he paused to consider the suggestion.

"Nah," he said. "I'm fine."

I watched him work on his cock, palming the head. The kid behind me was all over my back and panting, licking me all over, his hands roaming up and down the front of me, never lighting anywhere for more than a few seconds. I could not say, though, that it was not pleasurable; I was as stiff as I get and wishing he'd pay more attention to my dick. He touched it lightly, playing with the greasy head and making it hop. I squatted a little more to help him hit the right spot, and when he did I had to hang my head. His pesky fingers found my nipples then and stayed there, bless him, and I found myself about to come without the aid of any manual manipulations. I tensed and spilled like a Brazilian in a Kristen Bjorn film.

"Whoa," Kyle breathed.

"Shit," I muttered.

Hal continued his assault on my asshole, and I grinned and took it until he squealed and pulled out, squirting my back with a hot spray.

"That was cool," Kyle said. He started shoving his boner back into his pants.

"Aren't you going to get off?" I asked.

He shook his head. "Hal already told you, I'm not a queer."

I dreamed about Kevin. He was wearing my father's flannel bathrobe, nothing else. He walked around the house with a beer bottle, going from window to window, waiting for something, someone. It was raining, but there was sun too, and everything was golden, misty. Where was I? I don't even think I was there. It was like watching a movie. He stepped away from the window, swinging his beer bottle, his robe opening, coming untied, more and more of his beautiful skin being revealed, his little cock, thick and stubby save for that gumdrop head. He scratched beside his balls—they were still smooth, freshly shaved; I could smell the soap he used. *That's strange,* I thought.

He turned his back, and the robe fell off his shoulders. On his back, tattooed there, was a portrait of his brother. *That's kind of nice,* I decided, thinking that it was some kind of tribute to brotherly love. He turned around then, and he wasn't Kevin anymore but Tim, leering sexily. "I could use a rim job," he said, laughing. "I heard Polsen likes sucking ass."

Hal walked in then, naked, laughing too. "He likes getting fucked too."

"Who doesn't?" Kyle said, peering up over the back of the sofa.

And then a woman's voice from upstairs: "You boys ought to be sleeping!"

The friends all shushed each other, giggling like schoolboys. Kyle laughed out loud.

"Don't make me send your father down!" the woman shrieked.

The young men giggled more. Tim made farting noises, and Hal hooted.

"That's it!" I heard the lady say, and then there were footfalls on the stairs. A naked man walked into the living room, his cock hard. He was big and hairy, pot-bellied. He carried a belt in one hand, a big dildo in the other. He turned his face into the light. It was my face. He was me.

I opened my eyes. It was still dark. I felt warm air, breath, and flinched.

"You snore," Kevin said.

"What are you doing here?" I said, catching my breath. He'd scared the shit out of me, but I'd be damned if I'd let him know it. I felt his hand slip under the bedclothes and rest on the center of my chest.

"Were you dreaming?" he asked. His face was very close to mine, and I smelled his chewing gum. He licked the corner of my mouth. "Have you ever dreamed of me?"

"I don't remember my dreams," I told him, opening my mouth. His tongue slipped in, long and snaky. I thought about his brother, how he'd sat on the sofa with his dick in his hand, the pink tip of his tongue sliding across his lips.

He started undressing. *This is becoming complicated,* I thought. *I moved here because it was quiet and pretty.* Things were getting to be mathematical all of a sudden, and there were too many equations, too many young men.

"This place is crazy," I said.

"This place sucks," Kevin said. He knelt on the soft mattress, and I rolled toward him. I found his cock with my mouth. It was hard and smelled already of spit. Had someone already sucked him off, or had he been jacking off? It hardly mattered. It was dark, and I was horny again, and dick was the great pacifier. I closed my eyes and sucked him to the back of my throat.

In-Tents Encounter
by Christopher Morgan

Jack's hand was busy doing something that couldn't be mistaken for anything else. It pumped up and down in a steady long rhythm, and the length of each movement made me understand that the young man was hung the way only a Midwestern-raised football-playing giant can be. I sat there and watched, entranced, despite the light rain.

Though wet and chilled, I was reluctant to leave the vision of masculine perfection that lay stretched out in his own perfectly pitched tent, an ever-helpful lantern swinging inside. That lantern afforded me a perfect view of the goings-on: of Jack stripping down, reclining on a pile of packs and his bedroll, and then starting to work his huge cock.

I hate camping, but my friends had all implored me to get out of my apartment, out of the city. I ask you, Why on earth did I move to the city if I didn't want to get away from the damn woods? I was raised in Mississippi—and that state's got enough woods, swamps, meadows, and lakes to shake a stick at. If stick shaking is your kind of thing. Me, I prefer shaking martinis and double mocha lattes.

But I was tired of the bars and the dance clubs, meeting one glossy gym boy after another—hard pecs, firm abs, and empty skull. One-night stands were becoming too much of a hassle—I'd enjoy fucking them but couldn't stand to have breakfast with them too. I kept having wet dreams about the kind of fellows I knew at home—strong and quiet and shy, with shaggy hair and strong bodies that were tanned by the sun, not by lamps.

So gradually my friends convinced me to head off to this gay campground. They eagerly loaded me down with a borrowed tent and sleeping bag and a battered knapsack full of essential camping things. I personally provided myself a cooler full of beer—I knew what was essential to me! I also brought along condoms and lube.

But the camping trip didn't get off to a sexy—or happy—start. I tromped around getting lost for about two hours and then spent another two hours trying to figure out how to pitch the "easy to use" tent. I finally pitched it, all right—I pitched the fucking mess into the woods with a string of curses.

I was starting to repack all my supplies when I heard someone approaching through the trees. I looked up in time to see a huge guy. The man who stepped into my little clearing was the stud of my wet dreams. Easily six and a half feet of hard-workin', load-liftin' muscle, well-dressed in the kind of layered sensible clothing I really should have brought instead of my chic designer pseudo-country getup. His feet were laced into strong leather hiking boots, and his long hairy legs were strong and firm and deeply tanned. A baseball cap was tilted back on his forehead over a shock of almost-white blond hair.

He was holding a crumpled pile of green canvas: my tent. "Did you lose this?" he asked. My heart melted, and my cock hardened. "I found it back in those trees. Is it ripped or something? I've got a patch kit in my pack; you can borrow it."

I managed to figure out how to talk after a moment or two of just admiring him. "Um," I said brilliantly. "I was—it's not torn, it's defective!"

"Oh?"

"Yeah. It won't stand up by itself," I said quickly. And I almost blushed, because it must have been obvious that other things in my campsite did not share that problem!

But he ignored my clearly defined hard-on. "Well, maybe I can give you a hand," he suggested. And without a single bit of help from me, damned if he didn't toss that stupid thing down, tie a few knots, and flip a few sticks into position, and—*boom*—there it was: my home away from home.

I was very impressed—and anxious to keep this guy around. We exchanged introductions, and I found out that his name was Jack, he was 22 years old (my 30-year-old body experienced a huge pang of guilt and longing), and he was from Virginia.

Then he asked, "I was wondering if you'd mind if I pitched my tent over there?" He pointed to a clear spot directly across from my tent.

Mind?

I shook out my borrowed sleeping bag, wondering if it smelled too funky for a guest, and then decided that he wouldn't mind once I was sucking his cock. While he set up camp, I scarfed down some gourmet freeze-dried camping food. *How,* I wondered, *do the ad copywriters sleep at night, knowing their prose sells such a wretched product?*

By the time night fell, I could smell something delicious in the campsite across from mine and knew that the man of my dreams also cooked. Grabbing two cans of beer from my six-pack, I took them over as an offering.

But after I'd filled myself on his scrumptious grilled chicken and beans and we'd finished the beers, I was no closer to fucking him than before. All my polished lines fell flat, and all my innuendo seemed to go straight over this young man's head.

Wondering if he had a steady boyfriend back home, I gave up and slunk back to my tent. My cock was as stiff as a log and twice as ready for action as ever before. And as I snuffed out my lantern and rolled over in the darkness, I saw Jack's clearly outlined form against the side wall of his tent!

I hadn't realized that these canvas homes away from home could so clearly show what was going on inside them. But the minute I turned off my light, I could see every inch of Jack's outline, from his broad chest to his shock of hair to the jutting salami that extended from his body.

Oh, yeah, Jack was well-hung.

I watched, fascinated, as he rubbed his cock and ran a hand over his nipples. I scooted onto my side so I could drag my cock out of my jeans—it had been too cold to undress all the way. My cock fell into my hand with a heavy slap, and I knew the chances of my lasting as long as Jack were slim. I fisted my cock and stifled a groan as I felt the familiar heat of my own hand. But I had to do something—it was jerk off or cream right in my pants.

So I watched as Jack took a good long time to play with himself. I tried to follow all the movements as well as I could. That hunching movement must mean he was cupping his balls. My hand felt warm and rough over my own balls, and as I gave them a gentle squeeze, I had a sudden image of sucking Jack's heavy sac into my mouth and tugging on the twin orbs until he had to stuff his big fat cock back into my mouth.

But it was when he got up on his knees and turned away—making a large dark lump in the tent—that I realized that Jack was showing me his hot and hairy ass, spread wide and humping up and down as he fucked his own fist! I gasped and shot a load of jism straight onto my tent wall and almost screamed with pleasure. Just the thought of the crack of Jack's ass made me want to run over there and pounce!

But I didn't. I shoved my wet cock back into my pants and watched him until he shot his load as well. Then he finally snuffed his lantern, and I was alone in the complete and silent darkness. I fell asleep almost immediately, despite my frustration.

I was dreaming about large ferocious bears romping through the forest when I felt something furry pass my nose. I jerked away in panic, thinking, *Oh, my God, I* am *gonna be eaten by a bear!*—and then I opened my eyes. What was before my face was not some woodland creature but a carnivore that was bred in my neck of the woods!

It was my neighbor, Jack, and he was lying down next to me! I decided I was still dreaming.

"I can't sleep," he said, his voice low and urgent. "Wanna get it on with me for a while? It always helps me relax, you know?"

Yes, it had to be a dream. But I wasn't one to waste any dream as sweet as that one, so I reached out for him, forgetting that I was wrapped in layers of polyester and cotton. He chuckled and unzipped me, one zipper at a time.

By the time he got to my jeans, I had my mouth on his mouth and my hands in his fine light hair. He tasted like ginger and mint. I breathed him in as he grasped hold of my cock, and then I realized that this was no dream. Jack was really right there with me in my tent! I fumbled for my lantern and snapped it on. I was right—he was real!

"I've wanted you since the first time I saw you," I whispered, groping for his clothes. To my surprise and delight, he was wearing only a light pair of shorts. I ran my fingers through his luxurious chest hair and nibbled on his neck. "You're so hot!"

"You're the hot one," he murmured back. "I want to see you out of these jeans!"

We obliged by stripping down completely and exploring each other's bodies, hands entwined sometimes, legs wrapped around one another. Wet kisses seemed especially loud in the mountain air, and we shared a lot of them, making obscene sucking noises that must have scared every critter for miles.

Somehow I managed to grab a strip of condoms, and I tore one open while I was sucking on one of his nipples. But as soon as I had it in my hand, I dived for his huge cock and slurped around it, sucking the head into my mouth with the slow, deliberate movements I'd promised myself earlier.

But that wasn't enough for him—he moved and shifted so that I was on my back and then turned around so that he could take my cock into his mouth! I remembered seeing that he liked to come belly-down and moaned around the thick cock head. I felt the pressure of the rubber as it slid over my cock and then the sheer ecstasy of his hot, wet mouth following it.

We devoured each other for what seemed like hours, and for once I was grateful that we'd both jerked off earlier. I was able to hold back, even when his sucking mouth smacked off my cock and started nuzzling my nuts. I just did the same, and we played follow-the-leader on our crotches.

Soon we had to roll over so I was on top, and the pleasure of sliding my cock into his willing mouth became too much to bear. He was making little desperate sounds as I sucked him now, and I knew that he was eager to be on his hands and knees again, so I pulled up sharply and drew my cock out of his throat.

"Your ass," I hissed, slathering his spit all over the length of my cock. "I'm gonna come in your ass!"

"Oh, yeah!" he cried, twisting up onto his knees. "Drive it into me hard! Make me feel it!"

His hairy butt hole was exactly the way I'd imagined it except even more inviting than I could have believed. One quick thrust, and I was sliding through him like an oiled ear of corn through a tight fist. And as I sank deep, he squirmed and panted and started to push back at me, taking me all the way to the root.

"Fuck me, man, fuck me," he chanted, slamming back at me with every word. I didn't have to move—I could let him do all the fucking. The pressure in my nuts was building and building until I was ready to explode, so I grabbed on to his hips and began to slam back at him.

"Take my cock," I growled, shaking with need and desire. "And shoot your scum all over the fucking ground! Show me how much you like it!"

"Oh, yeah, oh, yeah," he whined, wiggling and fucking. "You got it, you got it!" He gave a short shout of almost anguish, and then I felt his butt muscles clenching at my cock, drawing the come out by the gallon! I shot into him like a fucking cannon, even as his cock exploded into the condom that had slipped almost halfway off.

I found the sight of it, dripping with my spit and full of his spunk, very erotic.

I gathered him in my arms, and we sank down into the smelly sleeping bag.

Somewhat belatedly I remembered to turn off my flashlight. I should have remembered sooner. From not too far away came the unmistakable sound of two men applauding. I think I blushed until dawn!

Traction
by Lew Dwight

My buddy Lew, crazy Lew.

Skinny, absurd Lew. Nuts.

I wouldn't have him any other way.

Always showing me something new, that Lew. Something risky.

He can take a bad, bad situation and make it…pay.

Take the accident. Or its aftermath, rather.

We were on our Kawasakis returning from a motorcycle convention (not bad people, bikers—if you like sweat, tattoos, and attitude). We were almost home, turning down a one-way street a few blocks from our neighborhood. I was riding out ahead of Lew and to his left. Suddenly there's a van coming the wrong way. I remember seeing only the out-of-state license plate before I pitched forward into silence. Luckily, I had my helmet on. Luckily, we were going only about 25 miles an hour. Still too fast to plow into a van.

I remember bits and pieces—the ride in the ambulance, the utter calm…except for Lew's falling apart beside me. He wasn't even permitted to touch me. They didn't know what was wrong with me yet.

A long stay in the hospital. Concussion, contusions. Two broken arms. That's right, two. Lucky me. At least I wasn't killed.

Immobilization: mummified arms hanging from a contraption overhead. Bedridden, only a paper napkin for clothes. Tube in my dick. Thought I'd lose it. On top of it all, a warthog of a nurse.

She has the lily-white uniform, a silver cross around her neck (this is Mercy Hospital, so no surprise there). She's efficient, prompt, caring—but hates fags (secretly). She can't help it. She thinks she's doing the right thing, monitoring my visitors. I long for Lew's buzz cut and toothy smile to appear at the door. I long for his long, lean body.

She has this uncanny habit of appearing out of nowhere, like a poltergeist, whenever Lew is visiting. Never when it's family, friends, or relatives, with whom I can chat unbothered, uninhibited. But as soon as Lew is there, sitting on the edge of the bed, attempting (at last!) to slide his leather wristband under the sheet...here comes the warthog. The wildebeest.

I shouldn't talk about her like that. She's been a kind lady, grandmotherly even. It's not easy to take care of a crabby, horny queer with his arms stuck up in the air and a tube stuck up his dick. She must feel saddled with me.

Lew just puts his hand back in his lap and sits there glumly.

"How are those arms doing?" the warthog says.

"The arms are fine, OK?"

"Let me see those fingers move."

I sigh. "All right." My fingers wiggle at the top of my casts like the legs of a half-dead centipede.

"There, see?" I say. "Fine."

"Just checking. *You.* Don't sit on the bed. How many times do I have to tell you? You might pull his tube loose."

Lew slides his skinny ass over to the chair.

Bitch, I *want* him to pull the damned tube loose!

We say nothing as the warthog flings herself about the room doing I don't know what, but it's always something that needs to be done. She's so official. Hospital nazi.

She's like this until Lew goes away. Then I don't see her until designated hours.

After a miserable three weeks of this, I could scream...and finally do.

Every so often I get to move the few joints in my upper body that haven't been smashed. Physical therapy, they call it. I weep with gratitude every time. But then it's back to traction, arms stuck up in a perpetual gesture of surrender. *I give up!*

It's back to the unwanted (but necessary) attentions of the warthog-in-waiting. I want to say, "Can I *please* jack off?"

One time she shows up to check the tube, and my hard dick has burst out of its tape restraints. Imagine Gulliver waking, all pissed off, in the land of Lilliput with all those strings binding him to the ground. He heaves and rolls and breaks his bonds, seething mad.

Such is my dick.

"Lew!" it sings. "Oh, Lew! Where are you, buddy? I miss your soft palm, your silky mouth, your skinny ass…"

"Oh, dear," the warthog says, pulling back the sheet.

I am near tears. I am wearing only a paper napkin. My dick has done nothing but piss through a tube for weeks. And it hurts like hell when it gets hard and starts to pull against the blue of the tape, finally ripping itself free to lie there, heaving, like some beached sea creature yearning for the deep.

"Just leave it, damn it! I don't want your stinking hands on my dick again!"

"Now, honey, you know you have to wear your tube. Other-wise, you'd just—"

"So I'd piss myself. You can change the sheets instead of putting your stinking hands on me. And that shitty hair-pulling tape! Never again! Do you hear me? Never again!"

But what am I going to do? Slap her out of the way like a horse-fly? My arms are not mine. They are in sarcophagi dangling from pulleys. I give up! I surrender!

Nothing makes poor Gulliver shrink and shrivel and submit to his bonds like that warthog's touch. Expertly she gets the tube back into place with fresh tape strapped on. As if Gulliver has to submit to a perpetual enema.

"This is sexual abuse. I am going to sue this fucking hospital."
She reads me the riot act.

"You're the one who's abusive. I have a job to do, and I mean to do it, or I'll have the head nurse down here. She'll take care of you. I don't have to take this from you."

But I do. I have to lie there and take it. I just turn my eyes up to my casts, concentrating on my pink wiggling fingers.

Below, Gulliver tries to speak through the tube: "Wew! Oh, Wew! Hepp me, Wew!"

Next time Lew shows up, he's beaming.

Usually he's hollow-eyed, depressed. Our conversation is strained. He goes home and jerks off. I piss through my tube.

But this time there's that toothy idiot grin of his. His face is flushed with good humor. He's wearing cutoff Army shorts, a baggy T-shirt, sneakers with no socks. Almost naked. He puts a bouquet of stinking flowers on the bedside table.

"What the hell are you so happy about?"

He just smiles, looks out the door, closes it.

"She'll just show up and open it again," I say. "She can smell you, you know."

He whips something out of his back pocket and holds it up before me: a wedge of wood.

He slides the wedge into the crack under the door and kicks it into place.

"Lew, what are you doing?"

He comes around and situates himself on the bed beside me. Just the weight of his ass sinking into the bed sends a chill through my guts.

"Oh, Lew." I start to cry. "Do you know what that wildebeest did today?"

He just softly, softly presses the palm of his hand against my mouth. He thumbs away my tears.

I have this overwhelming need to hug him. But like a mad dog running to the end of its tether...

I give up! I surrender!

He slides the other hand under the sheet, then up under the napkin.

His warm hand on my hairy belly.

It's like, *Oh, my fucking God.*

I puff and hum against the palm of his hand.

We stop and listen for a moment. It feels like my heart's in my brain. Like barbarians are beating the ram against the castle door.

Lew's hand passes over my chest, tweaks my hot nipples, then down, down it goes to within inches of my pubes. Something kicks in my groin and turns over.

Lew pulls the sheet back.

Lew pushes the napkin up to my neck.

Aah! Air against my body. I feel like I'm hanging naked by the arms. I *am* hanging naked by the arms.

"Lew, don't. The warthog."

He's smiling so hard, it breaks my heart.

He's smiling because he sees how my dick has swollen against the tape and is trying to spit the tube out. Like a fish thrashing against the hook.

Lew picks at the edge of the tape. It hurts gloriously.

He begins to peel back the tape. The swelling of my dick does the rest, like an insect shedding its husk.

Free!

Sort of.

Still imprisoned in my cast, hung up in my armor.

He begins kissing my hairy belly gently, like he's picking up crumbs with his lips.

I have this urge to pull myself up for a better view.

I can't. I just lie there.

"Lew. Don't."

He gives me a hurt "Why not?" look, his eyes big as chestnuts.

"I can't. Look at me. I'm helpless."

This brings the smile back to his face, the shit-eating grin.

"Lew. You fucker, you."

He rubs his palms together before his face.

"You bastard, Lew."

He resumes his excruciating kisses. "Ugh! Ugh!" I look up at my casts, wiggle my fingers.

My dick is thumping against me, seeping and oozing like a running sore.

"Lew, I can't."

As he kisses the lower part of my abdomen, I arch my back, pulling against my helpless arms.

"Lew!"

He grips my cock at the base, stands it up next to his cheek—and I come all over the place.

I come hotly and repeatedly.

I feel like I'm melting. Lew laughs and begins to eat the stuff off my belly, suck it out of my pubes. He wipes his face and licks his fingers.

The he leans up, kisses me—his mouth is hot and wet. We tongue each other, my semen passing back and forth between our mouths. We swallow.

"More. It's been weeks, Lew."

He climbs, sneakers and all, onto the bed with me. He straddles me with his arms and knees, and soon all I can see is the top of his buzz cut. My dick finds itself engulfed in something warm and fluid, and I just hang there and fuck Lew's head. Immediately there's the telltale throbbing, then the knocking at my asshole—then out my dick it goes. Lew sucks it all down and squeezes out the last few drops with his fist and nurses the throbbing away.

"Oh, Lew."

He comes up for air, and we swap spit and come again until our throats burn with bitterness.

My dick is still hard and hot as a missile.

"More, Lew. Gimme some ass this time."

Lew gets off of me and sheds his skimpy clothing beside the bed. He's looking at me the whole time. I haven't seen his body in so long. His dick looks as promising as dessert, glossy and ripe and curved.

He clambers onto the bed and gets on his knees. He takes my dick in one hand, stands it up on end—and sits right on it. His hole is tough and dry at first, but the more he grunts and writhes, the sooner it closes like a fist right over my oozy cock head. Lew looks up at the ceiling as he works my dick deeper into his ass. His unshaven throat swallows, and he hums as we fuck. Soon we're able to drag it out and shove it back in. I fuck and buck against my restraints. This is when the knocking begins.

We stop and look over at the door. The knob is being turned back and forth. The wedge stays tight. Lew turns and gives me a big grin.

"Lew!"

He just eases his ass back onto my cock. He closes down over it and then pulls back up. Each stroke makes my joints ache.

The knocking resumes.

"What's wrong with this door?"

"Quick, Lew!"

But Lew fucks slowly. He closes his eyes and opens his mouth like a baby bird awaiting the worm. We make no noise. His ass gives like a cunt. It yields and unfolds, engulfs the length of my long-neglected cock.

"Are you all right in there?"

I attempt to sit up but am checked, strung out between fucking Lew below and my immobilized arms overhead.

"Yes, I'm all right. Now would you go away?"

"Who's in there with you?"

We can hear the warthog pushing against the wedge.

"Lew, you'd better get off!" I whisper.

Lew just picks up the pace. The hospital bed rocks as my cock slides in and out of his ass with some resistance.

"Doesn't that hurt?"

He closes his eyes and whips his buzz cut back and forth. I melt into his ass until I'm sliding freely in my own ooze. "Fuck, Lew. I just came."

Lew quickly gets up on his knees and jacks furiously on his dick, his leather wristband blurring. There's a buffeting sound against the door. He cranks his head back, thrusts his hips forward—and ejaculates five long streams onto my neck, chest, and belly. He finishes dribbling come onto my stomach, then goes to work with his mouth, cleaning me off. More come-tasting kisses. His come is stronger, almost yeasty. We swallow all the evidence.

"I'm going to get maintenance!"

Suddenly it's quiet at the door.

Lew leans up and lets me suck the last drops off his meaty, half-limp dick. He smells ripe now. He pulls away, gets off the bed, gets his shorts and shirt back on.

"Lew, you're such a good boy. Now cover me quick."

Lew pulls the moist napkin down under my armpits. I hang there, relieved, as a louder knock comes at the door.

A man's voice says, "Open up!"

Lew reaches down, pulls out the wedge, and slips it into his back pocket. Then he calmly opens the door to admit them.

"Bye," I say. "And thanks for the flowers."

Lew slips out between the nurse and the custodian.

"What seems to be the problem?" the man says.

"Nothing as far as I know," I say.

"But a minute ago the door was—"

"My tape seems to have slipped off again, nurse. Could you, please?"

The custodian goes away.

The warthog fumes into the room, ranting. "What little trick were you trying to pull in here?" She whips back the sheet.

"Trick?" I say, then sink back between my helpless arms.

When Luddy Goes
by R.J. March

When Luddy got his Camaro, he drove to my house and sat out in front, smoking cigarettes until one of my little brothers saw him there and said, "Jason, your friend's out there." We weren't friends anymore, hadn't been since he started going out with Erin Moyer and we got into a stupid fight over who was going to Darien Lake. All of a sudden we were supposed to be the Three Stooges or something. I didn't even like Erin Moyer—she was pushy and a bitch and talked with her tits. She used her tits the way other people use their hands.

Luddy said, "Hey, Tuck," and I just looked at him. He'd called me "fag" the last time we talked, and Erin was there, and she sort of laughed, making her tits jump just a little for emphasis. There was a split-rail fence around our yard and some flowers my mom had planted. I stepped through them and leaned on the shaky railing, looking at Luddy's new Camaro. I didn't know shit about cars; they were just a means of getting around.

Luddy leaned out the window. "Happy birthday," he said, because I'd just had one a couple of weeks ago.

"Me 'n' Erin broke up last night," he said, and I was thinking, *Is that my birthday present?*

"We could go for a ride," he said. He looked through the windshield. He flicked his naked-lady air freshener with his finger. I could hear my mom telling my brothers to knock it off. Luddy had his sleeves rolled up, his arm flexed. I could see his vaccination scar, a little brown crater set into the balled muscle of his shoulder.

"We could go to the driving range," he suggested, because he knew I loved hitting balls around like that.

"Left my clubs in Gossage's car," I said, watching his face. I knew he didn't like Kenny Gossage any more than I liked his girl-friend—his ex-girlfriend. My clubs were actually in the garage.

Luddy kept looking through the windshield, his arms across the steering wheel.

"Get in," he said.

"I've got to tell Mom," I said, running back to the house. "Luddy's here," I yelled through the door. "Be back later!" And I started back for Lud and his car, and I heard my mom yelling for me not to be too late.

I got into the Camaro, and Luddy turned to me then, and for a split second I thought he was going to kiss me or something, and in that fraction of a second I wanted to hug him and kiss his whole stupid face, his sharp little nose, his foxy mouth. He'd got-ten a haircut—his black hair trimmed down to a mean quarter inch. He looked, I thought, like a little Marine, and I told him so. He twitched a corner of his mouth and started the car, and we got going.

I had a feeling I knew where he was taking me. I didn't say any-thing, though—I wasn't sure what I could have said at that mo-ment. I was feeling everything just then, sitting in that bucket seat, listening to the noise the air made and the crickets and the car and Luddy humming something, then saying he was getting a stereo put in over the weekend.

I sat with my back to the door, which seemed a little dangerous and all, but I wanted to look at Luddy. It seemed like I hadn't seen him in months. I wanted to say to him, "Luddy, where have you been?" But I didn't really care to know. The thought of him bon-ing the Moyer chick was enough to tie my stomach in knots, which in turn made me sick of myself for being so queer.

I couldn't help it, though—I freaking loved Luddy, and I felt like a freak admitting it to myself, but it was the truth. I never would have told him—or anyone else, for that matter—but I think he knew it anyway.

He was bulking up with weights and protein drinks, and I could see how much he was loving his new body. He put his left hand up under his shirt, touching his belly, and I saw all the hair he'd had there was gone, and I wondered if he'd also trimmed clear around his nipples where it had grown like a dark fringe.

He turned onto Lakeshore Road, then pulled sharply into the Mayflower parking lot, going all the way back to the woods. On the other side of the trees was the Wysockie orchard. He turned off the car.

It was my mom who said Luddy had a foxy mouth. "See him grinning there, the way a little fox does? His lips disappear, and there's just that sneaky little line left." Then she went into her bedroom and pulled out a fox fur stole that had the little head and feet still on it, and we all agreed that Luddy was like a fox, and his face went red, and we all laughed, and under the table Luddy put his bare feet on top of mine.

I followed Luddy through the trees, watching his behind. He wore Levi's, filling them, and an old blue work shirt like my dad used to wear. I was wondering, stepping over a fallen tree, if Luddy had a boner yet. I had a big, aching one that banged the front of my khakis, and I wanted him to turn around and see it and smile the way he smiled, telling me everything was the same. He didn't turn, though, and continued marching through the woods as though we were on some sort of schedule.

He said without warning, "Are you going back to school?"

I didn't know. I didn't care at that moment. "My mom wants me to," I told him.

He didn't say anything else, but he slowed up some, and soon we were walking side by side. I could make out the rows of trees up ahead and the fence that marked Wysockie's land.

When we were kids we'd hike to the orchard and steal around like spies, climbing the trees and throwing apples at each other. One day we found a shed in overgrown weeds, for storage or something, in the middle of nowhere. Inside there'd been a moldy stack of dirty magazines. We flipped through the pages, and Luddy suddenly flicked out his cock. It was hard and pinkish, its head like a German soldier's helmet, rounded like that, with this deep split at the top. It wasn't so big then, his cock, not as big as it was now. When puberty hit for Luddy, it pretty much focused on his crotch. It seemed that only recently had his body started catching up with his dick. He stayed short, though, but he was getting broader, thicker. Still, he could go a week without needing to shave.

The last time I was with Luddy was the best time. Used to be, we would just jerk off looking at something—a magazine, a movie he got from his brother. We progressed to jerking each other off, which was nice enough—awesome, actually—having that big thing in my hand. The last time, though, Luddy put his hands on my chest and played with my nipples and stuck his dick right between my legs, pushing me back against the wall in his bedroom, dragging his dick in and out of the pussy he made of the inside of my thighs, my own dick rubbing up against his hard, flat, hairy belly.

Out in the open Luddy picked up his pace again, and I straggled behind, my cock wobbling, the sensitive head tingling with every step I took, flickering inside my baggy pants. I looked down and noticed an embarrassing arrangement of wet spots to the left of my fly.

"Luddy," I said, stopping. He kept walking, a man on a mission. "Luddy," I said, louder. He looked over his shoulder. The sun was going down. Crows cawed in the trees. I unzipped my khakis, and my dick popped out.

"What the fuck, Tuck," he said, looking around as though there were actually someone around to see.

I pulled my shirt up over my head and threw it on the grass. I unhooked my pants and let them drop. Sitting on my shirt I got my sneakers off, breathing up the smelly stink of my bare feet. I put my pants out on the grass and got up on my knees, waiting for Luddy, who stayed where he was, hands in his pockets. A flock of blackbirds lifted off a nearby tree, making Luddy flinch. He pulled his hands out of his pockets and swung them around a little, reminding me of a swimmer warming up. He walked slowly over to me.

When he was close enough, I grabbed the front of his jeans.

"I missed you," I said to him.

I saw a smirk twist his mouth.

"Missed my dick," he said.

I had. Tall and feverish, it fit the cup of my hand but would not be enclosed by my fingers. The shaft was goose-fleshed, and a few stray black hairs grew halfway up it. His balls were snugly wrapped in a nearly bald bag that did not ever slacken or swing the way mine did when it was warm. His pubes were amazing, though, the richness of black, the sheen, the smell. The hair that surrounded his cock was long and smooth, very nearly straight, looking like you'd want to run a comb through it.

"This ain't right," I heard Luddy say. I pressed my fingers against his hardened cock, knowing I was squeezing out a bunch of precome to mess up his shorts. I wished I leaked like Luddy— he didn't need to spit to jack off, his dick supplying all the lube he needed. He wouldn't let me taste it, though, leastwise not by licking it as it sprang from that deep slit.

"It's wide open," he said. He hugged himself. I pulled on the tab of his zipper. "Anyone can see us," he whispered. His pants came down.

"Nobody's looking, though," I said.

His dick appeared like a magician's wand. I slid my fist down it, watching the drool it made. I put my tongue on his thigh, my forehead pressed against his nuts. He bent his legs and lowered his hips, sliding his dick on my cheek. He pushed me back, and I lost my balance, and he stretched himself out on top of me. He lifted up once and shot a gob of spit between us, placing it just over my navel. He put his face on my shoulder and turned away so I couldn't kiss him, but he let me put my hands on him, and I played with his rear end and backside, the new breadth of his shoulders, the silky pit hair under his arms.

My own dick was being roughed up by Luddy's bunched-up jeans. I didn't care—I was blown away by the feel of Luddy's body on mine, the slick drag of his big dick and the noise it made. I felt his mouth open against my shoulder as he sank his teeth gently into the soft flesh there.

His hands moved up to cradle my head, and I heard him say my name. He started fucking my gut more quickly, his sticky head knocking against my rib cage. His face turned toward mine, and he sniffed around my ear. He was breathing hard.

"Turn over," he said.

I went on my belly and felt a warm drop of spit land between my spread ass cheeks. He slid his fat wiener up against the slippery channel, and he laid himself over me again, pressing his face between my shoulder blades. He humped me, just under my tailbone, while his fingers played in my hair, and I ground my dick against my khakis, against the earth. Every time he slid his pecker against my asshole, I wanted to get him in, but he wasn't going there, and he chugged over it, pile-driving against my fanny, licking up my back, saying my name.

He didn't say he was on the verge of coming, but I knew it was about to happen. His body went hard, and he seemed to stop breathing, and I felt a sudden warm wetness on the small of my back. I rolled us over so that I was laid out on top of him, on my back, with my legs spread and dick lunging skyward. I buried a finger up my butt and pulled on my sore, rocky prick, tipping my head back and finding his cheek, putting my lips against it, and his hands came around and stroked my belly, digging into my pubes, up and onto my nipples. I dug my heels in the grass, arched my back, and fired off a half-dozen rounds of thick, clotted come.

Luddy disappeared, didn't come home from work one night, and the next day his mom called my mom, wanting to speak with me.

"He didn't say anything to you? Didn't mention taking off with anyone?" I could hear the hysteria that tightened her voice and made her breathless.

"No, Mrs. Ludlow," I said. "He didn't say anything to me about anything."

"Who is this Jay he's been hanging out with?" She sounded ready to cry. I looked at my mother, who was eyeing me like I had something to do with all of this.

"I don't know him," I said, and I really didn't know him, had never heard of him.

Mrs. Ludlow said, "Thank you, Jason," and hung up.

I hung up too, and my mother put her hand on my shoulder and said, "Where do you think he'd go, Jason?" and I shrugged because I really didn't have a clue.

Gossage called and said, "What are you doing?" and I said, "Nothing." He said to come on over then, and I did.

We hung out in his garage. He sat on one of his dad's empty beer kegs and said Mrs. Ludlow had called his mom and said she knew Luddy didn't really like Kenny but did Kenny know where Luddy was or did he have any idea who this Jay person was? He played with the stringy ends of his faded denim cutoffs, his thighs flexed and showing the splits of muscle there. He toed the concrete in soccer shoes, no socks, which always made me think of nakedness.

"You don't think he's dead or anything?" Gossage said.

I shook my head—what could kill Luddy?

"And who's this Jay guy?"

"I don't know," I said, leaning against his dad's workbench, my hands getting covered with sawdust. I stretched my arms up over my head, and the dust fell before my eyes like snow.

Gossage said, "You been working out?"

"Some," I said. "I got a weight set for my birthday."

"I got a six-pack from my brother," Kenny said. His birthday was a couple of days after mine. He smiled, showing me his different-colored tooth, the real one lost on a hockey rink last year. It was one of the things I liked best about him.

"Your arms look good, gigantic," he said. He got up off the keg and came up to me, putting his hand on my biceps. I could see the press his dick made in his shorts, the hard downward point. He had always been popping wood in school, sitting behind me in English and whispering, "Hey, Tuck—*boing!*" and I'd have to turn around and look. He'd blame it on some girl usually, but I had him figured otherwise; I was pretty sure it was me to blame.

"You and Luddy were fucking around, I heard," he said. He was close enough to touch.

"Who said?" I asked. I knew he was fucking with me. Nobody but Kenny would have ever thought about Luddy and me screwing around. The thought had probably come to him when he was wanking off one night, I guessed.

His crotch came closer to mine, and I waited for him to touch me again. He didn't, though. He straightened his body and put his hands on his head. I saw his other-colored tooth again.

"Whatever," he said.

We passed his dad asleep on the couch. He was stripped down to his boxers and looked a little like a beached whale, but seeing him there like that gave me a hard-on anyway. Plus I could see the head of his cock poking from the leg of his shorts, and it was the size of a freaking tennis ball. The room smelled of beer and farts, and Kenny said his dad was passed out.

"Awesome piece, huh?" he whispered. "Like father, like son."

"You fucking wish," I said back, keeping my voice low.

I followed him to his room. He stood by the door, closing and locking it. I sat on his bed. It was covered with a red, white, and blue afghan his grandmother must have knitted and some dingy-looking New York Yankees sheets. He turned on his stereo, the volume turned way down. I could still see the lump of his dick in his shorts.

He put his thumbs into his pockets and covered his hard-on with curled fingers. He wouldn't look at me, so I could look at him as much as I wanted. He yawned and said it was hot, and he took off his shirt. He had little pink nipples like mosquito bites, and his torso was hairless.

He threw himself suddenly onto the bed with me, bouncing me around. He went up to the head, and I kept to the foot. He toed off his sneakers and threw them into a corner of the room where a pile of clothes lay. I watched him lean over his feet and start picking between his toes, and then he bunched up some pillows behind his back, making himself comfortable, spreading his legs, bending one and resting it against the wall and touching my butt with the other one.

"My brother joined a frat at school," he said.

I turned to face him. He still wouldn't look at me, pretending to find something interesting in his belly button.

"It was fucked-up, man. They made him jerk off with a bunch of other guys. They put them all in a room and gave them five rubbers and said whoever doesn't drop a load into his bag has to suck out everyone else's."

"No way," I said, instantly intrigued. "That is fucking nasty."

"I shit you not," he said back.

"Did he do it?" The idea of it, five guys in a room jacking together, practically made me dizzy, and I was thinking then that even if nothing were to happen between Kenny and me, I'd at least have something to think about when I got home.

"Fuck, yeah, like my brother would drink some guy's come."

"How'd he get it up in front of all those guys?" I wanted to know, not that I considered it much of a problem.

Kenny put one hand down the front of his jeans to scratch or something. "Said he closed his eyes and pretended he was in a room full of chicks watching."

Yeah, right, I thought. *He probably had his eyes wide open and couldn't stop looking at all the other dicks that surrounded him.* I was thinking then that everybody was a little like me, because even Kenny was sitting beside me with his hand down his pants, and then there was Luddy humping me in the middle of the orchard.

It was becoming plainer and plainer that Kenny was wanting to bust a nut. The itch he scratched failed to go away.

"You'd lose, I bet," he said, "if you had to do that."

"Do what?" I said, unable to follow him on account of all the concentrating I was doing on his hand in his shorts.

"What my brother had to do," he answered, and I laughed.

"Think so?" I said.

"Yeah. You're a fucking pussy, man. You wouldn't even be able to get it up, I bet."

I thought at first that he was putting me on, and then I saw what he was really up to, baiting me, trying to initiate a little action and pretending it was just a game, a stupid contest. *Whatever,* I thought, more than ready to play along.

"You're the fucking softie, man," I said.

"Bullshit," he said.

"Betcha five," I said.

"Sucker bet, and you're going to be the sucker."

"Whatever, asshole," I said. Kenny was grinning from ear to ear—I figured he was thinking everything was going his way.

"Tell you what, fucker—I mean Tucker," he said. "Last one to come has to eat the other's load."

I laughed at him for being so fucking eager. "What am I supposed to do, Kenny—hold the shit in my hand until you're finished or what?"

"I just hope you're hungry," he said. He arched his back and undid his shorts, pushing them down. His dick sprang up, looking very hard. It was ruddy and shaped like a torpedo, in between big and small. He didn't touch it—he didn't dare—I could tell he was closer to shooting than he cared to be. He managed to wait until I got undressed, and as I got back on the bed, I accidentally went in between his legs with my naked foot and toed his balls.

"Ha, Jesus crap," he said, come fountaining from his pecker. "Goddamn it!"

"Looks like you're the winner," I said. I got up on my knees and crawled unsteadily between his legs.

"You don't have to," he said.

"Bet's a bet," I replied, resigned to sucking up the sweet cream cooling on his belly. I took it up with long licks—it tasted better than anything I'd known and stayed in the back of my throat. I had it all over my face, feeling like a kid with a bowl of batter.

I started licking around his balls and across his hipbones, making him shiver. I moved my mouth up to his chest and tickled his nips with my tongue and even pushed his arms up to suck on his pits. He was groaning by now, and his cock, which hadn't bothered getting soft, burned between my pecs, its head all smeared with goo.

I decided to lick that off too. I held it at its hairy base and sucked hard on the buttery end. His legs relaxed and spread a little, and his balls dropped down to the afghan, hiding his little brown hole. After being with Luddy, who was so careful not to let me handle him, being with Kenny was like being given a body to play with. I picked up his nuts and squeezed them until he made a noise, and then I poked a finger into his little brownie. I opened my mouth to the whole of his pecker and looked up his long torso to see him playing with his titties, eyes closed, mouth open, head at an odd angle. I swooped up and down on his johnson, dragging my lips up his shaft and pinching them around his slippery end.

I didn't know how much fun he was having until he made me stop. He got up then and started working on my joint, and no wonder he made me stop—I felt as though I was going to blow a hole right through his head. He slurped down to my bush, eating me whole, making little moans that I barely heard, but they rattled the hell out of my bone. He held on to my balls and twisted the sac while he sped his mouth up and down my shaft. He smoothed his tongue over my sensitive cap, making me shudder. My knees shook, and I lifted my hips and forced my way into him until he was nosing my bush again and nearly choking.

He backed off, and it was like he hadn't breathed the whole time, and he had drool dripping off his fattened lips, and I saw his cock all red and curving upward, dried come flaking along the rim of its head.

I felt the same pressure in my groin and knew I had to unload soon. I grabbed him and pulled his face down to my knob, and while he was down there, he stuck a finger up my ass, making me holler. He pushed me back and kept poking some weird spot that made my legs open and my dick quiver, and I closed my eyes, feeling my cock explode, and he slurped and gurgled over me until I was sucked dry, and he straightened up and shot me an eyeful of jizz like he was shooting a blackbird.

"I think your dad's awake," I said, hearing something crash outside of Kenny's door.

"Probably needs another beer," Kenny said, cuddling down beside me. "We'll be all right." He wiped his come from my face and covered me with his afghan, and we fell asleep.

Luddy came back and showed up at my door.

"Hey," he said.

"Your mom's going crazy looking for you," I told him.

He looked over his shoulder; there was someone sitting in his Camaro, the smoke of his cigarette swirling up out of the open window.

"Who's that?" I asked him.

"Friend of mine," he said. Kenny stepped up beside me then. He and I were watching my little brothers, my mom gone to her bowling banquet. He was hanging out, waiting for my brothers to go to bed so that he could blow me. He slipped his hand in my back pocket.

"We went to Ocean City," Luddy said.

I nodded, feeling Kenny's fingers move.

"Just thought I'd see what you were up to," he said. He turned around, lifting a hand to say good-bye.

"Good seeing you, Lud," I said, feeling the sudden absence of Kenny's hand. The door closed. Luddy left a smoking patch of rubber.

I'm glad he's back, I said to myself. *I'm glad he's OK.* I went back to the TV room. Kenny's clothes were in a pile on the floor, and he was wrapped up in a blanket on the couch, my brothers sacked out and snoring.

"Come here," he whispered, and I did.

My mom said Luddy was on the phone.

"Hey," he said. "Meet me at Wysockie's."

"I was going to the driving range," I said.

"Your boyfriend going?" I could hear the pissiness in his voice and pictured his face. "I'll see you at 2," he said, hanging up.

I walked to the orchard because my mom was taking the car to work. She said, "You be back soon. I don't want the boys on their own for long."

I went to the shed where Lud and I first did it, expecting to find him in it. It was empty except for some rabbits that ran wild when I stepped inside. I heard whistling in the distance, though, and stepped out again and saw him down the path that cut through goldenrod and tall grasses, his dark head bobbing along, disembodied. I watched him as he got closer, coming into full view, his pants too big, his shirt a little tight. He was carrying something.

He stopped in front of me, putting his hands behind his back, his chest thrust out.

He said hey, and I said, "Hey, Lud."

"What's up?" he asked.

"Nothing," I said back. His eyes traced my face, and I felt as though he were trying to memorize it.

"I got you something," he said. He held out a little wooden box made out of driftwood. It said OCEAN CITY on the lid. "It's got sand in it and some shells and some sea glass I found," he said, sounding proud and embarrassed all at the same time.

"Cool," I said.

We didn't say anything for the longest time. I tried to think of something, but nothing came to mind. I kept looking at the box, thinking it was the coolest thing anyone had ever gotten me, thinking how much I wanted to kiss him.

I should have done it. I should have grabbed him and put my mouth on his. I should have thrown my arms around him, thrown him to the ground. I thought about Kenny and shook my head a little, and Luddy said, "What?" and I said nothing, and I felt as though I were holding something more than just sand and glass and shells. And then a breeze blew across the field, and the grasses waved and hissed, and Luddy stepped back, and I lost him forever.

Physical Therapy
by Bob Vickery

The doors of the ambulance swing open, and the two guys in white jump out. As they roll the gurney out, one of them loses his grip, and it comes down hard on the asphalt. My leg explodes in a shock of pain. "Fuck!" I cry out. Black spots burst across my vision. I think I pass out for a moment because the next things I'm aware of are fluorescent lights overhead and faces peering down at me.

Voices fade in and out. "It was a hit-and-run," I hear a man's voice say. "A truck slammed into his cycle, and he went flying."

Someone bends down over me and shakes my shoulder. "Can you hear me?" he asks.

My vision is swimming, and the face above me shifts in and out of focus. I squeeze my eyes shut and open them again. "Yeah," I mutter.

"You've been in an accident," the voice says. "You've got a badly broken leg, and you may have a concussion as well. Do you have any family or friends that we can contact?"

The room is spinning around again, and I struggle to maintain consciousness. "No," I manage to say. "Not in this city. I'm just passing through." I grab the arm of the guy leaning over me. "What about my bike?" I ask. "Where is it? Is it OK?"

The guy gives a sharp laugh of surprise. "Your bike's only good for scrap, buddy," someone behind him says. I think it's the ambulance driver.

"Ask him if he's got any health insurance," I hear a woman's voice say.

I fall back onto the gurney. *Damn, shit, fuck, piss,* I think. I immediately pass out.

A nurse wheels in a rolling rack loaded with trays. Feeding time at the zoo. There are five other guys here in the ward, all charity cases like myself: two knife fights, one DUI who ended up wrapped around a telephone pole, a shooting, and a fall out of a third-story window. At least I got the bed next to the window, along with its splendid view of the brick wall opposite us. The drugs they gave me are wearing off, and my leg is throbbing. Every pulse shoots up my body to my fingertips, my head, even my teeth. The nurse comes by with my lunch tray and places it on the stand next to me.

"Can you give me something more to kill the pain?" I ask her, keeping my voice as low and polite as I can manage.

She turns her eyes on me. She looks like she's looking at a piece of furniture. "I can't give you any more medication for another two hours," she says.

I feel the rage rise up, and I push it back down. "You don't understand," I say slowly, drawing out the words. "I can't wait for two hours. I need something now. "

"I'm sorry. Doctor's orders." Her eyes look like ball bearings. "Why don't you just finish your lunch and not make any more trouble?"

I sweep the tray off the table, and it goes flying onto the floor with a loud clatter. Food splatters everywhere. "All done," I say. We glare at each other for a few moments. She wheels around on her heel and stalks off. I fall back onto the bed, my eyes closed.

The guy across from me, the one who got shot, laughs. "What an asshole," he says.

"Eat shit," I reply without much conviction. I turn my head and stare out the window at the brick wall.

I don't know how much time's gone by when I hear footsteps approach. I don't look to see who it is. "Looks like you had a little accident here," a man's voice says. I turn to see a dude dressed in an orderly's smock holding a mop and pail. The fucker towers over me like an oak tree. He looks Latino, maybe Mexican: dark skin, brown eyes, mustache. He's got arms like tree trunks and a chest as wide as a semi's front grill. A black plastic tag is pinned to his shirt, the word MIGUEL engraved on it in white.

"It wasn't an accident," I say, glaring at him, waiting for him to give me a ration of shit. But Miguel just looks at me calmly. He bends down and picks up the tray, mops up the floor, and then walks out of the room, clutching the mop, pail, and tray in his giant hands.

The throbbing in my leg wakes me up. The clock on the nightstand says 2:17, and I know I'm not due for another dose of painkillers till 4. I lie there staring up at the ceiling. *Today is Monday,* I think. *The day I'm due at the construction site in Chicago.* Two days ago I was a high-rise iron man. Now I'm dog meat. A faint light streams in from the hallway outside, and I look around. My roommates are all sawing wood, sleeping the sleep of the painless—the sons of bitches. I reach over and grab my crutches. When the doctor gave them to me yesterday, he told me to use them only for trips to the john. But if I don't get out of bed, I'm going to go out of my fuckin' skull.

The hospital corridors are dimly lit and empty. I hobble down them, my crutches squeaking against the linoleum. After about 20 minutes of this, I turn a corner and see a sign on the wall reading AIDS WARD. My armpits are killing me, and I can feel the sweat on my forehead dripping down into my eyebrows. But it feels good to use my body; I keep pushing on. All the rooms are dark; all the patients seem to be sleeping. I hear a noise that sounds like a groan. *Another poor slob in pain,* I think. The noise is coming from a room up ahead and to my left. A faint light

streams from it. As I pass by I glance in. I stop, my mouth dropping open, all thoughts about my aching leg forgotten.

Miguel is standing next to the bed of a patient, his shirt hiked
up, his pants and Jockeys tangled down around his ankles. He's
jerking off, pulling on his dick with slow, deliberate strokes, his
eyes intently watching the face of the man in bed. Miguel's body
is beautifully muscled: His pecs are sharply defined, his abs sculpted into a neat six-pack, his biceps rounded and veined. His torso
is as brown and smooth as polished oak, his nipples two dark
acorns. But it's his dick that finally commands my attention. It
lives up to the promise of his giant's body: thick and uncut, its
round, dark knob the size and color of a ripe plum. Miguel slides
his fist up and down the shaft, his hips pushing forward slightly
with each downstroke of his hand, the head winking in and out of
its foreskin. His balls hang loose, swaying gently. He stands there
in a pool of light, darkness all around him. The patient raises a thin
arm and slides his hand across Miguel's body, kneading the flesh of
his torso. Miguel's expression is calm and tender; his face looks like
that of one of the plaster saints I used to see in church as a kid.

Miguel spits in his hand and slicks up his dick. I can see beads
of sweat forming on his forehead, and his breath is coming out in
ragged gasps. Suddenly his body shudders. Miguel groans and
closes his eyes as his load oozes out between his fingers. His body
convulses repeatedly as the orgasm sweeps through him and then
finally passes. He stands there for a moment, his muscular body
glistening with sweat, his jizz dripping down his hand, his thick,
long dick slowly softening. I feel my own dick stir at the sight,
making a tent in my hospital gown.

I suddenly realize that all Miguel has to do to see me is raise his
head. I back off slowly toward a less conspicuous position. Bad
mistake. My left crutch slips out from under me, and I go crash-
ing to the floor. The pain is like a sunburst in my head, and I cry
out. I lie there stunned for a few moments, unable to lift my head,
unable even to breathe.

Miguel's face hovers over me. "Are you all right?" he asks. He's pulled his pants up, but his fly is still open.

I take a couple of deep breaths. I want to utter a string of obscenities, but no sound comes out. I shake my head. The pain causes my eyes to brim with tears.

Miguel bends down and effortlessly picks me up in his arms. He walks down the empty corridors with long, even strides. When he gets to my room, he lays me gently on the bed, making sure not to cause me any more pain than I'm already experiencing. He pushes the call button, and after a couple of minutes the night nurse shows up. "He slipped while going to the toilet," Miguel says. "He's in a lot of pain. Can you get him something?"

The nurse shakes her head. "Not till 4."

But Miguel just smiles. "Jesus, Susan, we're talking half an hour here. I won't tell anybody." He winks at her.

The nurse relents and brings me some Demerol. Miguel lifts my head and holds a glass of water to my lips. I swallow the pills. The nurse leaves, and Miguel sits by the bed watching me. I close my eyes. After a while the pills kick in, and I fall asleep.

The next day Miguel comes by with a washcloth and a basin of soapy water. "I'm here to give you a sponge bath," he says. His tone is matter-of-fact, as if our encounter last night never happened. He draws the curtain around us. I look up at him with curiosity as he pulls down the bedclothes and removes my hospital gown. "How are you feeling?" he asks.

"Better than last night," I say, watching his face for a reaction.

But Miguel merely nods his head. "Good," he says. He squeezes the sponge in the basin and then proceeds to soap down my chest. He rubs the sponge against my torso in slow, widening circles. I wait for him to say something, to explain or plea for my silence, but he says nothing. Finally he glances up at my face. "You have a nice body," he says. "Do you work out?"

This catches me off-guard. "Yeah," I say. I nod toward my leg. "At least I did before this."

Miguel continues with the ritual of soaping down my body. After a while I can't stand it anymore. "What the hell were you doing last night?" I ask, my voice low so that the others outside the curtain can't hear me.

Miguel regards me calmly. "What the hell do you think?" he asks, smiling slightly.

I don't say anything for a couple of beats as I contemplate a response. I plaster a nasty little smirk on my face. "A special form of physical therapy, huh?"

Miguel is washing my armpits now. "You could say that, I guess," he says, ignoring the sarcasm in my voice. His gaze holds mine. "I was just trying to help the poor guy feel like a human being again. Instead of an 'AIDS patient.'"

Miguel scrubs my face and neck. I close my eyes, conjuring up the memory of Miguel fucking his fist, his muscular body gleaming in the light of the bedside lamp. I feel my dick stir, and I deliberately stoke the flames, grabbing on to any sexual fantasy I can think of. It's only a few seconds before I'm sporting a full hard-on. I take Miguel's wrist and place his hand on my dick. "How about giving me a little physical therapy?" I ask.

But Miguel just looks amused. "Knock it off," he says. He takes his hand away and sponges down my right leg, the one not in a cast. I don't say anything else. After he's done he drops the sponge into the basin. "What's your name?" he asks.

I hold his gaze. "Al."

"Look, Al," Miguel says. "What I was giving that patient last night is not what you need right now. If that was what you needed, I'd do it."

"Thanks," I say, "but I don't take charity hand jobs." Miguel shrugs and says nothing. He finishes and leaves a couple of minutes later.

I see a lot of Miguel the next couple of days. He wheels me down the hall to the hospital sunroom. He cleans me up. He brings my food to me. I find myself looking forward to whenever he next shows up; he's the only person in the fuckin' hospital who treats me like a human being. Once, while taking me down to get X-rayed, he asks me what I'm going to do when I'm released from the hospital.

I don't say anything for a long time. "I don't know," I finally answer.

"Don't you have any family? Friends?" he asks.

"I have a brother somewhere," I say. "I lost track of him a few years ago. I have some friends back East, I guess." I put my hands on the wheels, stop the chair, and turn to face him. "I'm a construction worker," I say. "I work on high-rises, traveling around the country looking for gigs. I'm never in one place long enough to make real friends. I was traveling to Chicago for a job when this accident happened. I've been out of work for five months, and this job was going to get me on my feet again."

"What did you do for the five months you were out of work?" Miguel asks.

I give him a long, level look. "I hustled," I finally say. "Sometimes I hung out at a porn store in Boston. For $20 a john could take me in a booth and suck my dick. For an extra $10 I'd suck his." I glance down at my cast and give a laugh with precious little humor in it. "I can't fall back on that this time, though. No john wants to make it with a gimp." We don't talk for the rest of the ride down.

The next day I wait for Miguel to show up with my breakfast. I'm hoping we can talk for a few minutes; I find that I miss his company. When 8 o'clock finally rolls around, some guy I've never seen before comes in with my tray. "Where's Miguel?" I ask.

The guy puts the tray on the stand next to me. "You mean that big Mexican guy?" he asks. He shrugs. "He got fired."

I bolt up to a sitting position. "Why?"

The guy gives a smutty little grin. "He got caught jerking off with one of the patients in the AIDS ward last night. Sick, eh?" He turns and walks out the door.

Later that day the doctor comes in and tells me I'm being discharged from the hospital first thing tomorrow.

"I suggest you make arrangements for your home care, Mr. Pulaski," he says. "It's going to take a while for your leg to heal."

I spend the afternoon staring at the ceiling, weighing my options: a broken leg, no money, no job, no bike, no friends. *So I'm finally hitting bottom,* I think. I always wondered what it'd feel like. I don't feel particularly bad, just numb. After a while I ask the nurse for a telephone book. I turn to the government listings and look up Social Services. A couple of phone calls later, I have a list of all the city's homeless shelters.

After a week at the shelter, I've pretty much got the hang of the system. The people who run it kick everybody out at 9 A.M. I hang out in a nearby park with the dopers and the drunks; it's one of the few places I can get to on crutches. There's a Baptist mission a block away that runs a soup kitchen, and I get my meals there after listening to sermons about Jesus. I don't think or feel much of anything. I've had the vague hope sometimes of getting another job once my leg heals, but lately I don't even think about that very much. Sometimes my fellow bums pass around a bottle of Thunderbird, and I take a swig. I usually don't talk to anybody.

I've just finished my dinner at the mission, and I'm hobbling back toward the shelter, where they open the doors again at 7. I've gained an intimate knowledge of the stretch of street between the mission and the shelter—every fuckin' liquor store, bar, and video store. (I've tried hustling back among the booths of a couple of these but found no takers; I was right when I told Miguel that johns don't want gimps.) I turn the last corner before the shelter. Miguel is standing there in front of the door. We look at each other.

"Well, this is a surprise," I say.

Miguel smiles. "I still have a few friends at the hospital. I heard you were discharged, and I've been looking for you." His eyes travel down the length of my body. "You look like shit, Al." He wrinkles his nose. "You smell like it too."

"Thanks."

Miguel takes me by the elbow. "Come on. My car is parked just a block away."

I pull back. "Where are we going?"

"Back to my place," Miguel says. "And I don't want to hear any argument."

I have to laugh at that one. "You honestly think I'm going to argue?"

Miguel lives in a small apartment over a garage behind a duplex. The first thing he does after we walk in is pull out a basin from under the sink. He starts filling it with hot water. He looks at me over his shoulder. "Take off your clothes," he says. "I'm going to give you a bath." I don't argue with him. I pull off my jacket and T-shirt and drop my jeans, then kick them off. When I'm naked Miguel nods toward the bed. "Lie down."

I obey. Miguel sits down on the side of the bed, placing the basin beside me. He drops a washcloth in it, squeezes it, and starts bathing my chest. We don't talk. I keep my eyes focused on Miguel's face, but he just looks down at the parts of my body he's washing. He washes my armpits, my arms, each finger. The washcloth travels down my torso. He washes my dick and balls. The feel of the warm, wet cloth on them gives me an instant hard-on, but Miguel pays no attention. He washes my asshole; I push up my hips to give him better access. He washes my right leg and both feet, working each toe like he did my fingers. When he's finally done he drops the washcloth in the basin. Only then does he look me in the face. He bends down and kisses me, his tongue pushing into my mouth. I break away.

"Is this more physical therapy for a poor pathetic, needy patient?" I ask.

Miguel looks down at me. "You know what your problem is, Al?" he says. "You talk too damn much." He kisses me again, and this time I tongue him back. I pull on his shirt, fumbling with the buttons.

"Get naked," I say.

Miguel stands up and pulls off his clothes. When he's finally naked he slips into bed beside me and wraps his arms around me. "Maybe you can give *me* some physical therapy," he murmurs. "I've had a hell of a week myself." I look hard at him, and for the first time I notice the lines of strain in his face, the anxiety in his eyes. I remember that he's lost his job. Without thinking, I reach up and lay a hand on his cheek, a gesture I don't ever remember making before.

Miguel takes my face in his hands and tenderly kisses my mouth, my eyelids, my cheeks, my hair. He shifts in the bed, and I feel his tongue on my left nipple, licking it, working it over. I sigh. He takes the nub between his teeth and nips softly. My sigh turns into a low groan. Miguel does the same with my right nipple, working the nub, making it stand erect. I close my eyes and let the sensations tingle through my body. It's been so long since I've been in bed with another man.

Miguel drags his tongue down my torso, sliding it across my abs into the forest of my pubes. He works his way down the bed so that his head is positioned between my legs. I feel his tongue slide across my balls, and then he opens his mouth and sucks my scrotum in. He looks up at me, my balls in his mouth, and I hold his gaze as I run my fingers through his curly hair. Miguel reaches up and twists my nipples as he rolls my balls around with his tongue. His tongue works its way down to my asshole. I feel its warm wetness as he probes against it.

"Christ almighty," I groan loudly.

Miguel wraps a hand around my dick and squeezes it. "I love your cock, Al," he says, looking up at me. "It fills my hand so nicely." He starts stroking it, sliding his hand up and down the shaft, his tongue working on my balls again. He presses his lips against the base of my dick, then moves on up, kiss by kiss, to the head. His lips open, and he plunges down, taking my dick into his mouth. His head starts bobbing up and down, and I push my hips up to meet him. I've got my fingers entwined in his hair now, anchoring his head as I skewer his warm, wet mouth with my dick.

"Swing around," I say.

Miguel pivots his body so that his dick is jutting out a few inches above me. His balls hang low and heavy; I raise my head and bury my face in them, breathing in their musky pungency. I open my mouth, and Miguel's ball sac drops in. As I continue to fuck his face, I suck on his balls, rolling them around with my tongue, savoring their fleshiness. I spit in my hand and curl my fingers around his dick, sliding them up and down the shaft. Miguel groans, his voice muffled by my dick down his throat.

Miguel pulls back and swings his legs around so that he's straddling my torso, facing me. He pumps his hips, pushing his fat dick against my belly. He leans back, and his dick sticks out in front of him, proud and hard. I drink it in with my eyes, marveling at how thick it is, how dark, how the veins run up the shaft, ending in that purple plum on top. I wrap my hands around both our dicks and squeeze them together. I've got the red working-class dick of your average Pole, much lighter in color than Miguel's, cut, maybe not as long but certainly nothing to be ashamed of. I love the feel of Miguel's dick against mine, the two warm blood-engorged shafts of meat touching each other. I start stroking them together, pulling Miguel's foreskin over his cock head. A drop of precome oozes out of his piss slit, then another. I run my fingers over the clear little pearls, slicking my palm with them so that my strokes slide down our cocks more easily.

Miguel looks down at me, his body towering over me like a wall of muscle, his dark eyes burning, his mouth slightly open. I can see the hunger and excitement in his eyes. I feel it too, perhaps even more so. Miguel reaches down and gently brushes my hair back from my forehead. "It is so nice to have you in my bed,

Al," he says, "to finally have you in my bed." He bends down and kisses me again, wrapping his huge arms around me in a bear hug, grinding his powerful body against mine.

"You feel like fucking me, Miguel?" I ask.

Miguel's grin broadens. He opens the drawer of his nightstand and pulls out a condom and a jar of lube. "That's just what I had in mind."

He scoops out some lube on two fingers and slides them into the crack of my ass. I can feel the fingers working their way to my hole, massaging it, playing with it. One of them penetrates me, sliding up my chute until it's completely in. I push up with my knees, exposing my asshole even more. He crooks his finger and pushes against my prostate; I give a laugh just from the sheer pleasure of the sensation.

Miguel pulls his finger out, rolls a condom down his dick, and slathers it with more lube. I take his dick in my hand, and as Miguel hovers over me, I guide it to my asshole. Miguel penetrates me slowly, inch by patient inch, his eyes intent on my face, watching my reaction. "Let me know if I'm hurting you," he murmurs, but I just shake my head, my eyes never leaving his. When he's fully in, Miguel lies motionless on top of me for a moment, his arms wrapped around my torso, his face buried against my neck. He starts pumping his hips with short, slow thrusts. I pull his face up to mine and kiss him. Miguel's thrusts become deeper, faster. I slide my hands down his smooth back, squeezing the hard muscles of his ass, feeling them clench and unclench with each push of his hips. Miguel's torso writhes against mine, and I can feel his muscles, like steel embedded in hard rubber, flex against my body.

We roll over, and now I'm on top, my plastered leg carefully positioned. I sit up so that I can look down at Miguel. I run my hands over his torso, squeezing his nipples, flicking them, pinching them. Miguel's lips are pulled back into a snarl, and his eyes have a fierceness that I've never seen in him before. There's an elec-

tricity passing between us, a connection that crackles with energy.
I squeeze my ass muscles tightly as Miguel thrusts his dick up my
ass. Miguel groans softly. I do it again with his next thrust, and
Miguel's groans rise in volume. He looks at me with startled eyes.

"Where did you learn to fuck like this?" he asks, his eyes wide.
I just laugh. I reach back and hold his balls in my hand, squeezing them gently, imagining their creamy load. They've pulled up
against his body, and I know it won't be long before he shoots.
Miguel's huge hand, slicked with lube, is wrapped around my
dick, stroking it in time with each thrust of his hips. He pulls his
dick almost all the way out of me, its head just inside my sphincter, holds the position for a second, and then plunges in hard, his
shaft sliding fully up my chute. I feel his body shudder, and he
cries out sharply. The orgasm sweeps over him, one spasm after
another, and I ride it out on top of his thrashing body, feeling his
hot load pump into the condom up my ass.

Miguel continues stroking my dick, and I feel myself getting
close. "Slide down," he says, "and let me suck on your balls."

I move down Miguel's chest and drop my balls in his mouth.
He tongues my scrotum as he continues stroking my dick. I lean
back, eyes closed, feeling Miguel draw me to the brink. When I
come I groan loudly, my load squirting out, splattering against
Miguel's face in a thick white rain. I collapse onto the bed beside
Miguel. We lie there silently, our bodies pressed together. After a
while I prop myself on my elbow and look down at him.

My load drips down his face. I kiss him, tasting my jizz on his
lips. "Jesus, you're a mess," I say, grinning.

Miguel laughs and pulls me to him again. We lie in bed for
what seems like a long time. I watch the patterns of sun and shadow move across the ceiling. "Miguel," I finally say, "what did you
have in mind when you found me and brought me here?"

"We don't have to talk about it now," Miguel says.

"I don't have any money. It'll be a while before I can work
again. Do you realize what you're taking on?"

Miguel pulls me more tightly against him. "Just shut up, OK?" he says gently. "I can handle it, believe me."

We don't say anything else. After a while I can tell by the steady rhythm of his breathing that Miguel has fallen asleep. *Let it go,* I think. *Whatever happens, happens.* I close my eyes, and it doesn't take long before I drift off into sleep myself.

Discretion Sought, Discretion Served
by Lew Dwight

If Rick wants discreet, he'll get discreet, but I refuse to hide.

It's just as well that he wants to meet two hours north of here, for while my partner knows I like my little sorties on the side, I don't want any of our acquaintances to find out. I know how fags like to talk. Should I care? No, but I do anyway. I'm still hung up on appearances.

My partner and I have an imperfect union. We talk, though, and respect each other's needs, and we love each other. He can't help it that he's now disabled, and I can't help it that I still have the sex drive of a teenager. I kiss him on the lips before I throw on my jacket and leave for my long drive north.

"Have fun," he says without irony.

This Rick is a little crazed. Can't call his house; he calls me only at designated hours. We'll have to meet at night at his camp north of here, where there's no paved road and no phone. I respect his need for "discretion," and I even tell him I like the idea of doing it on the sly, out of sight, in a little cabin in the woods, but I will not hide. Sneak, yes, but not hide. I originally circled his ad because he said he was bi. My fantasy has always been to find a bisexual daddy who wants to fuck men on the side. *Bi,* to me, means "probably gay but still closeted, wants nothing but sex." *Bi* means "no strings."

I love the purity of it: A "relationship" with a tight little circle drawn around it. As soon as we step outside that circle, we disappear from each other's worlds.

After a week of hushed talk on the phone (I could often hear traffic in the background), we finally met for a face-to-face chat in the parking lot of a trucking stop far from either of our homes. As soon as I beheld that "professional look"—clean-shaven baby face, geeky glasses, close-cropped hair; the manicured look of the company man—there was a strong pull in my loins. I hadn't felt this way toward someone in years. I wanted to defile him, mess up his hair, take away his glasses so he couldn't see, fuck him halfway to Canada and back, then wipe my dick on his expensive shirt.

"I'm not squeamish about anything," I told him, "as long as it's consensual, clean, and safe. I'll do it all."

His nervous tic: pushing his glasses up the bridge of his nose. "What exactly do you mean?" he asked.

"You know. Sucking. Fucking. Rimming. Spitting. Biting. Dirty talk. A little slapping around, maybe. Even some water sports, if the mood strikes us. Stuff my partner has never been interested in but I've always wanted to try. Why are we doing this if not to explore our limits?"

He just looked out the window awhile.

"What exactly is it *you're* looking for?" I pressed him.

He turned the gold band around his finger several times. "I'm not sure what I want at this point in my life. I'm 30. I've devoted the past 12 years to work, wife, and kids. All I know is, I just want someone to get together with every once in a while for some good times. No strings. I really have to be careful."

"Am I coming across a little too strong, Rick?"

He took off his glasses and rubbed his eyes. "I should probably tell you, my name's not Rick. It's Andrew."

"Andrew."

"It's just that if anyone in town who knows me were to answer my ad—"

I found this both absurd and touching. I wanted to laugh; I wanted to take him into my arms and tell him everything was going to be all right.

"So do you think you'd be interested in me, Andrew?"

He looked out the window again, thinking about something, wondering, perhaps, how he ended up in a truck-stop parking lot with another guy who wanted to fuck him.

I reached over and took him by the chin. "Look at me," I said. "I won't bite...well, unless you ask."

His eyes widened behind his lenses.

"Tell me if I look like someone you want to have sex with. Let's be honest with each other. It's the least we can do in such a limited relationship. If it's no, you owe me nothing but a handshake. I'll tell you right now, I had my doubts when we talked on the phone. But now that I have you right here in front of me... "

He swallowed. "You really think so, huh?"

I took in the stubbled temples, the slightly crooked wire-frame glasses, the knot of his tie pressing against his throat, and I nearly swooned. *Andrew.*

"Absolutely. Now tell me: What do you think?"

"I think...yes. Yes, I'd like to do it."

Andrew drew me a map to his camp.

It's late fall, and most of the camps are closed up for the winter, with no one around but crows and crickets—and even they're getting sparse now that several frosts have come and gone.

The drive seems to take forever, especially since I have a hard-on most of the way. I unbuckle my belt once I get on the turnpike, loosen the top button of my jeans, and gently stroke the tender head of my dick with my finger while thinking of Andrew. I do this for 15 miles.

Andrew.

A closet case, he doesn't understand how my partner can countenance these trysts. His mode has always been one of dishonesty, one life for the wife and kids, another—secret—one for himself only. Over the phone, he'd asked whether my parents know (yes), whether I'm concerned about what people at work might think (no), if I ever feel guilty or ashamed that people know I love men (not anymore), and he seemed not to understand how it could be so. He was taken aback that anyone could live *that way*; it must be so difficult. I tried to explain how shame is the by-product of secrecy, not the reason for secrecy, and how it begins to vanish as soon as you're open about your needs, how it's actually more difficult to hold things back, to live a lie, to let shame control your life. But my explanations went nowhere. *We're from different worlds,* I concluded. *I should really dislike this Andrew guy.*

Andrew.

I stop rubbing the tip of my dick when the throbbing starts in the seat of my pants.

Andrew reminds me of the quiet boy who used to sit at the back of the room in my high school algebra class. Geeky, four-eyed, always nicely dressed and groomed, he never spoke unless spoken to, and he always knew the right answers to questions the teacher put to him. I used to imagine (in what was then my stifled, repressed way) that the glasses and self-effacing manner were a ruse to cover up the real him; take this boy home, take off his glasses, peel off his clothes, and you'd find a wild, wiry animal underneath that would take a bite out of you if you weren't careful.

I resume fingering my glans as I drive.

I remember lying in bed with my fist encircling my cock and fantasizing about meeting the geeky kid in the locker room after the rest of the boys had split for home. As he quietly peeled off his socks, my heart rate quickened; I got up the nerve to rise from the bench and corner him near the lockers, and then the fantasy derailed, went out of my control. I slapped the glasses off his face; I shoved him down against the concrete floor and got on top of him. He looked up at me, scared, his mouth bloodied. I kissed it, tasting the salty sharpness of it, then I shoved my hand down his shorts...

I stop rubbing when I'm at the point of orgasm again.

Andrew.

The place is very private, a half mile of dirt road, and you don't even see the cottage behind the spruce and pine till you're in the driveway. Quite a place too: flagstone patio, terraced garden, long private dock out to the water. The house is all wood shingles with many gables and dormers, a wrap-around porch with balustrade and wicker furniture—not the typical Maine camp I remember visiting as a kid, with missing clapboards, soft porch decking, stovepipe out the window, walls that didn't go all the way up to the ceiling inside.

The presence of children lingers about the place. There's a net-less basketball hoop above the carriage shed, a well-worn path leading down the hillside to the lake (in spite of the boardwalk there), heaps of shells and stones and other flotsam lying about.

I walk up to the door and notice a single lamp on in the cottage. It's very warm and rustic-looking inside the window, a woodsy retreat for city people who vanish as soon as this state turns harsh and real.

Andrew's face, somewhat pale and drawn, meets me at the door. He quietly lets me in.

"Well. Quite a place."

"Did you have a hard time finding it?"

I look at the varnished matchboard ceiling, the stone fireplace, the mission-style furniture, and I think, *Who is this guy? Where'd he get his money?*

"No, I didn't have a hard time at all. And neither have you, looks like."

"The wife. She likes the finest stuff. Want a beer?"

"Sure."

Andrew gets a Beck's for me out of the refrigerator.

We sit in the boxy chairs and talk about the camp, the changes they (he and his wife) have made in the place over the years, the fun the children have had there, and I begin to wonder whether I've been hallucinating, whether I've really come to this place to have sex with this man sitting in front of me.

As the chitchat goes on, I get angrier and angrier. This Andrew guy has it all—too much for a mere 30-year-old.

He has a well-paying job, obviously.

He has expensive tastes—imported beer in the fridge.

He has a wife who enjoys fine stuff.

He has children who will grow up healthy and clean and white.

He even has a willing trick sitting in his camp furniture and getting hornier and angrier by the minute.

He has his life perfectly compartmentalized.

I'm just a fag who grew up in Westbrook, Maine, with a father who could barely stand me. I went to college to get out of the house. I now do computer-aided design work and support my disabled lover, who is not covered under any insurance policy of mine. I never went to summer camp while I was growing up, though some of my friends did. I'm feeling like I want to teach this Andrew guy a lesson, one he can take home and chew on awhile.

As if sensing my impatience with the empty chitchat, he puts down his beer, pushes his glasses up his face, and says, "Well. I'm at a business conference in Boston right now, can you believe that?" He laughs and passes his hand through his hair.

Suddenly I realize that I *am* here to fuck him.

"So your wife has no idea, then?"

He shakes his head, looks away.

This is where the little conversation ends. This is where I look around the perfectly appointed cottage, see pictures of grown boys on the mantel, hear the snap of hemlock kindling in the fireplace, catch a whiff of potpourri and beer and sweat—and realize that Andrew is a liar. That my fantasy is about to come true. My odd, dangerous fantasy. The fantasy I can't enact with my partner; I love him too much. Even if he weren't disabled, I could never do to him what I am about to do to this closeted fucker sitting in front of me.

I too shake my head. In disgust.

I push myself up slowly from the arms of the mission-style chair. I walk over to Andrew and stand in front of him. "Made in the shade, huh, *Rick?*"

He looks up at me from the chair, small and afraid and still young-looking. Enough to pass for 30.

"You know what you are?"

He says nothing.

I reach down, tug the front of his Polo shirt, and pull him up to his feet. We stand chin to chin. I press my hidden erection against his thigh. "You're a fake. A liar and a closet case. And I'm going to fuck the shit out of you, *Rick.*"

I throw him back into his boxy, stylish chair.

He has to push his glasses back up his nose. He looks at me in disbelief. "You know, maybe this wasn't such a—"

"Shut the fuck up." I unbuckle my belt and take it out of my pants. I strip off my shirt, revealing my bare chest.

Who am I? What am I about to do?

"Nice remote little place you have here, *Rick.* I guess I can make you scream a little."

I unzip my pants, take out my hard dick. He sits back in his chair, just watches it, me.

"OK, *Rick.* What I want you to do is get down on your knees in front of me."

He doesn't budge; his eyes are locked on my erect dick.

"I *said*"—pausing, I grab him out of the chair—"get down there and suck my dick."

"Oh, jeez!" he says.

"*Oh, jeez,*" I mock him. "What the fuck do you think we came up here for—to talk about your kids, your camp, about what a fucking fine father you are? No, we came here so I could fuck the shit out of you, and now it's time to get started."

I hold my cock out with one hand, grab the back of his head with the other, and bring head and cock together. His mouth accepts the whole length. He moans and breathes and drools while the cock goes in and out. He sucks. His glasses slide askew on his face. That hammering begins in my asshole.

"Enough." I push him away. I step on the backs of my shoes and kick them off. I pull my pants inside out over my legs, toss them aside. I stand over him and brandish my naked dick above his head.

"Get out of your clothes, *Rick*."

He looks down at his shirt, undoes the top button, then the next. Then he hesitates.

"What are you waiting for?" I reach down and grab the end of his shirt and rip it off over his head. His arms fly up helplessly, and his glasses get caught in the fabric. When he goes for them, I step on his hand. "Leave them, cunt."

I push him back on his ass, grab his feet, pull off the shoes, and peel the socks from his bare white skin. Then I loosen his pants, grasp them by the cuffs, and yank them off his ass. He's down to underwear now. Silk boxers.

"Look at you," I say, pulling him to his feet. "Rather stylish little fag, aren't you?"

"I'm not a—"

I slap him across the face. Not hard; just enough to take his breath away. And mine.

He holds his jaw and looks at me. His eyes seem large now that the glasses are gone.

"The lies stop right here. Got that, fucker?"

He just drops his hand and stands there groggily a moment in front of me.

"You're not a fag like I'm not a fag. Bi, my ass."

His chin falls to his chest. He begins sobbing.

I drop to my knees in front on him and reach for his boxers. There's a big, hard dick inside. I strip the boxers off him and begin sucking.

"Oh, God!" he says through his sobs. His knees buckle while I suck him, and he almost topples over. "Oh, God!"

I suck his dick, then pull on it awhile, then suck and pull at the same time and keep at it until his sobs diminish to little sniffles. As he nears orgasm his dick swells in my mouth. I can feel the swollen veins with my tongue. He begins to swear in a whisper.

"Oh, shit…oh, fuck."

But I don't let him come.

I shove him to the floor and take the boxers off his feet. I find a rubber in my pocket and stand before him, rolling it slowly onto my hard dick. "It's time," I say. "Show me your ass."

He doesn't know what to do, so I lift his legs and slam my open hand against his ass a few times. "I *said,* show it to me!"

He makes little hurt noises. Handprints bloom on his ass. He hooks his wrists under his knees and pulls back his thighs until his hairy asshole comes to light. I take his legs out of his grasp and push them over his head. He grunts in acquiescence. I slide my sheathed cock back and forth over the hair in his crack. "Daddy, this is your big day. This is the day you become a fag."

"I told you, I'm not—"

Instinctively—angrily—I spit in his face. He lies back on the rug. "You know, *Rick,* at this point the sound of your voice just makes me sick. It makes me *sick,* I'm telling you, and I don't want to hear another word out of that cunt face of yours until we're through, you hear?"

He says nothing. He does nothing. He is as inert as a lapdog.

I push his legs high over his head. I spit again, this time aiming it right down at that puckered hole. I jab my dick into where the spit went, and I hold it there, pushing until the dry tightness begins to give way. He hollers and grabs the sides of my head. It's like I've punched my own private hole in him.

I keep my dick halfway in his ass until he gets used to it. Then, slowly at first, I begin to fuck him. I drag it out and screw it back in. I go from short thrusts to long jabs. He rocks back and forth on his spine on the rug. The grunts and moans he makes while I fuck him please me.

Though I breathe heavily, I talk to him while I fuck. "This is it, *Rick*. All the fake shit in your life—house, kids, camp—none of it matters. Lies. This is what you want. This is what you are. Fucking liar. You want...this. And...*this*. And...I'm gonna give it to you. I'm gonna give you what you want. You fucking fag!"

I grasp him by the thighs and lift his ass off the floor. My asshole hammers. I sink in deep and hold it there until my come floods out. Then I drop his legs and fall on top of him. I strip off the rubber and come a little more on his stomach.

He starts to jack off while I unwind. When his jacking quickens I put my mouth on his cock. He spurts his load. It tastes like bitter rind. It burns my throat.

We lie there for a time falling into and out of sleep. The fire has died on the hearth.

"I'm sorry, Andrew," I say.

He's silent a moment. "Forget it," he says.

"No, I mean it. That was...not me. I don't know why it happened. It just did."

"It's OK. It felt like...I deserved it."

"It was bad."

"No, it was good. I liked it. You knew what you were doing. I just don't know how I'm ever..."

I turn to look at him. "What?"

He rolls off the floor. He picks up his silk boxers and rubs at my come spots on his stomach hair.

"My life," he says.

"Your life?"

His arm makes a gesture, taking in the cabin, the lake, whatever else beyond it I can't see.

"This. My life. Remember?"

"Yes. I remember. What are you going to do with it?"

"I...throw it away."

"Not throw it away."

"Not throw it away?"

He goes into the bathroom, leaves the door open while he pisses. There's only a trickle at first, then a hard, noisy stream.

He lies down beside me, rolls against me. We entwine arms, legs. His dick is wet, like a dog's nose.

"This is the good part, isn't it?"

"It can be," I tell him.

"That gives me some hope," he says.

Coaching Session
by Steven Lundquist

"Hey...Fleetfeet!"

I almost didn't turn around. Now that I was out of high school, I didn't plan to answer to *that* name anymore. I continued looking over the selection of video games on the shelf, tuning out the voice behind me.

"Lundquist...too much rock music deafen you?"

Suddenly I realized—it wasn't one of my fellow escapees from Prairie High. It was *him!*

I whirled around—a little too fast, a little too eager—and found myself barely three feet from the convivial grin of Coach Halvorsen.

"Spending your graduation money on games?" There was that amused smile lifting up one corner of his mouth. Coach often looked amused—at us, we assumed. My take on it was that he looked as if he knew a secret about us...and in my case that was entirely possible.

I *did* harbor a guilty secret, and the first time he smiled at me like that, I was convinced Coach knew the *real* reason I was on the football team. I nearly dropped out then and there in embarrassment. But desire kept me committed to the team. And not the desire to beat our archrival, Central.

My running prowess had earned me my nickname back in junior high. I didn't mind being called Fleetfeet till some wiseass started

calling me Fleet Enema instead. My evident annoyance prompted him to keep on calling me that name, and soon some of the
others followed suit. Now I hated being called even Fleetfeet, but
as fast as I could run, I was destined to be known for my speed.
The name stuck.

In high school everyone urged me to try out for track. I hadn't
the least interest in running for anything except the school bus,
and no matter who got on my case or how often they all begged,
I resisted all their entreaties.

Then I got my first look at Coach Halvorsen.

At 14 I didn't yet realize what the reason was for the way my
blood raced and my heart pounded whenever I was near Coach,
but I knew I wanted to be around him. Mr. Garofolos, the eccentric math teacher, was the track coach; but Coach Halvorsen
guided the football team. I immediately signed up.

Even Coach suggested my wiry body was better suited to track.
But I was determined, and when he saw my speed, he made me a
running back.

By my senior year I was fully aware of why my dick inflated
when Coach was around. A certain degree of knowledge usually
goes along with turning 18, and I knew exactly what I was—or
would be once I did something about it. But admitting it to myself and admitting it to another human being were two different
things. Even my best bud didn't know my secret. I certainly
couldn't admit it to Coach Halvorsen, though when he looked at
me with that amused smile and that knowing twinkle, I often
wondered if he guessed.

I graduated high school a complete virgin…the sum total of
my sexual experience was one hand job (from a girl) in the backseat of my buddy's car on a double date. I certainly never told her
that at the moment I spurted, the image in my mind was of
Coach Halvorsen's body, striated with muscles and speckled with
a fine dusting of blond hairs.

"So what're you up to now that you're a free man?" Coach asked in that friendly, disarming way of his.

I stood there staring at him, trying to make sense of the words, which at first buzzed around my head in a jumble. For some reason I was more buffaloed by his presence now than I had been during my four years on the team.

"You aren't talking to me now that you're a man of the world?" he said laughingly as I stood there silently open-mouthed like some flummoxed lummox.

My eyes bugged wider. Still no sound issued from my mouth. I'd thought I'd never see Coach again. Now that I found myself unexpectedly face-to-face with him, I was not only delighted, I was overwhelmed.

"Want to talk over a cup of coffee?" he invited. "My apartment's right around the corner. My sister sent me some home-baked cookies. Want some?"

I could hardly tell him what I *really* wanted. Nodding my head, I mutely trotted out the door behind him.

Seated on Coach's overstuffed sofa, I felt a cold sweat break out across my brow. It intensified when he sat down right next to me with the coffee. He was so close, I could feel the heat emanating from his beefy, muscular, hair-flecked leg. It was July, and he was wearing shorts. I watched, mesmerized, as his leg muscles flexed, tensing and relaxing, tensing and relaxing. *Why did* he *seem to be so edgy?* I wondered.

Coach spoke to me; I didn't even hear the words. Everything was filtered through a haze of lust. The man's simple presence, without his *doing* anything, was enough to swell the simmering column of flesh in my shorts. My head buzzed as if a colony of bees had taken up residence in my brain. My nipples stiffened and elongated, rubbing against the knit material of my shirt.

"So...what about it?" Coach asked, dropping a hand on my shoulder heartily.

A shiver scurried through my body at the feel of his warm, strong paw on my body. "Uh—what? Sorry." I hadn't heard a word of the question.

"Weren't you listening to me?" He sounded more amused than annoyed as he cuffed me gently, sending waves of lust ricocheting through me.

My dick began oozing lube. I glanced furtively at my crotch to see if my excitement was visible.

"Pay attention, or I'll make you drop and give me 20," he chuckled.

From force of habit I started to rise, prepared to get down on the floor and do push-ups.

"Relax," Coach laughed. "You're out of school now. Shit, but you're spooked today, boy. What's crawled up your shorts?"

That was too close to the truth! I crossed my legs, desperate to hide my raging hard-on. I succeeded only in calling Coach's attention to it.

"Have you got your mind on some hot date you've got tonight?" Coach asked with a nod to my blossoming erection. "Or...?" he left the question unfinished, but he moved a little closer to me on the sofa.

Our bodies were touching. The hairs on my body all stood on end, as erect as my dick. Then Coach slipped his arm around my shoulder.

Instinctively I snuggled in. As soon as I did, I was consumed with abject guilt and terror. But before I could react, Coach did. When he felt my body cuddle up to his, he squeezed me tighter and eased his other hand to my crotch.

"I always thought you wanted some one-on-one," he said. His hand began rhythmically squeezing my crotch till I was in danger of shooting off in my pants.

"What...what do we do now?" I asked. I really didn't know. I'd seen only a couple of porno films, neither of them gay, and had never read a gay magazine. I'd heard jokes about "cocksuckers" and about "ass-fucking queers," but my practical knowledge was severely limited.

"What do you *want* to do?" Coach asked, unzipping my pants and then his own.

"Show me."

"Never had a man before?"

I shook my head in embarrassment.

Coach smiled and opened a drawer in his end table, extracting what I recognized as two packets of rubbers. "Stand up," he instructed. "Strip." Then he did the same.

I got my first look at Coach's boner. Meaty and thick, it jutted out and up from his dense tangle of dark brown hairs, curving at an angle as it oozed thick droplets of opalescent precome.

I put a hesitant finger to his gaping piss slit and wet my finger in the oozing lube. Coach mussed my hair affectionately as my finger skated in his slippery goo. I played with the stuff, entranced. My own dick never leaked copiously; it exuded a drop or two at best. But Coach's boner was producing prodigious quantities of thick precome.

As my fingers became coated with the sticky substance, Coach urged me, "As long as you're lubed, jack it."

I'd never jacked another guy's dick before…had never even *touched* another dick. But I was certainly familiar enough with my own, pounding my pud two or three times a day. Awkward yet eager, I curled my fingers around Coach's fat bone. The warm column pulsated under my touch. Coach groaned as I finished wrapping my hand uncertainly around his dick and, even more uncertainly, began cautiously moving my hand back and forth.

"Don't be so hesitant, boy," Coach urged me. "It won't fall off, and it won't bite you."

I moved my hand faster, feeling his dick as a living thing squirming in my grasp. The tighter I gripped it and the faster I moved my hand up and down Coach's cock, the more it swelled, throbbed, and dribbled tears of precome.

I had never gotten so much pure pleasure—not to mention ear-roaring excitement—as from hefting that swollen cylinder of meat, knowing it belonged to my idol, and squeezing it in my grip. Eagerly I moved my hand faster, faster, even faster till I was speeding out of control. When my motions got too jerky and my rhythm got totally lost, I realized I had gone overboard and stopped until I could regain some self-control.

When I resumed my efforts, I made a conscious attempt to govern my own rhythm and settled into a fairly decent stroke.

"Yeah, boy," Coach panted, sounding like he'd just run 50 laps, "that's the way to go. C'mere," and he curled his hand around my own palpitating rod.

"You'd better not," I warned.

"Afraid you'll shoot off?" Coach chuckled. "So what? There's plenty of cream in those sacs. Fill one rubber, and we'll put another on you. I have a whole box in my bedroom."

"But don't guys do...other things?" I asked, remembering all the jokes I'd heard about cocksuckers and ass fucking. "I want you to show me."

"Why don't we get comfortable inside?" Coach suggested. "More rubbers in there too."

But before leading the way to the bedroom, Coach got around behind me and pressed his beefy body up against mine, snugging his fully engorged dick into the cleft of my buns.

At the feel of his thick, resilient flesh rubbing against my butt, I did lose it; my balls convulsed, my knees went weak, and suddenly I was spurting, my dick spewing wad after creamy wad of slick stuff into the condom. Coach reached around, grasped my dick, and jacked it as it continued to spurt. His jerky jacking on my spitting shaft intensified the sensations and made me pump longer, till my balls felt fully wrung out.

Even then my rod remained rigid, and when I lay down on Coach's bed, the two of us naked and eager, my just-come dick was every bit as hard as Coach's undrained one.

"Now what would you like to do?" Coach asked.

"You show me," I answered. "Teach me. Teach me how to make you feel good."

"There's quite a few plays in this playbook," Coach said. "You could suck me off...or I could fuck you..."

"I want to do both! Can you come twice?"

"I think I can manage," Coach laughed. "Which first?"

"How do I suck it?"

"Get familiar with it first," Coach said. "Kiss it. Lick it. Take just a little of it in your mouth. As you get used to it, try to take more. Then compress your lips around it, tighten them, and suck. Then just move your mouth up and down. You don't have to suck hard; you're not trying to extract my come by force."

I swirled my tongue across the latexed crown. The feel of his bulbous head beneath the stretched-thin rubber was so exciting that I got past the gross taste of the condom. Forgetting his admonitions to go slow, I gulped a goodly portion of his dick into my mouth and immediately started to gag. I backed off, but for an instant before I'd gagged I'd been so thrilled with the feel of Coach's dick in my mouth—*really in my mouth!*—that I eagerly returned and took his dick head once more between my lips.

This time I took it slower. I grew acclimated to the overwhelming taste of rubber, acclimated to having Coach's hugeness fill my mouth, acclimated to the feel of something big and overpowering pushing at the back of my throat. Slowly I took more and more in. No, I wasn't deep-throating him—far from it!—but I had more than half of his immense weapon in my jaw grip...and that was quite good enough for a first time—and for Coach's pleasure.

Cautiously he began to rock his hips, thrusting his demanding meat into my mouth. As his dick slid past my tongue, slithering up against it, I was inspired and began deliberately swiping at it with my tongue with each inward thrust.

I became aware of the scent emanating upward from Coach's forest of tangled pubes. His thicket of curls was rich with a masculine aroma that was part sweat, part musk, and 100% manly. It seemed to dart up my nostrils and from there seep right into my brain, where it set fire to my brain cells and rendered me incapable of thinking.

Coach was obviously getting closer to climax. Despite his efforts to control his motions out of thoughtfulness, he was hunching harder and faster, driving his dick deeper into my mouth with every thrust. Finally he grunted a verbal explosion to match his dick's explosion of warmth into the rubber in my mouth.

He panted his way down from his orgasmic high, then said, "How do you like this so far?"

I couldn't answer.

"Well, I think the glow on your face answers my question. Are you ready to see if you can take it up the ass?"

I guess my face gave away my answer again—a mixture of joy and fear.

"I'll take it slow," Coach continued. "Don't worry. You'll enjoy it as much as you think, and it won't hurt nearly as much as you're worried about. Just relax—that'll help."

Coach's hard-on had softened just slightly, and he stripped his used rubber off. He also removed the full rubber from my hard-as-ever dick. Then he replaced both, dipped his fingers in a glob of lube he squirted from a handy tube, and placed one greased-up finger against my quivering bung hole.

I immediately quivered with a rush of heat that blazed right down to my balls. The feel of his finger, which hadn't even begun to try to invade me yet, was...well, it's an overused word, but *thrilling*. Thrilling in its truest sense...it shot thrills right through me. Those thrills made me shiver, quiver, and shake.

Coach, standing behind me, put a hand on my neck to gentle me, as if I were a spooked colt, and at the same time he squirmed his finger just barely within the grasp of my anal clench.

"Feel that, boy?" he asked me. "That's where my big ol' dick is gonna be going...real soon. Want it?"

I nodded my head eagerly.

"Well, you're gonna get it. Now get used to the finger. There's something much bigger and *much,* much better coming up next."

He inserted a second finger and then, quickly, a third. He began sliding them in and out, hooking them so that every time they started to slide out, the crooked end caught on my rim and strummed the nerves there. My asshole blazed. My inner canal itched with an itch that only his dick could scratch.

"Stuff it up," I urged, immediately blushing at my wanton words. "Give it to me."

"You're sure you're ready?" Coach asked, surprised.

I nodded yes.

Coach put his thick cock's blunt head at the entryway to my hole and edged inward. My ungiving anal pucker resisted, surprising me. I had thought my eager ass would swallow his meat readily now.

"No—shove it up there," I groaned. "I need it. Make it go in!" I was desperate.

"Gonna hurt you if I force it."

"I don't care. Shove it in." And I backed up against Coach, trying to swallow his meat.

It still didn't go in. I felt like crying, suddenly convinced that I was destined to remain forever a virgin.

Then Coach shifted position, put a hand on his fat tool, guided it against my hole again, and slowly, insistently worked his way against my pucker. He pushed and wormed his way gradually within the clench of my never-entered opening, all the while admonishing me, "Hold still. Don't move. Don't even try to help."

With a pop his massive meat breached my entrance.

"*Now* work with me," Coach breathed against my neck.

The pain stung sharply, but the wonderful feeling of fullness overcame the pain. Gradually Coach inched up into my guts, stopping at every inch to give me a chance to get used to the feeling—and to stop him if I had to.

I didn't have to. Soon he was halfway into me.

But the biggest thrill was feeling him buried to the hilt, his scratchy pubes brushing my buns, his body close up to mine while I breathed hard to get used to the feeling of being so filled.

Coach reared back, shoved it in, pulled back faster, shoved it in harder, and then began ramming his spike deep into me with a vengeance.

It was as if I had never come in my life, let alone a mere few minutes ago. I was harder, hotter, and hornier than I had ever been. Coach too was as fired up as a bull released into a herd of cows in season. He rutted with me, plowing me deep, drilling me determinedly with a fierce drive till we both exploded into our rubbers.

When we had both come down from our orgasmic highs, Coach clapped my shoulder approvingly and said, "You move that ass almost as well as you move your legs, Fleetfeet."

I didn't mind hearing the name at all.

The Roommate
by Grant Foster

I rode the elevator to the seventh floor, surrounded by the boxes that contained all my possessions. The two guys who were sharing the ride with me were easily twice my size, with enough muscles to stop a speeding truck on a freeway. They were talking sports to each other over my head, ignoring me.

When the car came to 7, the doors opened, and I began struggling with the unwieldy cartons. By the time I had wrestled the last one out into the hallway, the alarm bell had begun to ring, signaling that the doors had been open entirely too long.

"Sorry," I muttered, my cheeks burning.

"You sure are," one of the men on the elevator retorted as the doors slid closed.

I let out a big sigh. I hoped the other residents of Kane Hall weren't quite as big and surly as the pair I had just encountered, but I had my doubts.

I had originally been slated for a room in Boyer Hall with a fellow classmate from my small-town high school, but my paperwork got all screwed up, and I didn't receive my acceptance letter on time, so Jack was paired with someone else. When my papers finally came through, it was too late to get back in with Jack. That had left me at the mercy of the administration to match me up with a roommate.

When I mentioned Kane Hall to Jack, he told me that he'd heard it was a jock dorm, a place where they housed all the guys who had been admitted to college to keep the sports teams among the most competitive in the country. I had a strong premonition that I wasn't exactly going to fit in.

I was the type of guy who was likely to get carded in a candy store. At five-six and 115 pounds, I was nobody's idea of a jock. My stature, coupled with my pale blond hair and rosy cheeks, made me look like I was pushing 15 instead of 19. I was strong academically, but I suspected that my brains would not be appreciated here at Kane.

I picked up the smallest of the boxes and trudged down the hall, looking for Room 718. It was at the far end of a hall as long as an airstrip. I knocked when I finally arrived, but there was no answer.

I unlocked the door and looked inside. My roommate had already moved in. His bed was a tangle of sheets, and the floor was strewn with athletic equipment. In one corner I saw a barbell with enough weights on it to sink a large boat. The shelves above the desk on his side of the room were full of balls—soccer, football, baseball, basketball—but no books. My heart sank.

After almost half an hour of steady hauling, I had stowed all but one box. It was huge, full of my favorite books from home. I had paid the taxi driver extra to take it to the elevator for me, but now I was on my own.

I knelt down and tried to pick it up. My arms weren't long enough to allow me to get a grip on it. I tried it from every angle but had no luck.

I finally resigned myself to pushing it down the long hallway, my shoulder against the side, my left cheek pressed against the top. I gave it a push, but it didn't budge. I backed off and tried again. My feet slipped, and I fell flat. I scrambled up and looked around—fortunately, the hall was empty. I took a deep breath and hunkered down, ready to try it again.

"Hey, Squirt. Need some help?"

I looked around toward the source of the deep baritone voice. The first thing I saw were long, bare, magnificently muscled legs.

I had never seen calves that thick or thighs with that degree of definition.

As my gaze continued to rise, I quickly discovered that the perfect legs were the least of this incredible specimen's endowments. His torso could have appeared in the reference books as the standard by which all others would be compared. The belly washboarded, the lats flared, the pectoral muscles jutted out like a shelf, and the shoulders loomed broad enough to block my view entirely. His upper arms were thicker than my thighs, and his forearms were, in the words of my younger brother, totally awesome.

As my gaze rose to his face, I began to feel I was in danger of toppling over backward, like a tourist looking at skyscrapers. The last thing this man needed was a model-handsome face, but he had one. It was all planes and angles, high cheekbones, strong chin, startlingly blue eyes, and lashes so long that they almost created a breeze when he blinked. His thick black hair was plastered to his skull. Sweat gleamed on his tanned skin and beaded the hairs that feathered the expanse of his massive chest. He was incredible—and totally intimidating.

"Uh, I'm just moving in," I mumbled, conscious of the need to say something, however obvious. "This is the last box. It's heavy."

"I'll help you with it, Squirt. What room?"

"Seven eighteen." I usually hated to be reminded of my size, but there was nothing mean in the way he referred to me. Besides, what was I going to do? Punch his lights out?

"Seven eighteen?"

I nodded.

He gave me a speculative look and shook his gorgeous head, then bent down, grabbed my box, and hoisted it up onto his right shoulder. For all the effort he displayed, it could have been filled with feathers.

"Come with me, Squirt." He turned and went striding down the long hallway.

I trotted beside him, looking up surreptitiously along his side to the fan of dark hairs in his right armpit and the mighty bulge of his biceps.

"Here we are." He stopped in front of the door to my room.

"Thanks," I replied, searching frantically for my key.

I needn't have bothered. He had a key of his own.

My heart skipped a beat. Could this paragon of all-American studliness be my new roommate? I wasn't sure I was equipped to deal with that.

He opened the door and motioned me in ahead of him. He followed after me and set the box on top of my desk.

"I'm Mark," he announced, his huge hand engulfing mine.

"Keith," I replied shakily.

"Looks like we're bunking together. My last roommate flunked out. You don't look like the flunking type."

"I...uh...I hope not," I stammered, doing my best not to drool on my shoes.

He had raised his arms over his head and stretched, knotting up muscles in places where I didn't even have places. After tickling the ceiling with his long thick fingers, he bent over and planted his palms on the floor. More muscles jumped and knotted, making me feel warmer than the temperature warranted.

"Maybe you could give me a few pointers, Squirt. Math doesn't like me very much."

"Sure, Mark. Anytime."

"Gotta go to soccer practice now," he said, glancing at the alarm clock on his desk. "See you later, Squirt."

"See you, Hercules," I blurted without thinking.

He turned at the door and looked at me. I stood there, hoping the first punch would be enough to do me in so I wouldn't suffer. But he just grinned, winked, and was gone.

I stood there, my heart pounding, looking out the window at the lawn in front of Kane Hall. A couple of minutes later Mark came bounding out of the front doors and loped across the lawn.

He turned, looked up, and waved at someone. I waved back, pretending it was me.

Once he was out of sight, I locked the door, stripped, and jacked off while sitting on his bed.

I had a feeling it was going to be a very long semester.

"God, my neck hurts. How about a little massage, Squirt?"

I put my hands on Mark's shoulders and began kneading his incredible muscles. I was helping him with his calculus again. It was slow going, but he was beginning to absorb the concepts.

We'd been working together a couple of hours a night for the past month, and I had to admit that explaining it to Mark was helping me as well. Of course, I would have happily spent the same amount of time standing knee-deep in dog shit if it allowed me to touch him as I was now doing.

I pressed my thumbs into a knot above his right shoulder blade, and he sighed.

"I'm afraid I'm about ready to give it up for the day, Squirt. Football practice was rough this afternoon."

"Sure, Mark. You're ready for that test tomorrow. I've got total confidence in you. Just don't freeze up."

"Thanks. You've been a great help."

He grabbed his toothbrush and towel and headed down the hall to the bathroom.

When he returned he stripped down to the buff, sprawled out on top of his unmade bed, and was snoring softly in less than a minute.

I read the same paragraph in my history text 32 times, closed the book, and looked over at him. I let my eyes follow the contours of his upper body—contours I had committed to memory weeks ago—then focused on his crotch.

In addition to all of his other physical attributes, Mark was hung like a horse. I'd always known that some men were hung bigger than others, but I had never imagined anyone with a cock like his. When it was soft, it looked like a big, wrinkled Italian salami. Hard, it became an incredibly long, immensely thick dusky brown club. It was hard a lot at night: I guess he had hot dreams.

At first I had tried to ignore it, turning my chair so that I sat with my back to his bed. I knew it was there though, and the temptation to look at it was strong. I could hold out for an hour or two, but then I'd find myself copping glances at it. A few minutes more, and I'd be staring, watching the veiny cylinder and hooded head hover above his belly. He leaked a lot when he was hard. The sticky goo oozed out of his gaping piss hole and drooled onto his gut, running down his sides like thick sweat.

I'm ashamed to admit it, but I jerked off looking at Mark's dick, getting so excited by his monster meat that I could shoot three times in a row without even losing my hard-on. One night I got brave and caught a drop of his lube on my finger, then smeared it on my cock. I came instantly, shooting my wad up over my shoulder, onto the wall. After that I wanted his juice on my rod every time I jerked it.

That night after our study session, I really lost my mind. Mark was deep asleep, and his dick was levitating big time. I had put my books away and was naked in my chair, facing his bed. His dick looked bigger than ever, the knob so swollen, it was pushing out of its cowl, the tip glowing a delicate pink. The veins lacing his cock shaft were bulging, and he was leaking like a broken pipe.

I reached over and held my fingertips under his knob, getting them sticky. I touched my dick, then raised my fingers to my lips. I sucked his slime into my mouth and felt it on my tongue, slippery against my teeth. The taste was an aphrodisiac, making my dick flex against my palm. I reached again, scooped, and sucked my fingers clean a second time.

The next thing I knew, I was kneeling beside his bed, close enough to smell his musky sweat, close enough to feel his body heat. His prick pulsed when I breathed on it, rising a fraction higher above his belly. His eyes were closed, his chest rising and falling steadily, his enormous balls twitching in their low-hanging bag.

With one hand firmly on my cock, I leaned closer and closer, finally daring to brush his dick with my lips. The sensation was like getting punched in the gut. My face got all hot, sweat began trickling down my sides, and my skin began to tingle. I touched his cock again, then began licking his knob. The honey smeared my lips and dribbled off my chin.

I wanted to put his dick in my mouth—so I did. Hell, if he woke up, he was unlikely to make a distinction between licking and sucking.

I opened my mouth wide and wedged his oversize glans between my lips. Everything about it was incredibly hot—the taste, the silky texture of his dick skin, the pulsing hardness of him, the sheer size! I ran my tongue over the spongy surface, felt his foreskin slide back and forth, felt the blood pounding through the swollen veins. My teeth slipped over the rim of the crown and raked the massive shaft.

I don't know how I did it, but I began to swallow, not even gagging when his dick slid past my tonsils. I could feel the muscles in my throat stretching, flexing around the hot shaft I was struggling to engulf. Mark kept snoring, muttering gibberish and rubbing his fuzzy chest. When I was halfway down on him, his hips pumped suddenly, ramming his dick deeper into my throat. I grabbed the side of the bed and hung on tightly.

By the time I was facedown in his pubes, I was so turned on that my whole body was throbbing. I was a heartbeat from coming, but I didn't jack myself. Instead I sucked Mark's dick, bobbing my head up and down, licking, stroking, probing in his deep, salty blowhole for more of the juice that kept bubbling up from his monster nuts.

The flow increased, and then he started to whimper. His balls snapped up and bumped against my nose. I backed off of him and began working on his knob, checking out his cock as it got ready to erupt. I could see the load of jism moving up his pipe and watched, fascinated, as it swelled the fat tube connecting his piss hole to his balls.

Mark let out a piercing squeal as his cream began blasting into my mouth. I was swallowing the thick spew when his cock flexed and got away from me, spurting jism all over my face and chest. When I finally got him capped again, I milked his stalk till he was drained dry and going limp in my hand. I sank back on my haunches, smeared his come on my cock, and got myself off, trembling like a leaf with a combination of fear and horniness.

Afterward I walked over to the window and stood looking out into the darkness. Once the horniness had begun to wear off, I started to feel depressed. I had betrayed Mark, a man I genuinely liked. I had sneaked around like a thief, violating his private space and his body while he slept. I had every right to admire him, even to lust after him, but I had no right to do what I'd done. Tears welled up in my eyes, and within moments I was sobbing uncontrollably.

Suddenly Mark was behind me, close behind. "Hey, Squirt, what's the matter?" I felt his hands, heavy on my shoulders, then his big body, hot and hard against my back.

"I'm sorry, Mark. I…I…" My voice failed me, cut off by a racking sob. What was I going to do? If he knew what I'd done, he'd kill me—not that I didn't deserve it. How could I ever even look him in the face again? I'd offer to move out immediately. It was the least I could do.

"I wasn't asleep, Squirt."

My heart slammed up into my throat, and my stomach began to churn. "You…you weren't?"

"Hey, buddy, I told you I was tired, not dead. That was one hell of a blow job."

I couldn't believe my ears. He didn't sound angry, and, fortunately for me, he hadn't folded me in half and stuffed my head up my ass. I was more than a little confused.

"I said you give great head."

He gripped my shoulders and turned me to face him. His big dick pressed against my belly, still moist with jizz and my spit. He raised his hand and wiped the tears off my cheeks and smiled down at me.

"You're a sexy little fucker, Squirt."

He latched on to my left tit and gave it a pinch. I jerked against him like he'd stuck an electrode up my butt.

"And if I've got a type, I'd have to say you're it." He pinched my tit again and winked at me.

Mark moved back, drawing me with him. He sat in his desk chair and pulled me down on top of him, straddling him, face-to-face. My cock and balls nestled against his belly, and the hairs on his thighs tickled the backs of my legs. I just stared at him, too dazed to speak.

"Go ahead, Squirt. Feel me up to your heart's content."

He clasped his hands on top of his head, and his biceps swelled to monumental proportions. I watched, fascinated, as he flexed. His pecs bulged, and the ridges of his abs were etched clearly beneath his belly fur. He was obviously serious—all this full-blown masculine beauty was mine to enjoy. If this was a dream—a wet dream!—I never wanted to wake up.

I began with his arms, stroking from wrist to armpit, savoring the solid strength of him, feeling the blood pulse in the prominent veins that snaked over his forearms. I pressed my fingers into the mossy hollows of his armpits, then trailed them down his sides, following the fan of his lats. When I rubbed his belly, his silky fur curled around my fingers.

I touched his rib cage and then, at last, his chest. He lowered his arms, clamped his hands on my waist, and took a deep breath, swelling the shelf of his pecs to the max.

I leaned forward and pressed my face into the rock-hard center of his chest. I inhaled. The scent of him—very sexy, very male—tickled my nostrils and made my cock go hard.

"Pinch my tits," he growled, his voice a husky rumble.

I rubbed the hard mounds of muscle, found the thick nubs, and applied a gentle pressure.

"Harder!"

I obeyed, squeezing my thumbs and forefingers together as tightly as I could.

"Oh!"

I looked up at him, wide-eyed.

"You like that, Squirt?"

I nodded.

When I pinched, his cock rose up and smacked soundly against my asshole. I pinched again and got another smack. Mark watched me through the fan of his eyelashes as I went to work on his nipples in earnest.

"Come here, Squirt." He lifted me, and his dick rose from between his thighs and stood up like a fleshy monolith. "God, I want to fuck you, buddy. Will you let me do that?"

"I...I don't think that's possible." I eyed his mammoth prick doubtfully.

"You got it down your throat easily enough. Please let me give it a try. You've got such a pretty ass."

I swallowed noisily, then nodded. How could I refuse a request like that from such an incredible man? I was willing to try anything if it would give him pleasure.

He smiled at me, then reached into one of his desk drawers and pulled out a big bottle.

"Lube it up. Then we'll see what happens."

I took the bottle from him, popped the top, and squeezed. A huge dollop splattered out, rolled across the broad dome of his knob, and down the shaft. I kept on squeezing and smearing until his entire cock gleamed. I tossed the bottle aside, wiped my fingers in my ass crack, took a deep breath, and nodded to Mark.

He put his hands on my hips and lifted me until I felt his immense cock knob press against my crack.

"I feel like I'm sitting on top of a flagpole," I quipped, trying to hide my misgivings. "Uh…don't ruin me for future encounters, buddy. OK?"

"Hey, Squirt, I wouldn't do anything to hurt you. Just relax and trust me."

I put my arms around his thick neck and laid my head on his shoulder. His chest pressed against mine, and I could feel the pounding of his heart. His strong fingers curved around my ass cheeks, kneading them gently. I felt the throbbing heat of his cock as it pressed insistently against my asshole.

"Am I hurting you?" His voice was soft in my ear.

"No, but I think I'm gonna come."

"Not yet, Squirt. Not yet."

It was amazing. I had felt no pain. None at all. There was this incredible sensation of fullness in my bowels, then an intense sexual rush that made me feel like I was going to lose it. I struggled to control the impulse, digging my nails into my palms, holding my breath, willing myself not to shoot.

"I…I'm OK," I panted, still teetering dangerously close to the edge. "I think."

"Man, your ass feels good, Squirt. So hot and tight." He put his big hands on my chest, then his thumbs pressed down hard against my nipples. I jerked around in his lap like an out-of-control puppet. "That's it, Squirt. Ride my dick. Bounce on it."

I braced my palms against the solid wall of his belly and tensed the muscles in my thighs. I rose up, then sank back down into his lap. I could definitely feel his hard-on inside of me. I rose up a second time, relaxed, and slid back onto him. A ball of heat began to grow deep in my gut, radiating through my body.

"That's good, Squirt. That's real good."

He pulled my head down onto his chest. The rubbery point of his tit rubbed against my lips. I caught it between my teeth and started sucking it. Mark growled and thrust his hips up off the chair, raising me into the air.

I stayed still when he started to pull out, his huge dick sliding from my chute till the head of it pulsed against my sphincter. I started to sit down on him again, but he thrust up hard, driving deep into me. I locked my hands behind his neck and held on tight, sucking his nipple frantically as he started to fuck me.

Within moments my whole body was vibrating. My hard-on was hugging my belly, squirting clear juice every time Mark thrust his cock into my body. I looked up at him, still sucking. He was moaning, his eyes closed tight, sweat glistening on his forehead. A flush of pink was rising in his neck, staining his cheeks crimson. His mouth gaped open, and his full, sensual lips pulled back from his teeth. His breathing was ragged.

His prick was jerking and flexing inside of me, getting harder and bigger as he got ready to blast off. The wall of his belly was rubbing against my cock, making control impossible.

My body began to convulse as I started to come. I felt my muscles tighten and go rigid, felt my balls snap up tight between my legs as my orgasm began. My jism gushed out onto Mark's belly, hot and thick and sticky. He felt it, rubbed his fingers in it, and licked them clean. He looked at me one last time, winked, then threw his head back and roared as he blew his heavy load deep up my ass.

I lay there on top of him afterward, not wanting to move. His prick slowly deflated and slipped out of my hole, leaving me feeling empty and incomplete. Mark rose from the chair and carried me over to his bed. He dumped me on top and climbed in beside me. I snuggled up against him and drifted off to sleep, thinking that the semester wasn't going to seem so long after all.

Tuesdays We Read Baudelaire
by R.J. March

Mr. Gerard said he was going to Paris. Luke and I nodded. "Paris is cool," Luke said. How he'd know, I didn't know. Maybe he saw something on MTV about it. I was wishing I had worn some other kind of underwear, because I knew Luke was going to tell me to take off my jeans any minute now. The briefs I was wearing belonged to my brother—too big and not at all sexy except to me. I watched Luke playing with the buttons of his jeans. I could see the outline of his dick under the denim, the way it moved slyly down his thigh. Luke had a big one. Mr. Gerard pretended not to notice, but I knew he could see it, liked seeing it. He sat on his chair with a cup of tea balanced on his knee. He was tall and thin, wearing wire-rimmed glasses. His hair was combed back with some gel. There was a volume of Baudelaire on the table beside him—that's what he called it; it wasn't a book, it was a "volume."

Luke and I were drinking beers. Luke said, "Could I have another?" and I said, "Me too." I'd finished mine a while ago but didn't want to ask for more. Luke was good at asking for more. That's what I liked about him.

"Of course," Mr. Gerard said, and he started to get up, but I said I'd get them. I liked walking through his house. The hallway to the kitchen was lined with pictures of men. The walls were painted a mossy green, and the trim was red, and it always reminded me of being inside a Christmas box.

The kitchen's ceiling was higher than the hall's, and there was a hanging fixture that looked like a streetlight. It had a soft shine, though, and everything looked neat and clean, the way it always looked. There was a box of cookies on the counter that wasn't opened, so I didn't take one, but I did look into a cupboard to see what was there. There wasn't anything but food. I don't know what I expected to find.

I got the beers and went back to where we were sitting. Mr. Gerard called it the sitting room. It was a living room and his bedroom all together, though. The bed was against the wall and piled with pillows, looking like a couch, kind of, and he had a couple of chairs that were huge and comfortable, roomy enough for Luke and me together, and a big table covered with things, mainly books and magazines. In this room the walls were red and the trim was green, and it wasn't like being in a box at all. It was more like some foreign country, what with the hanging silk-covered lamps, the odd drawings of chairs that hung on one wall, and a big gold-framed mirror. Luke liked standing in front of the mirror when he undressed. He was working out and was in love with his body, which seemed to change every day. I liked the mirror because it was like seeing a big picture of all of us together.

Luke and I worked together at Good Buys. He worked in the electronics department, and I was a cashier, mostly. We graduated from school together but didn't really know each other until we started working together; then it was like, "Hey, I know you," and we started hanging out together. He took me up to the top of the hill that overlooked Reading and pointed out where he lived now. He shared an apartment near the outlets with Kenny Farrell, who was turning out, Luke said, to be a real asshole. I didn't know it at the time, but the hill was real cruisy, and I noticed all the guys pulling up to us and sitting in their cars doing nothing, waiting for something to happen. Some of them waved at Luke. (One of them, it turned out, was Mr. Gerard. I didn't know it until later, though.) I didn't say anything because I still hadn't put two and two together, so Luke said, "Guys come up here to get their rocks off." He looked at me, and I could make out his face in the darkness but not what he was driving at. It must have shown on my face, though, the blankness, the "duh," because he laughed and said, "With other guys. In their cars or in the woods there, or you go home with them."

I said, "Oh," and he laughed again, harder this time, and I laughed too because I felt stupid, and he put his hand on my leg. It stayed there, and I got a boner. I was glad he started it, because I never, ever would have, even though I liked him so much that I dreamed about him and pretended he was in bed with me at night, one of his hands on my hard-on, the other farther down between my legs, fingering my butt. I would stare at him from across the sales floor when I could, and he'd catch me and make a stupid face or a jack-off hand sign, like "I'm so fucking bored," and I'd nod, loving him.

He leaned over me that night and started licking my face like a dog. I wasn't expecting that, but it wasn't so bad, and when he started on my neck, it made me crazy with wanting him, and I put my arms around him, getting my hands into the back of his jeans, finding him without underwear. I pulled him onto me, but his legs were stuck between the seat and the steering wheel. His ass cheeks felt smooth, like river rocks. I squeezed them hard. "Take it easy, he-man," he said, undoing the buttons of his jeans. His fanny felt cold in my hands, and I rubbed his cheeks to warm them. My fingers touched into the rough of his crack—he was hot there and a little sweaty. The smell of his butt was going to stay on my fingers for hours that night since I refused to wash it off, sniffing them through the night and making myself come two, three times.

What he did to me that night was rub his big cock against my stomach. He lifted my shirt and played with my nipples and pushed his groin against my gut and humped me that way. His balls rubbed against the waistband of my jeans, and I wanted to take them down, my jeans, to get my dick out too, but Luke held my hands up over my head, his elbows dug into my armpits. I squirmed under him, seeing the bars of headlights cutting through the night air all around us, Luke's hot breath falling down on me in blasts, some stupid song I hated on the radio. I pushed up with my crotch, my dick harder than steel, right up against his fanny. I'd never fucked anyone before, but I was sure that was what I wanted to do. He kept gut-fucking me, though, holding my hands and licking the insides of my arms, making these little noises that really turned me on, little grunts or something that made me think he was really getting into what he was doing. And then he said, "OK," and lifted himself, and I felt the spray of his come hit my face and the front of my shirt. He sat up, right on my crotch, and moved his butt around. Everyone could see him and knew what he was doing, even if they couldn't see me. He touched my nipples, just put his thumbs over them, finding them right away through my semen-spotted T-shirt, and I sauced in my jeans.

It was only a week or so later when he came up to me in the break room, touching the back of my neck even though there was a camera in the room up in the corner by the ceiling. (I think they even had them in the toilets.) He said that we were going to visit a friend of his and that he brought a joint for the ride.

"Where does this guy live?" I asked.

"Just in Flying Hills, man," Luke said. He sat at the table with me and got one of his shoes off and put his foot up in my crotch, and I got a hard-on that lasted all fucking day.

He tried to explain it to me in the car on the way to Mr. Gerard's, but the dope made me stupid and lame, and I just wanted to put my hands in his jeans and touch his cock. "He likes watching," Luke said, unbuttoning his jeans to let me into the warm confines of his underpants. "You sit and have tea with him, and he reads a couple of poems, and then we fuck around."

"Does he fuck around too?" I asked.

Luke shook his head. It was dark now, and his cock glowed green under the dashboard. I had it in my mouth and was sucking on it, lapping up the sweet seepage that leaked out. "Shit," he said. "That feels awesome, Billy." He put a hand on the top of my head, forcing my mouth down into his pubes, and I swallowed him. I did some serious head bobbing, riding his veiny shaft and leaving a pool of my spit in the hairy hollow where his belly and dick met. He slipped his hand inside my shirt and fingered one of my nipples and made me feel wild, unable to get enough of him into my mouth. I wanted to eat him up. I growled and moaned, and he pinched my tit hard, and I had to stop because I was close enough to make a mess of myself, humping the seat piggishly.

"You're a fucking animal, man," Luke said, pulling off to the side of the road. "We're here." He got out of the car, putting away his wet, sticky boner, and got himself ready to introduce me to his friend Mr. Gerard.

I had expected someone older, I think, someone less attractive. Mr. Gerard—I never learned his first name—looked to me like someone who was really hot trying to look like a total dweeb, like Clark Kent or something. He shook my hand, with this prissy smile on his face, and led us into the sitting room, asking Luke how he'd been, going on about how long it had been since he'd seen him even though Luke told me they'd gotten together the previous week. There was a tray on an ottoman set up for tea: the pot on top of some little burner, three cups all ready for us. The room flickered with candles.

Mr. Gerard didn't talk; he chatted. Every third word out of his mouth was "delightful," every fourth "fascinating," as he sat cross-legged in a chair going on and on about this and that, his eyes flicking between Luke and me.

And then he said, getting up, "I need to make a phone call. Would you excuse me?"

When he left the room, Luke nudged me. He unzipped his jeans, and his prong poked out from his shorts. "C'mon," he said, "get undressed."

"What for?" I asked.

"It's time to frolic," Luke said, looking at me with a little smile. "He'll be back to watch."

I stood up and took my pants down. Luke told me to leave my socks on. "Next time you have to wear tighty-whities like me." Luke left his briefs on, his dick sticking out through the pee hole. He looked very sexy to me, and I lunged at him, but he dodged me. I fell across the pillow-covered daybed, my rear end swatted. He fell on top of me, his cock going hotly between my butt cheeks. We hadn't fucked yet, but I was hoping we would some-time and liked letting him know I thought the idea was pretty awesome. He burrowed his dog into the channel of my crack, licking my back. I rolled over, flipping us so that I was on top, his cock still trapped between my cheeks. I wriggled my fanny, feel-ing the sudden ooze of slickness that had leaked out of his fat-tipped bone. He put his hands on my hips and slid me up and down against his shaft. He covered my belly, putting a finger into my belly button, rubbing me there, and then his hands moved up the ribbed cage of my middle to the chocolate kisses of my nip-ples. I had my eyes closed, my head tilted back. I could smell his hair, I could feel his lips against the back of my neck, and I heard him say, "Pretend you don't see him," and I looked up, and there was Mr. Gerard across the room with a gigantic hard-on sticking out of his pants. He was rubbing the end of it, peering at us like a museum exhibit. Candlelight reflected off the lenses of his glass-es. "Suck my cock, man," Luke prompted, and I slowly got off him, feeling the loss of his burning prick against my rear. I turned so that my butt was pointing at Mr. Gerard, and I made my little hole wink and purse, but Luke moved me with a finger, allowing a clear view of his dick sliding into my mouth. I sensed movement in Mr. Gerard's corner and glanced over to see him edging closer, getting himself behind one of his enormous chairs, hiding his fat pecker and the jacking he was doing. I was thinking it would have been more fun if he joined in. From the corner of my eye, he looked awesome, his black hair like one of those British movie stars who play pirates and Shakespeare, long and wavy like that.

Luke spread his legs, and I played with the taut cotton that covered his balls, giving them a good squeeze. I petted his thighs, which were all feathery with hair and hard with muscle from playing soccer or whatever he did when he was in school. I chugged down on his boner, feeling my throat constrict around the head, feeling him throb alongside my tonsils, and he put his hands on my head and did some pretty impressive moaning, saying my name, rolling his head from side to side like I was taking him to the edge of ecstasy or something. I lifted my head to look him in the eye, a drippy string of drool and precome connecting us.

"Bring it here," he said.

Up until now Luke hadn't really gone near my cock. He might have licked it once or twice while we were locked in a sixty-nine and his prick was rooting around in my esophagus, but I couldn't have said he ever really sucked it. It didn't make much difference to me up until then, but the thought of it happening made my dick ache with wanting to feel his lips around it. I crawled up the bed on my knees, sinking into the pillows, bringing him my cock. When I got it close enough for him to kiss the end, he looked up at me and said, "Take it easy." He took hold of my prick like it was a finger sandwich and stuck out his tongue at it. I steadied myself with one hand on the wall behind Luke's head. Mr. Gerard had moved again, getting a better view. I could see his great penis, pale and huge, with its rolling skin and bright red head. He held it with both hands and still couldn't cover all of its shaft. He pulled on his trouser snake, pinching out a flood of leakage, baring and covering the bulbous head. But I forgot about Mr. Gerard when I felt the first heat of Luke's mouth and the slide of my dick head over his flattened tongue.

I did my best to keep still, but I couldn't help myself and had to fuck that soft wetness. It was better than anything I'd ever felt, better than the cool and slippery slide of the percale pillowcase I'd been fucking ever since I could remember, better than the space between Eric Moser's hairless thighs, better even than the spitty cup of my hand. I loved the friction of his chin on my balls and the terror of his slight underbite when his bottom teeth caught on the sensitive underside of my cock head. Together the sensations combined and doubled, tripled; I was practically shaking but banging into his mouth with a vengeance. I started breathing hard, and Luke was tapping my thighs, then hitting my stomach, choking on me. I pulled out, out of control, and creamed across his face, practically bawling, and I felt the warm squirt of jizz on the backs of my thighs as Luke unloaded.

"That wasn't so bad," Luke said later in the car. "Was it?"

I shrugged. Actually it was the single most awesome experience of my life. I'd just had an orgasm that was like an explosion, and it was witnessed by a man wanking on a monster dick, watching me like television. "Not bad," I agreed.

I was surprised one day when I saw Mr. Gerard in the CD department of Good Buys. "I'm looking for a Puccini disc," he said when I came up to him. He looked different to me this day—his hair wasn't so gelled, his clothes not all black and woolly. He looked very much like a normal guy. "Luke is busy tonight, but I was wondering if you'd care to drop by."

I told him I didn't drive.

"I'd be happy to pick you up. Shall I? After work?"

I waited outside the store for half an hour and was just about ready to give up when he pulled up in a little black Jag. He apologized for being late. "I was at the gym," he said, and I noticed under his jacket that he wasn't wearing a shirt and tie but a stringy tank top. There was a dark brush of hair between his pecs, straight and shining. He had on a pair of sweats, old gray ones with a rip in one knee. He looked more normal than ever. I sank into the leather seat with a sort of awe. He hadn't shaved, and he was wearing, I thought, contacts. It was like being with another person altogether.

He kept quiet. Apparently he liked the song on the radio. He hummed bits and pieces of it, his eyes intent on the road.

Mr. Gerard excused himself to go to the bathroom once we arrived, and he took a really long time. I sat and leafed through some boring magazines. *Where's the porn?* I wondered and figured he was taking a bath or something. He came out the same way he went in, though, and sat down beside me on the bed made up as a couch.

"Take off your clothes for me," he said casually, as though he'd just asked me to get him a glass of water. I stood up, feeling a little shy, and moved away from him so he'd have a good view. I started stripping.

"Take your time," he said, leaning back on some pillows. The bulge in the crotch of his sweats was prominent, a mountain of a molehill. I unbuttoned my shirt slowly, getting down to my T-shirt. I still had shoes and socks and jeans and briefs to go, figuring it would be a long show, not really thinking about how fast clothes come off. I went for the shoes next, untying them, bent over, feeling the blood rush to my face. I saw his hand run over the lump in his sweats.

The shoes came off quicker than I'd expected. I straightened up and wondered what to take off next—shirt, socks, or pants. I did some mental head scratching and decided the socks would go next, but I was going to need some help. I stepped close to Mr. Gerard and put my foot on the cushion between his legs. He caught on quickly and didn't seem put off by the idea. He grasped my foot and gently peeled the sock off, rubbing the sole with his thumb, his other hand on my ankle and creeping higher. When I gave him the other foot to unsock, he pulled me onto him.

"You're better at this than you let on," he said, his mouth close to my ear. His hands went all over my backside, and it was becoming apparent that my cherry little behind wasn't meant for Luke after all. He ran his thumb along the seam of the ass of my jeans, applying pressure at my hole and again where my balls were flattened between my legs. His mouth worked all over mine, his tongue darting and stabbing, flat and slobbering, then hard and pointed, and he stuck it into my mouth so that it nearly went to the back of my throat, taking my breath away.

He let me up for air once, rolling us around so that he was on top, and then his sweats were gone, and he was humping me with that humongous tool of his. His legs were covered with fine black hairs. I could put my hands on the backs of his thighs and cup his ass cheeks, which were smooth and firm with muscle. He sighed when I put my fingers into his crack, and he pawed at my briefs, rolling them off my hips and pushing them down my thighs, and they turned into tight ropes around my knees. His cock rolled over mine, dwarfing it, leaking a sticky goo that made it slick between us. His balls dangled down in the V of my legs, banging against my little chestnuts, slapping against my pinched-up little hole.

He got up and stood over me. "Get on your hands and knees," he said quietly. He had his great prong in his hand, palming it, getting his juices flowing. I looked at the gigantic head and wondered how on earth he was going to get it into me without splitting me wide open. "Don't worry," he added. "I wouldn't dream of hurting you."

He got behind me and started eating out my butt. I could feel the ring of my anus flutter under the stroke of his tongue. He licked up and down my ditch, wild hairs springing up all over the place. He bit my ass cheeks and chinned my balls. He handled my prick gently, tugging on the end of it, his fingers smearing in the grease. I heard him say, "Ready?" and I thought, *I'll never be ready for that thing.*

He didn't fuck me, though—not with his cock, anyway. He fingered me with his left hand and jacked off with his right, and he told me to turn over. I think he was afraid I'd jizz up his bedspread; I'd already gotten plenty of dick drool on it. On my back I lifted my legs and put my feet on his chest. His finger poked at that spot I'd recently found on my own, and it was driving me crazy. Mr. Gerard looked down at me with this glazed look on his face, his eyes slitted. He licked his beautiful lips, working another finger in. He tapped my thigh with the heavy head of his dick, leaving wet marks.

"Jerk yourself off," he said, because I wasn't touching myself— I didn't need to, really. I was sure he was going to make me come, working his fingertips over that hardening ball up my ass. "I want to see you come," he said, and I said, "OK," and it just happened. I started squirting all over myself, clotty streams of white flying all over the place, landing on my face and in my hair and on the pillows behind me, which might have pissed him off if he hadn't been so horny.

Mr. Gerard bent over and started lapping up my come like a cat over spilled milk. I could feel his fisted cock between my legs, then the hot spray of jizz as his prick spit out all over my cock and bush and balls.

He fell back on the bed with a huge sigh, his stiffer looking like a candle dripping wax. I wanted to lick it off. He looked at me with sleepy eyes. I was fascinated by his cock, the enormity of it, the way it started falling, a tree in slow motion, big and white, across his thigh, slime still coming out of the fat head.

"You want to do it again, don't you?" he said to me. I nodded.

"Dinner first," he said. "We'll go to Joe's. And when we come back you can fuck my brains out. How does that sound?"

I shrugged. "OK, I guess," I said, though inside I was starting to boil. My dick was still hard, and I imagined what it would be like to be up inside that muscular ass and very nearly had a little accident.

Mr. Gerard got up and took my hand, pulling me up and leading me to the bathroom. He turned on the water and started filling the tub, pouring in this and that, turning the water a pretty green that smelled like limes and oranges and roses all together. He touched the pointed prong that wouldn't go away.

"Insistent," he said thoughtfully.

We got into the hot water, and he pulled me to him, getting me between his legs as though we were tobogganing, and he put his lips against my head.

"Have you read any Kaváfis?" he asked me, and I carefully shook my head no.

"Oh, you must," he said. "You must."

Looking for Mr. Right
by Michael Cavanaugh

"Honestly, Michael, I can't take much more of this." My room-mate stood over the sofa looking down at me, his fists clenched. "This has been going on entirely too long. You've got to pull your-self together—and the sooner, the better."

"You're right, Cal. You're absolutely right." I sat up and pushed my hair out of my eyes. "It just isn't worth it." I glanced over at the clock. I had been moping about Carlos for almost half an hour—far longer than he deserved. I flashed a weak grin at Cal, then stood up and stretched. "I think I'll go to the gym. It'll do me good."

"There, that's better." Cal beamed at me sunnily, then flopped down on the sofa I had just vacated. "Now maybe I can watch *Oprah* without having to listen to your pissing and groaning all afternoon long."

"You could be a little more sensitive, Cal. I really thought Car-los was the one."

"The one what?"

"The love of my life, Cal. Mr. Right. The man I could spend my life with."

"Michael, you say that about every man you go to bed with. How many does that make in the past five months—two dozen, at least?"

"Certainly not!" I was scandalized by the very idea. "I can't think of anyone other than Carlos."

"What about Tim? And Joe? Then there was Bill, Tom, Antho-
ny, Rich, Dave, Steve—"

"Stop it! Stop that shit right now!" Roommates can be so un-
kind, so unfair. "I sincerely believed that my relationship with
Carlos was serious."

"Come on, Michael. Give me a break. How could you take a
man like that seriously?"

"He was very romantic, Cal. I really thought—"

Cal interrupted me with a rude snort. "Romantic? Your first
date was when he fucked you in the steam room at the gym. You
call that romantic?"

"That isn't the way it happened," I protested hotly. "Not exactly, anyway."

"Is too. Everybody at the gym knows about it."

"Only because some asshole started that revolting rumor."

"Only because you let him fuck you right there in front of anybody who happened to wander into the steamer. You're just lucky
you didn't get your gym membership revoked." Cal grabbed the
remote from the coffee table and flipped on the TV.

I glared at him, then stalked off to my bedroom to gather up
my gym clothes.

Cal obviously didn't understand relationships the way I did.
OK, so maybe Carlos and I did meet in the steam room, but Cal
had the dynamics all wrong. It wasn't sex…well, it wasn't *just* sex.
It was… Anyway, you had to have been there to understand the
nature of the attraction between us.

The day I met Carlos, I'd had a really great workout, and I was
pumped to the max and looking damned good, if I do say so myself. I only went into the steam room that afternoon because the
showers were full, and I had to do something.

Carlos was sitting on an upper bench in the far corner, his olive
skin glistening with sweat. The skin was stretched over an awesome array of muscles, so naturally I looked over at him and
smiled. He smiled back and waved me over to him.

"Hi," I said brightly, going over and standing in front of him. He was built like a brick shithouse.

"Hey, dude," he said, shifting on the bench and flexing his pecs. He had a dynamite chest. "I saw you working out today. Looking good."

"Thanks."

"You gotta have the hottest fucking ass in this entire gym, man. I mean it."

"Thanks again." He really was sweet. Observant too.

"Why don't you turn around and give me a good look at it?"

How could I say no to such a reasonable request? I turned around and flexed my cheeks. He grunted; then I felt one of his big hands on my ass. Next thing I knew, he'd plunged a finger into me up to the second knuckle.

"Damn, man," he breathed. "Nice, tight hole. Look what I got here for you."

"Oh!" I looked over my shoulder. He spread his powerful thighs, and this absolutely enormous hard-on rose up and pointed right at me, the fat cap flaring out like a helmet. I'm usually the shy type, but the sight of all that hard cock (we're talking in excess of ten inches here), not to mention the huge, hairy balls that hung down over the edge of the bench, really got me going. I clenched my hole playfully around his invading digit and took a step back.

"Ugh!" Before I realized it, he had picked me up, pulled me onto his lap, and crammed about half of his immense schlong up my unlubricated butt hole. "Spit on it!" I squealed. "It's too fucking big! You're splitting me in half!"

"Yeah, baby. That's the way I like it." He thrust his hips forward and buried several more inches of man meat up my chute. I wriggled and squirmed, but that only drove him in deeper. If his fat knob hadn't punched me in the prostate at that instant, I don't know what I would've done. As it was, I grunted and bucked, then settled back against his hard, sweaty torso, ready to ride.

Carlos was the masterful type, that was clear from the beginning. He slapped my belly hard enough to leave a perfect imprint of his hand on my skin and started pinching my sensitive tits while he packed my ass with a vengeance. I looked down at my chest, watching in amazement as my nipples were stretched a good inch beyond the rise of my perfectly sculpted pecs. They'd never been pulled that hard before, and I only hoped they wouldn't be permanently stretched. I didn't think they'd look good dangling.

"Ride my fucking cock, man. Tighten up that hole. That's it. Squeeze it hard! Fuck!"

I was crouching on the lower bench, ass thrust back, every muscle tensed, getting the fuck of destiny. My own dick was hard now, arching up against my belly, twitching and throbbing as Carlos continued to plow my aching hole. His big balls had stopped swinging up and slapping against mine and were now knotted at the base of his prick, punching against my ass ring with every gut-wrenching thrust of his meat.

"Bounce on it, dick pig!" He was biting my neck now, snorting and grunting, the sweat pouring off of him in rivers. His prick felt as if it had doubled in size since he first shoved it up into me, and I half expected to feel it battering against my tonsils any second. My tits were numb, but my hole was feeling every hard, veiny inch of him as he plowed in and out, in and out, reaming me as if this were the last fuck in the civilized world.

"Here it comes, fucker! Take my hot load! Oh, yeah!" He jammed his dick in deep, and I could feel the heat as he let fly, pumping my hole full of his juice. I tensed up and popped my rocks as well, hitting the man sitting across from us right in the face. To be honest, I hadn't even heard the door to the steam room open and was totally surprised when I opened my eyes and saw the man with the come on his face, not to mention the 20 other guys who were crowded around, watching me get my ass packed. I doubt if any of them thought anything about it until that rumor got started about me a couple of days later.

Anyway, my relationship with Carlos blossomed after our first meeting. He was always horny, and we must have screwed at least four times a day.

I was at the point of letting Cal know that I was moving out when disaster struck. I showed up at Carlos's place one afternoon, about an hour earlier than usual, only to find the jerk in bed, packing his dick up the ass of some anonymous blond who just happened to have bigger biceps than I did. On the other hand, the blond didn't have nearly as nice an ass as mine, and his legs were embarrassingly skinny. Obviously, the taste Carlos displayed when he got together with me had been a fluke.

I shot Carlos this totally contemptuous look, then walked right into the bathroom, where I retrieved my toothbrush and the expensive soap I had bought for him the week before.

"You are a total jerk," I snapped on my way back through the bedroom.

"Hey, man, it ain't what it looks like," Carlos panted, not even slowing down. The blond had his face buried in the pillows and wasn't in any condition to say anything.

"So, Carlos, what is it? A proctological exam?"

He just stared blankly. He obviously didn't get it.

"We are officially finished."

"Fuck you, buddy," Carlos snapped, flipping me off.

"In your dreams," I replied with as much sarcasm as I could muster, walking out on him, my head held high.

Afterward I had come back home and practically suffered a nervous breakdown until Cal brought me back to my senses. He was right—Carlos hadn't been the one. Definitely not.

I got to the gym before the evening rush and put on my new workout gear. It was a white spandex unitard, as tight as a second skin. I had bought a size small instead of a medium, and the fit was perfect. The front was cut to below the navel, and the thin straps left my pecs totally bare. I walked over to the mirror and took a good look. All of my assets were highlighted, leaving nothing to the imagination. I mean, you could practically tell that I shaved my balls. I struck a pose, then, satisfied with the results, headed out to warm up.

I was working on my biceps when I first noticed him. He was just my type: tall, dark-haired, handsome, and built like a Greek god. He was at the bench press, doing 275 pounds. Every time he pumped out a rep, his pecs bulged out like big boulders, and his arms got absolutely huge. When he was finished he stood up, and I could see the thick veins that cabled his hairy forearms and snaked up over his gorgeous biceps. He had dark beard stubble and beautiful green eyes with long lashes. I checked out his basket and could tell that he was really hung, even under his baggy old shorts. Lumps that size don't stay hidden—not that they're all that important. Not really.

He saw me looking at him and flashed me a smile. I smiled back and started pumping reps like crazy, determined to add more bulk to my arms. He soon moved on to work on his legs, and I followed along. I figured my thighs could use a little toning, not to mention the fact that it gave me a chance to keep an eye on the dark-haired man.

He was concentrating on his calves, which didn't really need any additional development. I love a man with good legs, and this guy's were really superior. Every time he rose up on his toes, his calves would twitch and swell, every individual muscle showing clearly beneath the dark, glossy hairs that coated his long legs. I stood beside him, doing my best to duplicate his moves even though I was using only half the weight. I had to quit when my right calf started cramping, but he went on and on until I thought his muscles would burst right out of his skin.

I tailored my workout to coincide with his, noticing how he kept looking over at me from time to time. Obviously he was pretty interested, although he didn't say anything. The strong, silent type—better yet. When he finally finished up and headed back to the locker room, I limped along after him, wishing I had done about a dozen fewer squats. My thighs really hurt.

When I got to the shower, he was there, soaping his magnificent body. He really was incredible: huge, sculpted chest; a perfect six-pack of abs; narrow hips; tiny waist; cute furry butt; arms to die for; and, of course, those amazing legs. I beelined for the shower jet next to him, oblivious to the two guys who had seen it come available at about the same instant I did. I ignored their muttered remarks and turned on the water full blast.

I took a quick, discreet peek at his crotch. Below a dense tangle of dark pubes, his dick hung down, thick and heavy, the fat glans hitting him about mid-thigh. It curved over a pair of big balls that sagged down to the tip of his prick, the left riding on top of the right. His dick had the coolest blue vein running up the middle of the back. It branched about halfway along the shaft, wrapping around it like tiny blue fingers. Short hairs sprouted for a couple of inches along the base of his meat. I couldn't help thinking how they'd tickle a guy's lips if he managed to swallow it that far.

"Great workout," I said, hoping to spark a conversation.

"Light one today," the man replied. "Have to give the old bod a rest once in a while."

"Uh…yeah. Me too." I wondered what a heavy workout would be for this dude. Wow!

"I'm Michael."

"Dane." He was a man of few words. I tried to think of something else to say, but before I could get started Dane had turned all of his attention to washing his left armpit.

I soaped myself up as well, turning so that the big guy could steal a look at my ass if he felt the urge. I kept peeking over my shoulder at him and finally caught him staring at my twin globes of muscled flesh. I grinned at him, and he raised his eyebrows, then turned toward the shower jets to rinse himself off. When he turned off the water, I did the same and followed him into the locker room.

His locker was across from mine, so I got dressed in a hurry, then went out to the lobby to wait for him. Casually, of course.

When he came out he saw me and raised his eyebrows again.

"Waiting for someone?"

"Yeah. You." He chuckled at that and shrugged his thickly developed shoulders.

"What the hell? I've got a couple of hours to kill, and you look hot enough to melt paint. Let's go." The words weren't exactly romantic, but I could tell by the way he said them that he was a good deal more excited than he was letting on. I grabbed my bag and followed him out to the parking lot.

Dane lived in a big house in a nice section of the city. I trotted after him across a huge lawn with expensive landscaping. It looked pretty great already, but I figured I'd probably put in a bunch of red petunias after I moved in. I think petunias always add class to a front yard.

Dane showed me into the kitchen and offered me a Coke, then went off to change his clothes. I stood at the sink, looking out over the back. He actually had a swimming pool and a hot tub. The man was obviously a class act. Cal would simply piss green ink when I invited him over for a barbecue after I got settled in.

"You ready?"

I turned and looked at Dane. He was naked except for a leather strap cinched around his cock and balls. It was doing its job, and his cock was already at least two inches longer than when I'd seen it at the gym, although it wasn't anywhere near hard yet.

"I sure—whoops!"

He'd put his hands on my shoulders and pushed me to my knees. Before I could say another word, he grabbed my hair and tilted my head back, then began stuffing his cock down my throat. It was a huge cock and nearly cut off my air supply, not that I was going to complain. It tasted really hot, a blend of sweat, soap, and piss that got me revved up in a hurry.

After he'd ridden my face for a couple of minutes, bouncing his big balls off my chin, he pulled back, and I started nursing his fat piece of meat in earnest. I kissed the swollen fist-size knob perched on the end, teasing at the gaping piss hole with the tip of my tongue. I heard Dane growl and saw his balls try to rise. They rolled up a little, then sagged back down, way too heavy to climb the cords this early in the game.

Once I'd gotten the head all worked over, I went after the sexy vein, tracing it up into his bush, then back down to where it branched. I was licking his big cock, kissing it and slobbering all over it, when Dane grabbed my hair again, pulled my head back, and started slapping my face with his meat. He was getting really hard, and he popped me a couple of good ones that really stung. After about the fifth whack, he started leaking profusely, and hot lube juice began splattering across my forehead and cheeks.

I was just about to see stars when he grabbed me by the neck and hauled me to my feet. I was going to say something clever and witty and maybe even give him a big kiss, but he spun me around and bent me over the island counter in the middle of the kitchen. My head accidentally bumped against the tiled surface, and I saw stars for real.

I reached out and grabbed the edge of the counter at about the same instant that I felt the head of his cock bump my ass pucker. It was hard and hot and sticky, and I forgot whatever it was I'd been planning to say.

His cock slid up and down along my crack until his knob hit me about mid-spine, then slid back and butted my hole again. I heard him hawk a wad of spit and felt it land on my bull's-eye. He wedged his knees between my legs and splayed them wide apart, leaving me totally defenseless. I waited breathlessly for his next move, my dick rigid, my heart pounding.

"Aie-e-e!" He skewered me on his prong, punching it into me up to the hairy hilt. His balls crashed against mine, shooting sparks of pain and lust throughout my frame.

"Hold on tight, Steve."

"Michael," I corrected him.

"Whatever," Dane whispered, grinding his hips and stirring his massive cock around in my straining chute. "You are about to get your lights fucked out."

I felt his dick withdraw all the way, leaving me gaping. Then he slammed forward, driving his gigantic hard-on back in to the limit again.

He kept it up, all the way out, all the way in, leaving me clawing at the counter and gasping for air. Every time he thrust, he hit my prostate hard, soon reducing me to a whimpering mass of horny nerve endings. I could feel the hairs on his thighs against the backs of my legs, shooting little sparks right up to my belly, where they exploded in mind-numbing rushes of lust.

He was going at me like a pile driver when I heard voices in the hall. I opened my eyes and saw two men step into the kitchen, then stop and stare at the scene being played out in front of them on the counter.

"Hey, guys," Dane said casually, not even slowing down. "I'm getting this hot little piece all warmed up. There's a hole up front going to waste. Come and join me."

I thought that was rather presumptuous, his not asking me or anything, but before I could protest, the men began shedding their clothes, and I decided to keep quiet.

They both obviously subscribed to Dane's brand of working out. We're talking major muscles here, one set dusted with copper fur, the other totally hairless even at crotch level. They walked over to the side of the counter my head was hanging over and started smacking me in the face with their swelling dicks. I was going to get major bruises if I wasn't careful.

Once they both got hard, they started to fuck my face, taking turns at first, then cramming both of their bloated hard-ons down my throat at the same time. They both had fat, tasty pricks, and I wouldn't have complained even if I could have at that point.

Dane was still fucking my ass like wild, his belly slapping my ass cheeks, his big balls battering my aching nuts like hairy hammers. Then one of his buddies reached back and stuffed a finger up my ass alongside Dane's huge, pistoning prick. The other one got into the act as well, and pretty soon I had more fingers shoved up my ass than I cared to count. The thing was, it felt good. Dane really liked it too, judging by the way he was fucking me, which was so hard, it made the counter creak.

All of a sudden one of the guys up front yelled and popped his cock out of my mouth. He started pumping it and blew his wad. I felt it splattering down across my shoulders, hot and pungent. The guy still in my mouth grabbed my ears and really went for it, fucking my face like a wild man. I could feel his dick getting stiffer and bigger, and then he started shooting his load down my throat. I sucked and swallowed, eating every drop of his white-hot come.

He went over to stand by his buddy while Dane rode me into the homestretch. He bucked and thrust, pounding my ass royally. I heard him groan, then felt his cock flex. He stopped pumping, and the heat began to gush out of him, flooding my ass channel. He shot again and again, filling me up till the come was running down over my balls and dripping down my legs. When he pulled out of me, I slid off the counter and onto the floor.

Dane would've helped me get off, I'm sure, but the phone rang, and he had to answer it. I jerked myself off into a kitchen towel, then lay back on the cool linoleum, too dazed to move.

It turned out that Dane and his buddies had to go out to dinner at someone's house, so we couldn't sit and talk as long as he would've wanted to. Hell, he didn't even have time to give me a lift home. It was a long walk, but I didn't mind. It wasn't really raining all that hard.

"You look like you got beaten up," Cal remarked when I trudged through the living room on my way to the bathroom to take a shower. "Who ran over you?"

"I met a very nice man, smarty," I retorted, smiling smugly. "I think this one is serious. He even introduced me to a couple of his friends."

"Right." Cal looked at me and shook his head. "What happened to your face, Michael? It looks like somebody pistol-whipped you with a Polish sausage."

"Mind your own business, Cal," I snapped back at him. "If the phone rings, it'll probably be Dane." I had scrawled my telephone number on the message pad on his refrigerator before I left. I was sure he would find it. "I'm going to take a shower."

"Good. You smell like a sperm bank."

"Up yours, Cal." I stuck my head out of the bathroom door. "You're just jealous. I've got a feeling this is the one I've been waiting for. We really clicked. I may be moving in with him by the end of the month."

"Right, Michael. I'll put an ad in the paper for a new roommate." He picked up the remote and pointed it at the TV. "Try soaking your head in cold water, Michael. It'll help with that swelling."

"Cal, why don't—" I decided to shut my mouth and closed the door. He just didn't get it. Either you're a romantic or you're not. There are no two ways about it. Dane would understand; I just know he would.

Contributors

Derek Adams is the author of a popular series of detective novels featuring the intrepid Miles Diamond as well as over a hundred short stories, which, he insists, are ongoing chapters in his auto-biography. He lives near Seattle and works out whenever he can find a man willing to do a few push-ups with him.

Barry Alexander didn't start out as a writer. In fact, he was diligently working his way through divinity school when he strayed a bit. After stunt-dicking in dozens of videos, he moved to Iowa, where he wrote his first book. "Yes, it's true," he says, "porn writers write from experience, and we always have big dicks."

Cain Berlinger's erotica has appeared in such magazines as *GBM*, *Drummer*, *Mandate*, *Bunkhouse*, *Honcho*, *Torso*, and *Cuir*. He is the creator of the black sex action hero Hannibal Rex, which made its debut in the German magazine *Toy*. His popular leather bear series, *Daddy Ben*, which had a successful ruin in *Cuir* (now *Eagle*), is due to hit bookshelves sometime soon. He divides his time between New York City (as a massage therapist) and Chicago (where he writes the Tribe column for the *Windy City Times* and lives with his two life partners, Jack and Shadow). He is currently hard at work on a gay mystery novel and a stage play based on his adventures as a massage therapist.

Michael Boyd grew up in the pine forests of north-central Louisiana but has called Austin, Texas, his home for the past seven years.

A nude-beach enthusiast, he is editor and publisher of *Naked Places: A Guide for Gay Men to Nude Recreation and Travel.* He also publishes *Smooth Buddies,* a 'zine for guys into body shaving. He and his lover spend as much time as they can on the road, exploring remote places in the West, doing things like camping on a South Dakota cliff, four-wheel driving in Utah's Canyonlands, and making love in a remote hot spring in the eastern Oregon desert.

Mark Caldwell is the name the author uses because it is the name of the boy who was both the object of greatest desire and the source of greatest torment during the author's youth. He has written for *Stroke* magazine since 1980.

Leo Cardini is the author of *Mineshaft Nights,* a collection of short stories inspired by his experiences as doorman at the legendary gay sex club. His short stories and novellas have also appeared in many publications, including *Freshmen, Men, FirstHand,* and the *STARbooks* anthologies. Further information on him can be found on the walls of better men's rooms everywhere.

Michael Cavanaugh has worked as a waiter, a doorman at a luxury hotel, and a model. He is currently ready to set sail as a steward on board a private yacht bound for the South Seas. He is confident that Mr. Right is definitely out there somewhere.

Lew Dwight lives deep in the woods of northern New England. Despite the perversion evident in his tales, he leads a remarkably settled existence with his partner of 12 years on a farm: "We have horses, sheep, ducks, chickens, turkeys, and innumerable rats. Most now are in the freezer. Well, not the horses." His alter ego has a secret literary career, which he doesn't care to discuss.

Grant Foster has contributed short stories to a number of magazines and anthologies. In addition to his fiction, he also writes articles about travel and gay history. When not writing, traveling, or doing historical research, he gardens at his home in rural Washington State.

Steven Lundquist developed his interest in male erotica during college, when he began writing accounts of his peeping sessions outside dorm windows at ICU. Fellow students clamored for copies of his stories. The profits paid his senior tuition, though some of the proceeds also went toward the purchase of gallon drums of lube, which were used in research, Steven avers with a straight face—the only thing about him that is straight. In his senior year he hosted many teas for gay students, who swore he offered "the best teas in town." Deciding to live up to that name—the best tease in town—he became a male stripper upon graduation…and also upon his new boss, a studly bear with a beercan nine-incher, at least the way Steven tells it. But then, we all know Steven can tell a good story.

R.J. March is the pseudonym of a man who wrote his first erotica in sixth grade. He lives in Reading, Pennsylvania, with his lover and no dog.

Roddy Martin once kept a wall of literary pinups: David Leavitt, Christopher Bram, and handsome young Christopher Isherwood. His work has appeared in *Freshmen, Classifieds,* and *In Touch for Men.* He is amazed to find himself writing sex scenes and even more so to find editors remarkably supportive and idealistic.

Todd McGuire has been busy working as a freelance writer ever since selling his first short story in 1994. He is considering publishing a collection of the best of his over three dozen stories within the next few years. He's also interested in writing a novel one day. He lives for his art.

Christopher Morgan is a 30-something born-and-bred New Yorker who has been writing and editing gay erotica for ages. His first novel, *Musclebound,* has been an excellent seller in both English and Japanese and was cited in Will Roscoe's scholarly work, *Queer Spirits: A Gay Men's Myth Book,* in his chapter "The Way of Initiation." Other short stories of Morgan's have appeared in *Boy Next Door* and *Country Boy* magazines and in *Southern Comfort,* edited by David Laurents, and *Western Trails,* edited by Gary Bowen. His own collection of short stories, *Steamgauge,* received very positive reviews, his favorite being: "Morgan must have done inordinate amounts of research on dozens (no, hundreds) of men to be able to portray the realism of these blow jobs." Um, sure!

Lee Alan Ramsay was born Robert Lee Allen, in Providence, Rhode Island. At age 30 he moved to Los Angeles, where he found his leather persona: Daddy Bob Allen. With a 16th-century torture grotto carved out of his garage, he has built an international reputation as a leatherman. For many years his dungeon was booked six weeks in advance, and it has been said that he has forgotten more about S/M than most people will ever know. He has been writing for *The Leather Journal* since its inception in 1987 and is now its news editor as well as the fiction and photo editor of *Eagle.* He has two books in print: a collection of articles titled *The Only Reason I Mention This* (1995) and a novel, *The Wings of Icarus* (1996).

Evan Robertson is a Los Angeles native currently residing near San Francisco. He is the author of works published in *CMA (Chest Men of America), Mandate, Inches, Mach, Drummer, Torso, Playguy,* and *Honcho.* He has reportedly donated the West Coast's largest private collection of Maria Callas paraphernalia to the San Francisco Performing Arts Library and Museum.

Ron Templeton created his first-remembered work of fiction as a teenager while on a prank phone call to a Protestant help line.

After creating a life of horror, which he never lived, Ron felt incredibly guilty as the clergyman fervently prayed for his salvation. He has since repented his ways, abstains from prank calls, and instead writes fiction that he suspects would make most clergymen apoplectic. He lives a very contented life in the Pacific Northwest with his heavyset husband of over 11 years, a roommate, and three dogs.

Bob Vickery's stories have appeared in a wide variety of magazines, and he is currently a regular contributor to *Men*. Two anthologies of his stories have been published: *Skin Deep* and *Cock Tales*, and he has stories appearing in other anthologies, including Susie Bright's *The Best American Erotica of 1997, Up All Hours, Butch Boys*, and *Queer Dharma: A Gay Buddhist Anthology*. In his spare time he bakes muffins at a Zen Buddhist monastery in Northern California.

About the Magazines

Beau was first published in 1989 and is a quarterly, with 11 stories running in each issue. Annual subscriptions are $9.97. For more information, write to: Sportomatic Ltd., P.O. Box 470, Port Chester, NY 10573. "Checkmate" appeared under the title "Fortunes" in the May 1997 issue.

The Boy Next Door debuted in 1994. Like *Beau,* it is a quarterly publication. Annual subscriptions are $9.97. Each issue contains 14 stories. For more information, write to: Sportomatic Ltd., P.O. Box 470, Port Chester, NY 10573. "In-Tents Encounter" appeared under the title "Forest Fuck" in the June 1997 issue.

Classifieds was launched in 1992. With its September 30, 1997, issue, however, the magazine began publishing under the name *Unzipped.* It features one piece of fiction per issue and is currently running chapters of a serialized novel. *Unzipped* is published 26 times a year. For subscription information, call (800) 757-7069 toll-free, Monday through Friday, 7:30 A.M. to 10 P.M. Central time. Among the fiction pieces appearing in *Classifieds* in 1997 were "Looking for Mr. Right" (January 7), "Toddy's Twick" (February 4), "Discretion Sought, Discretion Served" (March 4), "Traction" (April 1), "Fantasies" (April 29), "When Luddy Goes" (June 10), "The Canadian Censor" (September 2), and "Fever" (September 16).

Coming Out was first published in 1994. Like its sister publications, *Beau* and *The Boy Next Door,* it is a quarterly, and annual subscriptions are $9.97. Each issue has 14 stories. For more information, write to: Sportomatic Ltd., P.O. Box 470, Port Chester, NY 10573. "Coaching Session" appeared in the October 1997 issue.

Drummer Tough Customers is published quarterly and features one piece of fiction per issue. Annual subscriptions are $19.95. For more information, write to: P.O. Box 410390, San Francisco, CA 94141. "The Innocent Predator" appeared in the March 1997 issue.

Eagle Magazine initially appeared under the name *Cuir Magazine* in 1992; the name change occurred in 1995. Generally four pieces of fiction appear in each issue, and the magazine is published bimonthly. Subscriptions are $33 in the United States; $45, outside. Write for more information to *Eagle Magazine,* 7985 Santa Monica Blvd., 109-368, West Hollywood, CA 90046, or fax (213) 656-3120. "Snowbound" appeared in the June/July 1997 issue.

Freshmen started publishing in 1991. It is a monthly magazine and usually features two pieces of fiction per issue. For subscription information, call toll-free (800) 757-7069, Monday through Friday, 7:30 A.M. to 10 P.M. Central time. Issues in 1997 featured "The Golden Boys" (January), "Boystown" (April), "Anyway" and "A Queer Turn" (May), and "Tuesdays We Read Baudelaire" (August).

GBM (Gay Black Men) began publishing in 1997. Each issue includes two to three pieces of erotic fiction. The magazine is published quarterly, and annual subscriptions are $24. For more information, write to: Brush Creek Media Inc., 367 Ninth St., San Francisco, CA 94103. "Liberation!" appeared in the magazine's May 1997 issue.

Heavy Duty first appeared in 1996. It is published quarterly, and each issue includes two short stories. Annual subscriptions are $30. For more information, write to: *Heavy Duty,* 592 Castro St., Suite A, San Francisco, CA 94114; or call toll-free (800) 783-2441. "Gaijin" appeared in the July–September 1997 issue.

Inches is published monthly and features two stories in each issue. Subscriptions can be ordered by calling (888) 664-7827 or writing to Jiffy Fulfillment Inc., 50 Lawrence Rd., Springfield, NJ 07081-3121. "The Roommate" appeared in the February 1997 issue.

International Drummer debuted in 1975. The monthly magazine runs two to three short stories in each issue. Annual subscriptions are $59. For more information, write to: P.O. Box 410390, San Francisco, CA 94141. "Taking Out the Trash" appeared in the May 1997 issue.

In Touch for Men's first issue appeared in 1973. The magazine is published monthly and usually features three stories per issue. Annual subscriptions are $47.50. Write to: *In Touch for Men,* 13122 Saticoy St., North Hollywood,. CA 91605. "Souvenir" appeared in the July 1997 issue.

Men debuted in 1984. It is published monthly and generally features three short stories per issue. For subscription information, call toll-free (800) 757-7069, Monday through Friday, 7:30 A.M. to 10 P.M. Central time. Among the fiction appearing in *Men* in 1997 were "Jock Talk" (March), "Dads" (April), "Karma" (May), "Blind Date" (July), "Pinch" (August), and "Physical Therapy" (October).

Stroke started publishing in 1980. The bimonthly magazine has one story per issue. Annual subscriptions are $85. For more information, write to: Magcorp, P.O. Box 801434, Santa Clarita, CA 91380-1454. "Bringing Up Robbie" appeared in the August 1997 issue.

Torso was created in 1982. The monthly magazine runs two stories per issue. Subscriptions can be ordered by calling (888) 664-7827 or writing to Jiffy Fulfillment Inc., 50 Lawrence Rd., Springfield, NJ 07081-3121. "The Man at the Gym" appeared in the April 1997 issue.